EVERYMAN,

I WILL GO WITH THEE,

AND BE THY GUIDE,

IN THY MOST NEED

TO GO BY THY SIDE

EVERYMAN'S POCKET CLASSICS

IRISH STORIES

EDITED BY CHRISTOPHER MORASH

EVERYMAN'S POCKET CLASSICS
Alfred A. Knopf New York London

THIS IS A BORZOI BOOK
PUBLISHED BY ALFRED A. KNOPF

This selection by Christopher Morash first published in
Everyman's Library, 2026
Copyright © 2026 by Everyman's Library

A list of acknowledgments to copyright owners appears at the back
of this volume.

Penguin Random House values and supports copyright. Copyright fuels
creativity, encourages diverse voices, promotes free speech, and creates a
vibrant culture. Thank you for buying an authorized edition of this book
and for complying with copyright laws by not reproducing, scanning,
or distributing any part of it in any form without permission. You are
supporting writers and allowing Penguin Random House to continue to
publish books for every reader. Please note that no part of this book may
be used or reproduced in any manner for the purpose of training artificial
intelligence technologies or systems.

Published in the United States by Alfred A. Knopf, a division of
Penguin Random House LLC, 1745 Broadway, New York, NY 10019.
Published in the United Kingdom by Everyman's Library, 50 Albemarle
Street, London W1S 4BD and distributed by Penguin Random House
UK, One Embassy Gardens, 8 Viaduct Gardens, London SW11 7BW.

everymanslibrary.com penguinrandomhouse.com
www.penguin.co.uk/about/publishing-houses/everyman

ISBN 979-8-217-00813-1 (US)
978-1-84159-641-9 (UK)

A CIP catalogue reference for this book is available from the
British Library

Typography by Peter B. Willberg and James Sutton

Typeset in the UK by Input Data Services Ltd, Bridgwater, Somerset

Printed and bound in Germany by GGP Media GmbH, Pössneck

The authorized representative in the EU for product safety and
compliance is Penguin Random House Ireland, Morrison Chambers, 32
Nassau Street, Dublin D02 YH68, Ireland, https://eu-contact.penguin.ie

Contents

FOREWORD   9

WILLIAM CARLETON (1794–1869)
   Wildgoose Lodge (1833)   17

JOSEPH SHERIDAN LE FANU (1814–73)
   The Fortunes of Sir Robert Ardagh (1838)   43

KATHARINE TYNAN (1859–1931)
   A Descendant of Irish Earls (1894)   57

EDITH SOMERVILLE (1858–1949) and
MARTIN ROSS (1862–1915)
   A Nineteenth-Century Miracle (1903)   67

LADY AUGUSTA GREGORY (1852–1932)
   The Priest That Was Called Mad (1906)   83

JAMES JOYCE (1882–1941)
   The Dead (1914)   87

PÁDRAIC Ó CONAIRE (1882–1928)
   Knitting ('An Chniotáil') (1922)   141

LIAM O'FLAHERTY (1897–1984)
   The Sniper (1923)   149

FRANK O'CONNOR (1903–66)
  Guests of the Nation (1931) — 157

SAMUEL BECKETT (1906–89)
  Ding-Dong (1934) — 175

ELIZABETH BOWEN (1899–1973)
  The Last Night in the Old Home (1934) — 189

SEAN O FAOLAIN (1900–91)
  A Broken World (1937) — 197

NORAH HOULT (1898–1984)
  The Story of Father Peter (1938) — 215

FLANN O'BRIEN (1911–66)
  John Duffy's Brother (1940) — 227

MAEVE BRENNAN (1917–93)
  The Barrel of Rumours (1954) — 237

JAMES PLUNKETT (1920–2003)
  Dublin Fusilier (1955) — 247

MARY LAVIN (1912–96)
  In a Café (1960) — 265

JOHN McGAHERN (1934–2006)
  Bank Holiday (1985) — 289

MIKE McCORMACK (b. 1965)
  The Terms (1996) — 313

CLAIRE KEEGAN (b. 1968)
Dark Horses (2006) — 327

ANNE ENRIGHT (b. 1962)
Green (2008) — 337

EDNA O'BRIEN (1930–2024)
Send My Roots Rain (2009) — 347

COLM TÓIBÍN (b. 1955)
The Empty Family (2010) — 365

RODDY DOYLE (b. 1958)
Two Pints × 4 (2011, 2012, 2016, 2019) — 377

ÉILÍS NÍ DHUIBHNE (b. 1954)
A Literary Lunch (2012) — 385

JOHN CONNOLLY (b. 1968)
A Dream of Winter (2015) — 401

KEVIN BARRY (b. 1969)
The Apparitions (2016) — 405

LUCY CALDWELL (b. 1981)
Here We Are (2016) — 413

CATHY SWEENEY (b. 1970)
The Door (2018) — 433

SALLY ROONEY (b. 1991)
Colour and Light (2019) — 445

EOIN McNAMEE (b. 1961)
　Sable (2020) 469

YAN GE (b. 1984)
　How I Fell in Love with the Well-Documented
　Life of Alex Whelan (2023) 481

LUCY SWEENEY BYRNE (b. 1989)
　Echolocations (2024) 503

ACKNOWLEDGMENTS 523

FOREWORD

For many years, there were two commonly accepted explanations for the extraordinary flourishing of the Irish short story – neither of which was either entirely wrong or entirely convincing.

The first starts from the premise that a centuries-old Irish-language oral story-telling tradition forms a sort of seed bed for the Irish short story, an endlessly fertile imaginative loam out of which tales continuously sprout. This is the kind of explanation that has, if nothing else, a satisfying narrative appeal of its own, and it is certainly true in some instances. The book you are holding opens with a tale by William Carleton, whose *Traits and Stories of the Irish Peasantry* were reworkings of the folk tales Carleton had heard growing up in rural County Tyrone, while the Irish-language short stories of Galway-born Pádraic Ó Conaire (one of whose stories is included here) show a deep debt to the folkloric tradition into which he was born. Other Irish writers from the early decades of the twentieth century, such as Lady Gregory, collected tales from what they saw as a disappearing folk culture, and 'The Priest That Was Called Mad' (1906), included here, has its origins in the cottages around her home in Coole Park, in County Galway.

However, like all good soils, this origin story is both rich and crumbly. It is less convincing when we turn to Carleton's near contemporary, Joseph Sheridan Le Fanu, who lived his entire life in Dublin's literary circles, far from folk tales told around a cottage hearth. His gothic stories – like 'The Fortunes of Sir Robert Ardagh' (1838), included here – may have the feel of a tale told around a fire, but only if we imagine the fire laid in the marble fireplace in one of Dublin's Georgian townhouses. In other words, even when the rural folk tradition was alive and thriving, it required an act of translation.

The second explanation for the continuing vitality of the Irish short story might be considered a version of the first, with a bit more historical and sociological elaboration. It goes like this: the fractured nature of Irish history, ruptured by centuries of colonization, rebellion and a devastating famine, made it difficult, if not impossible, for Irish writers to produce the long, developmental narratives – novels – that were common in other European countries with a more secure sense of their pasts and futures. Hence (the argument went), Irish writers were thrown back upon shorter forms – the lyric poem, the one-act play, and the short story.

For more than one generation of Irish writers in the aftermath of the Irish War of Independence (1919–21), and ensuing Civil War (1922–23), this was an enabling fiction. If nothing else, it helped to explain the profusion of great Irish short-story writers in the middle decades of the twentieth century, a list that includes Sean O'Faolain, Frank O'Connor, Liam O'Flaherty, Elizabeth Bowen, Mary Lavin, and Maeve Brennan, with Edna O'Brien appearing at the end of the period with her first stories in *The New Yorker* in the mid-1950s. In O'Faolain's case, his 1948 book, *The Short Story*, would establish him not simply as one of the most acclaimed practitioners of the short story in the world, but also one of its principal apologists.

Again, however, there is a problem with this argument, not least in the recognition that in those same years that the short story was being proclaimed the most appropriate literary form for the discontinuities of Irish history, there was no shortage of Irish novels, among them what is arguably the greatest novel of the twentieth century: James Joyce's *Ulysses*, from 1922.

With the passage of time, however, this argument, too, has lost its credibility. If Ireland in the middle decades of the twentieth was insular, under-developed, and facing an uncertain future, in the final decade of the century this situation would be completely reversed. As its post-industrial economy boomed in the mid-1990s, the conflict in Northern Ireland reached a kind of resolution in 1998, and the moral authority of the Catholic Church shattered like a plaster saint being knocked from a shelf, Ireland went from being an inward-looking, repressed society, hemmed in by literary censorship and enervated by decades of outward migration, to become a prosperous, liberal, globalized, and ethnically diverse country, subject to the same pressures of most of the rest of the developed world, but no longer an outlier. In the process, the rich peaty soil of Irish peasant culture has been well and truly laid with fibre-optic cables.

If the earlier theory connecting the flourishing of the short story in Ireland in the 1930s and 1940s to a fractured, under-developed culture were accurate, we should have expected the short story to have withered in the twenty-first century. Instead, however, it has thrived. What is more, it has thrived on its own terms, and not at the expense of the Irish novel, which is also experiencing a kind of golden age. Most of the recent short-story writers included in this volume are also novelists, among them recent winners of the Booker Prize and of the Dublin Literary Award, the world's richest for a single novel. Little wonder that there has been talk – and not just in the usual Dublin pubs – of a golden age of Irish fiction in the twenty-first century, cutting across forms, genres, and every imaginable version of Irishness.

The vibrant persistence of the short story in Ireland across such a history of profound social change might make us inclined to ask: is there anything that binds together the almost two centuries' worth of stories collected here as 'Irish short stories', other than the fact that their authors live or lived in Ireland, and that they are all writing about Ireland. Even the latter insistence that the stories must be set in Ireland is a self-imposed rule for this collection, and it would be equally possible to fill a book with short stories by Irish writers *not* set in Ireland.

And yet, if we take the longest (probably the most famous) story in the collection as a kind of exemplar – James Joyce's 'The Dead' (1914) – we begin to glimpse two distinctive features that echo across the decades.

The first is a certain insistence on the voice. 'The Dead' is a kind of symphony of voices, from its opening line: 'Lily, the caretaker's daughter, was literally run off her feet.' It has been pointed out that, in fact, Lily is not '*literally* run off her feet' (she is still standing). However, the phrase 'I'm literally run off my feet' is what Lily would say if she were asked, even though the sentence is ostensibly spoken by a neutral, omniscient third-person narrator. What has happened here is that the voice of the narrator has picked up the inflections, the turns of phrase, of a minor character. It is as if the voice itself were able to colour the language, like a drop of dye dripped into a glass of water, lasting only until another voice moves into earshot, is picked up and adds its tincture to a mix that is in turn shot through with overlapping threads of direct speech. The result is a story whose essential fabric is the human voice.

In this respect, Joyce's story is not alone in these pages.

The earliest story here, Carleton's 'Wildgoose Lodge' (1833), hinges around the contrasting voices of the self-righteous, very proper narrator, and the wild, phonetically rendered speech of the story's peasant characters; from the opposite side of the nineteenth-century social spectrum, Edith Somerville and Martin Ross's stories (such as 'A Nineteenth-Century Miracle', 1903) work in the same way. Flash forward almost two centuries to Lucy Sweeney Byrne's 'Echolocations' (2024), and what lingers in the mind after reading is not so much the plot, as the sense of a speaker. Dig deeper, and you will find no purer instance of writing that revels in the sound of the voice than Roddy Doyle's 'Two Pints' (2011–20). Originally published as a series of social media posts (four of which are included here), these short pieces are entirely made up of the conversations of two unnamed men, meeting regularly in a pub for a couple of pints, where the human voice is gloriously, hilariously, front and centre, and talk has scant regard for facts or logic.

Of course, it could be argued that this fascination with the voice has long been a distinctive feature of Irish novels as well, from Maria Edgeworth's *Castle Rackrent* (1800) with its garrulous narrator, to Anna Burns's *Milkman* (2018). However, returning to Joyce's 'The Dead' as a kind of paradigm, something else emerges as a constant that is a distinctive feature of the short story, cutting across the voices' insistence on their own importance. 'The Dead' is, among other things, a kind of ghost story, although this is not apparent until its final sweeping vision of an Ireland covered in snow. Sometimes, the ghosts that haunt the Irish short story are revenants from a broken past, returning to haunt the present, as in Le Fanu's tale, or in the flashbacks of James Plunkett's shell-shocked soldier in 'Dublin Fusilier' (1955). Elsewhere, the ghosts are personal, as in Eoin McNamee's atmospheric 'Sable' (2020), in which a woman returns to the decaying site of her past life. Across the decades, however, they keep on returning.

Throughout this collection, some of the ghosts we encounter are of Irish literature itself, so that we might even imagine the stories here talking to one another from very different Irelands. Lucy Sweeney Byrne's 'Echolocations' opens with a character watching a film of Elizabeth Bowen (although she is not named as such) walking for a final time in the 1930s through the gardens of her family's Big House, Bowen's Court, in County Cork – the same moment about which Bowen herself writes in 'The Last Night in the Old Home' (1934). Likewise, someone once told Sean O Faolain that they considered his story 'A Broken World' (1937) to be a version of Joyce's 'The Dead', whose main character, Gabriel, gives his name to the restaurant that is the setting for Éilís Ní Dhuibhne's delicious satire, 'A Literary Lunch' (2012). And then there is Kevin Barry's 'The Apparitions' (2016), where the ghosts of earlier Irish writers (Joyce, Beckett, Yeats) make an unnervingly literal appearance on the streets of Dublin, concluding with a suggestion that the final paragraph of 'The Dead' should be played on a continuous loop in the city.

The short story is often considered to be a slice of life; however, the Irish short story is typically more than that. As a brief, intense burst of writing, the short story flares up within the present of its own telling, much like lively conversation. However, what gives the short story its satisfying narrative form and emotional force is the intrusion into that all-absorbing present of something else just beyond the edge of language, something that disrupts what we thought we knew about the world, intimating that the world we thought that we were observing so closely is other than we think it to be. This awareness may erupt in the final paragraph, as happens in the classic short story, or it may seep out slowly, as happens in more recent writing; either way, this undertow is at the heart of the short story's particular magic.

Over the past two centuries Irish writers have found, in widely differing circumstances, that this aspect of the short story has been suited to the temper of their times. Whether we are considering the aftermath of the revolutionary period in the middle of the twentieth century, or the social revolution of the twenty-first century, the short story has consistently provided Irish writers with a form capable of comprehending their predicament and its attendant sense of living in an uncertain world transformed. In the end, it may be that the final line of Frank O'Connor's 'Guests of the Nation' (1931) best captures what a great short story leaves in its wake: 'And anything that ever happened me after I never felt the same about again.'

Chris Morash

WILLIAM CARLETON

WILDGOOSE LODGE

I HAD READ the anonymous summons, but from its general import I believed it to be one of those special meetings convened for some purpose affecting the usual objects and proceedings of the body; at least the terms in which it was conveyed to me had nothing extraordinary or mysterious in them, beyond the simple fact, that it was not to be a general but a select meeting: this mark of confidence flattered me, and I determined to attend punctually. I was, it is true, desired to keep the circumstances entirely to myself, but there was nothing startling in this, for I had often received summonses of a similar nature. I therefore resolved to attend, according to the letter of my instructions, 'on the next night, at the solemn hour of midnight, to deliberate and act upon such matters as should then and there be submitted to my consideration'. The morning after I received this message, I arose and resumed my usual occupations; but, from whatever cause it may have proceeded, I felt a sense of approaching evil hang heavily upon me; the beats of my pulse were languid, and an undefinable feeling of anxiety pervaded my whole spirit; even my face was pale, and my eye so heavy, that my father and brothers concluded me to be ill; an opinion which I thought at the time to be correct, for I felt exactly that kind of depression which precedes a severe fever. I could not understand what I experienced, nor can I yet, except by supposing that there is in human nature some mysterious faculty, by which, in coming calamities, the dread of some fearful evil is anticipated, and that it is possible to catch a dark presentiment of the sensations which they subsequently produce. For my part I can neither analyse nor define it; but on that day I knew it by painful experience, and so have a thousand others in similar circumstances.

It was about the middle of winter. The day was gloomy and tempestuous, almost beyond any other I remember; dark clouds rolled over the hills about me, and a close sleet-like rain fell in slanting drifts that chased each other rapidly towards the earth on the course of the blast. The outlying cattle sought the closest and calmest corners of the fields for shelter; the trees and young groves were tossed about, for the wind was so unusually high that it swept in hollow gusts through them, with that hoarse murmur which deepens so powerfully on the mind the sense of dreariness and desolation.

As the shades of night fell, the storm, if possible, increased. The moon was half gone, and only a few stars were visible by glimpses, as a rush of wind left a temporary opening in the sky. I had determined, if the storm should not abate, to incur any penalty rather than attend the meeting; but the appointed hour was distant, and I resolved to be decided by the future state of the night.

Ten o'clock came, but still there was no change: eleven passed, and on opening the door to observe if there were any likelihood of its clearing up, a blast of wind, mingled with rain, nearly blew me off my feet. At length it was approaching to the hour of midnight; and on examining it a third time, I found it had calmed a little, and no longer rained.

I instantly got my oak stick, muffled myself in my great coat, strapped my hat about my ears, and, as the place of meeting was only a quarter of a mile distant, I presently set out.

The appearance of the heavens was lowering and angry, particularly in that point where the light of the moon fell against the clouds, from a seeming chasm in them, through which alone she was visible. The edges of this chasm were faintly bronzed, but the dense body of the masses that hung piled on each side of her, was black and impenetrable to sight. In no other point of the heavens was there any part of the sky visible; a deep veil of clouds overhung the whole horizon, yet was the light sufficient to give occasional glimpses of the rapid shifting which took place in this dark canopy, and of the tempestuous agitation with which the midnight storm swept to and fro beneath it.

At length I arrived at a long slated house, situated in a solitary part of the neighbourhood; a little below it ran a small stream, which was now swollen above its banks, and rushing with mimic roar over the flat meadows beside it. The appearance of the bare slated building in such a night was particularly sombre, and to those, like me, who knew the purpose to which it was usually devoted, it was or ought to have been peculiarly so. There it stood, silent and gloomy, without any appearance of human life or enjoyment about or within it. As I approached, the moon once more had broken out of the clouds, and shone dimly upon the wet, glittering slates and windows, with a death-like lustre, that gradually faded away as I left the point of observation, and entered the folding-door. It was the parish chapel.

The scene which presented itself here was in keeping not only with the external appearance of the house, but with the darkness, the storm, and the hour, which was now a little after midnight. About forty persons were sitting in dead silence upon the circular steps of the altar. They did not seem to move; and as I entered and advanced, the echo of my footsteps rang through the building with a lonely distinctness, which added to the solemnity and mystery of the circumstances about me. The windows were secured with shutters on the inside, and on the altar a candle was lighted, which burned dimly amid the surrounding darkness, and lengthened the shadow of the altar itself, and those of six or seven persons who stood on its upper steps, until they mingled in the obscurity which shrouded the lower end of the chapel. The faces of the men who sat on the altar steps were not distinctly visible, yet their prominent and more characteristic features were in sufficient relief, and I observed, that some of the most malignant and reckless spirits in the parish were assembled. In the eyes of those who stood at the altar, and those whom I knew to be invested with authority over the others, I could perceive gleams of some latent and ferocious purpose, kindled, as I soon observed, into a fiercer expression of vengeance, by the additional excitement of ardent spirits, with which they had stimulated themselves to a point of determination that mocked at the apprehension of all future responsibility, either in this world or the next.

The welcome which I received on joining them was far different from the boisterous good-humour that used to mark our greetings on other occasions; just a nod of the head from this or that person, on the part of those who sat, with a dhud dhemur tha fhu?* in a suppressed voice, even below a common whisper: but from the standing group, who were evidently the projectors of the enterprise, I received a convulsive grasp of the hand, accompanied by a fierce and desperate look, that seemed to search my eye and countenance, to try if I were a person likely to shrink from whatever they had resolved to execute. It is surprising to think of the powerful expression which a moment of intense

* How are you?

interest or great danger is capable of giving to the eye, the features and the slightest actions, especially in those whose station in society does not require them to constrain nature, by the force of social courtesies, into habits that conceal their natural emotions. None of the standing group spoke; but as each of them wrung my hand in silence, his eye was fixed on mine, with an expression of drunken confidence and secrecy, and an insolent determination not to be gainsaid without peril. If looks could be translated with certainty, they seemed to say, 'We are bound upon a project of vengeance, and if you do not join us, remember we can revenge.' Along with this grasp, they did not forget to remind me of the common bond by which we were united, for each man gave me the secret grip of Ribbonism in a manner that made the joints of my fingers ache for some minutes afterwards.

There was one present, however – the highest in authority – whose actions and demeanour were calm and unexcited. He seemed to labour under no unusual influence whatever, but evinced a serenity so placid and philosophical, that I attributed the silence of the sitting group, and the restraint which curbed in the outbreaking passions of those who stood, entirely to his presence. He was a schoolmaster, who taught his daily school in that chapel, and acted also on Sunday, in the capacity of clerk to the priest – an excellent and amiable old man, who knew little of his illegal connections and atrocious conduct.

When the ceremonies of brotherly recognition and friendship were past, the Captain (by which title I shall designate the last-mentioned person) stooped, and, raising a jar of whiskey on the corner of the altar, held a wineglass to its neck, which he filled, and with a calm nod handed it to me to drink. I shrank back, with an instinctive horror, at the profaneness of such an act, in the house, and on the altar of God, and peremptorily refused to taste the proffered draught. He smiled mildly at what he considered my superstition, and added quietly, and in a low voice, 'You'll be wantin' it I'm thinkin', afther the wettin' you got.'

'Wet or dry,' said I—

'Stop, man!' he replied, in the same tone; 'spake low. But why wouldn't you take the whiskey? Sure there's as holy people to the fore as you: didn't they all take it? An' I wish we may never do worse nor dhrink a harmless glass o' whiskey, to keep the cowld out, any way.'

'Well,' said I, 'I'll jist trust to God and the consequences, for the cowld, Paddy, ma bouchal; but a blessed dhrop of it won't be crossin' my lips, avick; so no more ghostlier about it; – dhrink it yourself if you like. Maybe you want it as much as I do; wherein I've the patthern of a good big-coat upon me, so thick, your sowl, that if it was rainin' bullocks, a dhrop wouldn't get undher the nap of it.'

He gave me a calm, but keen glance as I spoke.

'Well, Jim,' said he, 'it's a good comrade you've got for the weather that's in it; but, in the manetime, to set you a dacent patthern, I'll just take this myself,' – saying which, with the jar still upon its side, and the fore-finger of his left hand in his neck, he swallowed the spirits – 'It's the first I dhrank to-night,' he added, 'nor would I dhrink it now, only to show you that I've heart an' spirit to do the thing that we're all bound an' sworn to, when the proper time comes'; after which he laid down the glass, and turned up the jar, with much coolness, upon the altar.

During our conversation, those who had been summoned to this mysterious meeting were pouring in fast; and as each person approached the altar, he received from one to two or three glasses of whiskey, according as he chose to limit himself; but, to do them justice, there were not a few of those present, who, in despite of their own desire, and the Captain's express invitation, refused to taste it in the house of God's worship. Such, however, as were scrupulous he afterwards recommended to take it on the outside of the chapel door, which they did, as, by that means, the sacrilege of the act was supposed to be evaded.

About one o'clock they were all assembled except six: at least so the Captain asserted, on looking at a written paper.

'Now, boys,' said he in the same low voice, 'we are all present except the thraitors, whose names I am goin' to read to you; not that we are to count thim thraitors, till we know whether or not it was in their power to come. Any how, the night's terrible – but, boys, you're to know, that neither fire nor wather is to prevint you, when duly summoned to attind a meeting – particularly whin the summons is widout a name, as you have been told that there is always something of consequence to be done thin.'

He then read out the names of those who were absent, in order that the real cause of their absence might be ascertained, declaring that they would be dealt with accordingly.

After this, with his usual caution, he shut and bolted the door, and having put the key in his pocket, ascended the steps of the altar, and for some time traversed the little platform from which the priest usually addresses the congregation.

Until this night I had never contemplated the man's countenance with any particular interest; but as he walked the platform, I had an opportunity of observing him more closely. He was slight in person, apparently not thirty; and, on a first view, appeared to have nothing remarkable in his dress or features. I, however, was not the only person whose eyes were fixed upon him at that moment; in fact, every one present observed him with equal interest, for hitherto he had kept the object of the meeting perfectly secret, and of course we all felt anxious to know it. It was while he traversed the platform that I scrutinized his features with a hope, if possible, to glean from them some evidence of what was passing within him. I could, however, mark but little, and that little was at first rather from the intelligence which seemed to subsist between him and those whom I have already mentioned as standing against the altar, than from any indication of his own. Their gleaming eyes were fixed upon him with an intensity of savage and demon-like hope, which blazed out in flashes of malignant triumph, as upon turning, he threw a cool but rapid glance at them, to intimate the progress he was making in the subject to which he devoted the undivided energies of his mind. But in the course of his meditation, I could observe, on one or two occasions, a dark shade come over his countenance, that contracted his brow into a deep furrow, and it was then, for the first time, that I saw the satanic expression of which his face, by a very slight motion of its muscles, was capable. His hands, during this silence, closed and opened convulsively; his eyes shot out two or three baleful glances, first to his confederates, and afterwards vacantly into the deep gloom of the lower part of the chapel; his teeth ground against each other, like those of a man whose revenge burns to reach a distant enemy, and finally, after having wound himself up to a certain determination, his features relapsed into their original calm and undisturbed expression.

At this moment a loud laugh, having something supernatural in it, rang out wildly from the darkness of the chapel; he stopped, and putting his open hand over his brows, peered down into the gloom, and said calmly in Irish, 'Bee dhu husth; ha nih anam inh: – hold your tongue, it is not yet time.'

Every eye was now directed to the same spot, but, in

consequence of its distance from the dim light on the altar, none could perceive the person from whom the laugh proceeded. It was, by this time, near two o'clock in the morning.

He now stood for a few moments on the platform, and his chest heaved with a depth of anxiety equal to the difficulty of the design he wished to accomplish.

'Brothers,' said he – 'for we are all brothers – sworn upon all that's blessed an' holy, to obey whatever them that's over us, manin' among ourselves, wishes us to do – are you now ready, in the name of God, upon whose althar I stand, to fulfil yer oaths?'

The words were scarcely uttered, when those who had stood beside the altar during the night, sprang from their places, and descending its steps rapidly turned round, and raising their arms, exclaimed, 'By all that's good an' holy we're willin'.'

In the meantime, those who sat upon the steps of the altar, instantly rose, and following the example of those who had just spoken, exclaimed after them, 'To be sure – by all that's sacred an' holy we're willin'.'

'Now, boys,' said the Captain, 'ar'n't ye big fools for your pains? an' one of ye doesn't know what I mane.'

'You're our Captain,' said one of those who had stood at the altar, 'an' has yer ordhers from higher quarthers; of coorse, whatever ye command upon us we're bound to obey you in.'

'Well,' said he, smiling, 'I only wanted to thry yez; an' by the oath ye tuck, there's not a captain in the county has as good a right to be proud of his min as I have. Well, ye won't rue it, maybe, when the right time comes; and for that same rason every one of ye must have a glass from the jar; thim that won't dhrink it in the chapel can dhrink it widout; an' here goes to open the door for thim.'

He then distributed another glass to every one who would accept it, and brought the jar afterwards to the chapel door, to satisfy the scruples of those who would not drink within. When this was performed, and all duly excited, he proceeded:—

'Now, brothers, you are solemnly sworn to obay me, and I'm sure there's no thraithur here that 'ud parjure himself for a thrifle; but I'm sworn to obay them that's above me, manin' still among ourselves; an' to show that I don't scruple to do it, here goes!'

He then turned round, and taking the Missal between his hands placed it upon the altar. Hitherto every word was uttered in a low precautionary tone; but on grasping the book he again turned round, and looking upon his confederates with the same satanic expression which marked his countenance before, he exclaimed, in a voice of deep determination, first kissing the book: 'By this sacred an' holy book of God, I will perform the action which we have met this night to accomplish, be that what it may; an' this I swear upon God's book, and God's althar!'

On concluding, he struck the book violently with his open hand, thereby occasioning a very loud report.

At this moment the candle which burned before him went suddenly out, and the chapel was wrapped in pitchy darkness; the sound as if of rushing wings fell upon our ears, and fifty voices dwelt upon the last words of his oath with wild and supernatural tones, that seemed to echo and to mock what he had sworn. There was a pause, and an exclamation of horror from all present; but the Captain was too cool and steady to be disconcerted. He immediately groped about until he got the candle, and proceeding calmly to a remote corner of the chapel, took up a half-burned peat which lay there, and after some trouble succeeded in lighting it again.

He then explained what had taken place; which indeed was easily done, as the candle happened to be extinguished by a pigeon which sat directly above it. The chapel, I should have observed, was at this time, like many country chapels, unfinished inside, and the pigeons of a neighbouring dovecote had built nests among the rafters of the unceiled roof; which circumstance also explained the rushing of the wings, for the birds had been affrighted by the sudden loudness of the noise. The mocking voices were nothing but the echoes, rendered naturally more awful by the scene, the mysterious object of the meeting, and the solemn hour of the night.

When the candle was again lighted, and these startling circumstances accounted for, the persons whose vengeance had been deepening more and more during the night, rushed to the altar in a body, where each, in a voice trembling with passionate eagerness, repeated the oath, and as every word was pronounced, the same echoes heightened the wildness of the horrible ceremony, by their long and unearthly tones. The countenances of these human tigers were livid with suppressed rage; their knit brows, compressed lips, and kindled eyes, fell under the dim light of the taper, with an expression calculated to sicken any heart not absolutely diabolical.

As soon as this dreadful rite was completed, we were again startled by several loud bursts of laughter, which proceeded from the lower darkness of the chapel; and the Captain, on hearing them, turned to the place, and reflecting for a moment, said in Irish, 'Gutsho nish, avohenee – come hither now, boys.'

A rush immediately took place from the corner in which they had secreted themselves all the night; and seven men appeared, whom we instantly recognized as brothers and cousins of certain persons who had been convicted, some time before, for breaking into the house of an honest poor man in the neighbourhood, from whom, after having treated him with barbarous violence, they took away such fire-arms as he kept for his own protection.

It was evidently not the Captain's intention to have produced these persons until the oath should have been generally taken, but the exulting mirth with which they enjoyed the success of his scheme betrayed them, and put him to the necessity of bringing them forward somewhat before the concerted moment.

The scene which now took place was beyond all power of description; peals of wild, fiendlike yells rang through the chapel, as the party which stood on the altar and that which had crouched in the darkness met; wringing of hands, leaping in triumph, striking of sticks and fire-arms against the ground and the altar itself, dancing and cracking of fingers, marked the triumph of some hellish determination. Even the Captain for a time was unable to restrain their fury; but, at length, he mounted the platform before the altar once more, and with a stamp of his foot, recalled their attention to himself and the matter in hand.

'Boys,' said he, 'enough of this, and too much; an' well for us it is that the chapel is in a lonely place, or our foolish noise might do us no good. Let thim that swore so manfully jist now, stand a one side, till the rest kiss the book one by one.'

The proceedings, however, had by this time taken too fearful a shape for even the Captain to compel them to a blindfold oath; the first man he called flatly refused to answer, until he should hear the nature of the service that was required. This was echoed by the remainder, who, taking courage from the firmness of this person, declared generally that, until they first knew the business they were to execute, none of them would take the oath. The Captain's lip quivered slightly, and his brow again became knit with the same hellish expression, which I have remarked gave him so much the appearance of an embodied fiend; but this speedily passed away, and was succeeded by a malignant sneer, in which lurked, if there ever did in a sneer, 'a laughing devil', calmly, determinedly atrocious.

'It wasn't worth yer whiles to refuse the oath,' said he, mildly, 'for the truth is, I had next to nothing for yez to do. Not a hand, maybe, would have to rise, only jist to look on, an' if any resistance would be made, to show yourselves; yer numbers would soon make them see that resistance would be no use whatever in the present case. At all evints, the oath of secrecy must be taken, or woe be to him that will refuse that; he won't know the day, nor the hour, nor the minute, when he'll be made a spatch-cock of.'

He then turned round, and, placing his right hand on the Missal, swore, 'In the presence of God, and before his holy altar, that whatever might take place that night he would keep secret, from man or mortal, except the priest, and that neither bribery, nor imprisonment, nor death, would wring it from his heart.'

Having done this, he again struck the book violently, as if to confirm the energy with which he swore, and then calmly descending the steps, stood with a serene countenance, like a man conscious of having performed a good action. As this oath did not pledge those who refused to take the other to the perpetration of any specific crime, it was readily taken by all present. Preparations were then made to execute what was intended: the half-burned turf was placed in a little pot; another glass of whiskey was distributed; and the door being locked by the Captain, who kept the key as parish clerk and schoolmaster, the crowd departed silently from the chapel.

The moment those who lay in the darkness, during the night, made their appearance at the altar, we knew at once the persons we were to visit; for, as I said before, they were related to the miscreants whom one of those persons had convicted, in consequences of their midnight attack upon himself and his family. The Captain's object in keeping them unseen was, that those present, not being aware of the duty about to be imposed on them, might have less hesitation about swearing to its fulfilment. Our conjectures were correct; for on leaving the chapel we directed our steps to the house in which this devoted man resided.

The night was still stormy, but without rain: it was rather dark, too, though not so as to prevent us from seeing the clouds careering swiftly through the air. The dense curtain which had overhung and obscured the horizon was now broken, and large sections of the sky were clear, and thinly studded with stars that looked dim and watery, as did indeed the whole firmament; for in some places black clouds were still visible, threatening a continuance of tempestuous weather. The road appeared washed and gravelly; every dike was full of yellow water; and every little rivulet and larger stream dashed its hoarse murmur into our ears; every blast, too, was cold, fierce, and wintry, sometimes driving us back to a standstill, and again, when a turn in the road would bring it in our backs, whirling us along for a few steps with involuntary rapidity. At length the fated dwelling became visible, and a short consultation was held in a sheltered place, between the Captain and the two parties who seemed so eager for its destruction. Their fire-arms were now loaded, and their bayonets and short pikes, the latter shod and pointed with iron, were also got ready. The live coal which was brought in the small pot had become extinguished; but to remedy this, two or three persons from a remote part of the county entered a cabin on the wayside, and, under pretence of lighting their own and their comrades' pipes, procured a coal of fire, for so they called a lighted turf. From the time we left the chapel until this moment a profound silence had been maintained, a circumstance which, when I considered the number of persons present, and the mysterious and dreaded object of their journey, had a most appalling effect upon my spirits.

At length we arrived within fifty perches of the house, walking in a compact body, and with as little noise as possible; but it seemed as if the very elements had conspired to frustrate our design, for on advancing within the shade of the farm-hedge, two or three persons found themselves up to the middle in water, and on stooping to ascertain more accurately the state of the place, we could see nothing but one immense sheet of it – spread like a lake over the meadows which surrounded the spot we wished to reach.

Fatal night! The very recollection of it, when associated with the fearful tempests of elements, grows, if that were possible, yet more wild and revolting. Had we been engaged in any innocent or benevolent enterprise, there was something in our situation just then that had a touch of interest in it to a mind imbued with a relish for the savage beauties of nature. There we stood, about a hundred and thirty in number, our dark forms bent forward, peering into the dusky expanse of water, with its dim gleams of reflected light, broken by the weltering of the mimic waves into ten thousand fragments, whilst the few stars that overhung it in the firmament appeared to shoot through it in broken lines, and to be multiplied fifty-fold in the gloomy mirror on which we gazed.

Over us was a stormy sky, and around us, a darkness through which we could only distinguish, in outline, the nearest objects, whilst the wild wind swept strongly and dismally upon us. When it was discovered that the common pathway to the house was inundated, we were about to abandon our object and return home. The Captain, however, stooped down low for a moment, and, almost closing his eyes, looked along the surface of the waters; and then, rising himself very calmly, said, in his usually quiet tone, 'Ye needn't go back, boys, I've found a way; jist follow me.'

He immediately took a more circuitous direction, by which we reached a causeway that had been raised for the purpose of giving a free passage to and from the house, during such inundations as the present. Along this we had advanced more than half way, when we discovered a breach in it, which, as afterwards appeared, had that night been made by the strength of the flood. This, by means of our sticks and pikes, we found to be about three feet deep, and eight yards broad. Again we were at a loss how to proceed, when the fertile brain of the Captain devised a method of crossing it.

'Boys,' said he, 'of coorse you've all played at leap-frog; very well, strip and go in, a dozen of you, lean one upon the back of another from this to the opposite bank, where one must stand facing the outside man, both their shoulders agin one another, that the outside man may be supported. Then we can creep over you, an' a dacent bridge you'll be, any way.'

This was the work of only a few minutes, and in less than ten we were all safely over.

Merciful Heaven! how I sicken at the recollection of what is to follow! On reaching the dry bank, we proceeded instantly, and in profound silence, to the house; the Captain divided us into companies, and then assigned to each division its proper station. The two parties who had been so vindictive all the night, he kept about himself; for of those who were present, they only were in his confidence, and knew his nefarious purpose; their number was about fifteen.

Having made these dispositions, he, at the head of about five of them, approached the house on the windy side, for the fiend possessed a coolness which enabled him to seize upon every possible advantage. That he had combustibles about him was evident, for in less than fifteen minutes nearly one-half of the house was enveloped in flames. On seeing this, the others rushed over to the spot where he and his gang were standing, and remonstrated earnestly, but in vain; the flames now burst forth with renewed violence, and as they flung their strong light upon the faces of the foremost group, I think hell itself could hardly present anything more satanic than their countenances, now worked up into a paroxysm of infernal triumph at their own revenge. The Captain's look had lost all its calmness, every feature started out into distinct malignity, the curve in his brow was deep, and ran up to the root of the hair, dividing his face into two segments, that did not seem to have been designed for each other. His lips were half open, and the corners of his mouth a little brought back on each side, like those of a man expressing intense hatred and triumph over an enemy who is in the death-struggle under his grasp. His eyes blazed from beneath his knit eyebrows with a fire that seemed to be lighted up in the infernal pit itself. It is unnecessary, and only painful, to describe the rest of his gang; demons might have been proud of such horrible visages as they exhibited; for they worked under all the power of hatred, revenge, and joy; and these passions blended into one terrible scowl, enough almost to blast any human eye that would venture to look upon it.

When the others attempted to intercede for the lives of the inmates, there were at least fifteen guns and pistols levelled at them.

'Another word,' said the Captain, 'an' you're a corpse where you stand, or the first man who will dare to spake for them; no, no, it wasn't to spare them we came here. "No mercy" is the pass-word for the night, an' by the sacred oath I swore beyant in the chapel, any one among yez that will attempt to show it, will find none at my hand. Surround the house, boys, I tell ye, I hear them stirring. "No quarter – no mercy," is the ordher of the night.'

Such was his command over these misguided creatures, that in an instant there was a ring round the house to prevent the escape of the unhappy inmates, should the raging element give them time to attempt it; for none present durst withdraw themselves from the scene, not only from an apprehension of the Captain's present vengeance, or that of his gang, but because they knew that even had they then escaped, an early and certain death awaited them from a quarter against which they had no means of defence. The hour now was about half-past two o'clock. Scarcely had the last words escaped from the Captain's lips, when one of the windows of the house was broken, and a human head, having the hair in a blaze, was descried, apparently a woman's, if one might judge by the profusion of burning tresses, and the softness of the tones, notwithstanding that it called, or rather shrieked aloud for help and mercy. The only reply to this was the whoop from the Captain and his gang, of 'No mercy – no mercy!' and that instant the former, and one of the latter, rushed to the spot, and ere the action could be perceived, the head was transfixed with a bayonet and a pike, both having entered it together. The word 'mercy' was divided in her mouth; a short silence ensued, the head hung down on the window, but was instantly tossed back into the flames.

This action occasioned a cry of horror from all present, except the gang and their leader, which startled and enraged the latter so much, that he ran towards one of them, and had his bayonet, now reeking with the blood of its innocent victim, raised to plunge it in his body, when, dropping the point, he said in a piercing whisper, that hissed in the ears of all: 'It's no use now, you know; if one's to hang, all will hang; so our safest way, you persave, is to lave none of them to tell the story. Ye may go now, if you wish; but it won't save a hair of your heads. You cowardly set! I knew if I had tould yez the sport, that none of you, except my own boys, would come, so I jist played a thrick upon you; but remimber what you are sworn to, and stand to the oath ye tuck.'

Unhappily, notwithstanding the wetness of the preceding weather, the materials of the house were extremely combustible; the whole dwelling was now one body of glowing flame, yet the shouts and shrieks within rose awfully above its crackling and the voice of the storm, for the wind once more blew in gusts, and with great violence. The doors and windows were all torn open, and such of those within as had escaped the flames rushed towards them, for the purpose of further escape, and of claiming mercy at the hands of their destroyers; but whenever they appeared, the unearthly cry of 'no mercy' rang upon their ears for a moment, and for a moment only, for they were flung back at the points of the weapons which the demons had brought with them to make the work of vengeance more certain.

As yet there were many persons in the house, whose cry for life was strong as despair, and who clung to it with all the awakened powers of reason and instinct. The ear of man could hear nothing so strongly calculated to stifle the demon of cruelty and revenge within him, as the long and wailing shrieks which rose beyond the elements, in tones that were carried off rapidly upon the blast, until they died away in the darkness that lay behind the surrounding hills. Had not the house been in a solitary situation, and the hour the dead of night, any person sleeping within a moderate distance must have heard them, for such a cry of sorrow rising into a yell of despair was almost sufficient to have awakened the dead. It was lost, however, upon the hearts and ears that heard it: to them, though in justice be it said, to only comparatively a few of them, it appeared as delightful as the tones of soft and entrancing music.

The claims of the surviving sufferers were now modified; they supplicated merely to suffer death by the weapons of their enemies; they were willing to bear that, provided they should be allowed to escape from the flames; but no – the horrors of the conflagration were calmly and malignantly gloried in by their merciless assassins, who deliberately flung them back into all their tortures. In the course of a few minutes a man appeared upon the side-wall of the house, nearly naked; his figure, as he stood against the sky in horrible relief, was so finished a picture of woebegone agony and supplication, that it is yet as distinct in my memory as if I were again present at the scene. Every muscle, now in motion by the powerful agitation of his sufferings, stood out upon his limbs and neck, giving him an appearance of desperate strength, to which by this time he must have been wrought up; the perspiration poured from his frame, and the veins and arteries of his neck were inflated to a surprising thickness. Every moment he looked down into the flames which were rising to where he stood; and as he looked, the indescribable horror which flitted over his features might have worked upon the devil himself to relent. His words were few:—

'My child,' said he, 'is still safe, she is an infant, a young crathur that never harmed you, or any one – she is still safe. Your mothers, your wives, have young innocent childhre like it. Oh, spare her, think for a moment that it's one of your own; spare it, as you hope to meet a just God, or if you don't, in mercy shoot me first – put an end to me, before I see her burned!'

The Captain approached him coolly and deliberately. 'You'll prosecute no one now, you bloody informer,' said he: 'you'll convict no more boys for takin' an ould gun an' pistol from you, or for givin' you a neighbourly knock or two into the bargain.'

Just then, from a window opposite him, proceeded the shrieks of a woman, who appeared at it with the infant in her arms. She herself was almost scorched to death; but, with the presence of mind and humanity of her sex, she was about to put the little babe out of the window. The Captain noticed this, and, with characteristic atrocity, thrust, with a sharp bayonet, the little innocent, along with the person who endeavoured to rescue it, into the red flames, where they both perished. This was the work of an instant. Again he approached the man: 'Your child is a coal now,' said he, with deliberate mockery; 'I pitched it in myself, on the point of this,' – showing the weapon – 'an' now is your turn,' – saying which, he clambered up, by the assistance of his gang, who stood with a front of pikes and bayonets bristling to receive the wretched man, should he attempt, in his despair, to throw himself from the wall. The Captain got up, and placing the point of his bayonet against his shoulder, flung him into the fiery element that raged behind him. He uttered one wild and terrific cry, as he fell back, and no more. After this nothing was heard but the crackling of the fire, and the rushing of the blast; all that had possessed life within were consumed, amounting either to eight or eleven persons.

When this was accomplished, those who took an active part in the murder, stood for some time about the conflagration; and as it threw its red light upon their fierce faces and rough persons, soiled as they now were with smoke and black streaks of ashes, the scene seemed to be changed to hell, the murderers to spirits of the damned, rejoicing over the arrival and the torture of some guilty soul. The faces of those who kept aloof from the slaughter were blanched to the whiteness of death: some of them fainted, and others were in such agitation that they were compelled to lean on their comrades. They became actually powerless with horror: yet to such a scene were they brought by the pernicious influence of Ribbonism.

It was only when the last victim went down, that the conflagration shot up into the air with most unbounded fury. The house was large, deeply thatched, and well furnished; and the broad red pyramid rose up with fearful magnificence towards the sky. Abstractedly it had sublimity, but now it was associated with nothing in my mind but blood and terror. It was not, however, without a purpose that the Captain and his gang stood to contemplate its effect. 'Boys,' said he, 'we had betther be sartin that all's safe; who knows but there might be some of the sarpents crouchin' under a hape o' rubbish, to come out an' gibbet us to-morrow or next day: we had betther wait a while, anyhow, if it was only to see the blaze.'

Just then the flames rose majestically to a surprising height. Our eyes followed their direction; and we perceived, for the first time, that the dark clouds above, together with the intermediate air, appeared to reflect back, or rather to have caught the red hue of the fire. The hills and country about us appeared with an alarming distinctness; but the most picturesque part of it was the effect of reflection of the blaze on the floods that spread over the surrounding plains. These, in fact, appeared to be one broad mass of liquid copper, for the motion of the breaking-waters caught from the blaze of the high waving column, as reflected in them, a glaring light, which eddied, and rose, and fluctuated, as if the flood itself had been a lake of molten fire.

Fire, however, destroys rapidly. In a short time the flames sank – became weak and flickering – by and by, they shot out only in fits – the crackling of the timbers died away – the surrounding darkness deepened – and, ere long, the faint light was overpowered by the thick volumes of smoke that rose from the ruins of the house and its murdered inhabitants.

'Now, boys,' said the Captain, 'all is safe – we may go. Remember, every man of you, what you've sworn this night, on the book an' altar of God – not on a heretic Bible. If you perjure yourselves, you may hang us; but let me tell you, for your comfort, that if you do, there is them livin' that will take care the lease of your own lives will be but short.'

After this we dispersed every man to his own home.

Reader, – not many months elapsed ere I saw the bodies of this Captain, whose name was Patrick Devann, and all those who were actively concerned in the perpetration of this deed of horror, withering in the wind, where they hung gibbeted, near the scene of their nefarious villainy; and while I inwardly thanked Heaven for my own narrow and almost undeserved escape, I thought in my heart how seldom, even in this world, justice fails to overtake the murderer, and to enforce the righteous judgment of God – that 'whoso shedeth man's blood, by man shall his blood be shed.'

This tale of terror is, unfortunately, too true. The scene of hellish murder detailed in it lies at Wildgoose Lodge, in the county of Louth, within about four miles of Carrickmacross, and nine of Dundalk. No such multitudinous murder has occurred, under similar circumstances, except the burning of the Sheas, in the county of Tipperary. The name of the family burned in Wildgoose Lodge was Lynch. One of them had, shortly before this fatal night, prosecuted and convicted some of the neighbouring Ribbonmen, who visited him with severe marks of their displeasure, in consequence of his having refused to enrol himself as a member of their body. The language of the story is partly fictitious; but the facts are pretty closely such as were developed during the trial of the murderers. Both parties were Roman Catholics, and either twenty-five or twenty-eight of those who took an active part in the burning, were hanged and gibbeted in different parts of the county of Louth. Devann, the ringleader, hung for some months in chains, within about a hundred yards of his own house, and about half a mile from Wildgoose Lodge. His mother could neither go into nor out of her cabin without seeing his body swinging from the gibbet. Her usual exclamation on looking at him was— 'God be good to the sowl of my poor marthyr!' The peasantry, too, frequently exclaimed, on seeing him, 'Poor Paddy!' A gloomy fact that speaks volumes!

JOSEPH SHERIDAN LE FANU

THE FORTUNES OF SIR ROBERT ARDAGH

> *'The earth hath bubbles as the water hath –*
> *And these are of them.'*

IN THE SOUTH of Ireland, and on the borders of the county of Limerick, there lies a district of two or three miles in length, which is rendered interesting by the fact that it is one of the very few spots throughout this country in which some vestiges of aboriginal forests still remain. It has little or none of the lordly character of the American forest, for the axe has felled its oldest and its grandest trees; but in the close wood which survives live all the wild and pleasing peculiarities of nature: its complete irregularity, its vistas, in whose perspective the quiet cattle are browsing; its refreshing glades, where the grey rocks arise from amid the nodding fern; the silvery shafts of the old birch-trees; the knotted trunks of the hoary oak, the grotesque but graceful branches which never shed their honours under the tyrant pruning-hook; the soft green sward; the chequered light and shade; the wild luxuriant weeds; the lichen and the moss – all are beautiful alike in the green freshness of spring or in the sadness and sere of autumn. Their beauty is of that kind which makes the heart full with joy – appealing to the affections with a power which belongs to nature only. This wood runs up, from below the base, to the ridge of a long line of irregular hills, having perhaps, in primitive times, formed but the skirting of some mighty forest which occupied the level below.

But now, alas! whither have we drifted? whither has the tide of civilization borne us? It has passed over a land unprepared for it – it has left nakedness behind it; we have lost our forests, but our marauders remain; we have destroyed all that is picturesque, while we have retained everything that is revolting in barbarism. Through the midst of this woodland there runs a deep gully or glen, where the stillness of the scene is broken in upon by the brawling of a mountain-stream, which, however, in the winter season, swells into a rapid and formidable torrent.

There is one point at which the glen becomes extremely deep and narrow; the sides descend to the depth of some hundred feet, and are so steep as to be nearly perpendicular. The wild trees which have taken root in the crannies and chasms of the rock are so intersected and entangled, that one can with difficulty catch a glimpse of the stream which wheels, flashes, and foams below, as if exulting in the surrounding silence and solitude.

This spot was not unwisely chosen, as a point of no ordinary strength, for the erection of a massive square tower or keep, one side of which rises as if in continuation of the precipitous cliff on which it is based. Originally, the only mode of ingress was by a narrow portal in the very wall which overtopped the precipice, opening upon a ledge of rock which afforded a precarious pathway, cautiously intersected, however, by a deep trench cut out with great labour in the living rock; so that, in its pristine state, and before the introduction of artillery into the art of war, this tower might have been pronounced, and that not presumptuously, impregnable.

The progress of improvement and the increasing security of the times had, however, tempted its successive proprietors, if not to adorn, at least to enlarge their premises, and about the middle of the last century, when the castle was last inhabited, the original square tower formed but a small part of the edifice.

The castle, and a wide tract of the surrounding country, had from time immemorial belonged to a family which, for distinctness, we shall call by the name of Ardagh; and owing to the associations which, in Ireland, almost always attach to scenes which have long witnessed alike the exercise of stern feudal authority, and of that savage hospitality which distinguished the good old times, this building has become the subject and the scene of many wild and extraordinary traditions. One of them I have been enabled, by a personal acquaintance with an eye-witness of the events, to trace to its origin; and yet it is hard to say whether the events which I am about to record appear more strange and improbable as seen through the distorting medium of tradition, or in the appalling dimness of uncertainty which surrounds the reality.

Tradition says that, sometime in the last century, Sir Robert Ardagh, a young man, and the last heir of that family, went abroad and served in foreign armies; and that, having acquired considerable honour and emolument, he settled at Castle Ardagh, the building we have just now attempted to describe. He was what the country people call a *dark* man; that is, he was considered morose, reserved, and ill-tempered; and, as it was supposed from the utter solitude of his life, was upon no terms of cordiality with the other members of his family.

The only occasion upon which he broke through the solitary monotony of his life was during the continuance of the racing season, and immediately subsequent to it; at which time he was to be seen among the busiest upon the course, betting deeply and unhesitatingly, and invariably with success. Sir Robert was, however, too well known as a man of honour, and of too high a family, to be suspected of any unfair dealing. He was, moreover, a soldier, and a man of intrepid as well as of a haughty character; and no one cared to hazard a surmise, the consequences of which would be felt most probably by its originator only.

Gossip, however, was not silent; it was remarked that Sir Robert never appeared at the race-ground, which was the only place of public resort which he frequented, except in company with a certain strange-looking person, who was never seen elsewhere, or under other circumstances. It was remarked, too, that this man, whose relation to Sir Robert was never distinctly ascertained, was the only person to whom he seemed to speak unnecessarily; it was observed that while with the country gentry he exchanged no further communication than what was unavoidable in arranging his sporting transactions, with this person he would converse earnestly and frequently. Tradition asserts that, to enhance the curiosity which this unaccountable and exclusive preference excited, the stranger possessed some striking and unpleasant peculiarities of person and of garb – though it is not stated, however, what these were – but they, in conjunction with Sir Robert's secluded habits and extraordinary run of luck – a success which was supposed to result from the suggestions and immediate advice of the unknown – were sufficient to warrant report in pronouncing that there was something *queer* in the wind, and in surmising that Sir Robert was playing a fearful and a hazardous game, and that, in short, his strange companion was little better than the Devil himself.

Years rolled quietly away, and nothing very novel occurred in the arrangements of Castle Ardagh, excepting that Sir Robert parted with his odd companion, but as nobody could tell whence he came, so nobody could say whither he had gone. Sir Robert's habits, however, underwent no consequent change; he continued regularly to frequent the race meetings, without mixing at all in the convivialities of the gentry, and immediately afterwards to relapse into the secluded monotony of his ordinary life.

It was said that he had accumulated vast sums of money – and, as his bets were always successful and always large, such must have been the case. He did not suffer the acquisition of wealth, however, to influence his hospitality or his house-keeping – he neither purchased land, nor extended his establishment; and his mode of enjoying his money must have been altogether that of the miser – consisting merely in the pleasure of touching and telling his gold, and in the consciousness of wealth.

Sir Robert's temper, so far from improving, became more than ever gloomy and morose. He sometimes carried the indulgence of his evil dispositions to such a height that it bordered upon insanity. During these paroxysms he would neither eat, drink, nor sleep. On such occasions he insisted on perfect privacy, even from the intrusion of his most trusted servants; his voice was frequently heard, sometimes in earnest supplication, sometimes raised, as if in loud and angry altercation with some unknown visitant. Sometimes he would for hours together walk to and fro throughout the long oak-wainscoted apartment which he generally occupied, with wild gesticulations and agitated pace, in the manner of one who has been roused to a state of unnatural excitement by some sudden and appalling intimation.

These paroxysms of apparent lunacy were so frightful, that during their continuance even his oldest and most faithful domestics dared not approach him; consequently his hours of agony were never intruded upon, and the mysterious causes of his sufferings appeared likely to remain hidden for ever.

On one occasion a fit of this kind continued for an unusual time; the ordinary term of their duration – about two days – had been long past, and the old servant who generally waited upon Sir Robert after these visitations, having in vain listened for the well-known tinkle of his master's hand-bell, began to feel extremely anxious; he feared that his master might have died from sheer exhaustion, or perhaps put an end to his own existence during his miserable depression. These fears at length became so strong, that having in vain urged some of his brother servants to accompany him, he determined to go up alone, and himself see whether any accident had befallen Sir Robert.

He traversed the several passages which conducted from the new to the more ancient parts of the mansion, and having arrived in the old hall of the castle, the utter silence of the hour – for it was very late in the night – the idea of the nature of the enterprise in which he was engaging himself, a sensation of remoteness from anything like human companionship, but, more than all, the vivid but undefined anticipation of something horrible, came upon him with such oppressive weight that he hesitated as to whether he should proceed. Real uneasiness, however, respecting the fate of his master, for whom he felt that kind of attachment which the force of habitual intercourse not unfrequently engenders respecting objects not in themselves amiable, and also a latent unwillingness to expose his weakness to the ridicule of his fellow-servants, combined to overcome his reluctance; and he had just placed his foot upon the first step of the staircase which conducted to his master's chamber, when his attention was arrested by a low but distinct knocking at the hall-door. Not, perhaps, very sorry at finding thus an excuse even for deferring his intended expedition, he placed the candle upon a stone block which lay in the hall and approached the door, uncertain whether his ears had not deceived him. This doubt was justified by the circumstance that the hall entrance had been for nearly fifty years disused as a mode of ingress to the castle. The situation of this gate also, which we have endeavoured to describe, opening upon a narrow ledge of rock which overhangs a perilous cliff, rendered it at all times, but particularly at night, a dangerous entrance. This shelving platform of rock, which formed the only avenue to the door, was divided, as I have already stated, by a broad chasm, the planks across which had long disappeared, by decay or otherwise; so that it seemed at least highly improbable that any man could have found his way across the passage in safety to the door, more particularly on a night like this, of singular darkness. The old man, therefore, listened attentively, to ascertain whether the first application should be followed by another. He had not long to wait. The same low but singularly distinct knocking was repeated; so low that it seemed as if the applicant had employed no harder or heavier instrument than his hand, and yet, despite the immense thickness of the door, with such strength that the sound was distinctly audible.

The knock was repeated a third time, without any increase of loudness; and the old man, obeying an impulse for which to his dying hour he could never account, proceeded to remove, one by one, the three great oaken bars which secured the door. Time and damp had effectually corroded the iron chambers of the lock, so that it afforded little resistance. With some effort, as he believed, assisted from without, the old servant succeeded in opening the door; and a low, square-built figure, apparently that of a man wrapped in a large black cloak, entered the hall. The servant could not see much of this visitor with any distinctness; his dress appeared foreign, the skirt of his ample cloak was thrown over one shoulder; he wore a large felt hat, with a very heavy leaf, from under which escaped what appeared to be a mass of long sooty-black hair; his feet were cased in heavy riding-boots. Such were the few particulars which the servant had time and light to observe. The stranger desired him to let his master know instantly that a friend had come, by appointment, to settle some business with him. The servant hesitated, but a slight motion on the part of his visitor, as if to possess himself of the candle, determined him; so, taking it in his hand, he ascended the castle stairs, leaving the guest in the hall.

On reaching the apartment which opened upon the oak-chamber he was surprised to observe the door of that room partly open, and the room itself lit up. He paused, but there was no sound; he looked in, and saw Sir Robert, his head and the upper part of his body reclining on a table, upon which two candles burned; his arms were stretched forward on either side, and perfectly motionless; it appeared that, having been sitting at the table, he had thus sunk forward, either dead or in a swoon. There was no sound of breathing; all was silent, except the sharp ticking of a watch, which lay beside the lamp. The servant coughed twice or thrice, but with no effect; his fears now almost amounted to certainty, and he was approaching the table on which his master partly lay, to satisfy himself of his death, when Sir Robert slowly raised his head, and, throwing himself back in his chair, fixed his eyes in a ghastly and uncertain gaze upon his attendant. At length he said, slowly and painfully, as if he dreaded the answer,—

'In God's name, what are you?'

'Sir,' said the servant, 'a strange gentleman wants to see you below.'

At this intimation Sir Robert, starting to his feet and

tossing his arms wildly upwards, uttered a shriek of such appalling and despairing terror that it was almost too fearful for human endurance; and long after the sound had ceased it seemed to the terrified imagination of the old servant to roll through the deserted passages in bursts of unnatural laughter. After a few moments Sir Robert said,—

'Can't you send him away? Why does he come so soon? O Merciful Powers! let him leave me for an hour; a little time. I can't see him now; try to get him away. You see I can't go down now; I have not strength. O God! O God! let him come back in an hour; it is not long to wait. He cannot lose anything by it; nothing, nothing, nothing. Tell him that! Say anything to him.'

The servant went down. In his own words, he did not feel the stairs under him till he got to the hall. The figure stood exactly as he had left it. He delivered his master's message as coherently as he could. The stranger replied in a careless tone:

'If Sir Robert will not come down to me, I must go up to him.'

The man returned, and to his surprise he found his master much more composed in manner. He listened to the message, and though the cold perspiration rose in drops upon his forehead faster than he could wipe it away, his manner had lost the dreadful agitation which had marked it before. He rose feebly, and casting a last look of agony behind him, passed from the room to the lobby, where he signed to his attendant not to follow him. The man moved as far as the head of the staircase, from whence he had a tolerably distinct view of the hall, which was imperfectly lighted by the candle he had left there.

He saw his master reel, rather than walk, down the stairs, clinging all the way to the banisters. He walked on, as if about to sink every moment from weakness. The figure advanced as if to meet him, and in passing struck down the light. The servant could see no more; but there was a sound of struggling, renewed at intervals with silent but fearful energy. It was evident, however, that the parties were approaching the door, for he heard the solid oak sound twice or thrice, as the feet of the combatants, in shuffling hither and thither over the floor, struck upon it. After a slight pause, he heard the door thrown open with such violence that the leaf seemed to strike the side-wall of the hall, for it was so dark without that this could only be surmised by the sound. The struggle was renewed with an agony and intenseness of energy that betrayed itself in deep-drawn gasps. One desperate effort, which terminated in the breaking of some part of the door, producing a sound as if the door-post was wrenched from its position, was followed by another wrestle, evidently upon the narrow ledge which ran outside the door, overtopping the precipice. This proved to be the final struggle; it was followed by a crashing sound as if some heavy body had fallen over, and was rushing down the precipice through the light boughs that crossed near the top. All then became still as the grave, except when the moan of the night-wind sighed up the wooded glen.

The old servant had not nerve to return through the hall, and to him the darkness seemed all but endless; but morning at length came, and with it the disclosure of the events of the night. Near the door, upon the ground, lay Sir Robert's sword-belt, which had given way in the scuffle. A huge splinter from the massive door-post had been wrenched off by an almost superhuman effort – one which nothing but the gripe of a despairing man could have severed – and on the rocks outside were left the marks of the slipping and sliding of feet.

At the foot of the precipice, not immediately under the castle, but dragged some way up the glen, were found the remains of Sir Robert, with hardly a vestige of a limb or feature left distinguishable. The right hand, however, was uninjured, and in its fingers were clutched, with the fixedness of death, a long lock of coarse sooty hair – the only direct circumstantial evidence of the presence of a second person.

KATHARINE TYNAN

A DESCENDANT OF IRISH EARLS

HE SAT IN my little room on a brilliant day of May, despite that he wore a working-man's respectable cheap suit of tweeds, in face and gaze a reverend signior. The light blue eyes, that had just a film of dreams upon them, regarded me with grave dignity. The long slender olive face, with its finely-pointed beard, was the ideal one for doublet and ruff. Clap the head in an ancient picture frame, and place it alongside a gallery's length of Desmond's Earls, and you would at once recognize the relationship. Certainly not a pretender, and still less, one thought, marking his air of quiet belief in his assertions, a man who pretended to himself, or inwardly fell short of his pretensions. I suppose *noblesse oblige* will bind, or may bind, as surely the inheritor of proud blood and traditions fallen to a trade of glass-making, as one yet in possession of his inheritance. I do not know if my poor friend was a glass-blower *manqué* because of his Desmond blood; but sure am I that his dreams wove in the crystals such magic lines of rose and opal that if such things were tangible he were a finer craftsman than the finest of Salviatis. Sitting at his work I make no doubt he blew glass – and other things. Fairy iridescent things that floated between earth and sky, and had in them the glory of a prism. But presently he must needs go home to the tall tenement house in a grimy Dublin street, where wife and weans were depending on his mere prosaic glass-making; and there, no doubt, the poverty, the crying children, the poor room, would prick that rosy bubble that had floated home with him along the dark streets.

In Dublin one is not often out of sight of the mountains, nor out of smell of the sea. At least these things are nearly always easy to regain. From upper windows one can get a glimpse of the blue hills, these spring days glorified with the rose and purple of the East wind. These same East-windy mornings the salt breath of the sea comes up through the streets, reminding one delightfully that Dublin is a seaboard city. G —— Street, however, though the tenements be leaning over from height and ricketiness, affords one no glimpse of the mountains; and though a five minutes' walk will bring you in sight of Howth, like a sapphire in the bay, the seastrand you will come upon is little more than mud-banks and sewage deposit, and from that blows no sea-salt, bright and sweet.

On the street itself is writ large, as with many of its neighbours, *Ichabod*. These were the dwellings of the peers and gentlemen-commoners of Ireland in the palmy days before the Union, the days that no legislation will restore, any more than it will 'The glory that was Greece, and the grandeur that was Rome.' The houses have forlorn remnants of bygone splendour. Doors and window-shutters are of wine-red mahogany, rich and ancient. Ornate decorations in Italian stucco-work are on walls and ceiling. Why, here Angelica Kauffmann may have worked herself, for she came over in that reign of splendour, the Rutland Vice-royalty, to decorate some of these houses, the Irish nobility having singularly munificent ideas about decoration, and the best artists to perform it.

It was of a Bank-holiday my Desmond visited me. Any other day he had been at his glass-blowing. I suppose it was delightful to him to get out of the dark street, and come by lanes of bloomy hawthorn, and fields of white and gold, with scarce a grass-blade between, and to find at the end of that delightful journey – sympathy. I suppose the wife was a little intolerant of her earl-presumptive. I am sure the children were, especially the two elder ones, a boy and a girl grown enough to be employed respectably as a post-office sorter and an apprentice to the dressmaking, respectively. After all, when one is earning one's money, and well-content with the state of life in which God has placed one, it is somewhat irritating to have a father who is a pseudo-earl, and with very serious ideas of the ways and manners incumbent on one because there is in one's veins the blood of nobles, saints and warriors, who are come to be less than dust, and of no possible use to their descendants.

He came to me for sympathy because he had seen an article of mine about Youghal, once the seat of the Desmond power, in which I had been enthusiastic over that great line – a line rather of Irish princes than of Anglo-Irish earls. Between them and their cousins, the Kildare Fitzgeralds, they pretty well halved Ireland. Indeed all the great Southern and Eastern expanse of Ireland would have been theirs, except for a race sprung from a plaguy fellow who was Henry the Second's butler, and had founded a race of Butlers, great in brain-power as well as in thew and sinew. These and the Fitzgeralds hated each other with a bitter rivalry. However, my Fitzgerald of Desmond thought upon me as one likely to understand what he had inherited. And, poor soul, he had grown tired of trying to air in the columns of newspapers – mostly closed to him as a poor bore – the fact that he was the lineal descendant of the great Earls of Desmond, and that he would like to know on what basis certain ladies of wealth and position rested their claims to dispossess him of his honours.

He had come to prove his claims to one interested listener. Therefore he waved away all offer of refreshment; and producing from an old portfolio, which he carried as if it contained the Crown jewels, various documents, he demanded my attention for them. Each was tied and folded with scrupulous care; each wrapped in layers of tissue-paper. They were worn so thin that they needed such protection. 'I am in the habit of perusing them frequently, madam,' he said in his formal manner, and gazing at me over his great spectacles. It was easy to see that by the way he followed from a distance my reading of the MSS.

There was an elaborate and careful account of his derivation from Garrett Fitzgerald, nineteenth Earl of Desmond, and his wife Helen, daughter of Lord Richard Condon. His grandmother, Elizabeth Fitzgerald, was the grand-daughter of this last Fitzgerald to bear the title of Earl Desmond. They were three forlorn damsels, Elizabeth, Elleanora, and Helen, tricked of their inheritance as effectually as was their ancestor in 1589, by Sir Walter Raleigh, who was himself stript bare by the most astute Earl of Cork, thirteen years later. They had friends, however, if they had not gear, and no doubt were made much of in the gay Dublin of their time. The lovely Isabella, Duchess of Rutland, was their fast friend and sympathizer. One thinks of her protecting the wronged and innocent, for ever fresh and lovely, as Sir Joshua Reynolds painted her; or as she shines out of a contemporary record at a Rotunda Gardens fête, in a dress of pink silk with a stomacher and sleeve-knots of diamonds, and a great hat of brown velvet, sideways on her charming powdered head, set with a plume of feathers and an aigrette of diamonds. Perhaps the three damsels danced at those Rotunda balls, for their cousin, the Earl of Grandison, or their magnificent duchess, would surely never have allowed them to languish in genteel poverty.

Helen, a woman of spirit, proceeded against the Duke of Devonshire for the restoration of their lost acres. But being single-handed and a woman, she failed, poor soul, and taking her failure to heart, died of it. I have forgotten about Elleanora; but Elizabeth, my Desmond's grandmother, married a very gallant soldier, who afterwards was killed at the Battle of Bunker's Hill. So my Desmond has a lien with American earth.

If the Duke of Rutland had not taken a putrid fever after a gay progress through the North of Ireland, and died of it after a few days' illness, my sketch need never have been written. The duchess was so interested in her *protégées* that she had obtained the Duke's promise to settle a handsome pension upon them. No doubt, too, she would have been a powerful friend in any new effort they should make to win back their own. However, the Duke died; the gay days of the Rutland reign were over: her Grace fled back to England a forlorn widow; and there settled on Ireland the black shadow of the approaching Rebellion. And so the wrong went quite unrighted.

That it was acknowledged to a certain extent was shown by the fact that my Desmond's father enjoyed during his lifetime a small State pension, which, however, lapsed with his death.

I can see as I write the grave olive face with the eyes regarding me. What an unsettling thing for a common worker in glass to be lineal descendant of so proud a line! I have said they were Irish princes. They were; in their power, the extent of their territories, and their haughty bearing towards the race from whose loins they had sprung. More Irish than the Irish, such were the Fitzgeralds, alike of Desmond and

Kildare; but yet no Irish princes of a half-barbarous magnificence. Rather with all the stately splendour of the Courts of the Middle Ages superadded to their free life; with traditions of church-building and college-founding, as you will know, seeing their remains at Youghal, where is their college, and the Church of St Mary's, and the Warden's House of one magnificent foundation; and the town yet landmarked on North and South by the ruins of the abbeys built by them for the great mendicant Friars of the Middle Ages, Franciscan and Dominican. And along Blackwater, most lovely of rivers, all burnished copper and gold in the autumn because of the overhanging woods, every high crag has its castle in ruins, once the proud eyrie of a Desmond Earl.

The Atlantic roars like wild bulls at the strand of Youghal. On the mildest day the air is full of its thud and reverberation, and ever a shower of silver spray springs above the strong sea-wall. It must be magnificent in storm. Where the harbour of Youghal narrows to the mouth of Blackwater, one is ferried across to holy Ardmore of St Declan, with its church and holy well, and St Declan's stone. Across the ferry is county Waterford. In Ardmore long ugo they buried a Desmond Earl; but, exiled from his own Temple-Michael on the Blackwater, his spirit would not rest. So every night, over the breakers and the storm they heard a strange, great voice, crying terribly, 'Garoult arointha! arointha,' – which is 'Hurry over! Give Gerald a ferry.' So at last they took up the unquiet dead, and ferried him to Temple-Michael, where his sleep was sound.

A race of giants certainly. In Youghal streets, ghostly in the autumn weather, what shadows elbow each other! Knights Templars, Desmonds, Elizabethans, Spenser and Raleigh, Noll Cromwell and his Roundheads. The past of Youghal is great and misty, like a huge tapestry blown with the sea-wind, on which stir gigantic figures of knights and horsemen. But of the great and magnificent Desmonds remains this – an old man with a wallet of yellow papers, escaped from an irksome trade one hour of a summer day, to pour into the ears of a willing listener his mouldy old tale at which the well-fed, well-clad world had gaped and shrugged its impertinent shoulders.

EDITH SOMERVILLE
and MARTIN ROSS

A NINETEENTH-CENTURY MIRACLE

CAPTAIN 'PAT' NAYLOR, of the ——th Dragoons, had the influenza. For three days he had lain prostrate, a sodden and aching victim to the universal leveller, and an intolerable nuisance to his wife. This last is perhaps an over-statement; Mrs Naylor was in the habit of bearing other people's burdens with excellent fortitude, but she felt justly annoyed that Captain Pat should knock up before they had fairly settled down in their new quarters, and while yet three of the horses were out of sorts after the crossing from England.

Pilot, however, was quite fit, a very tranquillizing fact, and one that Mrs Pat felt was due to her own good sense in summering him on her father's broad pastures in Meath, instead of 'lugging him to Aldershot with the rest of the string, as Pat wanted to do', as she explained to Major Booth. Major Booth shed a friendly grin upon his fallen comrade, who lay, a deplorable object, on the horrid velvet-covered sofa peculiar to indifferent lodgings, and said vaguely that one of his brutes was right anyhow, and he was going to ride him at Carnfother the next day.

'You'd better come too, Mrs Pat,' he added; 'and if you'll drive me I'll send my chap on with the horses. It's too far to ride. It's fourteen Irish miles off, and fourteen Irish miles is just about the longest distance I know.'

Carnfother is a village in a remote part of the Co. Cork; it possesses a small hotel – in Ireland no hostelry, however abject, would demean itself by accepting the title of inn – a police barrack, a few minor public-houses, a good many dirty cottages, and an unrivalled collection of loafers. The stretch of salmon river that gleamed away to the distant heathery hills afforded the *raison d'être* of both hotel and loafers, but the fishing season had not begun, and the attention of both was therefore undividedly bestowed on Mrs Naylor and Major Booth. The former's cigarette and the somewhat Paradisaic dimensions of her apron skirt would indeed at any time have rivalled in interest the landing of a 20-lb fish, and as she strode into the hotel the bystanders' ejaculatory piety would have done credit to a revival meeting.

'Well, well, I'll say nothing for her but that she's quare!' said the old landlady, hurrying in from her hens to attend to these rarer birds whom fortune had sent to her net.

Mrs Pat's roan cob had attacked and defeated the fourteen Irish miles with superfluous zeal, and there were still several minutes before the hounds could be reasonably expected on the scene. The soda was bad, the whiskey was worse. The sound of a fiddle came in with the sunshine through the open door, and our friends strolled out into the street to see what was going on. In the centre of a ring of onlookers an old man was playing, and was, moreover, dancing to his own music, and dancing with serious, incongruous elegance. Round and round the circle he footed it, his long thin legs twinkling in absolute accord with the complicated jig that his long thin fingers were ripping out of the cracked and raucous fiddle. A very plain, stout young woman, with a heavy red face and discordantly golden hair, shuffled round after him in a clumsy pretence of dancing, and as the couple faced Mrs Pat she saw that the old man was blind. Steam was rising from his domed bald head, and his long black hair danced on his shoulders. His face was pale and strange and entirely self-absorbed. Had Mrs Pat been in the habit of instituting romantic parallels between the past and the present she might have thought of the priests of Baal who danced in probably just such measures round the cromlechs in the hills above Carnfother; as she wasn't, she remarked merely that this was all very well, but that the old maniac would have to clear out of that before they brought Pilot round, or there'd be trouble.

There was trouble, but it did not arise from Pilot, but from the yellow-haired woman's pertinacious demands for money from Mrs Naylor. She had the offensive fluency that comes of long practice in alternate wheedling and bullying, and although Major Booth had given her a shilling she continued to pester Mrs Pat for a further largesse. But, as it happened, Mrs Pat's purse was in her covert coat in the dog-cart, and Mrs Pat's temper was ever within easy reach, and on being too closely pressed for the one she exhibited the other with a decision that contracted the ring of bystanders to hear the fun, and loosened the yellow-haired woman's language, till unfortunate Major Booth felt that if he could get her off the field of battle for a sovereign it would be cheap at the price. The old man continued to walk round and round, fingering a dumb tune on his fiddle that he did not bow, while the sunlight glistened hot and bright in his unwinking eyes; there was a faint smile on his lips, he heard as little as he saw; it was evident that he was away where 'beyond these voices there is peace', in the fairy country that his forefathers called the Tir na'n Oge.

At this juncture the note of the horn sounded very sweetly from across the shining ford of the river. Hounds and riders came splashing up into the village street, the old man and his daughter were hustled to one side, and Mrs Pat's affability returned as she settled her extremely smart little person on Pilot's curveting back, and was instantly aware that there was nothing present that could touch either of them in looks or quality. Carnfother was at the extreme verge of the D—— Hounds' country; there were not more than about thirty riders out, and Mrs Pat was not far wrong when she observed to Major Booth that there was not much class about them. Of the four or five women who were of the field, but one wore a habit with any pretensions to conformity with the sacred laws of fashion, and its colour was a blue that, taken in connection with a red, brass-buttoned waistcoat, reminded the severe critic from Royal Meath of the head porter at the Shelburne Hotel. So she informed Major Booth in one of the rare intervals permitted to her by Pilot for conversation.

'All right,' responded that gentleman, 'you wait until you and that ramping brute of yours get up among the stone walls, and you'll be jolly glad if she'll call a cab for you and see you taken safe home. I tell you what – you won't be able to see the way she goes.'

'Rubbish!' said Mrs Pat, and, whether from sympathy or from a petulant touch of her heel, Pilot at this moment involved himself in so intricate a series of plunges and bucks as to preclude further discussion.

The first covert – a small wood on the flank of a hill – was blank, and the hounds moved on across country to the next draw. It was a land of pasture, and in every fence was a deep muddy passage, through which the field splashed in single file with the grave stolidity of the cows by whom the gaps had been made. Mrs Pat was feeling horribly bored. Her escort had joined himself to two of the ladies of the hunt, and though it was gratifying to observe that one wore a paste brooch in her tie and the other had an imitation cavalry bit and bridle, with a leather tassel hanging from her pony's throat, these things lost their savour when she had no one with whom to make merry over them. She had left her sandwiches in the dog-cart, her servant had mistaken whiskey for sherry when he was filling her flask; the day had clouded over, and already one brief but furious shower had scourged the curl out of her dark fringe and made the reins slippery.

At last, however, a nice-looking gorse covert was reached, and the hounds threw themselves into it with promising alacrity. Pilot steadied himself, and stood with pricked ears, giving an occasional snatch at his bit, and looking, as no one knew better than his rider, the very picture of a hunter, while he listened for the first note that should tell of a find. He had not long to wait. There came a thin little squeal from the middle of the covert, and a hound flung up out of the thicker gorse and began to run along a ridge of rock, with head down, and feathering stern.

'They've got him, my lady,' said a young farmer on a rough three-year-old to Mrs Pat, as he stuffed his pipe in his pocket. 'That's Patience; we'll have a hunt out o' this.'

Then came another and longer squeal as Patience plunged out of sight again, and then, as the glowing chorus rose from the half-seen pack, a whip, posted on a hillside beyond the covert, raised his cap high in the air, and a wild screech that set Pilot dancing from leg to leg broke from a country boy who was driving a harrow in the next field: 'Ga – aane away – ay!'

Mrs Pat forgot her annoyances. Her time had come. She would show that idiot Booth that Pilot was not to be insulted with impunity, and— But here retrospect and intention became alike merged in the present, and in the single resolve to get ahead and stay there. Half a dozen of Pilot's great reaching strides, and she was in the next field and over the low bank without putting an iron on it. The horse with the harrow, deserted by his driver, was following the hunt with the best of them, and, combining business with pleasure, was, as he went, harrowing the field with absurd energy. The Paste Brooch and the Shelburne Porter – so Mrs Pat mentally distinguished them – were sailing along with a good start, and Major Booth was close at their heels. The light soil of the tilled field flew in every direction as thirty or more horses raced across it, and the usual retinue of foot runners raised an ecstatic yell as Mrs Pat forged ahead and sent her big horse over the fence at the end of the field in a style that happily combined swagger with knowledge.

The hounds were streaking along over a succession of pasture fields, and the cattle gaps which were to be found in every fence vexed the proud soul of Mrs Pat. She was too good a sportswoman to school her horse over needless jumps when hounds were running, but it infuriated her to have to hustle with these outsiders for her place at a gap. So she complained to Major Booth, with a vehemence of adjective that, though it may be forgiven to her, need not be set down here.

'Is *all* the wretched country like this?' she inquired indignantly, as the Shelburne Porter's pony splashed ahead of her through a muddy ford, just beyond which the hounds had momentarily checked; 'you told me to bring out a big-jumped horse, and I might have gone the whole hunt on a bicycle!'

Major Booth's reply was to point to the hounds. They had cast back to the line that they had flashed over, and had begun to run again at right angles from the grassy valley down which they had come, up towards the heather-clad hills that lay back of Carnfother.

'Say your prayers, Mrs Pat!' he said, in what Mrs Pat felt to be a gratuitously offensive manner, 'and I'll ask the lady in the pretty blue habit to have an eye to you. This is a hill fox and he's going to make you and Pilot sit up!'

Mrs Pat was not in a mood to be trifled with, and I again think it better to omit her response to this inconvenient jesting. What she did was to give Pilot his head, and she presently found herself as near the hounds as was necessary, galloping in a line with the huntsman straight for a three-foot wall, lightly built of round stones. That her horse could refuse to jump it was a possibility that did not so much as enter her head; but that he did so was a fact whose stern logic could not be gainsaid. She had too firm a seat to be discomposed by the swinging plunge with which he turned from it, but her mental balance sustained a serious shake. That Pilot, at the head of the hunt, should refuse, was a thing that struck at the root of her dearest beliefs. She stopped him and turned him at the wall again; again he refused, and at the same instant Major Booth and the blue habit jumped it side by side.

'What did I tell you!' the former called back, with a laugh that grated on Mrs Pat's ear with a truly fiendish rasp; 'do you want a lead?'

The incensed Mrs Pat once more replied in forcible phraseology, as she drove her horse again at the wall. The average Meath horse likes stones just about as much as the average Co. Cork horse enjoys water, and the train of running men and boys were given the exquisite gratification of a contest between Pilot and his rider.

'Howld on, miss, till I knock a few shtones for ye!' volunteered one, trying to interpose between Pilot and the wall.

'Get out of the way!' was Mrs Pat's response to this civility, as she crammed her steed at the jump again. The volunteer, amid roars of laughter from his friends, saved his life only by dint of undignified agility, as the big horse whirled round, rearing and plunging.

'Isn't he the divil painted?' exclaimed another in highest admiration; 'wait till I give him a couple of slaps of my bawneen, miss!' He dragged off his white flannel coat and attacked Pilot in the rear with it, while another of the party flung clods of mud vaguely into the battle, and another persistently implored the maddened Mrs Pat to get off and let him lead the horse over 'before she'd lose her life': a suggestion that has perhaps a more thoroughly exasperating effect than any other on occasions such as this.

By the time that Pilot had pawed down half the wall and been induced to buck over, or into, what remained of it, Mrs Pat's temper was irretrievably gone, and she was at the heel instead of the head of the hunt. Thanks to this position there was bestowed on her the abhorred, but not to be declined, advantage of availing herself of the gaps made in the next couple of jumps by the other riders; but the stones they had kicked down were almost as agitating to Pilot's ruffled nerves as those that still remained in position. She found it the last straw that she should have to wait for the obsequious runners to tear these out of her way, while the galloping backs in front of her grew smaller and smaller, and the adulatory condolences of her assistants became more and more hard to endure. She literally hurled the shilling at them as she set off once more to try to recover her lost ground, and by sheer force of passion hustled Pilot over the next broken-down wall without a refusal. For she had now got into that stony country whereof Major Booth had spoken. Rough heathery fields, ribbed with rocks and sown with grey boulders, were all round. The broad salmon river swept sleekly through the valley below, among the bland green fields which were as far away for all practical purposes as the plains of Paradise. No one who has not ridden a stern chase over rough ground on a well-bred horse with his temper a bit out of hand will be able at all fitly to sympathize with the trials of Mrs Naylor. The hunt and all that appertained to it had sunk out of sight over a rugged hill-side, and she had nothing by which to steer her course save the hoof-marks in the occasional black and boggy intervals between the heathery knolls. No one had ever accused her of being short of pluck, and she pressed on her difficult way with the utmost gallantry; but short of temper she certainly was, and at each succeeding obstacle there ensued a more bitter battle between her and her horse. Every here and there a band of crisp upland meadow would give the latter a chance, but each such advantage would be squandered in the war dance that he indulged in at every wall.

At last the summit of the interminable series of hills was gained, and Mrs Pat scanned the solitudes that surrounded her with wrathful eyes. The hounds were lost, as completely swallowed up as ever were Korah, Dathan and Abiram. Not the most despised of the habits or the feeblest of the three-year-olds had been left behind to give a hint of their course; but the hoof-marks showed black on a marshy down-grade of grass, and with an angry clout of her crop on Pilot's unaccustomed ribs, she set off again. A narrow road cut across the hills at the end of the field. The latter was divided from it by a low, thin wall of sharp slaty stones, and on the further side there was a wide and boggy drain. It was not a nice place, and Pilot thundered down towards it at a pace that suited his rider's temper better than her judgment. It was evident, at all events, that he did not mean to refuse. Nor did he; he rose out of the heavy ground at the wall like a rocketing pheasant, and cleared it by more than twice its height; but though he jumped high he did not jump wide, and he landed half in and out of the drain, with his forefeet clawing at its greasy edge, and his hind legs deep in the black mud.

Mrs Pat scrambled out of the saddle with the speed of light, and after a few momentous seconds, during which it seemed horribly likely that the horse would relapse bodily into the drain, his and Mrs Pat's efforts prevailed, and he was standing, trembling, and dripping, on the narrow road. She led him on for a few steps; he went sound, and for one delusive instant she thought he had escaped damage; then, through the black slime on one of his hind legs the red blood began to flow. It came from high up inside the off hind leg, above the hock, and it welled ever faster and faster, a plaited crimson stream that made his owner's heart sink. She dipped her handkerchief in the ditch and cleaned the cut. It was deep in the fleshy part of the leg, a gaping wound, inflicted by one of those razor slates that hide like sentient enemies in such boggy places. It was large enough for her to put her hand in; she held the edges together, and the bleeding ceased for an instant; then, as she released them, it began again worse than ever. Her handkerchief was as inadequate for any practical purpose as ladies' handkerchiefs generally are, but an inspiration came to her. She tore off her gloves, and in a few seconds the long linen hunting-scarf that had been pinned and tied with such skilled labour in the morning was being used as a bandage for the wound. But though Mrs Pat could tie a tie with any man in the regiment, she failed badly as a bandager of a less ornamental character. The hateful stream continued to pump forth from the cut, incarnadining the muddy road, and in despair she took Pilot by the head and began to lead him down the hill towards the valley.

Another gusty shower flung itself at her. It struck her bare white neck with whips of ice, and though she turned up the collar of her coat, the rain ran down under the neck-band of her shirt and chilled her through and through. It was evident that an artery had been cut in Pilot's leg; the flow from the wound never ceased; the hunting-scarf, drenched with blood, had slipped down to the hock. It seemed to Mrs Pat that her horse must bleed to death, and, tough and unemotional though she was, Pilot was very near her heart; tears gathered in her eyes as she led him slowly on through the rain and the loneliness, in the forlorn hope of finding help. She progressed in this lamentable manner for perhaps half a mile; the rain ceased, and she stopped to try once more to readjust the scarf, when, in the stillness that had followed the cessation of the rain, she heard a faint and distant sound of music. It drew nearer, a thin, shrill twittering, and as Mrs Pat turned quickly from her task to see what this could portend, she heard a woman's voice say harshly:—

'Ah, have done with that thrash of music; sure, it'll be dark night itself before we're in to Lismore.'

There was something familiar in the coarse tones. The weirdness fell from the wail of the music as Mrs Pat remembered the woman who had bothered her for money that morning in Carnfother. She and the blind old man were tramping slowly up the road, seemingly as useless a couple to anyone in Mrs Pat's plight as could well be imagined.

'How far am I from Carnfother?' she asked, as they drew near to her. 'Is there any house near here?'

'There is not,' said the yellow-haired woman; 'and ye're four miles from Carnfother yet.'

'I'll pay you well if you will take a message there for me—' began Mrs Pat.

'Are ye sure have ye yer purse in yer pocket?' interrupted the yellow-haired woman with a laugh that succeeded in being as nasty as she wished; 'or will I go dancin' down to Carnfother—'

'Have done, Joanna!' said the old man suddenly; 'what trouble is on the lady? What lamed the horse?'

He turned his bright blind eyes full on Mrs Pat. They were of the curious green blue that is sometimes seen in the eyes of a grey collie, and with all Mrs Pat's dislike and suspicion of the couple, she knew that he was blind.

'He was cut in a ditch,' she said shortly.

The old man had placed his fiddle in his daughter's hands; his own hands were twitching and trembling.

'I feel the blood flowing,' he said in a very low voice, and he walked up to Pilot.

His hands went unguided to the wound, from which the steady flow of blood had never ceased. With one he closed the lips of the cut, while with the other he crossed himself three times. His daughter watched him stolidly; Mrs Pat, with a certain alarm, having, after the manner of her kind, explained to herself the incomprehensible with the all-embracing formula of madness. Yes, she thought, he was undoubtedly mad, and as soon as the paroxysm was past she would have another try at bribing the woman.

The old man was muttering to himself, still holding the wound in one hand. Mrs Pat could distinguish no words, but it seemed to her that he repeated three times what he was saying. Then he straightened himself and stroked Pilot's quarter with a light, pitying hand. Mrs Pat stared. The bleeding had ceased. The hunting-scarf lay on the road at the horse's empurpled hoof. There was nothing to explain the mystery, but the fact remained.

'He'll do now,' said the blind man. 'Take him on to Carnfother; but ye'll want to get five stitches in that to make a good job of it.'

'But – I don't understand—' stammered Mrs Pat, shaken for once out of her self-possession by this sudden extension of her spiritual horizon. 'What have you done? Won't it begin again?' She turned to the woman in her bewilderment: 'Is – is he mad?'

'For as mad as he is, it's him you may thank for yer horse,' answered the yellow-haired woman. 'Why, Holy Mother! did ye never hear of Kane the Blood-Healer?'

The road round them was suddenly thronged with hounds, snuffing at Pilot, and pushing between Mrs Pat and the fence. The cheerful familiar sound of the huntsman's voice rating them made her feel her feet on solid ground again. In a moment Major Booth was there, the Master had dismounted, the habits, loud with sympathy and excitement, had gathered round; a Whip was examining the cut, while he spoke to the yellow-haired woman.

Mrs Pat tie-less, her face splashed with mud, her bare hands stained with blood, told her story. It is, I think, a point in her favour that for a moment she forgot what her appearance must be.

'The horse would have bled to death before the lady got to Carnfother, sir,' said the Whip to the Master; 'it isn't the first time I seen life saved by that one. Sure, didn't I see him heal a man that got his leg in a mowing machine, and he half-dead, with the blood spouting out of him like two rainbows!'

This is not a fairy-story. Neither need it be set lightly down as a curious coincidence. I know the charm that the old man said. I cannot give it here. It will only work successfully if taught by man to woman or by woman to man; nor do I pretend to say that it will work for everyone. I believe it to be a personal and wholly incomprehensible gift, but that such a gift has been bestowed, and in more parts of Ireland than one, is a bewildering and indisputable fact.

LADY AUGUSTA GREGORY

THE PRIEST THAT WAS CALLED MAD

THERE WAS A miller of Connacht more than fifty years ago, and he had his mill near the roadside. And the people do be saying there came some man that was no right man to him one night, and asked him would he sooner his wife or his son to lose their wits. The miller made little of that question 'For as to my wife?' he said 'she is the most sensible woman in the whole parish, and as to my son, he is in the college now and within a week he will be a priest, and there is no danger of madness upon him.' 'Time is a good story-teller,' said the stranger. The first Sunday now the son that had been made a priest came home he read the Mass, that was the first and the last that ever he read. For that very night madness came upon him and he stripped off every bit of clothing, and out and away with him through the country, and he bare naked, and carrying on his head a very large book he himself had written in Irish and in Latin. He quieted after that, but nothing anyone could do would bring him back to the father's house, and he would use nothing but a bit of meal or of watercress. And every night he would go and sleep alone in the mill, and having but the big book under his head. And in the daytime it was his custom to go out to a wide field where there was a great flock of sheep and of lambs, and he used to sit down in the middle of the field, and there was not a sheep or a lamb but would gather to him, and he used to be reading to them out of his book until he would be tired. Then everyone of them would come to him and would be licking his hands. And one time some person was listening to him unknown, and could hear him giving out his sermon to the sheep. 'Listen to me' he was saying to them 'you that are without sin. You are under the care of God, and there is a grass growing for you and herbs, and there are nice white dresses upon you to keep you dry and warm; and there is no Judgment upon you after your death, and you are happier by far than the children of Eve.' And he told them of the coming of the Son of God to the earth, and the bad treatment and the abuse that he was given; and a great many other things he told them out of the book. One night late now his father was uneasy about him, and he got a lantern and went to the mill and another man along with him. And when they opened the door they saw the whole of the mill lit up as bright as if it was the sun was lighting it. And the mad priest was lying there in his sleep, and the big book under his head, and a great shining ram was standing on each side of him, guarding him.

# JAMES JOYCE

THE DEAD

LILY, THE CARETAKER'S daughter, was literally run off her feet. Hardly had she brought one gentleman into the little pantry behind the office on the ground floor and helped him off with his overcoat than the wheezy hall-door bell clanged again and she had to scamper along the bare hallway to let in another guest. It was well for her she had not to attend to the ladies also. But Miss Kate and Miss Julia had thought of that and had converted the bathroom upstairs into a ladies' dressing-room. Miss Kate and Miss Julia were there, gossiping and laughing, and fussing, walking after each other to the head of the stairs, peering down over the banisters and calling down to Lily to ask her who had come.

It was always a great affair, the Misses Morkan's annual dance. Everybody who knew them came to it, members of the family, old friends of the family, the members of Julia's choir, any of Kate's pupils that were grown up enough and even some of Mary Jane's pupils too. Never once had it fallen flat. For years and years it had gone off in splendid style as long as anyone could remember; ever since Kate and Julia, after the death of their brother Pat, had left the house in Stoney Batter and taken Mary Jane, their only niece, to live with them in the dark gaunt house on Usher's Island, the upper part of which they had rented from Mr Fulham, the corn-factor on the ground floor. That was a good thirty years ago if it was a day. Mary Jane, who was then a little girl in short clothes, was now the main prop of the household for she had the organ in Haddington Road. She had been through the Academy and gave a pupils' concert every year in the upper room of the Antient Concert Rooms. Many of her pupils belonged to the better-class families on the Kingstown and Dalkey line. Old as they were, her aunts also did their share. Julia, though she was quite grey, was still the leading soprano in Adam and Eve's, and Kate, being too feeble to go about much, gave music lessons to beginners on the old square piano in the back room. Lily, the caretaker's daughter, did housemaid's work for them. Though their life was modest they believed in eating well; the best of everything: diamond-bone sirloins, three-shilling tea and the best bottled stout. But Lily seldom made a mistake in the orders so that she got on well with her three mistresses. They were fussy, that was all. But the only thing they would not stand was back answers.

Of course they had good reason to be fussy on such a night. And then it was long after ten o'clock and yet there was no sign of Gabriel and his wife. Besides they were dreadfully afraid that Freddy Malins might turn up screwed. They would not wish for worlds that any of Mary Jane's pupils should see him under the influence; and when he was like that it was sometimes very hard to manage him. Freddy Malins always came late but they wondered what could be keeping Gabriel: and that was what brought them every two minutes to the banisters to ask Lily had Gabriel or Freddy come.

—O, Mr Conroy, said Lily to Gabriel when she opened the door for him, Miss Kate and Miss Julia thought you were never coming. Good-night, Mrs Conroy.

—I'll engage they did, said Gabriel, but they forget that my wife here takes three mortal hours to dress herself.

He stood on the mat, scraping the snow from his goloshes,

while Lily led his wife to the foot of the stairs and called out:

—Miss Kate, here's Mrs Conroy.

Kate and Julia came toddling down the dark stairs at once. Both of them kissed Gabriel's wife, said she must be perished alive and asked was Gabriel with her.

—Here I am as right as the mail, Aunt Kate! Go on up, I'll follow, called out Gabriel from the dark.

He continued scraping his feet vigorously while the three women went upstairs, laughing, to the ladies' dressing-room. A light fringe of snow lay like a cape on the shoulders of his overcoat and like toecaps on the toes of his goloshes; and, as the buttons of his overcoat slipped with a squeaking noise through the snow-stiffened frieze, a cold fragrant air from out-of-doors escaped from crevices and folds.

—Is it snowing again, Mr Conroy? asked Lily.

She had preceded him into the pantry to help him off with his overcoat. Gabriel smiled at the three syllables she had given his surname and glanced at her. She was a slim, growing girl, pale in complexion and with hay-coloured hair. The gas in the pantry made her look still paler. Gabriel had known her when she was a child and used to sit on the lowest step nursing a rag doll.

—Yes, Lily, he answered, and I think we're in for a night of it.

He looked up at the pantry ceiling, which was shaking with the stamping and shuffling of feet on the floor above, listened for a moment to the piano and then glanced at the girl, who was folding his overcoat carefully at the end of a shelf.

—Tell me, Lily, he said in a friendly tone, do you still go to school?

—O no, sir, she answered. I'm done schooling this year and more.

—O, then, said Gabriel gaily, I suppose we'll be going to your wedding one of these fine days with your young man, eh?

The girl glanced back at him over her shoulder and said with great bitterness:

—The men that is now is only all palaver and what they can get out of you.

Gabriel coloured as if he felt he had made a mistake and, without looking at her, kicked off his goloshes and flicked actively with his muffler at his patent-leather shoes.

He was a stout tallish young man. The high colour of his cheeks pushed upwards even to his forehead where it scattered itself in a few formless patches of pale red; and on his hairless face there scintillated restlessly the polished lenses and the bright gilt rims of the glasses which screened his delicate and restless eyes. His glossy black hair was parted in the middle and brushed in a long curve behind his ears where it curled slightly beneath the groove left by his hat.

When he had flicked lustre into his shoes he stood up and pulled his waistcoat down more tightly on his plump body. Then he took a coin rapidly from his pocket.

—O Lily, he said, thrusting it into her hands, it's Christmas-time, isn't it? Just . . . here's a little. . . .

He walked rapidly towards the door.

—O no, sir! cried the girl, following him. Really, sir, I wouldn't take it.

—Christmas-time! Christmas-time! said Gabriel, almost trotting to the stairs and waving his hand to her in deprecation.

The girl, seeing that he had gained the stairs, called out after him:

—Well, thank you, sir.

He waited outside the drawing-room door until the waltz

should finish, listening to the skirts that swept against it and to the shuffling of feet. He was still discomposed by the girl's bitter and sudden retort. It had cast a gloom over him which he tried to dispel by arranging his cuffs and the bows of his tie. He then took from his waistcoat pocket a little paper and glanced at the headings he had made for his speech. He was undecided about the lines from Robert Browning for he feared they would be above the heads of his hearers. Some quotation that they would recognize from Shakespeare or from the Melodies would be better. The indelicate clacking of the men's heels and the shuffling of their soles reminded him that their grade of culture differed from his. He would only make himself ridiculous by quoting poetry to them which they could not understand. They would think that he was airing his superior education. He would fail with them just as he had failed with the girl in the pantry. He had taken up a wrong tone. His whole speech was a mistake from first to last, an utter failure.

Just then his aunts and his wife came out of the ladies' dressing-room. His aunts were two small plainly dressed old women. Aunt Julia was an inch or so the taller. Her hair, drawn low over the tops of her ears, was grey; and grey also, with darker shadows, was her large flaccid face. Though she was stout in build and stood erect her slow eyes and parted lips gave her the appearance of a woman who did not know where she was or where she was going. Aunt Kate was more vivacious. Her face, healthier than her sister's, was all puckers and creases, like a shrivelled red apple, and her hair, braided in the same old-fashioned way, had not lost its ripe nut colour.

They both kissed Gabriel frankly. He was their favourite nephew, the son of their dead elder sister, Ellen, who had married T. J. Conroy of the Port and Docks.

—Gretta tells me you're not going to take a cab back to Monkstown to-night, Gabriel, said Aunt Kate.

—No, said Gabriel, turning to his wife, we had quite enough of that last year, hadn't we? Don't you remember, Aunt Kate, what a cold Gretta got out of it? Cab windows rattling all the way, and the east wind blowing in after we passed Merrion. Very jolly it was. Gretta caught a dreadful cold.

Aunt Kate frowned severely and nodded her head at every word.

—Quite right, Gabriel, quite right, she said. You can't be too careful.

—But as for Gretta there, said Gabriel, she'd walk home in the snow if she were let.

Mrs Conroy laughed.

—Don't mind him, Aunt Kate, she said. He's really an awful bother, what with green shades for Tom's eyes at night and making him do the dumb-bells, and forcing Eva to eat the stirabout. The poor child! And she simply hates the sight of it! . . . O, but you'll never guess what he makes me wear now!

She broke out into a peal of laughter and glanced at her husband, whose admiring and happy eyes had been wandering from her dress to her face and hair. The two aunts laughed heartily too, for Gabriel's solicitude was a standing joke with them.

—Goloshes! said Mrs Conroy. That's the latest. Whenever it's wet underfoot I must put on my goloshes. To-night even he wanted me to put them on, but I wouldn't. The next thing he'll buy me will be a diving suit.

Gabriel laughed nervously and patted his tie reassuringly while Aunt Kate nearly doubled herself, so heartily did she enjoy the joke. The smile soon faded from Aunt Julia's face and her mirthless eyes were directed towards her nephew's face. After a pause she asked:

—And what are goloshes, Gabriel?

—Goloshes, Julia! exclaimed her sister. Goodness me, don't you know what goloshes are? You wear them over your . . . over your boots, Gretta, isn't it?

—Yes, said Mrs Conroy. Guttapercha things. We both have a pair now. Gabriel says everyone wears them on the continent.

—O, on the continent, murmured Aunt Julia, nodding her head slowly.

Gabriel knitted his brows and said, as if he were slightly angered:

—It's nothing very wonderful but Gretta thinks it very funny because she says the word reminds her of Christy Minstrels.

—But tell me, Gabriel, said Aunt Kate, with brisk tact. Of course, you've seen about the room. Gretta was saying . . .

—O, the room is all right, replied Gabriel. I've taken one in the Gresham.

—To be sure, said Aunt Kate, by far the best thing to do. And the children, Gretta, you're not anxious about them?

—O, for one night, said Mrs Conroy. Besides, Bessie will look after them.

—To be sure, said Aunt Kate again. What a comfort it is to have a girl like that, one you can depend on! There's that Lily, I'm sure I don't know what has come over her lately. She's not the girl she was at all.

Gabriel was about to ask his aunt some questions on this point but she broke off suddenly to gaze after her sister who had wandered down the stairs and was craning her neck over the banisters.

—Now, I ask you, she said, almost testily, where is Julia going? Julia! Julia! Where are you going?

Julia, who had gone halfway down one flight, came back and announced blandly:

—Here's Freddy.

At the same moment a clapping of hands and a final flourish of the pianist told that the waltz had ended. The drawing-room door was opened from within and some couples came out. Aunt Kate drew Gabriel aside hurriedly and whispered into his ear:

—Slip down, Gabriel, like a good fellow and see if he's all right, and don't let him up if he's screwed. I'm sure he's screwed. I'm sure he is.

Gabriel went to the stairs and listened over the banisters. He could hear two persons talking in the pantry. Then he recognized Freddy Malins' laugh. He went down the stairs noisily.

—It's such a relief, said Aunt Kate to Mrs Conroy, that Gabriel is here. I always feel easier in my mind when he's here. . . . Julia, there's Miss Daly and Miss Power will take some refreshment. Thanks for your beautiful waltz, Miss Daly. It made lovely time.

A tall wizen-faced man, with a stiff grizzled moustache and swarthy skin, who was passing out with his partner said:

—And may we have some refreshment, too, Miss Morkan?

—Julia, said Aunt Kate summarily, and here's Mr Browne and Miss Furlong. Take them in, Julia, with Miss Daly and Miss Power.

—I'm the man for the ladies, said Mr Browne, pursing his lips until his moustache bristled and smiling in all his wrinkles. You know, Miss Morkan, the reason they are so fond of me is—

He did not finish his sentence, but, seeing that Aunt Kate was out of earshot, at once led the three young ladies into the back room. The middle of the room was occupied by two square tables placed end to end, and on these Aunt Julia and the caretaker were straightening and smoothing a large cloth. On the sideboard were arrayed dishes and plates, and glasses and bundles of knives and forks and spoons. The top of the closed square piano served also as a sideboard for viands and sweets. At a smaller sideboard in one corner two young men were standing, drinking hop-bitters.

Mr Browne led his charges thither and invited them all, in jest, to some ladies' punch, hot, strong and sweet. As they said they never took anything strong he opened three bottles of lemonade for them. Then he asked one of the young men to move aside, and, taking hold of the decanter, filled out for himself a goodly measure of whisky. The young men eyed him respectfully while he took a trial sip.

—God help me, he said, smiling, it's the doctor's orders.

His wizened face broke into a broader smile, and the three young ladies laughed in musical echo to his pleasantry, swaying their bodies to and fro, with nervous jerks of their shoulders. The boldest said:

—O, now, Mr Browne, I'm sure the doctor never ordered anything of the kind.

Mr Browne took another sip of his whisky and said, with sidling mimicry:

—Well, you see, I'm like the famous Mrs Cassidy, who is reported to have said: *Now, Mary Grimes, if I don't take it, make me take it, for I feel I want it.*

His hot face had leaned forward a little too confidentially and he had assumed a very low Dublin accent so that the young ladies, with one instinct, received his speech in silence. Miss Furlong, who was one of Mary Jane's pupils, asked Miss Daly what was the name of the pretty waltz she had played; and Mr Browne, seeing that he was ignored, turned promptly to the two young men who were more appreciative.

A red-faced young woman, dressed in pansy, came into the room, excitedly clapping her hands and crying:

—Quadrilles! Quadrilles!

Close on her heels came Aunt Kate, crying:

—Two gentlemen and three ladies, Mary Jane!

—O, here's Mr Bergin and Mr Kerrigan, said Mary Jane. Mr Kerrigan, will you take Miss Power? Miss Furlong, may I get you a partner, Mr Bergin. O, that'll just do now.

—Three ladies, Mary Jane, said Aunt Kate.

The two young gentlemen asked the ladies if they might have the pleasure, and Mary Jane turned to Miss Daly.

—O, Miss Daly, you're really awfully good, after playing for the last two dances, but really we're so short of ladies to-night.

—I don't mind in the least, Miss Morkan.

—But I've a nice partner for you, Mr Bartell D'Arcy, the tenor, I'll get him to sing later on. All Dublin is raving about him.

—Lovely voice, lovely voice! said Aunt Kate.

As the piano had twice begun the prelude to the first figure Mary Jane led her recruits quickly from the room. They had hardly gone when Aunt Julia wandered slowly into the room, looking behind her at something.

—What is the matter, Julia? asked Aunt Kate anxiously. Who is it?

Julia, who was carrying in a column of table-napkins, turned to her sister and said, simply, as if the question had surprised her:

—It's only Freddy, Kate, and Gabriel with him.

In fact right behind her Gabriel could be seen piloting Freddy Malins across the landing. The latter, a young man of about forty, was of Gabriel's size and build, with very round shoulders. His face was fleshy and pallid, touched with colour only at the thick hanging lobes of his ears and at the wide wings of his nose. He had coarse features, a blunt nose, a convex and receding brow, tumid and protruded lips. His heavy-lidded eyes and the disorder of his scanty hair made him look sleepy. He was laughing heartily in a high key at a story which he had been telling Gabriel on the stairs and at the same time rubbing the knuckles of his left fist backwards and forwards into his left eye.

—Good evening, Freddy, said Aunt Julia.

Freddy Malins bade the Misses Morkan good-evening in what seemed an offhand fashion by reason of the habitual catch in his voice and then, seeing that Mr Browne was grinning at him from the sideboard, crossed the room on rather shaky legs and began to repeat in an undertone the story he had just told to Gabriel.

—He's not so bad, is he? said Aunt Kate to Gabriel.

Gabriel's brows were dark but he raised them quickly and answered:

—O no, hardly noticeable.

—Now, isn't he a terrible fellow! she said. And his poor mother made him take the pledge on New Year's Eve. But come on, Gabriel, into the drawing-room.

Before leaving the room with Gabriel she signalled to Mr Browne by frowning and shaking her forefinger in warning to and fro. Mr Browne nodded in answer and, when she had gone, said to Freddy Malins:

—Now, then, Freddy, I'm going to fill you out a good glass of lemonade just to buck you up.

Freddy Malins, who was nearing the climax of his story,

waved the offer aside impatiently but Mr Browne, having first called Freddy Malins' attention to a disarray in his dress, filled out and handed him a full glass of lemonade. Freddy Malins' left hand accepted the glass mechanically, his right hand being engaged in the mechanical readjustment of his dress. Mr Browne, whose face was once more wrinkling with mirth, poured out for himself a glass of whisky while Freddy Malins exploded, before he had well reached the climax of his story, in a kink of high-pitched bronchitic laughter and, setting down his untasted and overflowing glass, began to rub the knuckles of his left fist backwards and forwards into his left eye, repeating words of his last phrase as well as his fit of laughter would allow him.

Gabriel could not listen while Mary Jane was playing her Academy piece, full of runs and difficult passages, to the hushed drawing-room. He liked music but the piece she was playing had no melody for him and he doubted whether it had any melody for the other listeners, though they had begged Mary Jane to play something. Four young men, who had come from the refreshment-room to stand in the doorway at the sound of the piano, had gone away quietly in couples after a few minutes. The only persons who seemed to follow the music were Mary Jane herself, her hands racing along the key-board or lifted from it at the pauses like those of a priestess in momentary imprecation, and Aunt Kate standing at her elbow to turn the page.

Gabriel's eyes, irritated by the floor, which glittered with beeswax under the heavy chandelier, wandered to the wall above the piano. A picture of the balcony scene in *Romeo and Juliet* hung there and beside it was a picture of the two murdered princes in the Tower which Aunt Julia had worked in red, blue and brown wools when she was a girl. Probably in the school they had gone to as girls that kind of work had been taught for one year his mother had worked for him as a birthday present a waistcoat of purple tabinet, with little foxes' heads upon it, lined with brown satin and having round mulberry buttons. It was strange that his mother had had no musical talent though Aunt Kate used to call her the brains carrier of the Morkan family. Both she and Julia had always seemed a little proud of their serious and matronly sister. Her photograph stood before the pierglass. She had an open book on her knees and was pointing out something in it to Constantine who, dressed in a man-o'-war suit, lay at her feet. It was she who had chosen the names for her sons for she was very sensible of the dignity of family life. Thanks to her, Constantine was now senior curate in Balbriggan and, thanks to her, Gabriel himself had taken his degree in the Royal University. A shadow passed over his face as he remembered her sullen opposition to his marriage. Some slighting phrases she had used still rankled in his memory; she had once spoken of Gretta as being country cute and that was not true of Gretta at all. It was Gretta who had nursed her during all her last long illness in their house at Monkstown.

He knew that Mary Jane must be near the end of her piece for she was playing again the opening melody with runs of scales after every bar and while he waited for the end the resentment died down in his heart. The piece ended with a trill of octaves in the treble and a final deep octave in the bass. Great applause greeted Mary Jane as, blushing and rolling up her music nervously, she escaped from the room. The most vigorous clapping came from the four young men in the doorway who had gone away to the refreshment-room at the beginning of the piece but had come back when the piano had stopped.

Lancers were arranged. Gabriel found himself partnered with Miss Ivors. She was a frank-mannered talkative young lady, with a freckled face and prominent brown eyes. She did not wear a low-cut bodice and the large brooch which was fixed in the front of her collar bore on it an Irish device.

When they had taken their places she said abruptly:

—I have a crow to pluck with you.

—With me? said Gabriel.

She nodded her head gravely.

—What is it? asked Gabriel, smiling at her solemn manner.

—Who is G. C.? answered Miss Ivors, turning her eyes upon him.

Gabriel coloured and was about to knit his brows, as if he did not understand, when she said bluntly:

—O, innocent Amy! I have found out that you write for *The Daily Express*. Now, aren't you ashamed of yourself?

—Why should I be ashamed of myself? asked Gabriel, blinking his eyes and trying to smile.

—Well, I'm ashamed of you, said Miss Ivors frankly. To say you'd write for a rag like that. I didn't think you were a West Briton.

A look of perplexity appeared on Gabriel's face. It was true that he wrote a literary column every Wednesday in *The Daily Express*, for which he was paid fifteen shillings. But that did not make him a West Briton surely. The books he received for review were almost more welcome than the paltry cheque. He loved to feel the covers and turn over the pages of newly printed books. Nearly every day when his teaching in the college was ended he used to wander down the quays to the second-hand booksellers, to Hickey's on Bachelor's Walk, to Webb's or Massey's on Aston's Quay, or to O'Clohissey's in the by-street. He did not know how to meet her charge. He wanted to say that literature was above politics. But they were friends of many years' standing and their careers had been parallel, first at the University and then as teachers: he could not risk a grandiose phrase with her. He continued blinking his eyes and trying to smile and murmured lamely that he saw nothing political in writing reviews of books.

When their turn to cross had come he was still perplexed and inattentive. Miss Ivors promptly took his hand in a warm grasp and said in a soft friendly tone:

—Of course, I was only joking. Come, we cross now.

When they were together again she spoke of the University question and Gabriel felt more at ease. A friend of hers had shown her his review of Browning's poems. That was how she had found out the secret: but she liked the review immensely. Then she said suddenly:

—O, Mr Conroy, will you come for an excursion to the Aran Isles this summer? We're going to stay there a whole month. It will be splendid out in the Atlantic. You ought to come. Mr Clancy is coming, and Mr Kilkelly and Kathleen Kearney. It would be splendid for Gretta too if she'd come. She's from Connacht, isn't she?

—Her people are, said Gabriel shortly.

—But you will come, won't you? said Miss Ivors, laying her warm hand eagerly on his arm.

—The fact is, said Gabriel, I have already arranged to go—

—Go where? asked Miss Ivors.

—Well, you know, every year I go for a cycling tour with some fellows and so—

—But where? asked Miss Ivors.

—Well, we usually go to France or Belgium or perhaps Germany, said Gabriel awkwardly.

—And why do you go to France and Belgium, said Miss Ivors, instead of visiting your own land?

—Well, said Gabriel, it's partly to keep in touch with the languages and partly for a change.

—And haven't you your own language to keep in touch with – Irish? asked Miss Ivors.

—Well, said Gabriel, if it comes to that, you know, Irish is not my language.

Their neighbours had turned to listen to the cross-examination. Gabriel glanced right and left nervously and tried to keep his good humour under the ordeal which was making a blush invade his forehead.

—And haven't you your own land to visit, continued Miss Ivors, that you know nothing of, your own people, and your own country?

—O, to tell you the truth, retorted Gabriel suddenly, I'm sick of my own country, sick of it!

—Why? asked Miss Ivors.

Gabriel did not answer for his retort had heated him.

—Why? repeated Miss Ivors.

They had to go visiting together and, as he had not answered her, Miss Ivors said warmly:

—Of course, you've no answer.

Gabriel tried to cover his agitation by taking part in the dance with great energy. He avoided her eyes for he had seen a sour expression on her face. But when they met in the long chain he was surprised to feel his hand firmly pressed. She looked at him from under her brows for a moment quizzically until he smiled. Then, just as the chain was about to start again, she stood on tiptoe and whispered into his ear:

—West Briton!

When the lancers were over Gabriel went away to a remote corner of the room where Freddy Malins' mother was sitting. She was a stout feeble old woman with white hair. Her voice had a catch in it like her son's and she stuttered slightly. She had been told that Freddy had come and that he was nearly all right. Gabriel asked her whether she had had a good crossing. She lived with her married daughter in Glasgow and came to Dublin on a visit once a year. She answered placidly that she had had a beautiful crossing and that the captain had been most attentive to her. She spoke also of the beautiful house her daughter kept in Glasgow, and of all the nice friends they had there. While her tongue rambled on Gabriel tried to banish from his mind all memory of the unpleasant incident with Miss Ivors. Of course the girl or woman, or whatever she was, was an enthusiast but there was a time for all things. Perhaps he ought not to have answered her like that. But she had no right to call him a West Briton before people, even in joke. She had tried to make him ridiculous before people, heckling him and staring at him with her rabbit's eyes.

He saw his wife making her way towards him through the waltzing couples. When she reached him she said into his ear:

—Gabriel, Aunt Kate wants to know won't you carve the goose as usual. Miss Daly will carve the ham and I'll do the pudding.

—All right, said Gabriel.

—She's sending in the younger ones first as soon as this waltz is over so that we'll have the table to ourselves.

—Were you dancing? asked Gabriel.

—Of course I was. Didn't you see me? What words had you with Molly Ivors?

—No words. Why? Did she say so?

—Something like that. I'm trying to get that Mr D'Arcy to sing. He's full of conceit, I think.

—There were no words, said Gabriel moodily, only she wanted me to go for a trip to the west of Ireland and I said I wouldn't.

His wife clasped her hands excitedly and gave a little jump.

—O, do go, Gabriel, she cried. I'd love to see Galway again.

—You can go if you like, said Gabriel coldly.

She looked at him for a moment, then turned to Mrs Malins and said:

—There's a nice husband for you, Mrs Malins.

While she was threading her way back across the room Mrs Malins, without adverting to the interruption, went on to tell Gabriel what beautiful places there were in Scotland and beautiful scenery. Her son-in-law brought them every year to the lakes and they used to go fishing. Her son-in-law was a splendid fisher. One day he caught a fish, a beautiful big big fish, and the man in the hotel boiled it for their dinner.

Gabriel hardly heard what she said. Now that supper was coming near he began to think again about his speech and about the quotation. When he saw Freddy Malins coming across the room to visit his mother Gabriel left the chair free for him and retired into the embrasure of the window. The room had already cleared and from the back room came the clatter of plates and knives. Those who still remained in the drawing-room seemed tired of dancing and were conversing quietly in little groups. Gabriel's warm trembling fingers tapped the cold pane of the window. How cool it must be outside! How pleasant it would be to walk out alone, first along by the river and then through the park! The snow would be lying on the branches of the trees and forming a bright cap on the top of the Wellington Monument.

How much more pleasant it would be there than at the supper-table!

He ran over the headings of his speech: Irish hospitality, sad memories, the Three Graces, Paris, the quotation from Browning. He repeated to himself a phrase he had written in his review: *One feels that one is listening to a thought-tormented music.* Miss Ivors had praised the review. Was she sincere? Had she really any life of her own behind all her propagandism? There had never been any ill-feeling between them until that night. It unnerved him to think that she would be at the supper-table, looking up at him while he spoke with her critical quizzing eyes. Perhaps she would not be sorry to see him fail in his speech. An idea came into his mind and gave him courage. He would say, alluding to Aunt Kate and Aunt Julia: *Ladies and Gentlemen, the generation which is now on the wane among us may have had its faults but for my part I think it had certain qualities of hospitality, of humour, of humanity, which the new and very serious and hypereducated generation that is growing up around us seems to me to lack.* Very good: that was one for Miss Ivors. What did he care that his aunts were only two ignorant old women?

A murmur in the room attracted his attention. Mr Browne was advancing from the door, gallantly escorting Aunt Julia, who leaned upon his arm, smiling and hanging her head. An irregular musketry of applause escorted her also as far as the piano and then, as Mary Jane seated herself on the stool, and Aunt Julia, no longer smiling, half turned so as to pitch her voice fairly into the room, gradually ceased. Gabriel recognized the prelude. It was that of an old song of Aunt Julia's – *Arrayed for the Bridal.* Her voice, strong and clear in tone, attacked with great spirit the runs which embellish the air and though she sang very rapidly she did not miss even the smallest of the grace notes. To follow the voice, without looking at the singer's face, was to feel and share the excitement of swift and secure flight. Gabriel applauded loudly with all the others at the close of the song and loud applause was borne in from the invisible supper-table. It sounded so genuine that a little colour struggled into Aunt Julia's face as she bent to replace in the music-stand the old leather-bound song-book that had her initials on the cover. Freddy Malins, who had listened with his head perched sideways to hear her better, was still applauding when every one else had ceased and talking animatedly to his mother who nodded her head gravely and slowly in acquiescence. At last, when he could clap no more, he stood up suddenly and hurried across the room to Aunt Julia whose hand he seized and held in both his hands, shaking it when words failed him or the catch in his voice proved too much for him.

—I was just telling my mother, he said, I never heard you sing so well, never. No, I never heard your voice so good as it is to-night. Now! Would you believe that now? That's the truth. Upon my word and honour that's the truth. I never heard your voice sound so fresh and so ... so clear and fresh, never.

Aunt Julia smiled broadly and murmured something about compliments as she released her hand from his grasp. Mr Browne extended his open hand towards her and said to those who were near him in the manner of a showman introducing a prodigy to an audience:

—Miss Julia Morkan, my latest discovery!

He was laughing very heartily at this himself when Freddy Malins turned to him and said:

—Well, Browne, if you're serious you might make a worse discovery. All I can say is I never heard her sing half so well as long as I am coming here. And that's the honest truth.

—Neither did I, said Mr Browne. I think her voice has greatly improved.

Aunt Julia shrugged her shoulders and said with meek pride:

—Thirty years ago I hadn't a bad voice as voices go.

—I often told Julia, said Aunt Kate emphatically, that she was simply thrown away in that choir. But she never would be said by me.

She turned as if to appeal to the good sense of the others against a refractory child while Aunt Julia gazed in front of her, a vague smile of reminiscence playing on her face.

—No, continued Aunt Kate, she wouldn't be said or led by anyone, slaving there in that choir night and day, night and day. Six o'clock on Christmas morning! And all for what?

—Well, isn't it for the honour of God, Aunt Kate? asked Mary Jane, twisting round on the piano-stool and smiling.

Aunt Kate turned fiercely on her niece and said:

—I know all about the honour of God, Mary Jane, but I think it's not at all honourable for the pope to turn out the women out of the choirs that have slaved there all their lives and put little whipper-snappers of boys over their heads. I suppose it is for the good of the Church if the pope does it. But it's not just, Mary Jane, and it's not right.

She had worked herself into a passion and would have continued in defence of her sister for it was a sore subject with her but Mary Jane, seeing that all the dancers had come back, intervened pacifically:

—Now, Aunt Kate, you're giving scandal to Mr Browne who is of the other persuasion.

Aunt Kate turned to Mr Browne, who was grinning at this allusion to his religion, and said hastily:

—O, I don't question the pope's being right. I'm only

a stupid old woman and I wouldn't presume to do such a thing. But there's such a thing as common everyday politeness and gratitude. And if I were in Julia's place I'd tell that Father Healey straight up to his face . . .

—And besides, Aunt Kate, said Mary Jane, we really are all hungry and when we are hungry we are all very quarrelsome.

—And when we are thirsty we are also quarrelsome, added Mr Browne.

—So that we had better go to supper, said Mary Jane, and finish the discussion afterwards.

On the landing outside the drawing-room Gabriel found his wife and Mary Jane trying to persuade Miss Ivors to stay for supper. But Miss Ivors, who had put on her hat and was buttoning her cloak, would not stay. She did not feel in the least hungry and she had already overstayed her time.

—But only for ten minutes, Molly, said Mrs Conroy. That won't delay you.

—To take a pick itself, said Mary Jane, after all your dancing.

—I really couldn't, said Miss Ivors.

—I am afraid you didn't enjoy yourself at all, said Mary Jane hopelessly.

—Ever so much, I assure you, said Miss Ivors, but you really must let me run off now.

—But how can you get home? asked Mrs Conroy.

—O, it's only two steps up the quay.

Gabriel hesitated a moment and said:

—If you will allow me, Miss Ivors, I'll see you home if you really are obliged to go.

But Miss Ivors broke away from them.

—I won't hear of it, she cried. For goodness sake go in to your suppers and don't mind me. I'm quite well able to take care of myself.

—Well, you're the comical girl, Molly, said Mrs Conroy frankly.

—*Beannacht libh*, cried Miss Ivors, with a laugh, as she ran down the staircase.

Mary Jane gazed after her, a moody puzzled expression on her face, while Mrs Conroy leaned over the banisters to listen for the hall-door. Gabriel asked himself was he the cause of her abrupt departure. But she did not seem to be in ill humour: she had gone away laughing. He stared blankly down the staircase.

At that moment Aunt Kate came toddling out of the supper-room, almost wringing her hands in despair.

—Where is Gabriel? she cried. Where on earth is Gabriel? There's everyone waiting in there, stage to let, and nobody to carve the goose!

—Here I am, Aunt Kate! cried Gabriel, with sudden animation, ready to carve a flock of geese, if necessary.

A fat brown goose lay at one end of the table and at the other end, on a bed of creased paper strewn with sprigs of parsley, lay a great ham, stripped of its outer skin and peppered over with crust crumbs, a neat paper frill round its shin and beside this was a round of spiced beef. Between these rival ends ran parallel lines of side-dishes: two little minsters of jelly, red and yellow; a shallow dish full of blocks of blancmange and red jam, a large green leaf-shaped dish with a stalk-shaped handle, on which lay bunches of purple raisins and peeled almonds, a companion dish on which lay a solid rectangle of Smyrna figs, a dish of custard topped with grated nutmeg, a small bowl full of chocolates and sweets wrapped in gold and silver papers and a glass vase in which stood some tall celery stalks. In the centre of the table there stood, as sentries to a fruit-stand which upheld a pyramid of oranges and American apples, two squat old-fashioned decanters of cut glass, one containing port and the other dark sherry. On the closed square piano a pudding in a huge yellow dish lay in waiting and behind it were three squads of bottles of stout and ale and minerals, drawn up according to the colours of their uniforms, the first two black, with brown and red labels, the third and smallest squad white, with transverse green sashes.

Gabriel took his seat boldly at the head of the table and, having looked to the edge of the carver, plunged his fork firmly into the goose. He felt quite at ease now for he was an expert carver and liked nothing better than to find himself at the head of a well-laden table.

—Miss Furlong, what shall I send you? he asked. A wing or a slice of the breast?

—Just a small slice of the breast.

—Miss Higgins, what for you?

—O, anything at all, Mr Conroy.

While Gabriel and Miss Daly exchanged plates of goose and plates of ham and spiced beef Lily went from guest to guest with a dish of hot floury potatoes wrapped in a white napkin. This was Mary Jane's idea and she had also suggested apple sauce for the goose but Aunt Kate had said that plain roast goose without apple sauce had always been good enough for her and she hoped she might never eat worse. Mary Jane waited on her pupils and saw that they got the best slices and Aunt Kate and Aunt Julia opened and carried across from the piano bottles of stout and ale for the gentlemen and bottles of minerals for the ladies. There was a great deal of confusion and laughter and noise, the noise of orders and counter-orders, of knives and forks, of corks and glass-stoppers. Gabriel began to carve second helpings as soon as he had finished the first round without serving himself. Every one protested loudly so that he compromised by taking a long draught of stout for he had found the carving hot work. Mary Jane settled down quietly to her supper but Aunt Kate and Aunt Julia were still toddling round the table, walking on each other's heels, getting in each other's way and giving each other unheeded orders. Mr Browne begged of them to sit down and eat their suppers and so did Gabriel but they said there was time enough so that, at last Freddy Malins stood up and, capturing Aunt Kate, plumped her down on her chair amid general laughter.

When everyone had been well served Gabriel said, smiling:

—Now, if anyone wants a little more of what vulgar people call stuffing let him or her speak.

A chorus of voices invited him to begin his own supper and Lily came forward with three potatoes which she had reserved for him.

—Very well, said Gabriel amiably, as he took another preparatory draught, kindly forget my existence, ladies and gentlemen, for a few minutes.

He set to his supper and took no part in the conversation with which the table covered Lily's removal of the plates. The subject of talk was the opera company which was then at the Theatre Royal. Mr Bartell D'Arcy, the tenor, a dark-complexioned young man with a smart moustache, praised very highly the leading contralto of the company but Miss Furlong thought she had a rather vulgar style of production. Freddy Malins said there was a negro chieftain singing in the second part of the Gaiety pantomime who had one of the finest tenor voices he had ever heard.

—Have you heard him? he asked Mr Bartell D'Arcy across the table.

—No, answered Mr Bartell D'Arcy carelessly.

—Because, Freddy Malins explained, now I'd be curious

to hear your opinion of him. I think he has a grand voice.

—It takes Teddy to find out the really good things, said Mr Browne familiarly to the table.

—And why couldn't he have a voice too? asked Freddy Malins sharply. Is it because he's only a black?

Nobody answered this question and Mary Jane led the table back to the legitimate opera. One of her pupils had given her a pass for *Mignon*. Of course it was very fine, she said, but it made her think of poor Georgina Burns. Mr Browne could go back farther still, to the old Italian companies that used to come to Dublin – Tietjens, Ilma de Murzka, Campanini, the great Trebilli, Giuglini, Ravelli, Aramburo. Those were the days, he said, when there was something like singing to be heard in Dublin. He told too of how the top gallery of the old Royal used to be packed night after night, of how one night an Italian tenor had sung five encores to *Let me Like a Soldier Fall*, introducing a high C every time, and of how the gallery boys would sometimes in their enthusiasm unyoke the horses from the carriage of some great *prima donna* and pull her themselves through the streets to her hotel. Why did they never play the grand old operas now, he asked, *Dinorah*, *Lucrezia Borgia*? Because they could not get the voices to sing them: that was why.

—O, well, said Mr Bartell D'Arcy, I presume there are as good singers to-day as there were then.

—Where are they? asked Mr Browne defiantly.

—In London, Paris, Milan, said Mr Bartell D'Arcy warmly. I suppose Caruso, for example, is quite as good, if not better than any of the men you have mentioned.

—Maybe so, said Mr Browne. But I may tell you I doubt it strongly.

—O, I'd give anything to hear Caruso sing, said Mary Jane.

—For me, said Aunt Kate, who had been picking a bone, there was only one tenor. To please me, I mean. But I suppose none of you ever heard of him.

—Who was he, Miss Morkan? asked Mr Bartell D'Arcy politely.

—His name, said Aunt Kate, was Parkinson. I heard him when he was in his prime and I think he had then the purest tenor voice that was ever put into a man's throat.

—Strange, said Mr Bartell D'Arcy. I never even heard of him.

—Yes, yes, Miss Morkan is right, said Mr Browne. I remember hearing of old Parkinson, but he's too far back for me.

—A beautiful pure sweet mellow English tenor, said Aunt Kate with enthusiasm.

Gabriel having finished, the huge pudding was transferred to the table. The clatter of forks and spoons began again. Gabriel's wife served out spoonfuls of the pudding and passed the plates down the table. Midway down they were held up by Mary Jane, who replenished them with raspberry or orange jelly or with blancmange and jam. The pudding was of Aunt Julia's making and she received praises for it from all quarters. She herself said that it was not quite brown enough.

—Well, I hope, Miss Morkan, said Mr Browne, that I'm brown enough for you because, you know, I'm all brown.

All the gentlemen, except Gabriel, ate some of the pudding out of compliment to Aunt Julia. As Gabriel never ate sweets the celery had been left for him. Freddy Malins also took a stalk of celery and ate it with his pudding. He had been told that celery was a capital thing for the blood and he was just then under doctor's care. Mrs Malins, who had been silent all through the supper, said that her son was going down to Mount Melleray in a week or so. The table then spoke of Mount Melleray, how bracing the air was down there, how hospitable the monks were and how they never asked for a penny-piece from their guests.

—And do you mean to say, asked Mr Browne incredulously, that a chap can go down there and put up there as if it were a hotel and live on the fat of the land and then come away without paying a farthing?

—O, most people give some donation to the monastery when they leave, said Mary Jane.

—I wish we had an institution like that in our Church, said Mr Browne candidly.

He was astonished to hear that the monks never spoke, got up at two in the morning and slept in their coffins. He asked what they did it for.

—That's the rule of the order, said Aunt Kate firmly.

—Yes, but why? asked Mr Browne.

Aunt Kate repeated that it was the rule, that was all. Mr Browne still seemed not to understand. Freddy Malins explained to him, as best he could, that the monks were trying to make up for the sins committed by all the sinners in the outside world. The explanation was not very clear for Mr Browne grinned and said:

—I like that idea very much but wouldn't a comfortable spring bed do them as well as a coffin?

—The coffin, said Mary Jane, is to remind them of their last end.

As the subject had grown lugubrious it was buried in a silence of the table during which Mrs Malins could be heard saying to her neighbour in an indistinct undertone:

—They are very good men, the monks, very pious men.

The raisins and almonds and figs and apples and oranges and chocolates and sweets were now passed about the table and Aunt Julia invited all the guests to have either port or sherry. At first Mr Bartell D'Arcy refused to take either but one of his neighbours nudged him and whispered something to him upon which he allowed his glass to be filled. Gradually as the last glasses were being filled the conversation ceased. A pause followed, broken only by the noise of the wine and by unsettlings of chairs. The Misses Morkan, all three, looked down at the tablecloth. Some one coughed once or twice and then a few gentlemen patted the table gently as a signal for silence. The silence came and Gabriel pushed back his chair and stood up.

The patting at once grew louder in encouragement and then ceased altogether. Gabriel leaned his ten trembling fingers on the tablecloth and smiled nervously at the company. Meeting a row of upturned faces he raised his eyes to the chandelier. The piano was playing a waltz tune and he could hear the skirts sweeping against the drawing-room door. People, perhaps, were standing in the snow on the quay outside, gazing up at the lighted windows and listening to the waltz music. The air was pure there. In the distance lay the park where the trees were weighted with snow. The Wellington Monument wore a gleaming cap of snow that flashed westward over the white field of Fifteen Acres.

He began:

—Ladies and Gentlemen.

—It has fallen to my lot this evening, as in years past, to perform a very pleasing task but a task for which I am afraid my poor powers as a speaker are all too inadequate.

—No, no! said Mr Browne.

—But, however that may be, I can only ask you to-night to take the will for the deed and to lend me your attention for a few moments while I endeavour to express to you in words what my feelings are on this occasion.

—Ladies and Gentlemen. It is not the first time that we have gathered together under this hospitable roof, around this hospitable board. It is not the first time that we have been the recipients – or perhaps, I had better say, the victims – of the hospitality of certain good ladies.

He made a circle in the air with his arm and paused. Every one laughed or smiled at Aunt Kate and Aunt Julia and Mary Jane who all turned crimson with pleasure. Gabriel went on more boldly:

—I feel more strongly with every recurring year that our country has no tradition which does it so much honour and which it should guard so jealously as that of its hospitality. It is a tradition that is unique as far as my experience goes (and I have visited not a few places abroad) among the modern nations. Some would say, perhaps, that with us it is rather a failing than anything to be boasted of. But granted even that, it is, to my mind, a princely failing, and one that I trust will long be cultivated among us. Of one thing, at least, I am sure. As long as this one roof shelters the good ladies aforesaid – and I wish from my heart it may do so for many and many a long year to come – the tradition of genuine warm-hearted courteous Irish hospitality, which our forefathers have handed down to us and which we in turn must hand down to our descendants, is still alive among us.

A hearty murmur of assent ran round the table. It shot through Gabriel's mind that Miss Ivors was not there and that she had gone away discourteously: and he said with confidence in himself:

—Ladies and Gentlemen.

—A new generation is growing up in our midst, a generation actuated by new ideas and new principles. It is serious and enthusiastic for these new ideas and its enthusiasm, even when it is misdirected, is, I believe, in the main sincere. But we are living in a sceptical and, if I may use the phrase, a thought-tormented age: and sometimes I fear that this new generation, educated or hypereducated as it is, will lack those qualities of humanity, of hospitality, of kindly humour which belonged to an older day. Listening to-night to the names of all those great singers of the past it seemed to me, I must confess, that we were living in a less spacious age. Those days might, without exaggeration, be called spacious days: and if they are gone beyond recall let us hope, at least, that in gatherings such as this we shall still speak of them with pride and affection, still cherish in our hearts the memory of those dead and gone great ones whose fame the world will not willingly let die.

—Hear, hear! said Mr Browne loudly.

—But yet, continued Gabriel, his voice falling into a softer inflection, there are always in gatherings such as this sadder thoughts that will recur to our minds: thoughts of the past, of youth, of changes, of absent faces that we miss here tonight. Our path through life is strewn with many such sad memories and were we to brood upon them always we could not find the heart to go on bravely with our work among the living. We have all of us living duties and living affections which claim, and rightly claim, our strenuous endeavours.

—Therefore, I will not linger on the past. I will not let any gloomy moralizing intrude upon us here to-night. Here we are gathered together for a brief moment from the bustle and rush of our everyday routine. We are met here as friends, in the spirit of good-fellowship, as colleagues, also to a certain extent, in the true spirit of *camaraderie*, and as the guest of – what shall I call them? – the Three Graces of the Dublin musical world.

The table burst into applause and laughter at this sally.

Aunt Julia vainly asked each of her neighbours in turn to tell her what Gabriel had said.

—He says we are the Three Graces, Aunt Julia, said Mary Jane.

Aunt Julia did not understand but she looked up, smiling, at Gabriel, who continued in the same vein:

—Ladies and Gentlemen.

—I will not attempt to play to-night the part that Paris played on another occasion. I will not attempt to choose between them. The task would be an invidious one and one beyond my poor powers. For when I view them in turn, whether it be our chief hostess herself, whose good heart, whose too good heart, has become a byword with all who know her, or her sister, who seems to be gifted with perennial youth and whose singing must have been a surprise and a revelation to us all to-night, or, last but not least, when I consider our youngest hostess, talented, cheerful, hard-working and the best of nieces, I confess, Ladies and Gentlemen, that I do not know to which of them I should award the prize.

Gabriel glanced down at his aunts and, seeing the large smile on Aunt Julia's face and the tears which had risen to Aunt Kate's eyes, hastened to his close. He raised his glass of port gallantly, while every member of the company fingered a glass expectantly, and said loudly:

—Let us toast them all three together. Let us drink to their health, wealth, long life, happiness and prosperity and may they long continue to hold the proud and self-won position which they hold in their profession and the position of honour and affection which they hold in our hearts.

All the guests stood up, glass in hand, and, turning towards the three seated ladies, sang in unison, with Mr Browne as leader:

> *For they are jolly gay fellows,*
> *For they are jolly gay fellows,*
> *For they are jolly gay fellows,*
> *Which nobody can deny.*

Aunt Kate was making frank use of her handkerchief and even Aunt Julia seemed moved. Freddy Malins beat time with his pudding-fork and the singers turned towards one another, as if in melodious conference, while they sang with emphasis:

> *Unless he tells a lie,*
> *Unless he tells a lie,*

Then, turning once more towards their hostesses, they sang:

> *For they are jolly gay fellows,*
> *For they are jolly gay fellows,*
> *For they are jolly gay fellows,*
> *Which nobody can deny.*

The acclamation which followed was taken up beyond the door of the supper-room by many of the other guests and renewed time after time, Freddy Malins acting as officer with his fork on high.

The piercing morning air came into the hall where they were standing so that Aunt Kate said:

—Close the door, somebody. Mrs Malins will get her death of cold.

—Browne is out there, Aunt Kate, said Mary Jane.

—Browne is everywhere, said Aunt Kate, lowering her voice.

Mary Jane laughed at her tone.

—Really, she said archly, he is very attentive.

—He has been laid on here like the gas, said Aunt Kate in the same tone, all during the Christmas.

She laughed herself this time good-humouredly and then added quickly:

—But tell him to come in, Mary Jane, and close the door. I hope to goodness he didn't hear me.

At that moment the hall-door was opened and Mr Browne came in from the doorstep, laughing as if his heart would break. He was dressed in a long green overcoat with mock astrakhan cuffs and collar and wore on his head an oval fur cap. He pointed down the snow-covered quay from where the sound of shrill prolonged whistling was borne in.

—Teddy will have all the cabs in Dublin out, he said.

Gabriel advanced from the little pantry behind the office, struggling into his overcoat and, looking round the hall, said:

—Gretta not down yet?

—She's getting on her things, Gabriel, said Aunt Kate.

—Who's playing up there? asked Gabriel.

—Nobody. They're all gone.

—O no, Aunt Kate, said Mary Jane. Bartell D'Arcy and Miss O'Callaghan aren't gone yet.

—Someone is strumming at the piano, anyhow, said Gabriel.

Mary Jane glanced at Gabriel and Mr Browne and said with a shiver:

—It makes me feel cold to look at you two gentlemen muffled up like that. I wouldn't like to face your journey home at this hour.

—I'd like nothing better this minute, said Mr Browne stoutly, than a rattling fine walk in the country or a fast drive with a good spanking goer between the shafts.

—We used to have a very good horse and trap at home, said Aunt Julia sadly.

—The never-to-be-forgotten Johnny, said Mary Jane, laughing.

Aunt Kate and Gabriel laughed too.

—Why, what was wonderful about Johnny? asked Mr Browne.

—The late lamented Patrick Morkan, our grandfather, that is, explained Gabriel, commonly known in his later years as the old gentleman, was a glue-boiler.

—O, now, Gabriel, said Aunt Kate, laughing, he had a starch mill.

—Well, glue or starch, said Gabriel, the old gentleman had a horse by the name of Johnny. And Johnny used to work in the old gentleman's mill, walking round and round in order to drive the mill. That was all very well; but now comes the tragic part about Johnny. One fine day the old gentleman thought he'd like to drive out with the quality to a military review in the park.

—The Lord have mercy on his soul, said Aunt Kate compassionately.

—Amen, said Gabriel. So the old gentleman, as I said, harnessed Johnny and put on his very best tall hat and his very best stock collar and drove out in grand style from his ancestral mansion somewhere near Back Lane, I think.

Every one laughed, even Mrs Malins, at Gabriel's manner and Aunt Kate said:

—O now, Gabriel, he didn't live in Back Lane, really. Only the mill was there.

—Out from the mansion of his forefathers, continued Gabriel, he drove with Johnny. And everything went on beautifully until Johnny came in sight of King Billy's statue: and whether he fell in love with the horse King Billy sits on or whether he thought he was back again in the mill, anyhow he began to walk round the statue.

Gabriel paced in a circle round the hall in his goloshes amid the laughter of the others.

—Round and round he went, said Gabriel, and the old gentleman, who was a very pompous old gentleman, was highly indignant. *Go on, sir! What do you mean, sir? Johnny! Johnny! Most extraordinary conduct! Can't understand the horse!*

The peals of laughter which followed Gabriel's imitation of the incident were interrupted by a resounding knock at the hall-door. Mary Jane ran to open it and let in Freddy Malins. Freddy Malins, with his hat well back on his head and his shoulders humped with cold, was puffing and steaming after his exertions.

—I could only get one cab, he said.

—O, we'll find another along the quay, said Gabriel.

—Yes, said Aunt Kate. Better not keep Mrs Malins standing in the draught.

Mrs Malins was helped down the front steps by her son and Mr Browne and, after many manœuvres, hoisted into the cab. Freddy Malins clambered in after her and spent a long time settling her on the seat, Mr Browne helping him with advice. At last she was settled comfortably and Freddy Malins invited Mr Browne into the cab. There was a good deal of confused talk, and then Mr Browne got into the cab. The cabman settled his rug over his knees, and bent down for the address. The confusion grew greater and the cabman was directed differently by Freddy Malins and Mr Browne, each of whom had his head out through a window of the cab. The difficulty was to know where to drop Mr Browne along the route and Aunt Kate, Aunt Julia and Mary Jane helped the discussion from the doorstep with cross-directions and contradictions and abundance of laughter. As for Freddy Malins he was speechless with laughter. He popped his head in and out of the window every moment, to the great danger of his hat, and told his mother how the discussion was progressing, till at last Mr Browne shouted to the bewildered cabman above the din of everybody's laughter:

—Do you know Trinity College?

—Yes, sir, said the cabman.

—Well, drive bang up against Trinity College gates, said Mr Browne, and then we'll tell you where to go. You understand now?

—Yes, sir, said the cabman.

—Make like a bird for Trinity College.

—Right, sir, cried the cabman.

The horse was whipped up and the cab rattled off along the quay amid a chorus of laughter and adieus.

Gabriel had not gone to the door with the others. He was in a dark part of the hall gazing up the staircase. A woman was standing near the top of the first flight, in the shadow also. He could not see her face but he could see the terracotta and salmonpink panels of her skirt which the shadow made appear black and white. It was his wife. She was leaning on the banisters, listening to something. Gabriel was surprised at her stillness and strained his ear to listen also. But he could hear little save the noise of laughter and dispute on the front steps, a few chords struck on the piano and a few notes of a man's voice singing.

He stood still in the gloom of the hall, trying to catch the air that the voice was singing and gazing up at his wife. There was grace and mystery in her attitude as if she were a symbol of something. He asked himself what is a woman standing on the stairs in the shadow, listening to distant music, a symbol of. If he were a painter he would paint her in that attitude. Her blue felt hat would show off the bronze of her hair against the darkness and the dark panels of her skirt would show off the light ones. *Distant Music* he would call the picture if he were a painter.

The hall-door was closed; and Aunt Kate, Aunt Julia and Mary Jane came down the hall, still laughing.

—Well, isn't Freddy terrible? said Mary Jane. He's really terrible.

Gabriel said nothing but pointed up the stairs towards where his wife was standing. Now that the hall-door was closed the voice and the piano could be heard more clearly. Gabriel held up his hand for them to be silent. The song seemed to be in the old Irish tonality and the singer seemed uncertain both of his words and of his voice. The voice, made plaintive by distance and by the singer's hoarseness, faintly illuminated the cadence of the air with words expressing grief:

> *O, the rain falls on my heavy locks*
> *And the dew wets my skin,*
> *My babe lies cold . . .*

—O, exclaimed Mary Jane. It's Bartell D'Arcy singing, and he wouldn't sing all the night. O, I'll get him to sing a song before he goes.

—O, do, Mary Jane, said Aunt Kate.

Mary Jane brushed past the others and ran to the staircase but before she reached it the singing stopped and the piano was closed abruptly.

—O, what a pity! she cried. Is he coming down, Gretta?

Gabriel heard his wife answer yes and saw her come down towards them. A few steps behind her were Mr Bartell D'Arcy and Miss O'Callaghan.

—O, Mr D'Arcy, cried Mary Jane, it's downright mean of you to break off like that when we were all in raptures listening to you.

—I have been at him all the evening, said Miss O'Callaghan, and Mrs Conroy too and he told us he had a dreadful cold and couldn't sing.

—O, Mr D'Arcy, said Aunt Kate, now that was a great fib to tell.

—Can't you see that I'm as hoarse as a crow? said Mr D'Arcy roughly.

He went into the pantry hastily and put on his overcoat. The others, taken aback by his rude speech, could find nothing to say. Aunt Kate wrinkled her brows and made signs to the others to drop the subject. Mr D'Arcy stood swathing his neck carefully and frowning.

—It's the weather, said Aunt Julia, after a pause.

—Yes, everybody has colds, said Aunt Kate readily, everybody.

—They say, said Mary Jane, we haven't had snow like it for thirty years; and I read this morning in the newspapers that the snow is general all over Ireland.

—I love the look of snow, said Aunt Julia sadly.

—So do I, said Miss O'Callaghan. I think Christmas is never really Christmas unless we have the snow on the ground.

—But poor Mr D'Arcy doesn't like the snow, said Aunt Kate, smiling.

Mr D'Arcy came from the pantry, fully swathed and buttoned, and in a repentant tone told them the history of his cold. Every one gave him advice and said it was a great pity and urged him to be very careful of his throat in the night air. Gabriel watched his wife who did not join in the conversation. She was standing right under the dusty fan-light and the flame of the gas lit up the rich bronze of her hair which he had seen her drying at the fire a few days before. She was in the same attitude and seemed unaware of the talk about her. At last she turned towards them and Gabriel saw that there was colour on her cheeks and that her eyes were shining. A sudden tide of joy went leaping out of his heart.

—Mr D'Arcy, she said, what is the name of that song you were singing?

—It's called *The Lass of Aughrim*, said Mr D'Arcy, but I couldn't remember it properly. Why? Do you know it?

—*The Lass of Aughrim*, she repeated. I couldn't think of the name.

—It's a very nice air, said Mary Jane. I'm sorry you were not in voice to-night.

—Now, Mary Jane, said Aunt Kate, don't annoy Mr D'Arcy. I won't have him annoyed.

Seeing that all were ready to start she shepherded them to the door where good-night was said:

—Well, good-night, Aunt Kate, and thanks for the pleasant evening.

—Good-night, Gabriel. Good-night, Gretta!

—Good-night, Aunt Kate, and thanks ever so much. Good-night, Aunt Julia.

—O, good-night, Gretta, I didn't see you.

—Good-night, Mr D'Arcy. Good-night, Miss O'Callaghan.

—Good-night, Miss Morkan.

—Good-night, again.

—Good-night, all. Safe home.

—Good-night. Good-night.

The morning was still dark. A dull yellow light brooded over the houses and the river; and the sky seemed to be descending. It was slushy underfoot; and only streaks and patches of snow lay on the roofs, on the parapets of the quay and on the area railings. The lamps were still burning redly in the murky air and, across the river, the palace of the Four Courts stood out menacingly against the heavy sky.

She was walking on before him with Mr Bartell D'Arcy, her shoes in a brown parcel tucked under one arm and her hands holding her skirt up from the slush. She had no longer any grace of attitude but Gabriel's eyes were still bright with happiness. The blood went bounding along his veins; and the thoughts went rioting through his brain, proud, joyful, tender, valorous.

She was walking on before him so lightly and so erect that he longed to run after her noiselessly, catch her by the shoulders and say something foolish and affectionate into her ear. She seemed to him so frail that he longed to defend her against something and then to be alone with her. Moments of their secret life together burst like stars upon his memory. A heliotrope envelope was lying beside his breakfast-cup and he was caressing it with his hand. Birds were twittering in the ivy and the sunny web of the curtain was shimmering along the floor: he could not eat for happiness. They were standing on the crowded platform and he was placing a ticket inside the warm palm of her glove. He was standing with her in the cold, looking in through a grated window at a man making bottles in a roaring furnace. It was very cold. Her face, fragrant in the cold air, was quite close to his; and suddenly she called out to the man at the furnace:

—Is the fire hot, sir?

But the man could not hear her with the noise of the furnace. It was just as well. He might have answered rudely.

A wave of yet more tender joy escaped from his heart and went coursing in warm flood along his arteries. Like the tender fires of stars moments of their life together, that no one knew of or would ever know of, broke upon and illumined his memory. He longed to recall to her those moments, to make her forget the years of their dull existence together and remember only their moments of ecstasy. For the years, he felt, had not quenched his soul or hers. Their children, his writing, her household cares had not quenched all their souls' tender fire. In one letter that he had written to her then he had said: *Why is it that words like these seem to me so dull and cold? Is it because there is no word tender enough to be your name?*

Like distant music these words that he had written years before were borne towards him from the past. He longed to be alone with her. When the others had gone away, when he and she were in the room in the hotel, then they would be alone together. He would call her softly:

—Gretta!

Perhaps she would not hear at once: she would be undressing. Then something in his voice would strike her. She would turn and look at him. . . .

At the corner of Winetavern Street they met a cab. He was glad of its rattling noise as it saved him from conversation. She was looking out of the window and seemed tired. The others spoke only a few words, pointing out some building or street. The horse galloped along wearily under the murky morning sky, dragging his old rattling box after his heels, and Gabriel was again in a cab with her, galloping to catch the boat, galloping to their honeymoon.

As the cab drove across O'Connell Bridge Miss O'Callaghan said:

—They say you never cross O'Connell Bridge without seeing a white horse.

—I see a white man this time, said Gabriel.

—Where? asked Mr Bartell D'Arcy.

Gabriel pointed to the statue, on which lay patches of snow. Then he nodded familiarly to it and waved his hand.

—Good-night, Dan, he said gaily.

When the cab drew up before the hotel Gabriel jumped out and, in spite of Mr Bartell D'Arcy's protest, paid the driver. He gave the man a shilling over his fare. The man saluted and said:

—A prosperous New Year to you, sir.

—The same to you, said Gabriel cordially.

She leaned for a moment on his arm in getting out of the cab and while standing at the kerbstone, bidding the others good-night. She leaned lightly on his arm, as lightly as when she had danced with him a few hours before. He had felt proud and happy then, happy that she was his, proud of her grace and wifely carriage. But now, after the kindling again of so many memories, the first touch of her body, musical and strange and perfumed, sent through him a keen pang of lust. Under cover of her silence he pressed her arm closely to his side; and, as they stood at the hotel door, he felt that they had escaped from their lives and duties, escaped from home and friends and run away together with wild and radiant hearts to a new adventure.

An old man was dozing in a great hooded chair in the hall. He lit a candle in the office and went before them to the stairs. They followed him in silence, their feet falling in soft thuds on the thickly carpeted stairs. She mounted the stairs behind the porter, her head bowed in the ascent, her frail shoulders curved as with a burden, her skirt girt tightly about her. He could have flung his arms about her hips and held her still for his arms were trembling with desire to seize her and only the stress of his nails against the palms of his hands held the wild impulse of his body in check. The porter halted on the stairs to settle his guttering candle. They halted too on the steps below him. In the silence Gabriel could hear the falling of the molten wax into the tray and the thumping of his own heart against his ribs.

The porter led them along a corridor and opened a door. Then he set his unstable candle down on a toilet-table and asked at what hour they were to be called in the morning.

—Eight, said Gabriel.

The porter pointed to the tap of the electric-light and began a muttered apology but Gabriel cut him short.

—We don't want any light. We have light enough from the street. And I say, he added, pointing to the candle, you might remove that handsome article, like a good man.

The porter took up his candle again, but slowly for he was surprised by such a novel idea. Then he mumbled goodnight and went out. Gabriel shot the lock to.

A ghostly light from the street lamp lay in a long shaft from one window to the door. Gabriel threw his overcoat and hat on a couch and crossed the room towards the window. He looked down into the street in order that his emotion might calm a little. Then he turned and leaned against a chest of drawers with his back to the light. She had taken off her hat and cloak and was standing before a large swinging mirror, unhooking her waist. Gabriel paused for a few moments, watching her, and then said:

—Gretta!

She turned away from the mirror slowly and walked along the shaft of light towards him. Her face looked so serious and weary that the words would not pass Gabriel's lips. No, it was not the moment yet.

—You looked tired, he said.

—I am a little, she answered.

—You don't feel ill or weak?

—No, tired: that's all.

She went on to the window and stood there, looking out. Gabriel waited again and then, fearing that diffidence was about to conquer him, he said abruptly:

—By the way, Gretta!

—What is it?

—You know that poor fellow Malins? he said quickly.

—Yes. What about him?

—Well, poor fellow, he's a decent sort of chap, after all, continued Gabriel in a false voice. He gave me back that sovereign I lent him and I didn't expect it really. It's a pity he wouldn't keep away from that Browne, because he's not a bad fellow at heart.

He was trembling now with annoyance. Why did she seem so abstracted? He did not know how he could begin. Was she annoyed, too, about something? If she would only turn to him or come to him of her own accord! To take her as she was would be brutal. No, he must see some ardour in her eyes first. He longed to be master of her strange mood.

—When did you lend him the pound? she asked, after a pause.

Gabriel strove to restrain himself from breaking out into brutal language about the sottish Malins and his pound. He longed to cry to her from his soul, to crush her body against his, to overmaster her. But he said:

—O, at Christmas, when he opened that little Christmas-card shop in Henry Street.

He was in such a fever of rage and desire that he did not hear her come from the window. She stood before him for an instant, looking at him strangely. Then, suddenly raising herself on tiptoe and resting her hands lightly on his shoulders, she kissed him.

—You are a very generous person, Gabriel, she said.

Gabriel, trembling with delight at her sudden kiss and at the quaintness of her phrase, put his hands on her hair and began smoothing it back, scarcely touching it with his fingers. The washing had made it fine and brilliant. His heart was brimming over with happiness. Just when he was wishing for it she had come to him of her own accord. Perhaps her thoughts had been running with his. Perhaps she had felt the impetuous desire that was in him and then the yielding mood had come upon her. Now that she had fallen to him so easily he wondered why he had been so diffident.

He stood, holding her head between his hands. Then, slipping one arm swiftly about her body and drawing her towards him, he said softly:

—Gretta dear, what are you thinking about?

She did not answer nor yield wholly to his arm. He said again, softly:

—Tell me what it is, Gretta. I think I know what is the matter. Do I know?

She did not answer at once. Then she said in an outburst of tears:

—O, I am thinking about that song, *The Lass of Aughrim*.

She broke loose from him and ran to the bed and, throwing her arms across the bed-rail, hid her face. Gabriel stood stock-still for a moment in astonishment and then followed her. As he passed in the way of the cheval-glass he caught sight of himself in full length, his broad, well-filled shirt-front, the face whose expression always puzzled him when he saw it in a mirror and his glimmering gilt-rimmed eye-glasses. He halted a few paces from her and said:

—What about the song? Why does that make you cry?

She raised her head from her arms and dried her eyes with the back of her hand like a child. A kinder note than he had intended went into his voice.

—Why, Gretta? he asked.

—I am thinking about a person long ago who used to sing that song.

—And who was the person long ago? asked Gabriel, smiling.

—It was a person I used to know in Galway when I was living with my grandmother, she said.

The smile passed away from Gabriel's face. A dull anger began to gather again at the back of his mind and the dull fires of his lust began to glow angrily in his veins.

—Someone you were in love with? he asked ironically.

—It was a young boy I used to know, she answered, named Michael Furey. He used to sing that song, *The Lass of Aughrim*. He was very delicate.

Gabriel was silent. He did not wish her to think that he was interested in this delicate boy.

—I can see him so plainly, she said after a moment. Such eyes as he had: big dark eyes! And such an expression in them – an expression!

—O then, you were in love with him? said Gabriel.

—I used to go out walking with him, she said, when I was in Galway.

A thought flew across Gabriel's mind.

—Perhaps that was why you wanted to go to Galway with that Ivors girl? he said coldly.

She looked at him and asked in surprise:

—What for?

Her eyes made Gabriel feel awkward. He shrugged his shoulders and said:

—How do I know? To see him perhaps.

She looked away from him along the shaft of light towards the window in silence.

—He is dead, she said at length. He died when he was

only seventeen. Isn't it a terrible thing to die so young as that?

—What was he? asked Gabriel, still ironically.

—He was in the gasworks, she said.

Gabriel felt humiliated by the failure of his irony and by the evocation of this figure from the dead, a boy in the gasworks. While he had been full of memories of their secret life together, full of tenderness and joy and desire, she had been comparing him in her mind with another. A shameful consciousness of his own person assailed him. He saw himself as a ludicrous figure, acting as a pennyboy for his aunts, a nervous well-meaning sentimentalist, orating to vulgarians and idealizing his own clownish lusts, the pitiable fatuous fellow he had caught a glimpse of in the mirror. Instinctively he turned his back more to the light lest she might see the shame that burned upon his forehead.

He tried to keep up his tone of cold interrogation but his voice when he spoke was humble and indifferent.

—I suppose you were in love with this Michael Furey, Gretta, he said.

—I was great with him at that time, she said.

Her voice was veiled and sad. Gabriel, feeling now how vain it would be to try to lead her whither he had purposed, caressed one of her hands and said, also sadly:

—And what did he die of so young, Gretta? Consumption, was it?

—I think he died for me, she answered.

A vague terror seized Gabriel at this answer as if, at that hour when he had hoped to triumph, some impalpable and vindictive being was coming against him, gathering forces against him in its vague world. But he shook himself free of it with an effort of reason and continued to caress her hand. He did not question her again for he felt that she would tell him of herself. Her hand was warm and moist: it did not respond to his touch but he continued to caress it just as he had caressed her first letter to him that spring morning.

—It was in the winter, she said, about the beginning of the winter when I was going to leave my grandmother's and come up here to the convent. And he was ill at the time in his lodgings in Galway and wouldn't be let out and his people in Oughterard were written to. He was in decline, they said, or something like that. I never knew rightly.

She paused for a moment and sighed.

—Poor fellow, she said. He was very fond of me and he was such a gentle boy. We used to go out together, walking, you know, Gabriel, like the way they do in the country. He was going to study singing only for his health. He had a very good voice, poor Michael Furey.

—Well; and then? asked Gabriel.

—And then when it came to the time for me to leave Galway and come up to the convent he was much worse and I wouldn't be let see him so I wrote a letter saying I was going up to Dublin and would be back in the summer and hoping he would be better then.

She paused for a moment to get her voice under control and then went on:

—Then the night before I left I was in my grandmother's house in Nuns' Island, packing up, and I heard gravel thrown up against the window. The window was so wet I couldn't see so I ran downstairs as I was and slipped out the back into the garden and there was the poor fellow at the end of the garden, shivering.

—And did you not tell him to go back? asked Gabriel.

—I implored of him to go home at once and told him he would get his death in the rain. But he said he did not want to live. I can see his eyes as well as well! He was standing at the end of the wall where there was a tree.

—And did he go home? asked Gabriel.

—Yes, he went home. And when I was only a week in the convent he died and he was buried in Oughterard where his people came from. O, the day I heard that, that he was dead!

She stopped, choking with sobs, and, overcome by emotion, flung herself face downward on the bed, sobbing in the quilt. Gabriel held her hand for a moment longer, irresolutely, and then, shy of intruding on her grief, let it fall gently and walked quietly to the window.

She was fast asleep.

Gabriel, leaning on his elbow, looked for a few moments unresentfully on her tangled hair and half-open mouth, listening to her deep-drawn breath. So she had had that romance in her life: a man had died for her sake. It hardly pained him now to think how poor a part he, her husband, had played in her life. He watched her while she slept as though he and she had never lived together as man and wife. His curious eyes rested long upon her face and on her hair: and, as he thought of what she must have been then, in that time of her first girlish beauty, a strange friendly pity for her entered his soul. He did not like to say even to himself that her face was no longer beautiful but he knew that it was no longer the face for which Michael Furey had braved death.

Perhaps she had not told him all the story. His eyes moved to the chair over which she had thrown some of her clothes. A petticoat string dangled to the floor. One boot stood upright, its limp upper fallen down: the fellow of it lay upon its side. He wondered at his riot of emotions of an hour before. From what had it proceeded? From his aunt's supper, from his own foolish speech, from the wine and dancing, the merry-making when saying good-night in the hall, the pleasure of the walk along the river in the snow. Poor Aunt

Julia! She, too, would soon be a shade with the shade of Patrick Morkan and his horse. He had caught that haggard look upon her face for a moment when she was singing *Arrayed for the Bridal*. Soon, perhaps, he would be sitting in that same drawing-room, dressed in black, his silk hat on his knees. The blinds would be drawn down and Aunt Kate would be sitting beside him, crying and blowing her nose and telling him how Julia had died. He would cast about in his mind for some words that might console her, and would find only lame and useless ones. Yes, yes: that would happen very soon.

The air of the room chilled his shoulders. He stretched himself cautiously along under the sheets and lay down beside his wife. One by one they were all becoming shades. Better pass boldly into that other world, in the full glory of some passion, than fade and wither dismally with age. He thought of how she who lay beside him had locked in her heart for so many years that image of her lover's eyes when he had told her that he did not wish to live.

Generous tears filled Gabriel's eyes. He had never felt like that himself towards any woman but he knew that such a feeling must be love. The tears gathered more thickly in his eyes and in the partial darkness he imagined he saw the form of a young man standing under a dripping tree. Other forms were near. His soul had approached that region where dwell the vast hosts of the dead. He was conscious of, but could not apprehend, their wayward and flickering existence. His own identity was fading out into a grey impalpable world: the solid world itself which these dead had one time reared and lived in was dissolving and dwindling.

A few light taps upon the pane made him turn to the window. It had begun to snow again. He watched sleepily the flakes, silver and dark, falling obliquely against the lamplight. The time had come for him to set out on his journey westward. Yes, the newspapers were right: snow was general all over Ireland. It was falling on every part of the dark central plain, on the treeless hills, falling softly upon the Bog of Allen and, farther westward, softly falling into the dark mutinous Shannon waves. It was falling, too, upon every part of the lonely churchyard on the hill where Michael Furey lay buried. It lay thickly drifted on the crooked crosses and headstones, on the spears of the little gate, on the barren thorns. His soul swooned slowly as he heard the snow falling faintly through the universe and faintly falling, like the descent of their last end, upon all the living and the dead.

PÁDRAIC Ó CONAIRE

KNITTING ('AN CHNIOTÁIL')

Translated by Thomas Murphy

I'M DOWN AND my heart is heavy throughout the day, and it's not without reason.

And yesterday I was laughing with the springtime of the year, and life laughing along with me, as I travelled the seashore from dawn to dusk. But today is a different story and I cannot lift myself out of its gloom.

At the fall of night, last night, I went to the house of a couple that were very great with me one time but, life being what it is, I hadn't had tide or tidings of them for ten years. But they would be the one to have the welcome for me, and wouldn't we have the great stories to exchange! I began to think, gathering my best and strangest adventures so as to set the pair of them laughing. And I'd have the right stories for the children too. . . . Yes, how many of them were in it? They had three sons ten years ago; they'd be fine tall boys by now, and maybe the house filled with other children as well. But, for the life of me, if I could remember the names of the three sons. I'd be ashamed of that.

No matter, my spirits were soaring, going to become re-acquainted with my old friends.

The man was in the parlour when I was let in and, though it was only dusk, he had the lamp lit on the table and the same with the candles in the windows. It struck me at first sight that he was looking worn, and older than his years. Somehow life had weighed heavily upon him. And he a fine tall man only into his middle years.

But the biggest wonder of all was what he was doing. There were gloves and mittens and all classes of garments on the table before him; they were knitted from the finest silken thread. And the business that was occupying my friend so earnestly was unravelling the knitted garments and winding up the thread again.

You'd know that he felt ashamed at being discovered in such work, for no sooner did he see me but he threw it from him in a way as if to hide the matter, and then he welcomed me in his own generous manner. I was curious to ask what had him so occupied but the question would embarrass him.

'Here is a man,' I said to myself, 'suffering the pains of hell.'

After a while I asked how was his wife. He seemed reluctant to reply but kept silent, looking into the fire as one in lingering thought.

I let the matter rest. Some disagreement or falling-out that was between them, I thought, and he didn't want to talk about it. That was a pity, because if there was a man in Ireland had the love and affection for his wife, that man was my friend. But isn't that the way with the story always, there's no cure for love but marriage.

And the fondness they had for each other ten years ago!

We talked about the world. It's hard to become re-acquainted with a person after ten years.

'And the family,' I said, 'are ye all well?'

He sighed.

'May the Son of God help me,' he said pitifully, 'but I'll have to tell you the whole story.'

He prepared himself, making ready to talk, but no sooner was he started than the door opened and who came in but his wife.

I stood up to greet her but she walked past me without as much as a glance. Indeed, she didn't even raise her eyes, but she knitting away earnestly the whole while. And wasn't I in great wonder to see that it was a silken shawl she was knitting, and wasn't it a silken shawl that her husband was unravelling!

The man had stood up too. He greeted her in his princely manner but she paid no more attention to him than she did to myself.

He arranged the big cosy chair in front of the fire. He couldn't have been more attentive if it was out of a sick bed she was after getting. And there was no colour or resemblance of sickness about her. On the contrary, she looked the picture of health, tall and stately, with a black dress of silk on her. She was past the forty mark but you wouldn't take her for much more than thirty.

She remained standing, her eyes cast down, still knitting away, until he took her arm gently and seated her. It wasn't because of anything between them or any falling-out that had made him reluctant to talk about her earlier: it was plain to see – it would be clear to the blind – that he was as fond of her now as he was in his youth.

But what was the matter with her? What sense could there be in this eternal knitting, and to be heedless of all else?

The place and the silent pair of them in the room were beginning to unsettle and weigh on me. If someone spoke it would have eased me and scattered the gloom that was in it. But no word was spoken since the woman had entered, and there was nothing to be heard but the sound of the knitting-needles knocking one against the other, and the occasional sigh from the man sitting beside me, his head bowed in sorrow.

Now and again the knitting fell to the floor; but in no way

did this upset her. She went on with her labour, working her fingers as if she was still holding the needles in her hands. And when the sound of the needles was not to be heard the man would know what had happened, and he'd stoop and hand the knitting back to her without a word being spoken. And though more often than not his head was bowed, there was hardly a stir from her that he'd miss, and his only care was to assist her in every way he could.

Hadn't I the pity for them when I realized that the gentle graceful woman he had given his heart to was gone clean out of her mind!

But that knitting, and the click-click of the needles knocking one against the other! And the sighs escaping from the man when his thoughts descended to scald the heart of him.

After a long time (long years they seemed to me) the knitting stopped and the woman craned her neck, listening.

'Is that Seán calling me?' she said.

'I expect it is,' said the man.

I wondered at them hearing a call for I heard no sound.

The woman stood up.

'I think the poor creature has a cold,' she said. 'The world itself wouldn't keep him out of the puddles.'

She went to the door, the knitting in her hands. The man arose and opened the door as you would for a queen.

'That's the way she is this two years,' he said, returning to the fire. 'Her mind and sense are gone clean from her.'

What good seeking to offer condolences on such an occasion!

I recalled that Seán was the eldest son and to make conversation I said, 'But I didn't hear him call.'

'My regret and misfortune that you didn't,' said he.

He looked at me.

'But did you not hear of the great sorrow that blighted the life in this house on us?'

I said I hadn't heard.

'It was a fine day at the end of spring two years ago that my heart was broken.' The poor man had a catch in his throat. He was silent a nice while. 'That day my three sons went out in an old boat. . . . the boat was leaking. . . . the three of them were drowned. . . . it was myself that brought the bodies ashore. . . .

'And my beautiful Sinéad is without mind or reason since. In her own strange way she thinks the three of them are still with us in the house, and she's forever knitting for them. . . . but for myself unravelling what she does from time to time, the house would be filled with mittens and gloves. . . .'

We were silent for a long while. Then I arose and took hold of his hand; we looked into each other's eyes and he understood the sympathy I had for him and for his handsome stately wife on whom God had laid a heavy hand.

LIAM O'FLAHERTY

THE SNIPER

THE LONG JUNE twilight faded into night. Dublin lay enveloped in darkness, but for the dim light of the moon, that shone through fleecy clouds, casting a pale light as of approaching dawn over the streets and the dark waters of the Liffey. Around the beleaguered Four Courts the heavy guns roared. Here and there through the city machine guns and rifles broke the silence of the night, spasmodically, like dogs barking on lone farms. Republicans and Free Staters were waging civil war.

On a roof-top near O'Connell Bridge, a Republican sniper lay watching. Beside him lay his rifle and over his shoulders were slung a pair of field-glasses. His face was the face of a student – thin and ascetic, but his eyes had the cold gleam of the fanatic. They were deep and thoughtful, the eyes of a man who is used to look at death.

He was eating a sandwich hungrily. He had eaten nothing since morning. He had been too excited to eat. He finished the sandwich, and taking a flask of whiskey from his pocket, he took a short draught. Then he returned the flask to his pocket. He paused for a moment, considering whether he should risk a smoke. It was dangerous. The flash might be seen in the darkness and there were enemies watching. He decided to take the risk. Placing a cigarette between his lips, he struck a match, inhaled the smoke hurriedly and put out the light. Almost immediately, a bullet flattened itself against the parapet of the roof. The sniper took another whiff and put out the cigarette. Then he swore softly and crawled away to the left.

Cautiously he raised himself and peered over the parapet. There was a flash and a bullet whizzed over his head. He dropped immediately. He had seen the flash. It came from the opposite side of the street.

He rolled over the roof to a chimney stack in the rear, and slowly drew himself up behind it, until his eyes were level with the top of the parapet. There was nothing to be seen – just the dim outline of the opposite housetop against the blue sky. His enemy was under cover.

Just then an armoured car came across the bridge and advanced slowly up the street. It stopped on the opposite side of the street fifty yards ahead. The sniper could hear the dull panting of the motor. His heart beat faster. It was an enemy car. He wanted to fire, but he knew it was useless. His bullets would never pierce the steel that covered the grey monster.

Then round the corner of a side street came an old woman, her head covered by a tattered shawl. She began to talk to the man in the turret of the car. She was pointing to the roof where the sniper lay. An informer.

The turret opened. A man's head and shoulders appeared, looking towards the sniper. The sniper raised his rifle and fired. The head fell heavily on the turret wall. The woman darted toward the side street. The sniper fired again. The woman whirled round and fell with a shriek into the gutter.

Suddenly from the opposite roof a shot rang out and the sniper dropped his rifle with a curse. The rifle clattered to the roof. The sniper thought the noise would wake the dead. He stopped to pick the rifle up. He couldn't lift it. His forearm was dead. 'Christ', he muttered, 'I'm hit.'

Dropping flat on to the roof, he crawled back to the parapet. With his left hand he felt the injured right forearm. The blood was oozing through the sleeve of his coat. There was no pain – just a deadened sensation, as if the arm had been cut off.

Quickly he drew his knife from his pocket, opened it on the breastwork of the parapet and ripped open the sleeve. There was a small hole where the bullet had entered. On the other side there was no hole. The bullet had lodged in the bone. It must have fractured it. He bent the arm below the wound. The arm bent back easily. He ground his teeth to overcome the pain.

Then, taking out his field dressing, he ripped open the packet with his knife. He broke the neck of the iodine bottle and let the bitter fluid drip into the wound. A paroxysm of pain swept through him. He placed the cotton wadding over the wound and wrapped the dressing over it. He tied the end with his teeth.

Then he lay still against the parapet, and closing his eyes, he made an effort of will to overcome the pain.

In the street beneath all was still. The armoured car had retired speedily over the bridge, with the machine gunner's head hanging lifeless over the turret. The woman's corpse lay still in the gutter.

The sniper lay for a long time nursing his wounded arm and planning escape. Morning must not find him wounded on the roof. The enemy on the opposite roof covered his escape. He must kill that enemy and he could not use his rifle. He had only a revolver to do it. Then he thought of a plan.

Taking off his cap, he placed it over the muzzle of his rifle. Then he pushed the rifle slowly upwards over the parapet, until the cap was visible from the opposite side of the street.

Almost immediately there was a report, and a bullet pierced the centre of the cap. The sniper slanted the rifle forward. The cap slipped down into the street. Then, catching the rifle in the middle, the sniper dropped his left hand over the roof and let it hang, lifelessly. After a few moments he let the rifle drop to the street. Then he sank to the roof, dragging his hand with him.

Crawling quickly to the left, he peered up at the corner of the roof. His ruse had succeeded. The other sniper seeing the cap and rifle fall, thought that he had killed his man. He was now standing before a row of chimney pots, looking across, with his head clearly silhouetted against the western sky.

The Republican sniper smiled and lifted his revolver above the edge of the parapet. The distance was about fifty yards – a hard shot in the dim light, and his right arm was paining him like a thousand devils. He took a steady aim. His hand trembled with eagerness. Pressing his lips together, he took a deep breath through his nostrils and fired. He was almost deafened with the report and his arm shook with the recoil.

Then, when the smoke cleared, he peered across and uttered a cry of joy. His enemy had been hit. He was reeling over the parapet in his death agony. He struggled to keep his feet, but he was slowly falling forward, as if in a dream. The rifle fell from his grasp, hit the parapet, fell over, bounded off the pole of a barber's shop beneath and then cluttered on to the pavement.

Then the dying man on the roof crumpled up and fell forward. The body turned over and over in space and hit the ground with a dull thud. Then it lay still.

The sniper looked at his enemy falling and he shuddered. The lust of battle died in him. He became bitten by remorse. The sweat stood out in beads on his forehead. Weakened by his wound and the long summer day of fasting and watching on the roof, he revolted from the sight of the shattered mass of his dead enemy. His teeth chattered. He began to gibber to himself, cursing the war, cursing himself, cursing everybody.

He looked at the smoking revolver in his hand and with an oath he hurled it to the roof at his feet. The revolver went off with the concussion, and the bullet whizzed past the sniper's head. He was frightened back to his senses by the shock. His nerves steadied. The cloud of fear scattered from his mind and he laughed.

Taking the whiskey flask from his pocket, he emptied it at a draught. He felt reckless under the influence of the spirits. He decided to leave the roof and look for his company commander to report. Everywhere around was quiet. There was not much danger in going through the streets. He picked up his revolver and put it in his pocket. Then he crawled down through the sky-light to the house underneath.

When the sniper reached the laneway on the street level, he felt a sudden curiosity as to the identity of the enemy sniper whom he had killed. He decided that he was a good shot whoever he was. He wondered if he knew him. Perhaps he had been in his own company before the split in the army. He decided to risk going over to have a look at him. He peered around the corner into O'Connell Street. In the upper part of the street there was heavy firing, but around here all was quiet.

The sniper darted across the street. A machine gun tore up the ground around him with a hail of bullets, but he escaped. He threw himself face downwards beside the corpse. The machine gun stopped.

Then the sniper turned over the dead body and looked into his brother's face.

FRANK O'CONNOR

GUESTS OF
THE NATION

I

AT DUSK THE big Englishman Belcher would shift his long legs out of the ashes and ask, 'Well, chums, what about it?' and Noble or me would say, 'As you please, chum' (for we had picked up some of their curious expressions), and the little Englishman 'Awkins would light the lamp and produce the cards. Sometimes Jeremiah Donovan would come up of an evening and supervise the play, and grow excited over 'Awkins's cards (which he always played badly), and shout at him as if he was one of our own, 'Ach, you divil you, why didn't you play the tray?' But, ordinarily, Jeremiah was a sober and contented poor devil like the big Englishman Belcher, and was looked up to at all only because he was a fair hand at documents, though slow enough at these, I vow. He wore a small cloth hat and big gaiters over his long pants and seldom did I perceive his hands outside the pockets of that pants. He reddened when you talked to him, tilting from toe to heel and back and looking down all the while at his big farmer's feet. His uncommon broad accent was a great source of jest to me, I being from the town as you may recognize.

I couldn't at the time see the point of me and Noble being with Belcher and 'Awkins at all, for it was and is my fixed belief you could have planted that pair in any untended spot from this to Claregalway and they'd have stayed put and flourished like a native weed. I never seen in my short experience two men that took to the country as they did.

They were handed on to us by the Second Battalion to keep when the search for them became too hot, and Noble and myself, being young, took charge with a natural feeling of responsibility. But little 'Awkins made us look right fools when he displayed he knew the countryside as well as we did and something more. 'You're the bloke they calls Bonaparte?' he said to me. 'Well, Bonaparte, Mary Brigid Ho'Connell was arskin abaout you and said 'ow you'd a pair of socks belonging to 'er young brother.' For it seemed, as they explained it, that the Second used to have little evenings of their own, and some of the girls of the neighbourhood would turn in, and, seeing they were such decent fellows, our lads couldn't well ignore the two Englishmen, but invited them in and were hail-fellow-well-met with them. 'Awkins told me he learned to dance 'The Walls of Limerick' and 'The Siege of Ennis' and 'The Waves of Tory' in a night or two, though naturally he could not return the compliment, because our lads at that time did not dance foreign dances on principle.

So whatever privileges and favours Belcher and 'Awkins had with the Second they duly took with us, and after the first evening we gave up all pretence of keeping a close eye on their behaviour. Not that they could have got far, for they had a notable accent and wore khaki tunics and overcoats with civilian pants and boots. But it's my belief they never had an idea of escaping and were quite contented with their lot.

Now, it was a treat to see how Belcher got off with the old woman of the house we were staying in. She was a great warrant to scold, and crotchety even with us, but before ever she had a chance of giving our guests, as I may call them, a lick of her tongue, Belcher had made her his friend for life. She was breaking sticks at the time, and Belcher, who hadn't been in the house for more than ten minutes, jumped up out of his seat and went across to her.

'Allow me, madam,' he says, smiling his queer little smile; 'please allow me', and takes the hatchet from her hand. She was struck too parlatic to speak, and ever after Belcher would be at her heels carrying a bucket, or basket, or load of turf, as the case might be. As Noble wittily remarked, he got into looking before she leapt, and hot water or any little thing she wanted Belcher would have it ready before her. For such a huge man (and though I am five foot ten myself I had to look up to him) he had an uncommon shortness – or should I say lack – of speech. It took us some time to get used to him walking in and out like a ghost, without a syllable out of him. Especially because 'Awkins talked enough for a platoon, it was strange to hear big Belcher with his toes in the ashes come out with a solitary 'Excuse me, chum,' or 'That's right, chum.' His one and only abiding passion was cards, and I will say for him he was a good card-player. He could have fleeced me and Noble many a time; only if we lost to him, 'Awkins lost to us, and 'Awkins played with the money Belcher gave him.

'Awkins lost to us because he talked too much, and I think now we lost to Belcher for the same reason. 'Awkins and Noble would spit at one another about religion into the early hours of the morning; the little Englishman as you could see worrying the soul out of young Noble (whose brother was a priest) with a string of questions that would puzzle a cardinal. And to make it worse, even in treating of these holy subjects, 'Awkins had a deplorable tongue; I never in all my career struck across a man who could mix such a variety of cursing and bad language into the simplest topic. Oh, a terrible man was little 'Awkins, and a fright to argue! He never did a stroke of work, and when he had no one else to talk to he fixed his claws into the old woman.

I am glad to say that in her he met his match, for one day when he tried to get her to complain profanely of the drought she gave him a great comedown by blaming the drought upon Jupiter Pluvius (a deity neither 'Awkins nor I had ever even heard of, though Noble said among the pagans he was held to have something to do with rain). And another day the same 'Awkins was swearing at the capitalists for starting the German war, when the old dame laid down her iron, puckered up her little crab's mouth and said, 'Mr 'Awkins, you can say what you please about the war, thinking to deceive me because I'm an ignorant old woman, but I know well what started the war. It was that Italian count that stole the heathen divinity out of the temple in Japan, for believe me, Mr 'Awkins, nothing but sorrow and want follows them that disturbs the hidden powers!' Oh, a queer old dame, as you remark!

II

SO ONE EVENING we had our tea together, and 'Awkins lit the lamp and we all sat in to cards. Jeremiah Donovan came in too, and sat down and watched us for a while. Though he was a shy man and didn't speak much, it was easy to see he had no great love for the two Englishmen, and I was surprised it hadn't struck me so clearly before. Well, like that in the story, a terrible dispute blew up late in the evening between 'Awkins and Noble, about capitalists and priests and love for your own country.

'The capitalists,' says 'Awkins, with an angry gulp, 'the capitalists pays the priests to tell you all abaout the next world, so's you waon't notice what they do in this!'

'Nonsense, man,' says Noble, losing his temper, 'before ever a capitalist was thought of people believed in the next world.'

'Awkins stood up as if he was preaching a sermon. 'Oh, they did, did they?' he says with a sneer. 'They believed all the things you believe, that's what you mean? And you believe that God created Hadam and Hadam created Shem and Shem created Jehoshophat? You believe all the silly hold fairy-tale abaout Heve and Heden and the happle? Well, listen to me, chum. If you're entitled to 'old to a silly belief like that, I'm entitled to 'old to my own silly belief – which is, that the fust thing your God created was a bleedin' capitalist with mirality and Rolls Royce complete. Am I right, chum?' he says then to Belcher.

'You're right, chum,' says Belcher, with his queer smile, and gets up from the table to stretch his long legs into the fire and stroke his moustache. So, seeing that Jeremiah Donovan was going, and there was no knowing when the conversation about religion would be over, I took my hat and went out with him. We strolled down towards the village together, and then he suddenly stopped, and blushing and mumbling, and shifting, as his way was, from toe to heel, he said I ought to be behind keeping guard on the prisoners. And I, having it put to me so suddenly, asked him what the hell he wanted a guard on the prisoners at all for, and said that so far as Noble and me were concerned we had talked it over and would rather be out with a column. 'What use is that pair to us?' I asked him.

He looked at me for a spell and said, 'I thought you knew we were keeping them as hostages.' 'Hostages—?' says I, not quite understanding. 'The enemy', he says in his heavy way, 'have prisoners belong to us, and now they talk of shooting them. If they shoot our prisoners we'll shoot theirs, and serve them right.' 'Shoot them?' said I, the possibility just beginning to dawn on me. 'Shoot them, exactly,' said he. 'Now,' said I, 'wasn't it very unforeseen of you not to tell me and Noble that?' 'How so?' he asks. 'Seeing that we were acting as guards upon them, of course.' 'And hadn't you reason enough to guess that much?' 'We had not, Jeremiah Donovan, we had not. How were we to know when the men were on our hands so long?' 'And what difference does it make? The enemy have our prisoners as long or longer, haven't they?' 'It makes a great difference,' said I. 'How so?' said he sharply; but I couldn't tell him the difference it made, for I was struck too silly to speak. 'And when may we expect to be released from this anyway?' said I. 'You may expect it tonight,' says he. 'Or tomorrow or the next day at latest. So if it's hanging round here that worries you, you'll be free soon enough.'

I cannot explain it even now, how sad I felt, but I went back to the cottage, a miserable man. When I arrived the discussion was still on, 'Awkins holding forth to all and sundry that there was no next world at all and Noble answering in his best canonical style that there was. But I saw 'Awkins was after having the best of it. 'Do you know what, chum?' he was saying, with his saucy smile, 'I think you're jest as big a bleedin' hunbeliever as I am. You say you believe in the next world and you know jest as much abaout the next world as I do, which is sweet damn-all. What's 'Eaven? You dunno. Where's 'Eaven? You dunno. Who's in 'Eaven? You dunno. You know sweet damn-all! I arsk you again, do they wear wings?'

'Very well then,' says Noble, 'they do; is that enough for you? They do wear wings.' 'Where do they get them then? Who makes them? 'Ave they a fact'ry for wings? 'Ave they a sort of store where you 'ands in your chit and tikes your bleedin' wings? Answer me that.'

'Oh, you're an impossible man to argue with,' says Noble. 'Now listen to me—'. And off the pair of them went again.

It was long after midnight when we locked up the Englishmen and went to bed ourselves. As I blew out the candle I told Noble what Jeremiah Donovan had told me. Noble took it very quietly. After we had been in bed about an hour he asked me did I think we ought to tell the Englishmen. I having thought of the same thing myself (among many others) said no, because it was more than likely the English wouldn't shoot our men, and anyhow it wasn't to be supposed the Brigade who were always up and down with the second battalion and knew the Englishmen well would be likely to want them bumped off. 'I think so,' says Noble. 'It would be sort of cruelty to put the wind up them now.' 'It was very unforeseen of Jeremiah Donovan anyhow,' says I, and by Noble's silence I realized he took my meaning.

So I lay there half the night, and thought and thought, and picturing myself and young Noble trying to prevent the Brigade from shooting 'Awkins and Belcher sent a cold sweat out through me. Because there were men on the Brigade you daren't let nor hinder without a gun in your hand, and at any rate, in those days disunion between brothers seemed to me an awful crime. I knew better after.

It was next morning we found it so hard to face Belcher and 'Awkins with a smile. We went about the house all day scarcely saying a word. Belcher didn't mind us much; he was stretched into the ashes as usual with his usual look of waiting in quietness for something unforeseen to happen, but little 'Awkins gave us a bad time with his audacious gibing and questioning. He was disgusted at Noble's not answering him back. 'Why can't you tike your beating like a man, chum?' he says. 'You with your Hadam and Heve! I'm a Communist – or an Anarchist. An Anarchist, that's what I am.' And for hours after he went round the house, mumbling when the fit took him, 'Hadam and Heve! Hadam and Heve!'

III

I DON'T KNOW clearly how we got over that day, but get over it we did, and a great relief it was when the tea-things were cleared away and Belcher said in his peaceable manner, 'Well, chums, what about it?' So we all sat round the table and 'Awkins produced the cards, and at that moment I heard Jeremiah Donovan's footsteps up the path, and a dark presentiment crossed my mind. I rose quietly from the table and laid my hand on him before he reached the door. 'What do you want?' I asked him. 'I want those two soldier friends of yours,' he says reddening. 'Is that the way it is, Jeremiah Donovan?' I ask. 'That's the way. There were four of our lads went west this morning, one of them a boy of sixteen.' 'That's bad, Jeremiah,' says I.

At that moment Noble came out, and we walked down the path together talking in whispers. Feeney, the local intelligence officer, was standing by the gate. 'What are you going to do about it?' I asked Jeremiah Donovan. 'I want you and Noble to bring them out: you can tell them they're being shifted again; that'll be the quietest way.' 'Leave me out of that,' says Noble suddenly. Jeremiah Donovan looked at him hard for a minute or two. 'All right so,' he said peaceably. 'You and Feeney collect a few tools from the shed and dig a hole by the far end of the bog. Bonaparte and I'll be after you in about twenty minutes. But whatever else you do, don't let anyone see you with the tools. No one must know but the four of ourselves.'

We saw Feeney and Noble go round to the houseen where the tools were kept, and sidled in. Everything if I can so express myself was tottering before my eyes, and I left Jeremiah Donovan to do the explaining as best he could, while I took a seat and said nothing. He told them they were to go back to the Second. 'Awkins let a mouthful of curses out of him at that, and it was plain that Belcher, though he said nothing, was duly perturbed. The old woman was for having them stay in spite of us, and she did not shut her mouth until Jeremiah Donovan lost his temper and said some nasty things to her. Within the house by this time it was pitch dark, but no one thought of lighting the lamp, and in the darkness the two Englishmen fetched their khaki topcoats and said good-bye to the woman of the house. 'Just as a man mikes a 'ome of a bleedin' place,' mumbles 'Awkins shaking her by the hand, 'some bastard at headquarters thinks you're too cushy and shunts you off.' Belcher shakes her hand very hearty. 'A thousand thanks, madam,' he says, 'a thousand thanks for everything . . .' as though he'd made it all up.

We go round to the back of the house and down towards the fatal bog. Then Jeremiah Donovan comes out with what is in his mind. 'There were four of our lads shot by your fellows this morning so now you're to be bumped off.' 'Cut that stuff out,' says 'Awkins flaring up. 'It's bad enough to be mucked about such as we are without you plying at soldiers.' 'It's true,' says Jeremiah Donovan, 'I'm sorry, 'Awkins, but 'tis true,' and comes out with the usual rigmarole about doing our duty and obeying our superiors. 'Cut it out,' says 'Awkins irritably, 'cut it out!'

Then, when Donovan sees he is not being believed he

turns to me. 'Ask Bonaparte here,' he says. 'I don't need to arsk Bonaparte. Me and Bonaparte are chums.' 'Isn't it true, Bonaparte?' says Jeremiah Donovan solemnly to me. 'It is,' I say sadly, 'it is.' 'Awkins stops. 'Now, for Christ's sike. . . .' 'I mean it, chum,' I say. 'You daon't saound as if you mean it. You knaow well you don't mean it.' 'Well, if he don't I do,' says Jeremiah Donovan. 'Why the 'ell sh'd you want to shoot me, Jeremiah Donovan?' 'Why the hell should your people take out four prisoners and shoot them in cold blood upon a barrack square?' I perceive Jeremiah Donovan is trying to encourage himself with hot words.

Anyway, he took little 'Awkins by the arm and dragged him on, but it was impossible to make him understand that we were in earnest. From which you will perceive how difficult it was for me, as I kept feeling my Smith and Wesson and thinking what I would do if they happened to put up a fight or ran for it, and wishing in my heart they would. I knew if only they ran I would never fire on them. 'Was Noble in this?' 'Awkins wanted to know, and we said yes. He laughed. But why should Noble want to shoot him? Why should we want to shoot him? What had he done to us? Weren't we chums (the word lingers painfully in my memory)? Weren't we? Didn't we understand him and didn't he understand us? Did either of us imagine for an instant that he'd shoot us for all the so-and-so brigadiers in the so-and-so British Army? By this time I began to perceive in the dusk the desolate edges of the bog that was to be their last earthly bed, and, so great a sadness overtook my mind, I could not answer him. We walked along the edge of it in the darkness, and every now and then 'Awkins would call a halt and begin again, just as if he was wound up, about us being chums, and I was in despair that nothing but the cold and open grave made ready for his presence would convince him that we meant it all. But all the same, if you can understand, I didn't want him to be bumped off.

IV

AT LAST WE saw the unsteady glint of a lantern in the distance and made towards it. Noble was carrying it, and Feeney stood somewhere in the darkness behind, and somehow the picture of the two of them so silent in the boglands was like the pain of death in my heart. Belcher, on recognizing Noble, said ' 'Allo, chum' in his usual peaceable way, but 'Awkins flew at the poor boy immediately, and the dispute began all over again, only that Noble hadn't a word to say for himself, and stood there with the swaying lantern between his gaitered legs.

It was Jeremiah Donovan who did the answering. 'Awkins asked for the twentieth time (for it seemed to haunt his mind) if anybody thought he'd shoot Noble. 'You would,' says Jeremiah Donovan shortly. 'I wouldn't, damn you!' 'You would if you knew you'd be shot for not doing it.' 'I wouldn't, not if I was to be shot twenty times over; he's my chum. And Belcher wouldn't – isn't that right, Belcher?' 'That's right, chum,' says Belcher peaceably. 'Damned if I would. Anyway, who says Noble'd be shot if I wasn't bumped off? What d'you think I'd do if I was in Noble's place and we were out in the middle of a blasted bog?' 'What would you do?' 'I'd go with him wherever he was going. I'd share my last bob with him and stick by 'im through thick and thin.'

'We've had enough of this,' says Jeremiah Donovan, cocking his revolver. 'Is there any message you want to send before I fire?' 'No, there isn't, but . . .' 'Do you want to say your prayers?' 'Awkins came out with a cold-blooded remark that shocked even me and turned to Noble again. 'Listen to me, Noble,' he said. 'You and me are chums. You won't come over to my side, so I'll come over to your side. Is that fair? Just you give me a rifle and I'll go with you wherever you want.'

Nobody answered him.

'Do you understand?' he said. 'I'm through with it all. I'm a deserter or anything else you like, but from this on I'm one of you. Does that prove to you that I mean what I say?' Noble raised his head, but as Donovan began to speak he lowered it again without answering. 'For the last time have you any messages to send?' says Donovan in a cold and excited voice.

'Ah, shut up, you, Donovan; you don't understand me, but these fellows do. They're my chums; they stand by me and I stand by them. We're not the capitalist tools you seem to think us.'

I alone of the crowd saw Donovan raise his Webley to the back of 'Awkins's neck, and as he did so I shut my eyes and tried to say a prayer. 'Awkins had begun to say something else when Donovan let fly, and, as I opened my eyes at the bang, I saw him stagger at the knees and lie out flat at Noble's feet, slowly, and as quiet as a child, with the lantern-light falling sadly upon his lean legs and bright farmer's boots. We all stood very still for a while watching him settle out in the last agony.

Then Belcher quietly takes out a handkerchief, and begins to tie it about his own eyes (for in our excitement we had forgotten to offer the same to 'Awkins), and, seeing it is not big enough, turns and asks for a loan of mine. I give it to him and as he knots the two together he points with his foot at 'Awkins. ''E's not quite dead,' he says, 'better give 'im another.' Sure enough 'Awkins's left knee as we see it under the lantern is rising again. I bend down and put my gun to his ear; then, recollecting myself and the company of Belcher, I stand up again with a few hasty words. Belcher understands what is in my mind. 'Give 'im 'is first,' he says, 'I don't mind. Poor bastard, we dunno what's 'appening to 'im now.' As by this time I am beyond all feeling I kneel down again and skilfully give 'Awkins the last shot so as to put him for ever out of pain.

Belcher who is fumbling a bit awkwardly with the handkerchiefs comes out with a laugh when he hears the shot. It is the first time I have heard him laugh, and it sends a shiver down my spine, coming as it does so inappropriately upon the tragic death of his old friend. 'Poor blighter,' he says quietly, 'and last night he was so curious abaout it all. It's very queer, chums, I always think. Naow, 'e knows as much abaout it as they'll ever let 'im know, and last night 'e was all in the dark.'

Donovan helps him to tie the handkerchiefs about his eyes. 'Thanks, chum,' he says. Donovan asks him if there are any messages he would like to send. 'Naow, chum,' he says, 'none for me. If any of you likes to write to 'Awkins's mother you'll find a letter from 'er in 'is pocket. But my missus left me eight years ago. Went away with another fellow and took the kid with her. I likes the feelin' of a 'ome (as you may 'ave noticed) but I couldn't start again after that.'

We stand around like fools now that he can no longer see us. Donovan looks at Noble and Noble shakes his head. Then Donovan raises his Webley again and just at that moment Belcher laughs his queer nervous laugh again. He must think we are talking of him; anyway, Donovan lowers his gun. ''Scuse me, chums,' says Belcher, 'I feel I'm talking the 'ell of a lot . . . and so silly . . . abaout me being so 'andy abaout a 'ouse. But this thing come on me so sudden. You'll forgive me, I'm sure.' 'You don't want to say a prayer?' asks Jeremiah Donovan. 'No, chum,' he replies, 'I don't think that'd 'elp. I'm ready if you want to get it over.' 'You understand,' says Jeremiah Donovan, 'it's not so much our doing. It's our duty, so to speak.' Belcher's head is raised like a real blind man's, so that you can only see his nose and chin in the lamplight. 'I never could make out what duty was myself,' he said, 'but I think you're all good lads, if that's what you mean. I'm not complaining.' Noble, with a look of desperation, signals to Donovan, and in a flash Donovan raises his gun and fires. The big man goes over like a sack of meal, and this time there is no need of a second shot.

I don't remember much about the burying, but that it was worse than all the rest, because we had to carry the warm corpses a few yards before we sunk them in the windy bog. It was all mad lonely, with only a bit of lantern between ourselves and the pitch-blackness, and birds hooting and screeching all round disturbed by the guns. Noble had to search 'Awkins first to get the letter from his mother. Then having smoothed all signs of the grave away, Noble and I collected our tools, said good-bye to the others, and went back along the desolate edge of the treacherous bog without a word. We put the tools in the houseen and went into the house. The kitchen was pitch-black and cold, just as we left it, and the old woman was sitting over the hearth telling her beads. We walked past her into the room, and Noble struck a match to light the lamp. Just then she rose quietly and came to the doorway, being not at all so bold or crabbed as usual.

'What did ye do with them?' she says in a sort of whisper, and Noble took such a mortal start the match quenched in his trembling hand. 'What's that?' he asks without turning round. 'I heard ye,' she said. 'What did you hear?' asks Noble, but sure he wouldn't deceive a child the way he said it. 'I heard ye. Do you think I wasn't listening to ye putting the things back in the houseen?' Noble struck another match and this time the lamp lit for him. 'Was that what ye did with them?' she said, and Noble said nothing – after all what could he say?

So then, by God, she fell on her two knees by the door, and began telling her beads, and after a minute or two Noble went on his knees by the fireplace, so I pushed my way out past her, and stood at the door, watching the stars and listening to the damned shrieking of the birds. It is so strange what you feel at such moments, and not to be written afterwards. Noble says he felt he seen everything ten times as big, perceiving nothing around him but the little patch of black bog with the two Englishmen stiffening into it; but with me it was the other way, as though the patch of bog where the two Englishmen were was a thousand miles away from me, and even Noble mumbling just behind me and the old woman and the birds and the bloody stars were all far away, and I was somehow very small and very lonely. And anything that ever happened me after I never felt the same about again.

SAMUEL BECKETT

DING-DONG

MY SOMETIME FRIEND Belacqua enlivened the last phase of his solipsism, before he toed the line and began to relish the world, with the belief that the best thing he had to do was to move constantly from place to place. He did not know how this conclusion had been gained, but that it was not thanks to his preferring one place to another he felt sure. He was pleased to think that he could give what he called the Furies the slip by merely setting himself in motion. But as for sites, one was as good as another, because they all disappeared as soon as he came to rest in them. The mere act of rising and going, irrespective of whence and whither, did him good. That was so. He was sorry that he did not enjoy the means to indulge this humour as he would have wished, on a large scale, on land and sea. Hither and thither on land and sea! He could not afford that, for he was poor. But in a small way he did what he could. From the ingle to the window, from the nursery to the bedroom, even from one quarter of the town to another, and back, these little acts of motion he was in a fair way of making, and they certainly did do him some good as a rule. It was the old story of the salad days, torment in the terms and in the intervals a measure of ease.

Being by nature however sinfully indolent, bogged in indolence, asking nothing better than to stay put at the good pleasure of what he called the Furies, he was at times tempted to wonder whether the remedy were not rather more disagreeable than the complaint. But he could only suppose that it was not, seeing that he continued to have recourse to it, in a small way it is true, but nevertheless for years he continued to have recourse to it, and to return thanks for the little good it did him.

The simplest form of this exercise was boomerang, out and back; nay, it was the only one that he could afford for many years. Thus it is clear that his contrivance did not proceed from any discrimination between different points in space, since he returned directly, if we except an occasional pause for refreshment, to his point of departure, and truly no less recruited in spirit than if the interval had been whiled away abroad in the most highly reputed cities.

I know all this because he told me. We were Pylades and Orestes for a period, flattened down to something very genteel; but the relation abode and was highly confidential while it lasted. I have witnessed every stage of the exercise. I have been there when he set out, springing up and hastening away without as much as by your leave, impelled by some force that he did not care to gainsay. I have had glimpses of him enjoying his little trajectory. I have been there again when he returned, transfigured and transformed. It was very nearly the reverse of the author of the Imitation's 'glad going out and sad coming in'.

He was at pains to make it clear to me, and to all those to whom he exposed his manoeuvre, that it was in no way cognate with the popular act of brute labour, digging and such like, exploited to disperse the dumps, an antidote depending for its efficaciousness on mere physical exhaustion, and for which he expressed the greatest contempt. He did not fatigue himself, he said; on the contrary. He lived a Beethoven pause, he said, whatever he meant by that. In his anxiety to explain himself he was liable to come to grief. Nay, this anxiety in itself, or so at least it seemed to me, constituted a break-down in the self-sufficiency which he never wearied of arrogating to himself, a sorry collapse of my little internus homo, and alone sufficient to give him away as inept ape of his own shadow. But he wriggled out of everything by pleading that he had been drunk at the time, or that he was an incoherent person and content to remain so, and so on. He was an impossible person in the end. I gave him up in the end because he was not *serious*.

One day, in a positive geyser of confidence, he gave me an account of one of these 'moving pauses'. He had a strong weakness for oxymoron. In the same way he over-indulged in gin and tonic-water.

Not the least charm of this pure blank movement, this 'gress' or 'gression', was its aptness to receive, with or without the approval of the subject, in all their integrity the faint inscriptions of the outer world. Exempt from destination, it had not to shun the unforeseen nor turn aside from the agreeable odds and ends of vaudeville that are liable to crop up. This sensitiveness was not the least charm of this roaming that began by being blank, not the least charm of this pure act the alacrity with which it welcomed defilement. But very nearly the least.

Emerging, on the particular evening in question, from the underground convenience in the maw of College Street, with a vague impression that he had come from following the sunset up the Liffey till all the colour had been harried from the sky, all the tulips and aerugo expunged, he squatted, not that he had too much drink taken but simply that for the moment there were no grounds for his favouring one direction rather than another, against Tommy Moore's plinth. Yet he durst not dally. Was it not from brooding shill I, shall I, dilly, dally, that he had come out? Now the summons to move on was a subpoena. Yet he found he could not, any more than Buridan's ass, move to right or left, backward or forward. Why this was he could not make out at all. Nor was it the moment for self-examination. He had experienced little or no trouble coming back from the Park Gate along the north quay, he had taken the Bridge and Westmoreland Street in his stride, and now he suddenly found himself good for nothing but to loll against the plinth of this bull-necked bard, and wait for a sign.

There were signs on all hands. There was the big Bovril sign to begin with, flaring beyond the Green. But it was useless. Faith, Hope and – what was it? – Love, Eden missed, every ebb derided, all the tides ebbing from the shingle of Ego Maximus, little me. Itself it went nowhere, only round and round, like the spheres, but mutely. It could not dislodge him now, it could only put ideas into his head. Was it not from sitting still among his ideas, other people's ideas, that he had come away? What would he not give now to get on the move again! Away from ideas!

Turning aside from this and other no less futile emblems, his attention was arrested by a wheel-chair being pushed rapidly under the arcade of the Bank, in the direction of Dame Street. It moved in and out of sight behind the bars of the columns. This was the blind paralytic who sat all day near to the corner of Fleet Street, and in bad weather under the shelter of the arcade, the same being wheeled home to his home in the Coombe. It was past his time and there was a bitter look on his face. He would give his chairman a piece of his mind when he got him to himself. This chairman, hireling or poor relation, came every evening a little before the dark, unfastened from the beggar's neck and breast the placard announcing his distress, tucked him up snugly in his coverings and wheeled him home to his supper. He was well advised to be assiduous, for this beggar was a power in the

Coombe. In the morning it was his duty to shave his man and wheel him, according to the weather, to one or other of his pitches. So it went, day after day.

This was a star the horizon adorning if you like, and Belacqua made off at all speed in the opposite direction. Down Pearse Street, that is to say, long straight Pearse Street, its vast Barrack of Glencullen granite, its home of tragedy restored and enlarged, its coal merchants and Florentine Fire Brigade Station, its two Cervi saloons, ice-cream and fried fish, its dairies, garages and monumental sculptors, and implicit behind the whole length of its southern frontage the College. Perpetuis futuris temporibus duraturum. It was to be hoped so, indeed.

It was a most pleasant street, despite its name, to be abroad in, full as it always was with shabby substance and honest-to-God coming and going. All day the roadway was a tumult of buses, red and blue and silver. By one of these a little girl was run down, just as Belacqua drew near to the railway viaduct. She had been to the Hibernian Dairies for milk and bread and then she had plunged out into the roadway, she was in such a childish fever to get back in record time with her treasure to the tenement in Mark Street where she lived. The good milk was all over the road and the loaf, which had sustained no injury, was sitting up against the kerb, for all the world as though a pair of hands had taken it up and set it down there. The queue standing for the Palace Cinema was torn between conflicting desires: to keep their places and to see the excitement. They craned their necks and called out to know the worst, but they stood firm. Only one girl, debauched in appearance and swathed in a black blanket, fell out near the sting of the queue and secured the loaf. With the loaf under her blanket she sidled unchallenged down Mark Street and turned into Mark Lane. When she got back to the queue her place had been taken of course. But her sally had not cost her more than a couple of yards.

Belacqua turned left into Lombard Street, the street of the sanitary engineers, and entered a public-house. Here he was known, in the sense that his grotesque exterior had long ceased to alienate the curates and make them giggle, and to the extent that he was served with his drink without having to call for it. This did not always seem a privilege. He was tolerated, what was more, and let alone by the rough but kindly habitués of the house, recruited for the most part from among dockers, railwaymen and vague joxers on the dole. Here also art and love, scrabbling in dispute or staggering home, were barred, or, perhaps better, unknown. The aesthetes and the impotent were far away.

These circumstances combined to make of this place a very grateful refuge for Belacqua, who never omitted, when he found himself in its neighbourhood with the price of a drink about him, to pay it a visit.

When I enquired how he squared such visits with his anxiety to keep on the move and his distress at finding himself brought to a standstill, as when he had come out of the underground in the mouth of College Street, he replied that he did not. 'Surely' he said 'my resolution has the right to break down.' I supposed so indeed. 'Or' he said 'if you prefer, I make the raid in two hops instead of non-stop. From what' he cried 'does that disqualify me, I should very much like to know.' I hastened to assure him that he had a perfect right to suit himself in what, after all, was a manoeuvre of his own contriving, and that the raid, to adopt his own term, lost nothing by being made in easy stages. 'Easy!' he exclaimed, 'how easy?'

But notice the double response, like two holes to a burrow. Sitting in this crapulent den, drinking his drink, he gradually ceased to see its furnishings with pleasure, the bottles, representing centuries of loving research, the stools, the counter, the powerful screws, the shining phalanx of the pulls of the beer-engines, all cunningly devised and elaborated to further the relations between purveyor and consumer in this domain. The bottles drawn and emptied in a twinkling, the casks responding to the slightest pressure on their joysticks, the weary proletarians at rest on arse and elbow, the cash register that never complains, the graceful curates flying from customer to customer, all this made up a spectacle in which Belacqua was used to take delight and chose to see a pleasant instance of machinery decently subservient to appetite. A great major symphony of supply and demand, effect and cause, fulcrate on the middle C of the counter and waxing, as it proceeded, in the charming harmonics of blasphemy and broken glass and all the aliquots of fatigue and ebriety. So that he would say that the only place where he could come to anchor and be happy was a low public-house, and that all the wearisome tactics of gress and dud Beethoven would be done away with if only he could spend his life in such a place. But as they closed at ten, and as residence and good faith were viewed as incompatible, and as in any case he had not the means to consecrate his life to stasis, even in the meanest bar, he supposed he must be content to indulge this whim from time to time, and return thanks for such sporadic mercy.

All this and much more he laboured to make clear. He seemed to derive considerable satisfaction from his failure to do so.

But on this particular occasion the cat failed to jump, with the result that he became as despondent as though he were sitting at home in his own great armchair, as anxious to get on the move and quite as hard put to it to do so. Why this was he could not make out. Whether the trituration of the child in Pearse Street had upset him without his knowing it, or whether (and he put forward this alternative with a truly insufferable complacency) he had come to some parting of the ways, he did not know at all. All he could say was that the objects in which he was used to find such recreation and repose lost gradually their hold upon him, he became insensible to them little by little, the old itch and algos crept back into his mind. He had come briskly all the way from Tommy Moore, and now he suddenly found himself sitting paralysed and grieving in a pub of all places, good for nothing but to stare at his spoiling porter, and wait for a sign.

To this day he does not know what caused him to look up, but look up he did. Feeling the impulse to do this strong upon him, he forced his eyes away from the glass of dying porter and was rewarded by seeing a hatless woman advancing slowly towards him up the body of the bar. No sooner had she come in than he must have become aware of her. That was surely very curious in the first instance. She seemed to be hawking some ware or other, but what it was he could not see, except that it was not studs or laces or matches or lavender or any of the usual articles. Not that it was unusual to find a woman in that public-house, for they came and went freely, slaking their thirst and beguiling their sorrows with no less freedom than their men-folk. Indeed it was always a pleasure to see them, their advances were always most friendly and honourable, Belacqua had many a delightful recollection of their commerce.

Hence there was no earthly reason why he should see in the advancing figure of this mysterious pedlar anything untoward, or in the nature of the sign in default of which he was clamped to his stool till closing-time. Yet the impulse to do so was so strong that he yielded to it, and as she drew nearer, having met with more rebuffs than pence in her endeavours to dispose of her wares, whatever they were, it became clear to him that his instinct had not played him false, in so far at least as she was a woman of very remarkable presence indeed.

Her speech was that of a woman of the people, but of a gentlewoman of the people. Her gown had served its time, but yet contrived to be respectable. He noticed with a pang that she sported about her neck the insidious little mock fur so prevalent in tony slumland. The one deplorable feature of her get up, as apprehended by Belacqua in his hasty survey, was the footwear – the cruel strait outsizes of the suffragette or welfare worker. But he did not doubt for a moment that they had been a gift, or picked up in the pop for a song. She was of more than average height and well in flesh. She might be past middle-age. But her face, ah her face, was what Belacqua had rather refer to as her countenance, it was so full of light. This she lifted up upon him and no error. Brimful of light and serene, serenissime, it bore no trace of suffering, and in this alone it might be said to be a notable face. Yet like tormented faces that he had seen, like the face in the National Gallery in Merrion Square by the Master of Tired Eyes, it seemed to have come a long way and subtend an infinitely narrow angle of affliction, as eyes focus a star. The features were null, only luminous, impassive and secure, petrified in radiance, or words to that effect, for the reader is requested to take notice that this sweet style is Belacqua's. An act of expression, he said, a wreathing or wrinkling, could only have had the effect of a dimmer on a headlight. The implications of this triumphant figure, the just and the unjust, etc., are better forgone.

At long last she addressed herself to Belacqua.

'Seats in heaven' she said in a white voice 'tuppence apiece, four fer a tanner.'

'No' said Belacqua. It was the first syllable to come to his lips. It had not been his intention to deny her.

'The best of seats' she said 'again I'm sold out. Tuppence apiece the best of seats, four fer a tanner.'

This was unforeseen with a vengeance, if not exactly vaudeville. Belacqua was embarrassed in the last degree, but transported also. He felt the sweat coming in the small of his back, above his Montrouge belt.

'Have you got them on you?' he mumbled.

'Heaven goes round' she said, whirling her arm, 'and round and round and round and round and round.'

'Yes' said Belacqua 'round and round.'

'Rowan' she said, dropping the *d*'s and getting more of a spin into the slogan, 'rowan an' rowan an' rowan.'

Belacqua scarcely knew where to look. Unable to blush he came out in this beastly sweat. Nothing of the kind had ever happened to him before. He was altogether disarmed, unsaddled and miserable. The eyes of them all, the dockers, the railwaymen and, most terrible of all, the joxers, were upon him. His tail drooped. This female dog of a pixy with her tiresome Ptolemy, he was at her mercy.

'No' he said 'no thank you, no not this evening thank you.'

'Again I'm sold out' she said 'an' buked out, four fer a tanner.'

'On whose authority . . .' began Belacqua, like a Scholar.

'For yer frien' ' she said 'yer da, yer ma an' yer motte, four fer a tanner.' The voice ceased, but the face did not abate.

'How do I know' piped Belacqua 'you're not sellin' me a pup?'

'Heaven goes rowan an' rowan . . .'

'Rot you' said Belacqua 'I'll take two. How much is that?'

'Four dee' she said.

Belacqua gave her a sixpence.

'Gobbless yer honour' she said, in the same white voice from which she had not departed. She made to go.

'Here' cried Belacqua 'you owe me twopence.' He had not even the good grace to say tuppence.

'Arragowan' she said 'make it four cantcher, yer frien', yer da, yer ma an' yer motte.'

Belacqua could not bicker. He had not the strength of mind for that. He turned away.

'Jesus' she said distinctly 'and his sweet mother preserve yer honour.'

'Amen' said Belacqua, into his dead porter.

Now the woman went away and her countenance lighted her to her room in Townsend Street.

But Belacqua tarried a little to listen to the music. Then he also departed, but for Railway Street, beyond the river.

ELIZABETH BOWEN

THE LAST NIGHT
IN THE OLD HOME

ANNABELLE, WHO HAD been searching about upstairs, pinching the corners of mattresses as though they ought to hold guineas and opening and shutting drawers, discovered a pair of gloves in the blue room wardrobe. So she came down to ask everyone whose these could be. From room to room she went: everyone soon learned to dread her step.

'It seems a pity,' she said, 'that they should be sold *with* the wardrobe. They are nice gloves – look.' They were fine suède gloves for narrow hands, worn at the finger-tips, doing up at the wrists with small pearl buttons. 'Someone should have the good of them.'

'Perhaps they're Delia's,' said Henry, her present victim.

'She says no. Hers don't *button* up.'

'I should keep them yourself.'

'Oh, no, Henry, I mustn't; besides, look, they are too small.'

Henry could have screamed. Throughout the house, disappearing in dusk, there reigned an unnatural silence that first he could not account for: all the clocks had been let run down. You cannot auction a ticking clock. The silence echoed, for against the dusty feet of tomorrow all carpets had been rolled up. Here in the morning-room hung a smell of stale notepaper; his mother had taken the family letters – from school, from London, from India – out of the bureau drawers to be read aloud. Now, thank God, they were burnt. Only the best, the jauntiest and most eloquent, had been put away in dispatch-cases. All Adrian's had been kept, because he was dead. (With the dispatch-cases no one knew what to do.) Had Henry been dead, his might have acquired some kind of morbid value. As it was, they put up a poor show at the hearing by mother and sisters and had been unostentatiously burnt. Absent or present, he was constrained with his family: too civil, nervous. He was humiliated by Annabelle's oddness, that all the others took calmly. His embarrassment was unforgivable: Annabelle was not 'afflicted'; she simply did not grow up. Inside the big, bustling form of a woman she was a girl of ten. So she remained their home-girl.

After Annabelle, Delia looked into the morning-room. 'How funny it is,' she said briskly, 'with all the pictures down!' Smoke had dimmed, sun faded, the wall-paper; fresh flowery squares stared oddly.

Delia always put balm on the rawest of situations by saying something quite brilliantly superficial. She had been clicking round on her high heels, applying this happy touch to the family's nerves, all today and yesterday. Quite beautiful, she had married and left home young: she cared for no one at all. Henry liked her the best of them; she was as gay as a stranger; between these two convention was comfortably present. 'There's a fire,' she said, 'in the library.'

'Who's in there?'

'Mother and father and poor dear John.'

'Doing what?'

'That's the difficulty,' she said brightly; 'there's nothing much they *can* do. Oh, mother is trying to rub out the places where we all used to be measured against the door.'

Something more than her constant wish to be social accounted for Delia's brightness: she felt a profound relief. Something let go of her conscience. Delia was no good; to her husband, who bored her, she had for years been unfaithful; she was as light as a little cat. With home still going on here, some fiction of innocence had always unnerved her. Now mother and father and Annabelle would be people in a hotel; the cuckoo-clock, the scrap screen, the big chintz chairs rumpled by dogs, would all be auctioned tomorrow and carted away. There *it* went – pouf! Its grip relaxed on her spirit . . . Delia asked Henry to give her a cigarette, and, balancing with a hand on his shoulder as they stood over the grate cold with papery ashes, she began to tell him, amazingly, all about her life. Once or twice she glanced defiantly round the morning-room. Henry, having had no idea she was such a bad woman, violently registered shock.

She concluded: 'I've always wanted to ask you – do you have love-affairs?'

He looked at her queerly. 'No,' he said.

'How *wise*, but how silly.'

Annabelle went into the kitchen, where cook, for her final credit, was giving a final scrub to the copper and zinc saucepans, then ranging them back in their lots on the dresser and tables. All the other servants had wept and gone. Annabelle turned the handle of the mincing-machine and looked regretfully into a colander. 'Oh, dear,' she sighed. Cook took the mincing-machine firmly away from Annabelle and put it back on a shelf.

'I used to make cakes here, usen't I?'

'You did indeed, miss, and very nice cakes they were. Now let that strainer alone, there's a good girl!'

'Cook, whose gloves *can* these be? No one seems to care.'

No doubt, said cook, they had belonged to a visitor. Her eyes, always watery in their scorched lids from the heat of so many fires, looked smaller and dull, like a dead porcupine's; it was hard to tell if she had been crying. Tomorrow she was going straight on to another gentleman's family. If she felt at all, it was angry sorrow for John. He was her darling: it seemed a direct hit at cook that it should be John who had ruined the family. He had a way with him. He never told cook how much, these days, he detested apricot jam, or that her puddings and cakes made him flatulent.

Decency had required John's presence at the obsequies of the home. He felt this unduly hard; his parents' brave brightness affected him. Their silence from all reproach became sinister, like the silence of clocks. He felt prickly all over and drank a good deal of whisky. When Henry told him, that rationally, this was for the best, that the old place had no place now they were all grown up and there were no grandchildren, and that their parents would do much better out of this valley climate, John became very angry. He felt that it was in spirit Henry who ruined the home. Hard-hit, John felt really innocent. Not once had he been deliberate: if mess-bills ran up, horses he backed turned out rotten, cards he held worthless and women he loved exacting, was John to blame? He told himself he had had no real fun. It had always helped him to think of his old home; after a thick night it made him feel good and squashy.

The marks where the children were measured would not rub off the door; John suggested scratching them out with a pocket-knife, but his mother said that would spoil the paint. So he left the library, where the books were stacked up in lots, and went upstairs to look out of the landing window. Here the garden poplars were visible through the dusk, but he saw more plainly his figure reflected against the sky. He turned from the window; the gas was lit on the landing; outside the nursery door John saw the rocking-horse. So mounted, John as a little fellow had charged impressively, hurling himself on enemies. But, when you got off, those red-painted nostrils were always scoffing away. Maddened, John kicked the rocking-horse.

The rocking-horse, stirrups flying, bumped noisily on its rollers. 'Oh, you *mustn't*!' screamed Annabelle, darting out of the nursery, the suède gloves still in her hand. Kneeling, she crooned on the horse's neck. 'Darling . . . poor darling . . . Wicked, unkind John!'

'Damn!' muttered John, unnerved.

Annabelle heard him. Wild with affront, she scrambled heavily to her feet with a cowlike movement and dashed down the naked stairs. 'Mother, mother,' she wailed. Her mother came out of the library. 'Oh, mother, John said "Damn" to me!'

'Never mind,' said her mother, patting the convulsed home-girl.

'He *looked* so awful.'

'We must be kind to him.'

All the doors were open. Henry and Delia glanced at each other; she smiled at a crease in her sleeve, he fumbled a cigarette out and went quite white. They both felt home had lasted a day too long. John came downstairs; his hand shook on the banisters. He looked in at Delia, mouth twisted as though he wanted to laugh, then pushed past into the dining-room where the decanters were.

'He's right,' said Delia. 'I think I should like one too.'

'Our horse,' Annabelle wailed, 'our old darling horse. . . .'

'This is intolerable,' said Henry. But their mother looked at him with expressionless eyes over Annabelle's heaving shoulder. 'Never mind,' she murmured, and Henry knew that he had been ordered away.

Only the drawing-room, where they were all always polite, remained unentered, untroubled. It was prepared for tomorrow, its last occasion, when crowds would bid for the piano, the sofas, the clock. The rugs were rolled up and numbered, the chairs stood in rows; statues' unwearied arms upheld unlit lamps on the mantelpiece. Twilight came in through the unshuttered windows, hung in drops from the chandeliers, and shone in the mirrors.

A wind came up; creepers began to tap on the south windows; draughts crept through the house, fluttering here and there a ticket on objects already bespoken. A door slammed upstairs. Henry went up to shut the windows; the rocking-horse was still rocking. A straw from some packing-case blew past his feet in the dark, which was melodramatic.

SEAN O FAOLAIN

A BROKEN WORLD

'THAT'S A LONELY PLACE!' said the priest suddenly. He was rubbing the carriage window with his little finger. He pointed with the stem of his pipe through the window, and the flutter of snow and the blown steam of the engine, at the mountainy farm to his right. He might have been talking to himself, for he did not stir his head or remove his elbow from its rest. He was a skeleton of a man, and the veins of his temples bulged out like nerves. Peering I could barely see, below the pine forest of 'The Department', through the fog of the storm, a lone chapel and a farmhouse, now a tangle of black and white. Although it was the middle of the day a light shone yellow in a byre. Then the buildings swivelled and were left behind. The land was blinding.

'Aye!' I said. 'It is lonely. But,' I said easily, 'sure every parish is a world in itself.'

He grunted and pulled at his cherrywood pipe and kept looking out the window at the whirling dots of white.

Then, without looking at me – looking down at the flap of my trousers, instead – he leaned forward, one bony hand gripping his left knee, and his elbow resting on the other knee so that he might still hold and smoke his pipe in comfort. I could see that he spoke less for the sake of conversation than from a desire to instruct me, for he seemed to get no other pleasure out of his talk.

'That used to be a credo with me, too,' he said, 'that every parish is a world in itself. But where there is no moral unity there is no life.'

'Moral unity?'

There were ten notes in the wind, boom and whistle and groan and sigh. Listening to them I hardly heard him. The snow had stopped.

'Yes.' He was cock-assuredly positive. 'Life is a moral unity with a common thought. The *compositum* of one's being, emerging from the Divine Essence, which is harmony itself, cannot, unless it abdicates its own intelligence and lives in chaos, that is to say, in sin, be in disunity with itself. Since society, however, is an entity composed of many members, life becomes a moral unity with a common thought. You can see that?'

'Yes.'

He went on, while I wondered if he was a professor in some seminary trying out something he had been studying. He enunciated his ideas with indrawn lips. That gave him a hellish, pedagogic look. The glare outside turned him into marble.

'In places like that you have a broken world, and there is no unity.'

In spite of this abstract way of talking the next thing he said showed me that he was not a professor.

'Let me give you an example of what life is like in those isolated places,' jerking his head. 'When I was ordained my first parish was a lonely parish in the County Wicklow. From my presbytery window I could see the entire coast, a long straight beach, miles to the north, miles to the south, with a headland at each end stuck out into the sea. By the sea it is marsh. Then comes the first wave of highland around villages like Newtownmountkennedy. The land isn't bad on those hills, though it isn't what you would call really good land. They grow good turnips and potatoes and marigolds; the greens are not bad; but they cannot grow wheat. You need a good marl bottom for wheat. I was a young man then, and keen, so I studied these questions.'

(Whatever else you were, I said to myself, you must have been a bloody bore.)

'Look!' he said, pointing through the opposite window.

A vast white plain, level as a sea, mapped with black hedgerows, all diminishing in size, spread away and away, maybe twenty miles, to a much lower range of mountains.

'My parish was in the same relation to that good land as these mountains here' – nodding over his shoulder – 'in relation to that plain. That is to say, it was mountain bog, reclaimed by much labour, but always badly drained. Last of all, beyond me, was the utterly, miserably' – his voice was almost oratorical here – 'wretched moor. Miles and miles of it on the plateau of the mountaintops. The native tribes lived as freebooters up there as late as the end of the eighteenth century. It was wooded then, and untouched by any road. Then, in ninety-eight, two so-called military roads cut it across and across like a scissors. They were fifty miles long, and straight as rulers. By the way,' he asked suddenly, catching me looking idly out through the window, 'were you ever in County Wicklow?'

'Oh, no, Father,' I replied, as suddenly. I forced myself to attend. Just then my eye caught the eye of an old farmer seated opposite me in the carriage; he was midway on the same seat as the priest, and, so, near enough to hear everything. A pool of water had gathered around each boot. Spits starred the dry patch between. Seeing me look at him he took from his mouth, with his entire fist, a bit of a cigarette he was smoking, and winked at me. Then he put back the cigarette and contemplated the priest's face with an air of child-like wonderment. At that wink I began to listen more carefully. Evidently my priest was a local 'character'.

'They are remarkable roads,' went on the priest. 'Well, the people of my parish were all poor. The interesting thing about them is that there were two sets of names – either the old tribal names, like O'Toole or O'Byrne or Doyle, or foreign names like Ryder, Nash, Greene, Pugh, Spink, Empie, Gascon, Latour.'

A little smile took the corners of his mouth as he said those names; but he never raised his eyes.

'The Greenes and Ryders and Pughs, and the rest of them, were soldiers who long ago trickled down into the houses of the poor, intermarried there, and became poor themselves as a result. However, they brought the people respect for law and order. Or, if you like, they knocked the last bit of rebel spirit out of them.'

'Interesting!' I said, politely. I was beginning to enjoy the joke, for I could see the old farmer getting cross, and at the end of that last bit he had spat out his butt end of cigarette.

'But the middle land, the good land, remained in the possession of the big people who never intermarried. When I went there to take over my duties I looked up the history of these wealthy people in *Debrett* and *Who's Who*, and *Burke's Landed Gentry*.'

His palm became an imaginary book, and with his pipe-stem he followed the lines and pretended to read:

' "Lord Blank, family name of Baron Blank. Fifth baron. Created in eighteen hundred and one. Lieutenant of the Seventeenth Hussars. Married Dorothy, oldest daughter of, let's say something like James Whipple Teaman of Grange House, Dilworth, Dorsetshire, you know the kind of thing.

Succeeded his father in nineteen-eighteen. Educated at Eton and Sandhurst. Address, Grosvenor Square, London. Club – Travellers' or Brooks's. Recreations? Oh, as usual, hunting, shooting, fishing, racquets, riding." '

Again the thin smile. The farmer was gob-open.

'My parishioners were their stableboys, gate-lodge keepers, woodmen, beaters, farmhands, lady's maids, et cetera. They were always intermarrying. Their bits of farms, reclaimed from the furze, were always being divided. I've seen people live on a bit of land about twice the size of this carriage.'

The farmer leaned forward, listening now with great interest. Our three heads nodded with the jolt of the train.

'Then there was emigration. In the five years I spent there I had one solitary marriage. I had sixty schoolchildren on roll when I went there. I had thirty-five when I left. Last year I heard they were reduced to eleven, and five of those were all one family. No wonder the county is full of ruins. You come on them in scores on scores, with, maybe, a tree growing out of the hearth, and the marks of the ridges they ploughed still there, now smooth with grass.'

'Begobs, then, they're here too, Father,' said the old farmer. The priest nodded sideways to him and proceeded:

'I liked the people. They were clean, hard-working, respectful. Too respectful – tipping their hats to everybody. They were always making what we call "the poor mouth" – a mendicant habit of centuries, I suppose. They gave me no trouble, except for two things. They had a habit of writing anonymous letters, and I couldn't stop it. They were at it all the time. They wrote them to one another.'

He paused. I prompted him.

'The other thing?' I asked.

The farmer leaned closer and closer.

'The other thing?' he said irritably to his pipe bowl. 'In every one of these cabins they earned money by taking boarded-out children – children unwanted by poor parents, or simply illegitimates. There was hardly a cottage without one, two, or three of these stranger children. They were well looked after, and the people often grew so fond of them they wouldn't part with them; and, I suppose, that was a nice trait too. But the point is that the only fresh blood coming into the county was . . . Well – a curious county, as you can see, and the morals were a bit curious too. However, that's enough about them.'

And he had at least enough sense to go no further with that.

'Well, there you are. That was my parish, and you can't say it was a world in itself. It was too incomplete. Too many things left out. The human dignity of men is always impaired when, like that, they're depending on other people who can make or break them. They weren't men. They were servants. That's the whole of it.'

'But did that make their lives lonely? You said they were lonely?'

For the first time he looked up at me. The veins on his temples, swollen from holding his head down, throbbed with relief.

'I didn't say *they* were lonely.'

His eyes wavered sideways to the farmer. I easily followed him over the hiatus when he jumped to –

'One day, after three years without stepping out of the parish, I decided to see if the neighbouring parish was any better.' (When I heard the personal note come into his voice I wished the farmer was not there; as it was he kept to his cold, factual description.)

'Do you know, the contrast was amazing! When I climbed down to the valley and the good land! And it was the trees that made me realize it. Beeches instead of pines. Great, old beeches with roots like claws on the double ditches. The farmhouses, too. They were large and prosperous with everything you might expect to find in a sturdy English farm – barns, ducks in the pond, thick-packed granaries, airy lofts, a pigeon croft, a seat under an arbour, fruit gardens.

'All that was good. But it was those beeches that really impressed me. They were so clean and old, not like the quick-growing pines of the mountains – dirty trees that scatter their needles into the shoots of the houses and block them up three times every winter.'

'Oh, they're buggers, Father!' agreed the farmer earnestly.

'I climbed lower still and came to the gates of the houses where the gentry used to live.'

'Used to?'

'Used to. I should have expected it, but somehow it hadn't occurred to me. It's funny how we all forget how time passes. But there they were – the gateposts falling. The lodges boarded up. Notices, *For Sale*. Fifteen years of grass on the avenues. You see? "Owns ten thousand acres in Ireland. Address, Grosvenor Square, London."'

The pipestem travelled across the palm.

'I met an old man who took me down one of those avenues to see the ruins of a big house burned out during the troubled times. It was a lovely spring evening. The sky was like milk. The rooks were cawing about the roofless chimneys just like the flakes of soot come to life again. I spotted a queer little building at the end of a cypress avenue. The old man called it "the oftaphone". He meant octagon. It was a kind of peristyle. He said, "The Lord" – just like that – "The Lord used to have tea parties and dances there long ago." I went into it and it had a magnificent view, a powerful view, across the valley over at my mountainy parish, yes, and beyond it to the ridges of the mountains, and even beyond that again to the very moors behind with their last little flecks and drifts of snow. They could have sat there and drunk their tea and seen my people – the poor Ryders, and Greenes, and O'Tooles – making little brown lines in the far-off fields in the ploughing time.'

'They could! Oh, begobs, Father, so they could!' – and a mighty spit.

'Or at night, of summer evenings, they could have sipped their brandy and coffee and seen the little yellow lights of our cabin windows, and said, "How pretty it is!"'

'Begobs, yes! That's true!'

If anyone entered the carriage then he would have taken us for three friends, we were huddled together so eagerly. The priest went on:

' "They must have had good times here, once?" I said to the man who was with me. "The best, Father!" says he. "Oh, the best out. The best while they lasted. And there were never any times like the old times. But they're scattered now, Father," says he, "to the four winds. And they'll never come back." "Who owns the land now?" I asked him. "They own it always, but who wants it?" says he. "The people here don't want it. They'd rather live in the towns and cities and work for wages." '

'That's right,' said the farmer, as if we were really discussing his own county. 'Begobs, you're talking sense now, Father!'

' "The land was kept from them too long," says he. "And now they have lost the knack of it. I have two grown sons of my own," says he, "and they're after joining the British Army." '

'Begobs, yes!' said the farmer, leaning to catch every word; but the priest stopped and leaned back.

The white, cold fields were singing by us. The cabins so still they might be rocks clung to the earth. The priest was looking at them and we were all looking at them, and at the flooded and frozen pools of water divided by the hedgerows. By his talk he had evoked a most powerful sense of comradeship in that carriage, whether he meant to or not: we felt one. Then, as quickly, he proceeded to break it.

'Well?' I asked eagerly. 'Well?'

'Why, that's all!' said the priest. 'I came back from my voyage of exploration much refreshed. Much improved in spirits. You see, I had extended the pattern of life of my own poor parish. I saw how, how – I mean, how the whole thing had worked, hung together, made up a real unity. It was like putting two halves of a broken plate together. As I walked up another one of those hill roads on my way home I passed more prosperous houses – smaller houses this time, what you would call private houses. They had neat, green curtains with fine, polished brassware inside on the polished mahogany. And through another window three aluminium hot-water bottles shining on a dark hall table, signs of comfort, as you might say. Yes! I had completed the pattern. That parish and my parish made up a world, as neither did by itself, rich and poor, culture and . . .'

'But,' I cried angrily, 'where's your moral unity? Your common thought? It's absurd.'

'Oh, yes! I realized that even before I got home. I just tell you the thing as it happened. But they in their octagon and we in our lighted cabins, I mean to say, it was two halves of a world . . .'

The farmer was looking at us both with dull, stupid eyes. He had lost the thread of the talk.

'Yes, I suppose so,' I agreed, just as lightly. 'But now that the gentry are gone, won't the people, the mountainy people, and so on, begin to make a complete world of their own?'

He shook his head. The farmer listened again.

'I refuse to believe they won't,' I said.

He shrugged his shoulders.

'And is there no possible solution, then?' I asked him.

He was looking out of the window, his poll to the farmer. He rolled up his eyes under his brows – a warning look – and faintly indicated the man behind him. Then he actually began to laugh, a cold, cackling laugh, an extraordinary, inhuman kind of laugh that ended in a noise like a little groan.

The train slowed up, and we were in a station, and he was gathering his bags. He got out without even saying 'Good day' to us, and his face was coldly composed. A manservant, touching his cap, took the bags. The stationmaster touched his cap to him. The porter receiving the tickets touched his cap to him. The jarvey, who was waiting for him, bowed as he received the bags from the manservant. Black, tall, thin, and straight as a lamp post, he left the lit, snow-bright station with every downlooking lounger there bowing and hat touching as he passed. When I turned away, the train was moving out, and the old farmer, in his own place, had lit another cigarette.

'Do you know his Reverence?' I asked – as irritated as somebody from whom a book has been snatched before the end of the tale.

'Oh, aye!' said the old man, and he added, without interest. 'He's silenced.'

There was a touch of dread in that word, *silenced*.

'What did they silence him for?'

'Politics.'

'Oh? He was too extreme?'

'Aye!' Still without interest.

'A clever man?'

No answer. His mind had gone to sleep. I looked at him in annoyance.

'What kind of ideas had he? I mean, what did he want?'

'Begobs, I dunno.'

Then he added, as if it was a matter of no importance:

'He wanted the people to have the land.'

'What land?'

'The land. The gentry's land.'

I leaned to him eagerly –

'But isn't that what ye want? Isn't that what the whole trouble is? Isn't that what the government wants?'

'Aye I suppose it is, you know? But he wanted it to be a sudden business.'

'They didn't silence him for that?'

'Maybe they didn't. Ach, he's odd. Sure, he took ten or twenty foolish young lads and, one night, he thrun down the walls of Lord Milltown's estate. He started some sort of a league, too. He's odd. God help him.'

'What did he want to do with this league of his?'

'I dunno. It was some kind of faddy business. He wanted halls ... and ... some kind of halls he wanted. Halls. I dunno what he wanted 'em for. Ah, he's a decent poor man.'

I tried another line.

'I suppose it's true for his Reverence – ye have a hard time of it up here on the poor land?'

Puffing at his ease he was looking idly at the passing fields. A woman and two small boys, crushed into the doorway of a cabin, waved to us. He looked, and when they were gone his eyes were still fixed; seeing whatever passed beneath them with equal interest – or disinterest?

He tilted his head, but he said nothing. I made one last effort to shake him from his lethargic mood – possibly, most likely indeed, the mood in which he spent the greater part of his life.

'You know,' I said, warmly, 'I think I'd die in this lonely place. That priest is right!'

He looked at it, and scratched his ear, and said:

'Aye!' And then, suddenly, he added a second 'Aye!' – and then, when I thought he was finished, he actually added, 'I suppose 'tis quiet,' and relapsed into indifference.

Angrily I burst out at him:

'But damn it all, don't you mind, or is it that ye don't want to stir, ye're too damn lazy to stir?'

He took the butt end from his mouth, and he looked at me, and by the way he looked up and down at me, I was hoping he would say something bitter and strong. But his stare was childish, and the eyes wavered, as if he was very tired. He just dropped one last, vast spit on the wet floor, snuggled into his corner, and went to sleep under his hat.

In his sleep he was as motionless as a rock; but you could not say he was 'like a rock' because he was like nothing on earth but himself, everything about him was so personal to him. Unless, because he was so much a random accumulation of work and season and all that belongs to the first human that was ever made, I chose to say, as I glared at him snoring in his corner, that time and nature had engendered something no more human than a rock. So I thought, as the dusk drew down, and the wind moaned in many keys, and the snow blew horizontally and stuck to the edges of the window. It was as if we two might have been jolting into a blank, beyond either sleep or night, and I wanted to get up and kick him. I felt that if I did he would only moo.

We halted at several stations, with their one or two silent white-shouldered figures. He slept on. I was just wondering if I should wake him when suddenly, at a station, identical with every other station, as if some animal magnetism in the place stirred him, he rose and stumbled out. He did not speak. He did not raise his head to see if it was his station. He saluted no one. Anyway, there was no one there but a muffled porter who silently waved a lantern over his head. As we moved off he was trudging in the middle of a road that glimmered with its own strange afterglow, passing between a row of pines whose sheltered sides were red and raw as with the cold. He was exactly like an old black mongrel loping home.

So I was left with the pool of water on the floor, dark under the carriage light, and the snow crumbling into the corners of the windows outside, and beyond that only the light leaping and falling along the hedges. And in another two hours or so, when I got out, the carriage would be racing along, empty, through the night – three bits of separateness, the priest and the farmer and myself, flung off it like bits of the *disjecta membra* of the wheel of life.

For those two hours I tried to refute the talk of that priest, thinking that he had merely spoken out of the snowy landscape, which above all other conditions of nature is so powerful to make life seem lonely, and all work futile, and time itself a form of decay; or thinking that, had it been the green dripping spring or the hot summer, we might all have shown different and more happy sides of our worlds; or thinking that the thin cheeks and the throbbing nerves of the man were nothing but the sign of twenty years of self-corrosion, and that even when he was a young man in his first parish, his heart must have been so bitter and vain that, like a leech, it began to destroy everything to preserve itself; or thinking that because of it he had joined us for a few moments until we seemed to crouch over a fire, and then deliberately scattered us and left us with his pox. But, though that might be all true, I could not deny to the wintry moment its own truth, and that under that white shroud, covering the whole of Ireland, life was lying broken and hardly breathing. His impress remained even when the train swished slowly into the city, when the arc lamps sizzled in the snow, and the sounds were muffled, and through every street a sharp, pure wind blew down from the Wicklow hills. Once their distant convex gleamed, far away, beyond the vista of a street. There were few people abroad, and as they walked against the wind with huddled backs they, too, seemed to be shrouding something within them that slept, and barely palpitated, and was hurt by the cold. What image, I wondered, as I passed through them could warm them as the Wicklow priest had warmed us for a few minutes in that carriage now chugging around the edge of the city to the sea? What image of life that would fire and fuse us all, what music bursting like the spring, what triumph, what engendering love, so that those breasting mountains that now looked cold should appear brilliant and gay, the white land that seemed to sleep should appear to smile, and these people who huddled over the embers of their lives should become like the peasants who held the hand of Faust with their singing one Easter morning? Perhaps it was foolish to wish for such an image – so magnificent that it would have the power of a resurrection call? Yet, there are times, as when we hear the percussion of some great music, or when we feel the shrivelling effect of the cold wind and snow, that leave us no other choice but to live splendidly, or gather up at least enough grace for a quick remove.

The train could be heard easily, in the rarefied air, chugging across the bridges that span the city, bearing with it an empty coach. In the morning, Ireland, under its snow, would be silent as a perpetual dawn.

NORAH HOULT

THE STORY OF FATHER PETER

AFTER THE FIRST day or two, there is an odd feeling about any return, a dissatisfied perplexed feeling as if one expected something more. At least that is how it was with me when I stood by O'Connell Bridge one Sunday evening, looking up and down, and thinking with one part of my mind that the rebuilding of Sackville Street – O'Connell Street, as it is now called – might have been done better: too modern it is now to my way of thinking.

And with the other part of my mind I was wishing something would happen, that somebody would greet me, that Dublin would show itself the friendly place I had always thought it when I was a lonely young man during those first years in London. Of course I'm married now, settled in Streatham, and there's a kid as well; but no place can quite come up to the recollections you have of your native place, if you know what I mean. There always seems something missing, and it's to find that something that you go back. Well, the old Liffey was still the same, and so were the flat-fronted shabby pink houses along the quays.

But I was glad when I saw a face coming towards me that I knew – Willy O'Donovan. He'd have passed me without seeing only that I slipped out and grabbed hold of his arm.

'Be the holy smoke, Frank Farrell!' he said recognizing me immediately. 'What in the name of God are you doing here?'

I told him I was over for a few days only, partly a sentimental sort of visit, though I wasn't neglecting business either. There were things going on in the Irish Free State that might prove interesting to my firm. And then, of course, came the idea that we might celebrate our reunion as the saying is.

'Wait, now, where'll I take you?' said Willy. 'Would you like to have a look in at Kennedy's? Since the new Mrs Kennedy came they've opened a grand big lounge: she often serves there herself. The spot is just near the quay here.'

'I don't mind looking at your Mrs Kennedy,' I said. 'But I'd rather look at a really bona-fide John Jameson. You've no notion what they do to whiskey over the other side.'

'So I've heard,' said Willy. 'You needn't fret. The liquor's good where I'm taking you, and I'm telling you no lie.'

The upstairs lounge at Kennedy's was comfortable enough, though dingy, when you've been used to bars in the West End of London. But Willy was right about showing Mrs Kennedy to me, for she was a fine-looking figure of a woman. She'd be about thirty, and fattening under the chin. But her skin was lovely in the way some Irish skins are. And her hair was black and shining.

Willy insisted on being the first to go up to the bar, and I watched him pass the time of day with her as he ordered our poisons. She had a smiling, yet reserved way of listening that rather took my fancy.

'Your Mrs Kennedy is a nice-looking woman,' I said a while later when I came back from the bar myself, and she'd given me a pleasant look.

'There's a story to her,' said he. 'Do you know it?'

'How would I know it?' I asked, 'when I've been out of Dublin for over ten years, ever since the troubled times made the place too warm for my temperature?'

'You were not the only one,' he said. 'And I don't blame you for being one of the cautious lads. In any case it would be before that it happened.'

'What happened?' I asked.

And with that he told me.

'She comes from County Meath,' he said. 'Bridget Kelly was her name in those days. And as a young girl it happened to her to be put into the priest's house. For she was a clean girl and willing, not to mention being a Child of Mary, and at that time, I believe, had thoughts of being a nun. Anyway, that's what I heard. As innocent as innocent.

'It might have been all right if the priest had been an old man, one who knew the world and had served his time. But Father – we'd best call him Father Peter, and leave his real name out of it. In case herself should catch a word.'

I nodded understanding.

'Well poor Father Peter was a young man, only lately ordained. And you can imagine that it was a hard road he had to tread, the spiritual care of a lonely village, for it *was* a lonely village. And with the young men all stirred up and bitter. More interested in war and politics than in anything a priest might have to say. And the doctor, the only other educated man in the place, was a surly old fellow who had little truck with anyone or anything outside doing his job. He had no one to speak to that counted. No one, of course, save the young girl, and she so meek and pretty with her, "Yes, Father," and "No, Father," and now and again perhaps, as she got to know him better, "Won't you have a rest, Father? You're looking tired, so you are."'

Willy stopped, and his eyes looked into the distance. When he gets warmed up he has a great way of telling a story, so that you seem to see it all inside of yourself, and it was as if I was looking into the old damp presbytery – I don't know why exactly I thought of it that way – and watching the young priest, and he lonely and bothered. It's hard for all young priests, come to that. I remember once, years ago, one of them saying to me: 'When everyone calls you "Father", it seems sometimes that you haven't a real friend in the world and never will have.' And, as I say, I seemed to see that young lad, likely bewildered and embarrassed by all the stories he'd be hearing in the Confessional, and the young girl opening the door to him with her kind smile, and bringing in his meals whenever he'd want them.

'Well, you're a man of the world, and not bigoted, and you can picture the state of affairs. If he'd had anyone to talk to, even if another priest had been near, but he hadn't and so he fell.'

I nodded my head, and we raised our glasses. The way I thought of the priest was as a dark young man with a bony serious face and black hair. I could see him tossing in his bed; I could see him gabbling prayer after prayer, asking to be saved from the temptation of immodesty in thought, of inclination towards the slightest impurity. I could imagine him being short with the young girl, so that she entered to him with a new shyness, hardly venturing on a word. And then hating himself because he might have hurt her feelings, and longing for her to come back into the room again, so that he might say he was sorry. And the way her face would come in between him and his sermon writing. And he would fling his pen away, and rise up and stand at the window, looking at the soft sky, or along the rich green fields of the county. And wherever he went and whatever he did, there was nothing but the itch in him to be putting his arms round the girl. Oh, I could see it all, and I raised my glass again with a sort of queer satisfaction.

'Well, there it was. But it didn't end there. One day, so it must have been, she came to him and told him that she was with child. I suppose things like that have happened before, and not once or twice in our fair island's story. And a priest in that predicament can't be too particular about finding a way out. There are ways and means of sending a girl to England, and keeping her quiet, or finding her a husband. You know what I mean. A priest after all isn't like an ordinary man, and if he's disgraced and silenced his life is over and he's like a bird that has its wings cut so that it can only hop in a melancholy way about a wee patch of earth with the other birds flying over its head, and never giving it a look, unless maybe it's a jeer.'

'Not that our people here are not very good and charitable towards a silenced priest,' I interposed.

'Charitable, yes! Charity's what they get, but nothing else. Leaves an ugly taste in your mouth so.'

That was true, of course. And I nodded.

'But this young man, Father Peter as we're calling him, rightly or wrongly, stuck by the girl. He was fond of her, you see, and, I suppose, about as inexperienced for all the talk he'd heard, and all the books he'd read, as he could well be. I take it he was in a blue funk all the while, but neither of them let out a word, and if there was any gossip it didn't get to the stage when it burst into a scandal. And then when her time was near, up he came with her to Dublin and saw her into a hospital, making up some tale, whatever it might be. Though not a good one I'd say! And so far you couldn't but admire him in a sort of way for all that he was showing himself so green and raw. Sure what was he after all when you take his trappings away? Nothing but the bookish son of a farmer, going about mostly with downcast eyes, And knowing as little of real life as a green pea in a pod.'

'That's true,' I agreed.

'Of course, it's true. And it was he himself that proved it. Though for that matter, in the heel of the hunt, he showed himself a priest as well, a true son of the Holy Roman and Apostolic Church!'

'How do you mean?'

'I'm telling you. Can't you listen? I suppose the time she was lying-in gave him time to think. And instead of thinking like a sensible man to some purpose, he just went and lost his head entirely. You'd hardly credit what he did! He met her when she came out of hospital, carrying the child in her arms, and then, as they were walking up together to the station, what must he do but take the child from its mother, and leave it down on a door-step.

'I suppose the way it was they thought no one was looking. But it was broad daylight itself, and however quiet the street might have been just at that moment, there's sure to be some old woman staring out from a window, or gaping out from a little shop. In Dublin there's always someone who isn't minding their own business. Anyhow they hadn't gone more than a step or two before there was a voice calling after them and then another voice screeching and asking what in the name of all that's holy they thought they were doing at all, at all?

'With that Father Peter lost his head altogether, and he began to run, pulling on the girl with him. He hadn't a blue chance of course. People in front heard the commotion and thought he'd stolen something. So one or two must have caught hold of them. Then up comes a whole crew of angry women carrying the baby with them, abusing them both, calling out names like child murderer and deserter. He tried to get away and drag the girl, who was crying as if her heart would break, but needless to say the old ones wouldn't hear of that, and in the struggle off came the mackintosh he was wearing. Or at least it was twisted on him enough to show his Roman collar.'

'That would be a queer shock to them,' I interrupted.

'It was so. You can just see all the old women falling back muttering, "O God save us it's a priest," "God help us, what are we doing at all?" O, they'd have let him go. We're still Catholic Ireland when all's said and done, and it being a poor quarter the people were specially superstitious about meddling with a priest. But it had gone too far. A guard had come up – a policeman or peeler he'd be called in those times – and he took them both into custody. And marched them along to the police station with all the tag-rag and bob-tail of Dublin following behind.'

Willy stopped to empty his glass. 'What'll you have?' he asked me, and when I'd said the same and while he was waiting at the bar, I thought of the scene he'd been telling me about. It was as if the procession passed in front of me. The scared white-faced young priest with his torn raincoat; the young girl sobbing and crying; the old women with their black shawls drawn round their faces, muttering and nodding, the old ravens! And the swarms of grimy children. For that was one of the things that had struck me this trip, the great quantity of children playing all over the streets, crowding out of the tenement houses so fast that you wondered how any place could hold them all. Living on the other side, I had got out of the way of accepting them as in the natural order of things.

And then as Willy came back I turned round, and I remember that it was at that moment I noticed that Mrs Kennedy had a nice back to her neck. Not every woman has.

'Well, what do you think of that?' he said, when he sat down. 'A nice scene for Holy Ireland. An Irish Hogarth should have been there to do the thing justice. That's what

Dublin has always lacked. A Hogarth to do pictorially what in a manner of speaking Joyce had done verbally.'

Willy was speaking a bit sententiously and bookishly now. After he's had a few it often takes him that way. I've noticed it before. So I just said: 'Well, what was the next item on the agenda?'

'A distressing one,' said Willy. 'A very distressing one. Poor Father Peter got six months' hard labour. As for the girl, she was let off with a caution. You see she was very young then. Not more than seventeen she wouldn't be. So the nuns took her and the baby in.'

'And was Father Peter silenced?'

'He was. And silenced in more ways than by Holy Church.'

'What do you mean?'

Willy drank before he answered. Then, setting down his glass with deliberation, he said: 'Soon after he came out of prison he went stark staring mad.'

'So that was the way of it?'

'That was the way of it. God have pity on him.'

We were quiet for a little while. There was a sorry feeling inside me. The young priest had sinned, but he'd suffered for it. As Willy had said the whole thing was worse for a priest than it would have been for an ordinary man. It was little wonder, perhaps, that with his head going round and round with remorse for the sin he'd done and the disgrace that had come upon him, madness had taken him for its own.

'Is he still in the madhouse?'

'I think he would be. I'm not sure. Wasn't someone telling me he'd died? Ah, I wouldn't like to say. You don't hear much more of anyone when they've been put away.'

I looked round at Mrs Kennedy. She was moving to the other end of the counter, and I could see she had a proud way with her. It was as if she was a woman apart. And why wouldn't she be? A woman that had ruined a priest!

'Well, she did all right for herself,' said Willy, following my glance. 'She got a job in this very public-house when the late Mrs Kennedy was alive. And I suppose Tom Kennedy had got used to seeing her about the place, and, of course, she was still a pretty girl with a way all her own. Anyway, he only waited a year after losing the first to wed with this one. That was about six years ago. And I think the child is with the nuns. Or in a home or somewhere. She's not with her here I do know. Ah, it would put people too much in mind of the old scandal. And the funny thing is that she hasn't had a child by Tom at all. Ah, well there's plenty of time.'

'So that's the story,' said I. 'Well, it's a queer pitiful old tale.'

'And now tell me about yourself. What have you been doing all this long time?' Willy asked me.

And I started to tell him something of my ups and downs. But, sure that story isn't very interesting to anyone.

FLANN O'BRIEN

JOHN DUFFY'S BROTHER

STRICTLY SPEAKING, THIS story should not be written or told at all. To write it or to tell it is to spoil it. This is because the man who had the strange experience we are going to talk about never mentioned it to anybody, and the fact that he kept his secret and sealed it up completely in his memory is the whole point of the story. Thus we must admit that handicap at the beginning – that it is absurd for us to tell the story, absurd for anybody to listen to it, and unthinkable that anybody should believe it.

We will, however, do this man one favour. We will refrain from mentioning him by his complete name. This will enable us to tell his secret and permit him to continue looking his friends in the eye. But we can say that his surname is Duffy. There are thousands of these Duffys in the world; even at this moment there is probably a new Duffy making his appearance in some corner of it. We can even go so far as to say that he is John Duffy's brother. We do not break faith in saying so, because if there are only one hundred John Duffys in existence, and even if each one of them could be met and questioned, no embarrassing enlightenments would be forthcoming. That is because the John Duffy in question never left his house, never left his bed, never talked to anybody in his life, and was never seen by more than one man. That man's name was Gumley. Gumley was a doctor. He was present when John Duffy was born and also when he died, one hour later.

John Duffy's brother lived alone in a small house on an eminence in Inchicore. When dressing in the morning he could gaze across the broad valley of the Liffey to the slopes of the Phoenix Park, peacefully. Usually the river was indiscernible but on a sunny morning it could be seen lying like a long glistening spear in the valley's palm. Like a respectable married man, it seemed to be hurrying into Dublin as if to work.

Sometimes recollecting that his clock was fast, John Duffy's brother would spend an idle moment with his father's spyglass, ranging the valley with an eagle eye. The village of Chapelizod was to the left and invisible in the depth but each morning the inhabitants would erect, as if for Mr Duffy's benefit, a lazy plume of smoke to show exactly where they were.

Mr Duffy's glass usually came to rest on the figure of a man hurrying across the uplands of the Park and disappearing from view in the direction of the Magazine Fort. A small white terrier bounced along ahead of him but could be seen occasionally sprinting to overtake him after dallying behind for a time on private business.

The man carried in the crook of his arm an instrument which Mr Duffy at first took to be a shotgun or patent repeating rifle, but one morning the man held it by the butt and smote the barrels smartly on the ground as he walked, and it was then evident to Mr Duffy – he felt some disappointment – that the article was a walking-stick.

It happened that this man's name was Martin Smullen. He was a retired stationary-engine driver and lived quietly with a delicate sister at Number Four Cannon Row, Parkgate. Mr Duffy did not know his name and was destined never to meet him or have the privilege of his acquaintance, but it may be worth mentioning that they once stood side by side at the counter of a public house in Little Easter Street, mutually unrecognized, each to the other a black stranger. Mr Smullen's call was whiskey, Mr Duffy's stout.

Mr Smullen's sister's name was not Smullen but Goggins, relict of the late Paul Goggins, wholesale clothier. Mr Duffy had never even heard of her. She had a cousin by the name of Leo Corr who was not unknown to the police. He was sent up in 1924 for a stretch of hard labour in connection with the manufacture of spurious currency. Mrs Goggins had never met him, but heard that he had emigrated to Labrador on his release.

About the spyglass. A curious history attaches to its owner, also a Duffy, late of the Mercantile Marine. Although unprovided with the benefits of a University education – indeed, he had gone to sea at the age of sixteen as a result of an incident arising out of an imperfect understanding of the sexual relation – he was of a scholarly turn of mind and would often spend the afternoons of his sea-leave alone in his dining-room thumbing a book of Homer with delight or annotating with erudite sneers the inferior Latin of the Angelic Doctor. On the fourth day of July, 1927, at four o'clock, he took leave of his senses in the dining-room. Four men arrived in a closed van at eight o'clock that evening to remove him from mortal ken to a place where he would be restrained for his own good.

It could be argued that much of the foregoing has little real bearing on the story of John Duffy's brother, but modern writing, it is hoped, has passed the stage when simple events are stated in the void without any clue as to the psychological and hereditary forces working in the background to produce them. Having said so much, however, it is now permissible to set down briefly the nature of the adventure of John Duffy's brother.

He arose one morning – on the 9th of March, 1932 – dressed, and cooked his frugal breakfast. Immediately afterwards, he became possessed of the strange idea that he was a train. No explanation of this can be attempted. Small boys sometimes like to pretend that they are trains, and there are fat women in the world who are not, in the distance, without some resemblance to trains. But John Duffy's brother was certain that he *was* a train – long, thunderous, and immense, with white steam escaping noisily from his feet and deep-throated bellows coming rhythmically from where his funnel was.

Moreover, he was certain that he was a particular train, the 9.20 into Dublin. His station was the bedroom. He stood absolutely still for twenty minutes, knowing that a good train is equally punctual in departure as in arrival. He glanced often at his watch to make sure that the hour should not go by unnoticed. His watch bore the words 'Shockproof' and 'Railway Timekeeper'.

Precisely at 9.20 he emitted a piercing whistle, shook the great mass of his metal ponderously into motion, and steamed away heavily into town. The train arrived dead on time at its destination, which was the office of Messrs Polter and Polter, Solicitors, Commissioners for Oaths. For obvious reasons, the name of this firm is fictitious. In the office were two men, old Mr Cranberry and young Mr Hodge. Both were clerks and both took their orders from John Duffy's brother. Of course, both names are imaginary.

'Good Morning, Mr Duffy,' said Mr Cranberry. He was old and polite, grown yellow in the firm's service.

Mr Duffy looked at him in surprise. 'Can you not see I am a train?' he said. 'Why do you call me Mr Duffy?'

Mr Cranberry gave a laugh and winked at Mr Hodge who sat young, neat and good-looking, behind his typewriter.

'Alright, Mr Train,' he said. 'That's a cold morning, sir. Hard to get up steam these cold mornings, sir.'

'It is not easy,' said Mr Duffy. He shunted expertly to his chair and waited patiently before he sat down while the company's servants adroitly uncoupled him. Mr Hodge was sniggering behind his roller.

'Any cheap excursions, sir?' he asked.

'No,' Mr Duffy replied. 'There are season tickets, of course.'

'Third-class and first-class, I suppose, sir?'

'No,' said Mr Duffy. 'In deference to the views of Herr Marx, all class distinctions in the passenger rolling-stock have been abolished.'

'I see,' said Mr Cranberry.

'That's communism,' said Mr Hodge.

'He means,' said Mr Cranberry, 'that it is now first-class only.'

'How many wheels has your engine?' asked Mr Hodge. 'Three big ones?'

'I am not a goods train,' said Mr Duffy acidly. 'The wheel formation of a passenger engine is four-four-two – two large driving wheels on each side, coupled, of course, with a four-wheel bogey in front and two small wheels at the cab. Why do you ask?'

'The platform's in the way,' Mr Cranberry said. 'He can't see it.'

'Oh, quite,' said Mr Duffy. 'I forgot.'

'I suppose you use a lot of coal?' Mr Hodge said.

'About half-a-ton per thirty miles,' said Mr Duffy slowly, mentally checking the consumption of that morning. 'I need scarcely say that frequent stopping and starting at suburban stations takes a lot out of me.'

'I'm sure it does,' said Mr Hodge, with sympathy.

They talked like that for half an hour until the elderly Mr Polter arrived and passed gravely into his back office. When that happened, conversation was at an end. Little was heard until lunch-time except the scratch of pens and the fitful clicking of the typewriter.

John Duffy's brother always left the office at one thirty and went home to his lunch. Consequently he started getting steam up at twelve forty five so that there should be no delay at the hour of departure. When the 'Railway Timekeeper' said that it was one thirty, he let out another shrill whistle and steamed slowly out of the office without a word or a look at his colleagues. He arrived home dead on time.

We now approach the really important part of the plot, the incident which gives the whole story its significance. In the middle of his lunch John Duffy's brother felt something important, something queer, momentous, and magical taking place inside his brain, an immense tension relaxing, clean light flooding a place which had been dark. He dropped his knife and fork and sat there for a time wild-eyed, a filling of potatoes unattended in his mouth. Then he swallowed, rose weakly from the table and walked to the window, wiping away the perspiration which had started out on his brow.

He gazed out into the day, no longer a train, but a badly frightened man. Inch by inch he went back over his morning. So far as he could recall he had killed no one, shouted no bad language, broken no windows. He had only talked to Cranberry and Hodge. Down in the roadway there was no dark van arriving with uniformed men infesting it. He sat down again desolately beside the unfinished meal.

John Duffy's brother was a man of some courage. When he got back to the office he had some whiskey in his stomach and it was later in the evening than it should be. Hodge and

Cranberry seemed preoccupied with their letters. He hung up his hat casually and said:

'I'm afraid the train is a bit late getting back.'

From below his downcast brows he looked very sharply at Cranberry's face. He thought he saw the shadow of a smile flit absently on the old man's placid features as they continued poring down on a paper. The smile seemed to mean that a morning's joke was not good enough for the same evening. Hodge rose suddenly in his corner and passed silently into Mr Polter's office with his letters. John Duffy's brother sighed and sat down wearily at his desk.

When he left the office that night, his heart was lighter and he thought he had a good excuse for buying more liquor. Nobody knew his secret but himself and nobody else would ever know.

It was a complete cure. Never once did the strange malady return. But to this day John Duffy's brother starts at the rumble of a train in the Liffey tunnel and stands rooted to the road when he comes suddenly on a level-crossing – silent, so to speak, upon a peak in Darien.

MAEVE BRENNAN

THE BARREL OF RUMOURS

IN DUBLIN, MY mother used to take parcels of food to a community of Poor Clare nuns who had their convent a long walk from our house in Ranelagh. Sometimes she used to send my sister and me with the parcels. The Poor Clares are silent. They never speak, to each other or to anyone, and they are a closed order, which means that they never see outsiders and no one ever sees them. These Dublin Poor Clares had no food except what their friends – women, mostly, people like my mother – brought to them. They were forbidden to ask for anything, but we heard that if their food supply got dangerously low, the Reverend Mother was allowed to signal their distress by ringing the bell in the steeple of their chapel. To my regret, our house was too far from the convent to let us hear the bell, but my mother assured me that there was no need to worry; the nuns had never yet been driven to ring for help.

One hall in the convent was open to visitors for a part of every day, and it was there we used to call with our offerings of food. A huge revolving barrel with an open section had been built upright into the narrow end wall that sealed the public hall away from the rest of the convent. We used to place our parcels on the floor of the barrel and then turn it around so that the open section faced the nun on the other side of the wall. The nun would immediately turn it back to us, always sending us a present of a few holy pictures or some medals.

The nun who attended the barrel was named Sister Bridget. She was the only member of the community who had permission to talk to visitors. A tiny square waiting room opened off the hall, and we used to go in there and hold conversations with her through a blind grille in the wall. One of my names is Bridget, and she had the idea that I would someday develop a vocation and maybe become a Poor Clare like herself. She used to offer many prayers for my vocation, and I enjoyed talking with her about it. I was about twelve then.

I had heard that the Poor Clares slept in their coffins, with stones under their heads. I had been told that they were measured for their coffins the first day they entered the convent and that they never knew any other bed afterwards. My mother liked to throw cold water on this story, but I could not forget it. I used to wonder if they had separate cells for sleeping, with a coffin in each cell, or if they slept in a dormitory, and if they had sheets and blankets and pillowcases, and, if so, how they made their beds in the morning. Also, I wondered, what about the coffin lids? Where were they kept? On the floor alongside the coffin? Or leaning, like hockey sticks and bicycles, against the wall? I knew that the nuns never slept more than a couple of hours at a time and that they arose at intervals during the night, even in the dead of winter, to go to their chapel and pray. It was a picture to dwell upon.

I asked my mother many questions about the nuns, but her answers were never satisfactory. One time that I remember asking her about them, her younger brother, my Uncle Matt, was lounging about the room. We were in the front sitting room, and she was trying to coax one of her precious ferns to twine itself around a long bamboo cane that she had stuck into its pot.

Q: Do the Poor Clare nuns have any other convent besides the one here in Dublin?

A: I think they have another convent somewhere in Ireland, and I believe they have one in England.

Q: If nobody is allowed to see them, what happens when they're moved from one convent to another?

A: How would I know? I suppose a car, a little van, maybe, backs up to the convent door, and the nun gets in and shuts herself in.

Q: Would she bring her coffin with her?

A: I wish you'd stop all this nonsense about the nuns sleeping in their coffins.

(UNCLE MATT: Of course she'd bring her coffin with her. Doesn't she have to get her sleep, like anybody else? She'd carry it under her arm like a music roll. Do you mean to tell me you've never seen a nun walking along the street with her coffin under her arm?)

Q: What if a Poor Clare gets sick and has to have the doctor?

A: I don't know.

Q: What about if they're dying, and the priest has to come?

A: I don't know. Besides, that would be different. A priest would be different.

Q: What about if they talk in their sleep? Would that be a sin for them?

(UNCLE MATT: Well, of course, it would depend what they said.)

A: That's enough of that, now. I don't want to hear another word out of either of you.

Lentils, dried peas, eggs, and flour were chiefly what my mother used to bring to the nuns. Sometimes she baked a cake for them. Once, she brought salt, and Sister Bridget thanked her particularly, telling her that the community had been without salt for two weeks. Although the walk to the convent was long, it was not lonely. We had to cross at least two busy main streets, full of traffic as we walked along, and the way was very pleasant, with trees lining the sidewalks in front of the houses, and benches to sit on in case we got tired.

The convent and its chapel formed three sides of a square court, which was carefully tended and had a small, smooth grass lawn and bright flower beds. The fourth side of the court was on the public road and was walled off, with an iron gate through which visitors entered. The wall was very high and you couldn't see through the gate. To the right of the gate was the gate lodge, where an old woman lived and attended to visitors who called during off hours.

Although the convent had fixed visiting hours, the chapel was always open, and people could go in there and pray any time. People who lived near the chapel used to attend Mass and Benediction there. It was a beautiful little chapel, the plainest I have ever seen, with a small, almost bare main altar flanked by two tall statues of nuns – Saint Clare on the left as you knelt facing the altar, and Saint Camillus on the right. Both saints wore the brown habit of the Poor Clares. To the right of the altar, a great grille was set into the wall, and through this grille the nuns used to witness Mass and receive Benediction, and through the grille people kneeling in the chapel could hear their voices answering the prayers and singing the Benediction hymns.

One Sunday afternoon, my mother took me to Benediction there. I watched the altar and listened to the voices of the nuns, but my real attention was given to a small old woman kneeling in the seat ahead of me. This old woman, dressed in black, had her head half turned, so that I could see her face, and she was listening to the voices from behind the grille with such concentration that she appeared desperate, her eyes wide open and her mouth working along with the words.

My mother saw me watching her, and as we left the chapel, she said, 'That poor old woman comes here every chance she gets. Her daughter has been in there fourteen years, and she's got so she imagines she can hear her daughter's voice out of all the others. We came out together one day, and she told me she can't hear any of the other voices any more, only her daughter's voice. It's like as if her daughter was in there alone, she says. It's sad to see her straining like that, to hear every word.'

'Was it her oldest daughter or the youngest?' I asked. Being the middle one, I was concerned with such things.

'I don't know that,' my mother said.

'Do you suppose the daughter thinks about her mother out there and doesn't think of anybody else?' I asked.

'She could hardly help thinking of her,' my mother said. 'After all, she's still her daughter. But, of course, once they're in there, they're in there,' she added, 'and they're not supposed to think about what they've left behind. It's hard to know what goes on in their heads. Maybe they try to forget about the outside world altogether.'

'Except for our sins,' I said. 'They have to pray for us.'

'That's true,' my mother said. 'They have to think about all the sins we commit.'

If this thought amused her, she gave no sign of it.

One sunny morning late in the summer, my mother called me into the kitchen, where she was packing a parcel for the Poor Clares.

'I was wondering if you would like to take Robert with

you,' she said. 'It's a long walk, but you could go slow. Then you could put him in the barrel and send him around to see the nuns.'

'Put Robert in the barrel?' I cried.

Robert, my brother, was at this time about two years old.

'Certainly,' my mother said. 'Children are allowed in the barrel until they're three years old. After that they're too old. You can take him if you like. I'll put his blue suit on him.'

A few minutes later, I started off, pushing Robert in his pram. He sat back placidly against his pillow and stared at me. The nun's parcel made a comfortable prop for his feet. He was very pink and cheerful. My mother had dressed him in a suit of pale blue wool that she had knitted herself and that fitted him very tightly all over and left his fat legs bare. He wore short white cotton socks and brown sandals. His hair, of which he did not have much, was brushed into a golden crest on top of his head, and he shone with health, contentment, and cleanliness. I was in a great hurry to get him into the barrel, and I sped along, almost skating behind the pram.

When I got to the convent, I rushed into the waiting room and told Sister Bridget I had brought Robert to see her. She was delighted and said she would call the other nuns. I didn't know, and didn't like to ask, whether she meant that she would call all the nuns or just a few of them. I imagined them, silent and swift, of all ages, descending upon Robert from every part of the convent. I hoped none of them would be in the chapel, because surely they would never be allowed to interrupt their prayers.

I went back to the hall and lifted Robert into the barrel, making sure he had his back against the wall. He sat very solidly where I placed him, a good deal larger than the parcels I was in the habit of bringing. As soon as I heard Sister

Bridget's voice, I revolved him out of sight. He didn't seem to mind disappearing. There was silence on the other side of the barrel. I couldn't hear a rustle – not even the suspicion of a whisper. Even Robert made no sound. I stared at the blank side of the barrel and wondered what was going on on the other side.

After a minute or two, the barrel began to move, and Robert gradually came into view, sitting exactly as I had placed him, looking very matter-of-fact and friendly. I lifted him out and put the parcel on the warmed-up spot where he had been sitting. When the barrel came back the second time, Sister Bridget had sent us more presents than usual. There were extra holy pictures and extra medals and a special present for Robert, a holy picture sewn by some nun to a square of white satin and embroidered with white-satin thread. I went back into the conversation room and received Sister Bridget's compliments about Robert and acknowledged the hopes she expressed for him, which I took to be blessings, considering their source. Then I heard a few words, perfunctory this time, about my vocation, and left.

As I trundled Robert home, I was exasperated to think that he had been where I might never go and that he didn't even realize his luck. He was in great good humour. He waved his arms and pointed at people and objects that interested him and even talked a little, but I could make no sense of his language, and anyway none of his remarks seemed to have to do with the barrel, which he had apparently forgotten. He was unable to tell me what he had seen, and by the time he got old enough to express himself, it would all have passed from his memory. Not from him would I ever learn how the nuns looked, if they were young or old, if they were pretty or ugly, if they smiled at him, or nodded to him, or tried to take his hand or stroke his head, as other strangers did. He never would be able to tell me what the inside of the convent looked like. Worst of all, I realized that no matter what I heard, I would never really know for sure if the nuns slept in their coffins, with stones for pillows.

JAMES PLUNKETT

DUBLIN FUSILIER

MARTY CAME SWINGING across town. Beneath the tall lamps and the broad white-faced clocks, by picture houses and odorous restaurant gratings, under the pillar where what was left of Nelson posed proudly against the sky, came what was left of Marty. The General Post Office pushed out its ponderous chest, and Marty did likewise. In the darkness white faces passed him, warm scents assailed him, shoulders brushed his shoulder. A newsboy bawled in his ear '*Herald* or *Mail*, sir.' But Marty walked his own path in his own city, the present like a soft mist trailing past him. For Marty and Nelson were aloof. Nelson on his pillar stuck his head a little higher up into the dark arch of the night, and his stony fingers were curled irrevocably on his sword. And beneath him marched Marty with his satchel of grenades. Both bore arms always.

Marty with his pale foxy face, the nose of a snipe, the chest of a pigeon, the gait of a halty mongrel, walked his own lonely inaccessible way. There was a drop on the end of his nose, which he removed from time to time by wiping with the back of his hand.

Tramp, tramp, tramp, came Marty the Dublin Fusilier. Pride in me heart, said Marty, and porter in me belly. Tramp, tramp, tramp, thunderously across the city came Marty.

'Tell me, me dear Lord Roberts,' says Queen Victoria, 'whose them?'

'Them, ma'am,' says Lord Roberts, 'is the Black Watch.'

'Hmm,' says the Queen.

Tramp, tramp, tramp.

'And who,' says the Queen, 'is them?'

'Them, ma'am,' says Lord Roberts, 'is the Coldstream Guards.'

'Hmm,' says the Queen.

Tramp, tramp, tramp.

'Quick,' says the Queen, plucking at his arm, 'whose them?'

'Them, ma'am,' says Lord Roberts, 'is the Dublin Fusiliers.'

'Jesus,' says the Queen, 'them's Troops!'

Marty began to sing *Tipperary*.

'It's a long way, to Tipperary, it's a long way to go.'

'Are you going far?' asked the voice. It was dark on the bridge and hard to see. Marty squinted from his height of five foot seven at a silver button and a big helmet. He halted. 'Atten-shun,' he bawled. So the policeman grinned broadly at the thin, sick face under the peaky cap, and the sharp nose with its pendulent drop.

'So that's the way it is,' he said.

That was on the wide bridge over the river. People passed and twisted to look closer, but did not stand because the breeze blew coldly from the river. Trams with lighted windows clanged past, with here half a man reading a paper or smoking, and there a girl staring straight ahead of her or perhaps patting her hair with deft fingers.

So the policeman grinned again and putting his fingers in his belt, turned and walked away.

Marty swung his grenades. Was he not Marty, an Irishman and a Dublin Fusilier? Son of no carey nor scab, but now and then the son of a seacook, and sometimes a son of a bitch, and always an oul' son of a gun. No sugarin' policeman would lay a hand on Marty. No dirty Jerry, nor snooping Boer, nor bloody Black and Tan. He'd banjax the whole issue, Marty would, all on his Barney Malone. But in the meanwhile, would you manage a pint, Marty? Would a duck swim, wha'? Willy is a bad fella. Right you are, oul' son, off we go for a loaf of Bolands.

Marty, letting out a shout, began to take his pint. A young man sat at the bar with his back to a partition, his raincoat unbuttoned, his hat on the back of his head. He had been talking to two men about music.

'I've been rehearsing for three solid hours,' he said. 'Bloody *Faust*. I've a thirst that a parish priest would sell his soul for.'

'All the same,' said the pavior, '*Faust* is a lovely opera.'

'It's lovely,' said the young man, 'because it gives you a lovely thirst after rehearsing it for three solid hours.'

'Mick and me,' said the pavior, 'used to play in the Trade Union band. We were thrown out for hocking the instruments when we were short for a few pints. We used to play selections from *Faust*.'

'Rehearsing *Faust*,' said Mick, 'used to give us a lovely thirst too.'

'What band was that?'

'Tell him what they called us, Tommy.'

'They used to call us The Sufferin' Ducks,' said the pavior reminiscently.

'It was very insultin' . . .' added Mick sadly.

Marty gave another yell out of him.

'That's Marty,' the pavior said, 'a harmless poor divil.' He put a finger to his temple and twisted it significantly. His left eye winked.

'That was a terrible man once,' said Mick, 'that was a holy terror.'

'Poor Marty,' said the pavior.

'I remember the band during the big strike. We were

marching down to a meeting at the docks. But when we got to Butt Bridge every bloody policeman in the country was there waiting for us.'

'Drawn in a cordon across the street,' put in Mick, 'standing about ten deep with their batons in their hands and murder in their hearts.'

'Your man Marty was the Bandmaster,' the pavior continued, 'and he gave us the order to halt. "Where do you think you're going?" the Inspector came up and asked him. "Down to a meeting," said Marty. "My men are drawn across there in front of you," said the Inspector, "and if you try to pass them they'll leave the lot of you for dead." "Will they?" said Marty, and the Inspector walked away. So Marty turned round to us. "Strike it up boys," he shouted, "and forward on the double tap." He waves his stick. "Close your eyes, boys," he says, "and you won't feel the pain."'

'It was slaughter, right enough,' Mick commented.

'The police didn't like music,' said the young man.

'They didn't like *our* music,' Mick said sadly. 'Marty had us playing *The Peeler and the Goat*.'

'That was Marty for you,' concluded the pavior, turning to consult his pint.

Marty crouched staring in his corner, his head at an angle.

The curate, who knew Marty of an old date, nodded his head towards him and then winked at the pavior.

'We're off,' said the pavior, 'pension on Wednesday and pop goes the thinking cabinet.'

'We're over the top all right,' said Mick. 'Next stop Blighty.'

'What's wrong with him?' asked the young man, upset because Marty was staring at him with violence and hatred in his eyes.

'Shellshock,' the pavior said. 'I soldiered with Marty in

France.' Then he said loudly, 'How's tricks, Marty oul' son?'

Marty continued to stare.

'He doesn't know you,' Mick said. 'Maybe he'll come round later.'

Marty lived in the same house as the pavior, and a married sister who lived there looked after him. The pavior said Marty was a fine Soccer player once. He played for St Patrick's when they won the Leinster Senior Cup. That was against Sligo. They had a dinner after it in a hotel and then drove out to the Strawberry Beds on hacks and played melodeons and drank a lot of porter. But that was in Oul' God's time. In those days you could get a pint for twopence and any amount of cheese and biscuits for nothing. They were on the counter. You wouldn't see the like of that to-day.

'Them days is done,' Mick declared. 'You'd see white blackbirds before you'd see that again.'

The pavior spat into the sawdust, and then scrubbed his heavy boot over it so that it made a trundling noise on the floor. The young man regarded Marty with curiosity. Marty, however, was watching the fellow with the machine gun. In France Marty had been going forward with his eye on that machine gun when the explosion blew him off his feet. He woke up blind, with a buzzing in his head. The blindness went away after a while but the buzzing remained intermittently. When it became bad Marty crouched and watched. Sometimes he would throw himself flat with a sudden wild movement, a loud obscenity. If he did this where there was concrete, Mrs White, his married sister, had to get the enamel basin and bathe away the blood. Quite often he did it where there was concrete.

Marty took a grenade from the satchel, bit out the pin and swung his arm in a slow loop. When the flame and smoke subsided he saw in front of him the three shiny handles, like rifle nozzles protruding above three shoulders, which were used for pulling pints, and beyond them the glass mirror with its gilt advertisement for DWD potstill whiskey, the yellow pear of the electric bulb with its white shade, hanging plumb and without movement from the ceiling and the pavior's broad back. He heard also the hum of conversation and cars blowing horns now and then in the street. He found his pint almost finished. Would you have another Marty? He would because a bird never flew on one wing. He fetched out a bright silver shilling from his pocket.

> O Brian you've been drinking Brian O
> I know it by your winking Brian O . . .
> I took the Saxon shillin' for to do their dirty killin'
> The oul' sergeant found me willin'
> > Molly O.

So Marty gave his bright silver shilling to the curate and in return he received his pint and a few pence in change.

'All the same,' the pavior said, '*Faust* is a fine opera.'

'I remember it well,' Mick said. 'The Devil has a bit to do with it.'

'Too much,' agreed the young man.

'He sells his soul to the devil,' continued the pavior thoughtfully, 'for the sake of a slip of a girl.'

'Shockin',' Mick said, 'a bloody poor bargain.'

'Many a man sold his soul for less, for a pint of porter or a piece of silver.'

'That's the truth,' Mick said.

'Yiz sold yer sowls for penny rolls and a cut of streaky bacon,' quoted the pavior.

'No doubt about it,' said Mick.

'Marty sold his soul for a shillin',' said the pavior with a finality which caused Mick, who did not quite follow, to shake his head in solemn agreement.

Marty gave his shilling. In the good days when he was young he would think himself well off with a shilling in his pocket of a Sunday morning.

One bright Sunday morning he left his mother's house in Patrick Street, his cap set gallantly, his shirt clean, his boots shining. Marty, young and vigorous, cocked an eye at the light cloud and the sun high up over the spire of the Cathedral. The clamouring bells shook the street, St Audeon's, St Patrick's, John's Lane and Christ Church, shouting and singing above the rattling cabs and the slaty cobbles, 'Come and worship all ye true followers of Christ.' He was going to Mass but he was thinking of other things. The bells he had grown up with made his head spin.

'Come and worship, Marty oul' son,' said John's Lane. 'Don't be dallying there with the sun warming your back and your eye giving the beck to the young girls with the feathers and the flowers in their hats.'

'And them on their way to holy Mass too,' said St Audeon's. 'Don't be hanging about there looking at the artificial sprays in the artificial ponds, and the dirty little urchins sailing paper boats in the close of St Patrick's, the little desecrators of the Blessed Sabbath.'

'He's dreaming about the medal he'll wear in his chain when they knock the stuffin' out of Sligo,' said St Patrick's. 'He's thinking he might give it to Annie.'

'Taking her out to the hollow in the park or maybe down the Shellybanks, God forgive him, that's what's occupying him.'

As he walked, the hand which was in his pocket holding the shilling sweated so that he felt a moist circle in his palm.

'Come in, Marty,' said John's Lane, 'and pray a while for your soul. It could do with it. And pray for the souls of them that's gone – a summer's day is a long day.'

Everybody harped at him.

'Marty Callaghan,' his mother had said to him previously, 'are you going to Mass at all?' He said he was ready, he had lashings of time. 'It's on your knees in the church you should be now, not polishing your boots. If it was a football match you'd be in time, never fear.' Marty whistled and winked at his young sister.

He stepped out of the sunlight into the porch of John's Lane, and taking off his cap and dipping his warm brown fingers in the holy water font, he crossed himself and sprinkled some at the door for the poor souls in purgatory. A large dim church cluttered with poor people. A warm place, the air shimmering with the tapering flame of candles and sour with the smell of devout bodies. He was in time for the first gospel and came out after the last, leaving the women to light their lamps to Saint Anne, patron of childing mothers, and the old men with rosary beads and yellow faces to keep watch against the thief who came by night. In the afternoon he walked with Annie through the Pigeon House fort where the soldiers practised firing, to the Shellybanks with their rough grasses which were sweet to lie in. They paddled in the shallow water and ate oranges, and Annie wore her blue dress. He asked her to marry him. Not immediately, he said, but soon. She said she didn't know really, she always thought she'd have liked a soldier. Dinny Andrews was a soldier and she thought it was a brave thing that, to be a soldier. He said he always thought she cared for him more than Dinny Andrews, and she said she did too, honest. Her eyes were blue and she laughed when she saw that he was moodily plucking at the grass. The grass cut his finger. She became very concerned, and made him bathe it in the salt water. After that she thought she might marry him. He went down to the men's place to swim, his heart singing, his lithe body pulsing with a new excitement. When he came back they bought oranges and sweets from the peddling women and ate them lying in the sandy grasses, watching the boats and the people who passed, laughing at the antics of little children and making love to one another.

In the evening he left her home, and that night he sat for a long time dreaming at the kitchen window, until it was midnight, and the bells of St Patrick's having struck the hour, began as they always did at that hour to play a little tune, which stole quietly to him over streets and roof-tops.

Some nights later he told his father. He didn't know what to say to his mother. His father told her.

'Ellen,' he said, 'Marty's took the shillin'.' He was sitting in a high armchair with his feet on the hob.

'I'm going to France, mother,' Marty said, twiddling his cap in his hands. 'I'm a soldier.'

That was in the kitchen where the picture of Parnell hung between two bronze horses with warriors tilting at one another across the mantelpiece, and the speech of Robert Emmet stood framed on age-spotted parchment. 'Let no man write my epitaph; for as no man who knows my motives dares now vindicate them, let not prejudice nor ignorance asperse them.' Lovely round phrases which rolled in splendour from the mouth of his grandfather when he had a few jars in him.

One for the road and a bit of a song, Marty. Why not? It was a long time waiting for the war to be over. What would it be? Make it something Irish, was what they used to say to him.

Marty closed his eyes and turned his white face upwards. The sunken mouth opened and yellow molars stood up like cartridges. He sang *Danny Boy*. His voice was cracked and wobbly, like his broken body. His voice was a thing sewn and stitched together, wrapped like a ragged bandage about his song.

'There's a bit of a tune now for you,' said Mick. Marty had his eyes fixed on the ceiling, displaying a scrawny neck where his Adam's apple ran to and fro between two deep ridges when he paused for breath after each line. The three of them turned to stare.

'He's putting his heart into it,' said the pavior. They laughed.

> O Danny Boy, the pipes the pipes is callin'
> From glen to glen and down the mountain side,
> The summer's gone and all the flowers is dying
> 'Tis you must go, and so 'tis I must bide . . .

Two big tears rolled from Marty's eyes and lay on his cheeks on either side of his nose, matching the drop which now hung unmolested. The lower lids of both eyes, which sagged slightly outwards, were blood rimmed.

It was a sad song. Often his father had sung it at parties in their house in Patrick Street, because of course it was his father's song. It used to make his mother cry. It was always sad to think of the brave soldier marching off to the wars, leaving his father and his poor mother and the good kind people he loved. And his sweetheart too, who would wait for him until he came back.

> In sunshine or in shadow,
> And I will stand still waiting there for you.

But as like as not, he never came back.

A very sad, beautiful song, just like all the old songs. *When the fields are white with daisies I'll return* had been his mother's song. Marty had a face which made the barman exchange another nod and a wink with the three, who looked on happily, and a heart which was broken for love of poor dead days and their poor dead people, a spirit which groped back, always back with tearing and torture to his mother, God bless her, and his good father who drank come-day-go-day God-send-pay-day may the sod rest light on him, to Mick his brother who'd give the shirt off his back and Little One his sister who said give us a penny Marty there's a darlin' Marty for to buy seedy cake and he always gave it to her, and to other poor souls dead and gone this many a long day, may perpetual light shine upon them, may they rest in peace. Amen.

Marty stared at the ceiling. His mouth remained open. He found he was walking down by Dublin Castle and the clock striking midnight. A moon stared down at him from the cloud-racked sky. His grandfather stepped out from the shadows.

'Remember your oul' grandfather,' said the voice, 'I cobbled boots for fifty years in Nash's Court. You used to laugh at me when my mouth was full of nails. You were only a dawny chisler then, Marty.' He laughed again heartily at his grandfather, remembering the green baize apron and the cock of his hawky face over the boot. 'An oul' cod,' said Marty. He swung down the steep cobbles of Lord Edward Street.

'What about me,' said a Callaghan with a greasy cloak, 'that carried the keg of dynamite to the castle gate the time they pulled Kilwarden from his coach. They stuck twenty pitchforks in him to make sure he wouldn't remember who done it. Emmet was bloody annoyed, I can tell you.'

'That was a wrong thing to do,' Marty said, 'even though he was only a Protestant.' His boots rang on the cobbles. Under a guttering lamp another joined him. He was long and broad shouldered, but he had the hawky face.

'Did I ever tell you about 1534, Marty? I was keeping an eye on things after piling a bit of hay and me and Silken Thomas was having a drink together. "Well, Fitzgerald," says I, "how's tricks?" "Bad, Callaghan," says he. "They're after murdering the poor father. Do you see me sword of office?" "I do," I says. "Well," says he, "as soon as I finish this mouthful I'm going straight over to the Abbey, and do you know what I'll do then?"

' "I don't."

' "I'm going to take it off and throw it at the bloody Archbishop."

' "You'd be a foolish young man to do that," I says.

' "Foolish or not," says he, "that's the programme; and what's more, I hope it takes the bloody head off him, mitre an' all." '

Marty yelled out loud at the idea of it. But a vague figure was following, whining and pulling at his sleeve. It had a death's head of a face, and a scrawny neck. 'Fine talk,' it said, 'and fine men. But my potatoes withered in the ground and my youngest died with the green ooze of grass on his lips.'

'They broke the house about my head,' said another, 'and the bailiff stood watching them and laughing.'

'What odds; didn't you tie him to a gate afterwards and roast him over a fire?'

'We did – and when he died with God's mercy he went on roasting. I declare to God his carcase turned black as his heart.'

Said the Inspector to him, 'My men are drawn across in

front of you, Marty, and if you try to pass them they'll leave the lot of you for dead.'

But that was poor Erin for you, the tear and the smile in her eye.

He would meet Annie on some cool summer's evening out at the Strawberry Beds. In the distance someone would play a melodeon. Or once again perhaps in Phoenix Park on a day when the fields were white with daisies and golden with buttercups he'd return and the sky would be wide and blue above them, and the river a silver girdle far below. But it was a long time waiting for the war to be over.

The glass he was holding was flung violently to the ground. Mick and the barman jumped. 'My Christ, Marty,' said the barman, rushing out, 'what the hell do you think you're doing?'

Marty swung both arms out wide.

'Atten-shun,' he bawled.

'Attenshun nothing,' said the barman, 'that bloody glass cost eight pence.' Marty screwed up his face and glared.

'Forward,' he commanded. 'At the double,' he bawled.

'Leave him alone,' said the pavior, 'you might as well talk to the wall.'

'He's over the top,' averred Mick sadly.

'Breaking glasses is a new one. What the hell am I to do if everyone that has a pint can smash hell out of me glasses without an after you or a by your leave? It's all bloody fine.'

'He couldn't help it, Joe,' said the pavior soothingly.

'*Non compass mensit*,' explained Mick.

Marty, brushing aside the commotion, drew himself up and with dignity demanded a pint.

'There you are,' the barman complained bitterly. 'Now he has the bloody neck to ask me for a pint.'

'Give it to him,' they said, 'he's all right now.' Marty got his pint. He was talking to himself. They heard him arguing and swearing. Then he swung his grenades into position and marched out.

Tramp, tramp, tramp, went Marty the Dublin Fusilier. Pride in his heart and porter in his belly. The night hung mildly over the city, the streets were quiet, the dark houses stood up like tall sentries. Some taxi men, who were waiting for the theatres to close, stood smoking at the great gate of Stephen's Green. A faint scent of flowers hung in the air. Marty stood still at the corner. He stared ahead of him. Then he motioned with his arm. Then he stood still again. Then he howled an obscenity and began to lope forward. Now and then his arm swung in a wide loop. The noise of battle was about him. Once more in front of him was the fellow with the machine gun. His cheeks were grey and streaky with sweat and dust but his bared teeth were blinding white. Marty shouted out Tipperary, flung grenades, ran and stopped. But the machine gun continued to swing to and fro. When its black unwinking eye cocked itself wickedly in the centre of his regimental belt, Marty shouted and flung himself violently to the ground. His head struck on stone steps.

They said it was disgraceful that a man should get into such a condition. It was hard to know who was more to blame, the man himself or the publican who served him. A small knot had gathered when the pavior came along with Mick and the young man. The pavior knelt down and lifted him up. The pavior was the slightest bit tipsy.

'Marty oul' son,' he said. Marty stirred.

'Come on, Marty, never say die. Old soldiers like you and me never die, Marty, we only fade away.'

Marty murmured, 'Attenshun.'

'That's the spirit, Marty oul' son, that's the stuff to give the troops.' He said to Mick, 'For the love of God, will you take one side of him and don't stand there like a bloody statue.'

Some money fell from his pocket as they lifted him, which Mick and the young man searched for while the pavior wiped blood from his face with his cap. There were traces of foam on Marty's mouth which he removed gently. 'Have you his few ha'pence?' asked the pavior.

Mick, after peering around helplessly two or three times, said he didn't see any more. They helped him home. The spot where Marty had fallen was marked a little with blood, and in a corner by the iron railings where a little mound of dust had gathered winked a silver shilling. It lay waiting to be found by some passer-by with sharper eyesight than Mick. They took Marty up the broad carpetless stairs, their boots kicking each step and echoing as they struggled with their burden. Mrs White, his sister, was in tears. 'His poor face,' she said when she saw him, 'me poor Marty, what did they do to you?' And she got her green enamel basin and washed his face, and with her husband they put him to bed. Then she said there was tea waiting on the hob and they might as well have a cup.

'You're a good neighbour, God bless you,' she said to the pavior. So they sat round drinking tea and saying Marty would be right as rain again to-morrow morning. But she kept saying, 'What am I to do with him at all, at all? I can't be managing him for ever.' And again she said, looking at her husband, 'Wouldn't it be an unnatural thing to have him put away?' They talked until midnight in that way.

Marty lay in the little room. The window was open and let in the night noises, and the curtain stirred now and then faintly. The muscles of his hawky face twitched nervously, his mouth moved unceasingly. Sometimes his hands groped out for his satchel of grenades. St Patrick's sounded midnight and the room reverberated. The bells died away. It was quiet and peaceful once more, with only the murmur of voices from the next room to break the silence. Marty slept. Then the bells of St Patrick's, with their time-mellowed tongues, begun to play a little tune.

MARY LAVIN

IN A CAFÉ

THE CAFÉ WAS in a back street. Mary's ankles ached and she was glad Maudie had not got there before her. She sat down at a table near the door.

It was a place she had only recently found, and she dropped in often, whenever she came up to Dublin. She hated to go anywhere else now. For one thing, she knew that she would be unlikely ever to have set foot in it if Richard were still alive. And this knowledge helped to give her back a semblance of the identity she lost willingly in marriage, but lost doubly, and unwillingly, in widowhood.

Not that Richard would have disliked the café. It was the kind of place they went to when they were students. Too much water had gone under the bridge since those days, though. Say what you liked, there was something faintly snobby about a farm in Meath, and together she and Richard would have been out of place here. But it was a different matter to come here alone. There could be nothing – oh, nothing – snobby about a widow. Just by being one, she fitted into this kind of café. It was an unusual little place. She looked around.

The walls were distempered red above and the lower part was boarded, with the boards painted white. It was probably the boarded walls that gave it the peculiarly functional look you get in the snuggery of a public-house or in the confessional of a small and poor parish church. For furniture there were only deal tables and chairs, with black-and-white checked tablecloths that were either unironed or badly ironed. But there was a decided feeling that money was not so much in short supply as dedicated to other purposes – as witness the paintings on the walls, and a notice over the fire-grate to say that there were others on view in a studio overhead, in rather the same way as pictures in an exhibition. They were for the most part experimental in their technique.

The café was run by two students from the Art College. They often went out and left the place quite empty – as now – while they had a cup of coffee in another café – across the steet. Regular clients sometimes helped themselves to coffee from the pot on the gas-ring, behind a curtain at the back; or, if they only came in for company and found none, merely warmed themselves at the big fire always blazing in the little black grate that was the original grate when the café was a warehouse office. Today, the fire was banked up with coke. The coffee was spitting on the gas-ring.

Would Maudie like the place? That it might not be exactly the right place to have arranged to meet her, above all under the present circumstances, occurred vaguely to Mary, but there was nothing that could be done about it now. When Maudie got there, if she didn't like it, they could go somewhere else. On the other hand, perhaps she might like it? Or perhaps she would be too upset to take notice of her surroundings? The paintings might interest her. They were certainly stimulating. There were two new ones today, which Mary herself had not seen before: two flower paintings, just inside the door. From where she sat she could read the signature, Johann van Stiegler. Or at least they suggested flowers. They were nameable as roses surely in spite of being a bit angular. She knew what Richard would have said about them. But she and Richard were no longer one. So what would *she* say about them? She would say – she would say –

But what was keeping Maudie? It was all very well to be glad of a few minutes' time in which to gather herself together; it was a different thing altogether to be kept a quarter of an hour.

Mary leaned back against the boarding. She was less tired than when she came in, but she was still in no way prepared for the encounter in front of her.

What had she to say to a young widow recently bereaved? Why on earth had she arranged to meet her? The incongruity of their both being widowed came forcibly upon her. Would Maudie, too, be in black with touches of white? Two widows! It was like two magpies: one for sorrow, two for joy. The absurdity of it was all at once so great she had an impulse to get up and make off out of the place. She felt herself vibrating all over with resentment at being coupled with anyone, and urgently she began to sever them, seeking out their disparities.

Maudie was only a year married! And her parents had been only too ready to take care of her child, greedily possessing themselves of it. Maudie was as free as a girl. Then – if it mattered – ? – she had a nice little income in her own right too, apart from all Michael had left her. So?

But what was keeping her? Was she not coming at all?

Ah! the little iron bell that was over the door – it too, since the warehouse days – tinkled to tell there was another customer coming into the café.

It wasn't Maudie though. It was a young man – youngish anyway – and Mary would say that he was an artist. Yet his hands at which, when he sat down, he began to stare, were not like the hands of an artist. They were peculiarly plump soft-skinned hands, and there was something touching in the relaxed way in which, lightly clasped one in the other, they rested on the table. Had they a womanish look perhaps?

No; that was not the word, but she couldn't for the life of her find the right word to describe them. And her mind was teased by trying to find it. Fascinated, her eyes were drawn to those hands, time and again, no matter how resolutely she tore them away. It was almost as if it was by touch, not sight, that she knew their warm fleshiness.

Even when she closed her eyes – as she did – she could still see them. And so, innocent of where she was being led, she made no real effort to free her thoughts from them, and not until it was too late did she see before her the familiar shape of her recurring nightmare. All at once it was Richard's hands she saw, so different from those others, wiry, supple, thin. There they were for an instant in her mind, limned by love and anguish, before they vanished.

It happened so often. In her mind she would see a part of him, his hand – his arm, his foot perhaps, in the finely worked leather shoes he always wore – and from it, frantically, she would try to build up the whole man. Sometimes she succeeded better than others, built him up from foot to shoulder, seeing his hands, his grey suit, his tie, knotted always in a slightly special way, his neck, even his chin that was rather sharp, a little less attractive than his other features—

—But always at that point she would be defeated. Never once voluntarily since the day he died had she been able to see his face again.

And if she could not remember him, at will, what meaning had time at all? What use was it to have lived the past, if behind us it fell away so sheer?

In the hour of his death, for her it was part of the pain that she knew this would happen. She was standing beside him when, outside the hospital window, a bird called out with a sweet, clear whistle, and hearing it she knew that he was dead, because not for years had she really heard bird-song or bird-call, so loud was the noise of their love in her ears. When she looked down it was a strange face, the look of death itself, that lay on the pillow. And after that brief moment of silence that let in the bird-song for an instant, a new noise started in her head; the noise of a nameless panic that did not always roar, but never altogether died down.

And now – here in the little café – she caught at the table-edge – for the conflagration had started again and her mind was a roaring furnace.

It was just then the man at the end of the table stood up and reached for the menu-card on which, as a matter of fact, she was leaning – breasts and elbows – with her face in her hands. Hastily, apologetically, she pushed it towards him, and at once the roar died down in her mind. She looked at him. Could he have known? Her heart was filled with gratitude, and she saw that his eyes were soft and gentle. But she had to admit that he didn't look as if he were much aware of her. No matter! She still was grateful to him.

'Don't you want this too?' she cried, thankful, warm, as she saw that the small small slip of paper with the speciality for the day that had been clipped to the menu-card with a paper-pin, had come off and remained under her elbow, caught on the rough sleeve of her jacket. She stood up and leant over the table with it.

'Ah! thank you!' he said, and bowed. She smiled. There was such gallantry in a bow. He was a foreigner, of course. And then, before she sat down again she saw that he had been sketching, making little pencil sketches all over a newspaper on the table, in the margins and in the spaces between the newsprint. Such intricate minutely involuted little figures – she was fascinated, but of course she could not stare.

Yet, when she sat down, she watched him covertly, and

every now and then she saw that he made a particular flourish: it was his signature, she felt sure, and she tried to make it out from where she sat. A disproportionate, a ridiculous excitement rushed through her, when she realized it was Johann van Stiegler, the name on the new flower paintings that had preoccupied her when she first came into the place.

But it's impossible, she thought. The sketches were so meticulous; the paintings so—

But the little bell had tinkled again.

'Ah! Maudie!'

For all her waiting, taken by surprise in the end, she got to her feet in her embarrassment, like a man.

'Maudie, my dear!' She had to stare fixedly at her in an effort to convey the sympathy, which, tongue-tied, she could express in no other way.

They shook hands, wordlessly.

'I'm deliberately refraining from expressing sympathy – you know that?' said Mary then, as they sat down at the chequered table.

'Oh, I do!' cried Maudie. And she seemed genuinely appreciative. 'It's so awful trying to think of something to say back! – Isn't it? It has to come right out of yourself, and sometimes what comes is something you can't even say out loud when you do think of it!'

It was so true. Mary looked at her in surprise. Her mind ran back over the things people had said to her, and the replies.

Them: It's a good thing it wasn't one of the children.

Her: I'd give them all for him.

Them: Time is a great healer.

Her: Thief would be more like: taking away even my memory of him.

> Them: God's ways are wonderful. Some day you'll see His plan in all this.
>
> Her: Do you mean, some day I'll be glad he's dead.

So Maudie apprehended these subtleties too? Mary looked hard at her. 'I know, I know,' she said. 'In the end you have to say what is expected of you – and you feel so cheapened by it.'

'Worse still, you cheapen the dead!' said Maudie.

Mary looked really hard at her now. Was it possible for a young girl – a simple person at that – to have wrung from one single experience so much bitter knowledge? In spite of herself, she felt she was being drawn into complicity with her. She drew back resolutely.

'Of course, you were more or less expecting it, weren't you?' she said, spitefully.

Unrepulsed, Maudie looked back at her. 'Does that matter?' she asked, and then, unexpectedly, she herself put a rift between them. 'You have the children, of course!' she said, and then, hastily, before Mary could say anything, she rushed on. 'Oh, I know I have my baby, but there seems so little link between him and his father! I just can't believe that it's me, sometimes, wheeling him round the park in his pram: it's like as if he was illegitimate. No! I mean it really. I'm not just trying to be shocking. It must be so different when there has been time for a relationship to be started between children and their father, like there was in your case.'

'Oh, I don't know that that matters,' said Mary. 'And you'll be glad to have him some day.' This time she spoke with deliberate malice, for she knew so well how those same words had lacerated her. She knew what they were meant to say: the children would be better than nothing.

But the poison of her words did not penetrate Maudie.

And with another stab she knew why this was so. Maudie was so young; so beautiful. Looking at her, it seemed quite inaccurate to say that she had lost her husband: it was Michael who had lost her, fallen out, as it were, while she perforce went outward. She didn't even look like a widow. There was nothing about her to suggest that she was in any way bereft or maimed.

'You'll marry again, Maudie,' she said, impulsively. 'Don't mind my saying it,' she added quickly, hastily. 'It's not a criticism. It's because I know how you're suffering that I say it. Don't take offence.'

Maudie didn't really look offended though, she only looked on the defensive. Then she relaxed.

'Not coming from you,' she said. 'You know what it's like.' Mary saw she was trying to cover up the fact that she simply could not violently refute the suggestion. 'Not that I think I will,' she added, but weakly. 'After all, you didn't!'

It was Mary who was put upon the defensive now.

'After all, it's only two years – less even,' she said stiffly.

'Oh, it's not altogether a matter of time,' said Maudie, seeing she had erred, but not clear how or where. 'It's the kind of person you are, I think. I admire you so much! It's what I'd want to be like myself if I had the strength. With remarriage it is largely the effect on oneself that matters I think, don't you? I don't think it really matters to – to the dead! Do you? I'm sure Michael would want me to marry again if he were able to express a wish. After all, people say it's a compliment to a man if his widow marries again, did you ever hear that?'

'I did,' said Mary, curtly. 'But I wouldn't pay much heed to it. A fat lot of good the dead care about compliments.'

So Maudie *was* already thinking about remarriage? Mary's

irritation was succeeded by a vague feeling of envy, and then the irritation returned tenfold.

How easily it was accepted that *she* would not marry again. This girl regards me as too old, of course. And she's right – or she ought to be right! She remembered the way, even two years ago, people had said she 'had' her children. They meant, even then, that it was unlikely, unlooked for, that she'd remarry.

Other things that had been said crowded back into her mind as well. So many people had spoken of the special quality of her marriage – hers and Richard's – their remarkable suitability one for the other, and the uniqueness of the bond between them. She was avid to hear this said at the time.

But suddenly, in this little café, the light that had played over those words, flickered and went out. Did they perhaps mean that if Richard had not appeared when he did, no one else would have been interested in her?

Whereas Maudie – ! If she looked so attractive now, when she must still be suffering from shock, what would she be like a year from now, when she would be 'out of mourning', as it would be put? Why, right now, she was so fresh and – looking at her there was no other word for it – virginal! Of course she was only a year married. A year! You could hardly call it being married at all.

But Maudie knew a thing or two about men for all that. There was no denying it. And in her eyes at that moment there was a strange expression. Seeing it, Mary remembered at once that they were not alone in the café. She wondered urgently how much the man at the other end of the table had heard and could hear of what they were saying. But it was too late to stop Maudie.

'Oh Mary,' cried Maudie, leaning forward, 'it's not what

they give us – I've got over wanting things like a child – it's what we have to give them! It's something—' and she pressed her hands suddenly to her breasts, 'something in here!'

'Maudie!'

Sharply, urgently, Mary tried to make her lower her voice, and with a quick movement of her head she did manage at last to convey some caution to her.

'In case you might say something,' she said, in a low voice.

'Oh, there was no fear,' said Maudie. 'I was aware all the time.' She didn't speak quite so low as Mary, but did lower her voice. 'I was aware of him *all the time*,' she said. 'It was *him* that put it into my mind – about what we have to give.' She pressed her hands to her breasts again. 'He looks so lonely, don't you think? He is a foreigner, isn't he? I always think it's sad for them; they don't have many friends, and even when they do, there is always a barrier, don't you agree?'

But Mary was too embarrassed to let her go on. Almost frantically she made a diversion.

'What are you going to have, Maudie?' she said, loudly. 'Coffee? Tea? And is there no one to take an order?'

Immediately she felt a fool. To whom had she spoken? She looked across at Johann van Stiegler. As if he were waiting to meet her glance, his mild and patient eyes looked into hers.

'There is no one there,' he said, nodding at the curtained gas-ring, 'but one can serve oneself. Perhaps you would wish that I—'

'Oh not at all,' cried Mary. 'Please don't trouble! We're in absolutely no hurry! Please don't trouble yourself,' she said, 'not on our account.'

But she saw at once that he was very much a foreigner, and that he was at a disadvantage, not knowing if he had not perhaps made a gaffe. 'I have perhaps intruded?' he said, miserably.

'Oh, not at all,' cried Mary, and he was so serious she had to laugh.

The laugh was another mistake though. His face took on a look of despair that could come upon a foreigner, it seemed, at the slightest provocation, as if suddenly everything was obscure to him – everything.

'Please,' she murmured, and then vaguely, '– your work,' meaning that she did not wish to interrupt his sketching.

'Ah, you know my work?' he said, brightening immediately, pleased and with a small and quite endearing vanity. 'We have met before? Yes?'

'Oh no, we haven't met,' she said, quickly, and she sat down, but of course after that it was impossible to go on acting as if he were a complete stranger. She turned to see what Maudie would make of the situation. It was then she felt the full force of her irritation with Maudie. She could have given her a slap in the face. Yes: a slap right in the face! For there she sat, remotely, her face indeed partly averted from them.

Maudie was waiting to be introduced! To be *introduced*, as if she, Mary, did not need any conventional preliminaries. As if it was all right that she, Mary, should begin an unprefaced conversation with a strange man in a café because – and of course that was what was so infuriating, that she knew Maudie's unconscious thought – it was all right for a woman of *her* age to strike up a conversation like that, but that it wouldn't have done for a young woman. Yet, on her still partly averted face, Mary could see the quickened look of interest. She had a good mind not to make any gesture to draw her into the conversation at all, but she had the young man to consider. She had to bring them together whether she liked it or not.

'Maudie, this is—' she turned back and smiled at van

Stiegler, 'this is—' But she was confused and she had to abandon the introduction altogether. Instead, she broke into a direct question.

'Those are your flower pictures, aren't they?' she asked.

It was enough for Maudie – more than enough you might say.

She turned to the young man, obviously greatly impressed; her lips apart, her eyes shining. My God, how attractive she was!

'Oh no, not really?' she cried. 'How marvellous of you!'

But Johann van Stiegler was looking at Mary.

'You are sure we have not met before?'

'Oh no, but you were scribbling your signature all over that newspaper,' she looked around to show it to him, but it had fallen on to the floor.

'Ah yes,' he said, and – she couldn't be certain, of course – but she thought he was disappointed.

'Ah yes, you saw my signature,' he said, flatly. He looked dejected. Mary felt helpless. She turned to Maudie. It was up to her to say something now.

Just then the little warehouse bell tinkled again, and this time it was one of the proprietors who came in, casually, like a client.

'Ah good!' said van Stiegler. 'Coffee,' he called out. Then he turned to Mary. 'Coffee for you too?'

'Oh yes, coffee for us,' said Mary, but she couldn't help wondering who was going to pay for it, and simultaneously she couldn't help noticing the shabbiness of his jacket. Well – they'd see! Meanwhile, he determined to ignore the plate of cakes that was put down with the coffee. And she hoped Maudie would too. She pushed the plate aside as a kind of hint to her, but Maudie leaned across and took a large bun filled with cream.

'Do you mind my asking you something – about your work—?' said Mary.

But Maudie interrupted.

'You are living in Ireland? I mean, you are not just here on a visit?'

There was intimacy and intimacy, and Mary felt nervous in case the young man might resent this question.

'I teach art in a college here,' he said, and he did seem a little surprised, but Mary could see too, that he was not at all displeased. He seemed to settle more comfortably into the conversation.

'It is very good for a while to go to another country,' he said, 'and this country is cheap. I have a flat in the next street to here, and it is very private. If I hang myself from the ceiling, it is all right – nobody knows; nobody cares. That is a good way to live when you paint.'

Mary was prepared to ponder. 'Do you think so?'

Maudie was not prepared to ponder. 'How odd,' she said, shortly, and then she looked at her watch. 'I'll have to go,' she said, inexplicably.

They had finished the coffee. Immediately Mary's thoughts returned to the problem of who was to pay for it. It was a small affair for which to call up all one's spiritual resources, but she felt enormously courageous and determined when she heard herself ask in a loud voice for her bill.

'My bill, please,' she called out, over the sound of spitting coffee on the gas stove.

Johann van Stiegler made no move to ask for his bill, and yet he was buttoning his jacket and folding his newspaper as if to leave too. Would his coffee go on her bill? Mary wondered.

It was all settled, however, in a second. The bill was for two eight-penny coffees, and one bun, and there was no charge for van Stiegler's coffee. He had some understanding with the owners, she supposed. Or perhaps he was not really going to leave then at all?

As they stood up, however, gloved and ready to depart, the young man bowed.

'Perhaps we go the same way?' and they could see he was anxious to be polite.

'Oh, not at all,' they said together, as if he had offered to escort them, and Maudie even laughed openly.

Then there was, of course, another ridiculous situation. Van Stiegler sat down again. Had they been too brusque? Had they hurt his feelings?

Oh, if only he wasn't a foreigner, thought Mary, and she hesitated. Maudie already had her hand on the door.

'I hope I will see some more of your work sometime,' said Mary. It was not a question, merely a compliment.

But van Stiegler sprung to his feet again though.

'Tonight after my classes I am bringing another picture to hang here,' he said. 'You would like to see it? I would be here—' he pulled out a large, old-fashioned watch, '—at ten minutes past nine.'

'Oh, not tonight – I couldn't come back tonight,' said Mary. 'I live in the country, you see,' she said, explaining and excusing herself. 'Another time perhaps? It will be here for how long?'

She wasn't really listening to what he said. She was thinking that he had not asked if Maudie could come. Perhaps it was that, of the two of them, she looked the most likely to buy a picture, whereas Maudie, although in actual fact more likely to do so, looked less so. Or was it that he coupled them so that he thought if one came, both came. Or was it really Maudie he'd like to see again, and that he regarded her as a chaperone? Or was it—?

There was no knowing, however, and so she said goodbye again, and the next minute the little bell had tinkled over the door and they were in the street. In the street they looked at each other.

'Well! if ever there was—' began Maudie, but she didn't get time to finish her sentence. Behind them the little bell tinkled yet again, and their painter was out in the street with them.

'I forgot to give you the address of my flat – it is also my studio,' he said. 'I would be glad to show you my paintings at any time.' He pulled out a notebook and tore out a sheet. 'I will write it down,' he said, concisely. And he did. But when he went to hand it to them, it was Maudie who took it. 'I am nearly always there, except when I am at my classes,' he said. And bowing, he turned and went back into the café.

They dared not laugh until they had walked some distance away, until they turned into the next street in fact.

'Well, I never!' said Maudie, and she handed the paper to Mary.

'Chatham Row,' Mary read, 'number 8.'

'Will you go to see them?' asked Maudie.

Mary felt outraged.

'What do you take me for?' she asked. 'I may be a bit unconventional, but can you see me presenting myself at his place? Would *you* go?'

'Oh, it's different for me,' said Maudie, enigmatically. 'And anyway, it was you he asked. But I see your point – it's a pity. Poor fellow! – he must be very lonely. I wish there was something we could do for him – someone to whom we could introduce him.'

Mary looked at her. It had never occurred to her that he might be lonely! How was it that the obvious always escaped her?

They were in Grafton Street by this time.

'Well, I have some shopping to do. I suppose it's the same with you,' said Maudie. 'I am glad I had that talk with you. We must have another chat soon.'

'Oh yes,' said Mary, over-readily, replying to their adieux though, and not as Maudie thought, to the suggestion of their meeting again! She was anxious all at once to be rid of Maudie.

And yet, as she watched her walk away from her, making her passage quickly and expertly through the crowds in the street, Mary felt a sudden terrible aimlessness descend upon herself like a physical paralysis. She walked along, passing to look in at the shop windows.

It was the evening hour when everyone in the streets was hurrying home, purposeful and intent. Even those who paused to look into the shop windows did so with direction and aim, darting their bright glances keenly, like birds. Their minds were all intent upon substantives; tangibles, while her mind was straying back to the student café, and the strange flower pictures on the walls; to the young man who was so vulnerable in his vanity: the legitimate vanity of his art.

It was so like Maudie to laugh at him. What did she know of an artist's mind? If Maudie had not been with her, it would have been so different. She might, for one thing, have got him to talk about his work, to explain the discrepancy between the loose style of the pictures on the wall and the exact, small sketches he'd been drawing on the margins of the paper.

She might even have taken up his invitation to go and see his paintings. Why had that seemed so unconventional – so laughable? Because of Maudie, that was why.

How ridiculous their scruples would have seemed to the young man. She could only hope he had not guessed them.

She looked up at a clock. Supposing, right now, she were to slip back to the café and suggest that after all she found she would have time for a quick visit to his studio? Or would he have left the café? Better perhaps to call around to the studio? He would surely be back there now!

For a moment she stood debating the arguments for and against going back. Would it seem odd to him? Would he be surprised? But as if it were Maudie who put the questions, she frowned them down and all at once purposeful as anyone in the street, began to go back, headlong, you might say, towards Chatham Street.

At the point where two small streets crossed each other she had to pause, while a team of Guinness's dray-horses turned with difficulty in the narrow cube of the intersection. And, while she waited impatiently, she caught sight of herself in the gilded mirror of a public-house. For a second, the familiar sight gave her a misgiving of her mission, but as the dray-horses moved out of the way, she told herself that her dowdy, lumpish, and unromantic figure vouched for her spiritual integrity. She pulled herself away from the face in the glass and hurried across the street.

Between two lock-up shops, down a short alley – roofed by the second storey of the premises overhead, till it was like a tunnel – was his door. Away at the end of the tunnel the door could clearly be seen even from the middle of the street, for it was painted bright yellow. Odd that she had never seen it in the times she had passed that way. She crossed the street.

Once across the street, she ran down the tunnel, her footsteps echoing loud in her ears. And there on the door, tied to the latchet of the letter-box, was a piece of white cardboard with his name on it. Grabbing the knocker, she gave three clear hammer-strokes on the door.

The little alley was a sort of cul-de-sac; except for the street behind her and the door in front of her, it had no outlet. There was not even a skylight or an aperture of any kind. As for the premises into which the door led, there was no way of telling its size or its extent, or anything at all about it, until the door was opened.

Irresponsibly, she giggled. It was like the mystifying doors in the trunks of trees that beguiled her as a child in fairy-tales and fantasies. Did this door, too, like those fairy doors, lead into rooms of impossible amplitude, or would it be a cramped and poky place?

As she pondered upon what was within, seemingly so mysteriously sealed, she saw that – just as in a fairy-tale – after all there was an aperture. The letter-box had lost its shutter, or lid, and it gaped open, a vacant hole in the wood, reminding her of a sleeping doll whose eyeballs had been poked back in its head, and creating an expression of vacancy and emptiness.

Impulsively, going down on one knee, she peered in through the slit.

At first she could see only segments of the objects within, but by moving her head, she was able to identify things: an unfinished canvas up against the splattered white wainscot, a bicycle-pump flat on the floor, the leg of a table, black iron bed-legs and, to her amusement, dangling down by the leg of the table, dripping their moisture in a pool on the floor, a pair of elongated, grey, wool socks. It was, of course, only possible to see the lower portion of the room, but it seemed enough to infer conclusively that this was indeed a little room in a tree, no bigger than the bulk of the outer trunk, leading nowhere, and – sufficient or no – itself its own end.

There was just one break in the wainscot, where a door ran down to the floor, but this was so narrow and made of roughly-jointed boards, that she took it to be the door of a press. And then, as she started moving, she saw something else, an intricate segment of fine wire spokes. It was a second before she realized it was the wheel of a bicycle.

So, a bicycle, too, lived here, in this little room in a tree-trunk!

Oh, poor young man, poor painter: poor foreigner, inept at finding the good lodgings in a strange city. Her heart went out to him.

It was just then that the boarded door – it couldn't have been a press after all – opened into the room, and she found herself staring at two feet. They were large feet, shoved into unlaced shoes, and they were bare to the white ankles. For, of course, she thought wildly, focusing her thoughts, his socks are washed! But her power to think clearly only lasted an instant. She sprang to her feet.

'Who iss that?' asked a voice. 'Did someone knock?'

It was the voice of the man in the café. But where was she to find a voice with which to reply? And who was she to say what she was? Who – to this stranger – was she?

And if he opened the door, what then? All the thoughts and words that had, like a wind, blown her down this tunnel, subsided suddenly, and she stood, appalled, at where they had brought her.

'Who iss that?' came the voice within, troubled.

Staring at those white feet, thrust into the unlaced shoes, she felt that she would die on the spot if they moved an inch. She turned.

Ahead of her, bright, shining and clear, as if it were at the end of a powerful telescope, was the street. Not caring if her feet were heard, volleying and echoing as if she ran through a mighty drain-pipe, she kept running till she reached the street, kept running even then, jostling surprised shoppers, hitting her ankles off the wheel-knobs of push-cars and prams. Only when she came to the junction of the streets again, did she stop, as in the pub mirror she caught sight again of her familiar face. That face steadied her. How absurd to think that anyone would sinisterly follow this middle-aged woman?

But suppose he had been in the outer room when she knocked! If he had opened the door? What would have happened then? What would she have said? A flush spread over her face. The only true words that she could have uttered were those that had sunk into her mind in the café; put there by Maudie.

'I'm lonely!' That was all she could have said. 'I'm lonely. Are you?'

A deep shame came over her with this admission and, guiltily, she began to walk quickly onward again, towards Grafton Street. If anyone had seen her, there in that dark alleyway! If anyone could have looked into her mind, her heart!

And yet, was it so unnatural? Was it so hard to understand? So unforgiveable?

As she passed the open door of the Carmelite Church she paused. Could she rid herself of her feeling of shame in the dark of the confessional? To the sin-accustomed ears of the wise old fathers her story would be light-weight; a tedious tale of scrupulosity. Was there no one, no one who'd understand?

She had reached Grafton Street once more, and stepped into its crowded thoroughfare. It was only a few minutes since she left it, but in the street the evasion of light had begun. Only the bustle of people, and the activity of traffic, made it seem that it was yet day. Away at the top of the street, in Stephen's Green, to which she turned, although the tops of the trees were still clear, branch for branch, in the last of the light, mist muted the outline of the bushes. If one were to put a hand between the railings now, it would be with a slight shock that the fingers would feel the little branches, like fine bones, under the feathers of mist. And in their secret nests the smaller birds were making faint avowals in the last of the day. It was the time at which she used to meet Richard.

Oh Richard! she cried, almost out loud, as she walked along by the railings to where the car was parked. Oh Richard! it's you I want.

And as she cried out, her mind presented him to her, as she so often saw him, coming towards her: tall, handsome, and with his curious air of apartness from those around him. He had his hat in his hand, down by his side, as on a summer day he might trail a hand in water from the side of a boat. She wanted to preserve that picture of him forever in an image, and only as she struggled to hold on to it did she realize there was no urgency in the search. She had a sense of having all the time in the world to look and look and look at him. That was the very way he used to come to meet her – indolently trailing the old felt hat, glad to be done with the day; and when they got nearer to each other she used to take such joy in his unsmiling face, with its happiness integral to it in all its features. It was the first time in the two years he'd been gone from her that she'd seen his face.

Not till she had taken out the key of the car, and gone straight around to the driver's side, not stupidly, as so often, to the passenger seat – not till then did she realize what she had achieved. Yet she had no more than got back her rights. No more. It was not a subject for amazement. By what means exactly had she got them back though – in that little café? That was the wonder.

JOHN McGAHERN

BANK HOLIDAY

IT HAD BEEN unusual weather, hot for weeks, and the white morning mist above the river, making ghostly the figures crossing the metal bridge, seemed a certain promise that the good weather was going to last beyond the holiday. All week in the Department he had heard the girls talking of going down the country, of the ocean, and the dances in the carnival marquees. Already, across the river, queues were forming for the buses that went to the sea – Howth, Dollymount, Malahide. He, Patrick McDonough, had no plans for the holiday, other than to walk about the city, or maybe to go out into the mountains later. He felt a certain elation of being loose in the morning, as if in space. The solid sound of his walking shoes on the pavement seemed to belong to someone else, to be going elsewhere.

A year ago he had spent this holiday in the country, among the rooms and fields and stone walls he had grown up with, as he had spent it every year going back many years. His mother was still living, his father had died the previous February. The cruellest thing about that last holiday was to watch her come into the house speaking to his father of something she had noticed in the yard – a big bullfinch feeding on the wild strawberries of the bank, rust spreading in the iron of one of the sheds – and then to see her realize in the midst of speech that her old partner of the guaranteed responses was no longer there. They had been close. His father had continued to indulge her once great good looks long after they had disappeared.

That last holiday he had asked his mother to come and live with him in the city, but she had refused without giving it serious thought. 'I'd be only in the way up there. I could never fit in with their ways now.' He had gone down to see her as often as he was able to after that, which was most weekends, and had paid a local woman to look in on her every day. Soon he saw that his visits no longer excited her. She had even lost interest in most of the things around her, and whenever that interest briefly gleamed she turned not to him but to his dead father. When pneumonia took her in a couple of days just before Christmas, and her body was put down beside her husband's in Aughawillian churchyard, he was almost glad. The natural wind now blew directly on him.

He sold the house and lands. The land had been rich enough to send him away to college, not rich enough to bring him back other than on holiday, and now this holiday was the first such in years that he had nowhere in particular to go, no one special to see, nothing much to do. As well as the dangerous elation this sense of freedom gave, he looked on it with some of the cold apprehension of an experiment.

Instead of continuing on down the quays, he crossed to the low granite wall above the river, and stayed a long time staring down through the vaporous mist at the frenzy and filth of the low tide. He could have stood mindlessly there for most of the morning but he pulled himself away and continued on down the quays until he turned into Webb's Bookshop.

The floor in Webb's had been freshly sprinkled and swept, but it was dark within after the river light. He went from stack to stack among the second-hands until he came on a book that caught his interest, and he began to read. He stood there a long time until he was disturbed by the brown-overalled manager speaking by his side.

'Would you be interested in buying the book, sir? We could do something perhaps about the price. The books in this stack have been here a long time.' He held a duster in his hand, some feathers tied round the tip of a cane.

'I was just looking.'

The manager moved away, flicking the feathers along a row of spines in a gesture of annoyance. The spell was ended, but it was fair enough; the shop had to sell books, and he knew that if he bought the book it was unlikely that he would ever give it the same attention again. He moved to the next stack, not wanting to appear driven from the shop. He pretended to inspect other volumes. He lifted and put down *The Wooing of Elizabeth McCrum*, examining other books cursorily, all the time moving towards the door. It was no longer pleasant to remain. He tried to ignore the manager's stare as he went out, to find himself in blinding sunshine on the pavement. The mist had completely lifted. The day was uncomfortably hot. His early excitement and sense of freedom had disappeared.

Afterwards he was to go over the little incident in the bookshop. If it had not happened would he have just ventured again out into the day, found the city too hot for walking, taken a train to Bray as he thought he might and walked all day in the mountains until he was dog-tired and hungry? Or was this sort of let-down the inescapable end of the kind of elation he had felt walking to the river in the early morning? He would never know. What he did know was that once outside the bookshop he no longer felt like going anywhere and he started to retrace his steps back to where he lived, buying a newspaper on the way. When he opened the door a telegram was lying on the floor of the hallway.

It was signed 'Mary Kelleher', a name he didn't know. It seemed that a very old friend, James White, who worked for the Tourist Board in New York, had given her his name. There was a number to call.

He put it aside to sit and read through the newspaper, but he knew by the continuing awareness of the telegram on the table that he would call. He was now too restless to want to remain alone.

James White and he had met when they were both young civil servants. White slightly the older – though they both seemed the same age now – the better read, the more forthright, the more sociable. They met at eight-thirty on the Friday night of every week for several years, the evening interrupted only by holidays and illnesses, proof against girlfriends, and later wives, ended only by White's transfer abroad. They met in bars, changing only when they became known to the barmen or regulars, and in danger of losing their anonymity. They talked about ideas, books, 'the human situation', and 'reality and consciousness' often surfaced with the second or third pint. Now he could hardly remember a sentence from those hundreds of evenings. What he did remember was a barman's face, white hair drawn over baldness, an avid follower of Christy Ring; a clock, a spiral iron staircase to the Gents, the cold of marble on the wristbone, footsteps passing outside in summer, the sound of heavy rain falling before closing time. The few times they had met in recent years they had both spoken of nothing but people and happenings, as if those early meetings were some deep embarrassment; that they had leaned on them too heavily once and were now like lost strength.

He rang. The number was that of a small hotel on the

quays. Mary Kelleher answered. He invited her to lunch and they arranged to meet in the hotel foyer. He walked to the hotel, and as he walked he felt again the heady, unreal feeling of moving in an unblemished morning, though it was now past midday.

When she rose to meet him in the foyer, he saw that she was as tall as he. A red kerchief with polka dots bound her blonde hair. She was too strong boned to be beautiful but her face and skin glowed. They talked about James White. She had met him at a party in New York. 'He said that I must meet you if I was going to Dublin. I was about to check out of the hotel when you rang.' She had relations in Dundalk that she intended to look up and Trinity College had manuscripts she wanted to see. They walked up Dame Street and round by the Trinity Railings to the restaurant he had picked in Lincoln Place. She was from Mount Vernon, New York, but had been living in Chicago, finishing her doctorate in medieval poetry at the University of Chicago. There were very pale hairs on the brown skin of her legs and her leather sandals slapped as she walked. When she turned her face to his, he could see a silver locket below the line of the cotton dress.

Bernardo's door was open on to the street, and all but two of the tables were empty.

'Everybody's out of town for the holiday. We have the place to ourselves.' They were given a table for four just inside the door. They ordered the same things, melon with Parma ham, veal Milanese, a carafe of chilled white wine. He urged her to have more, to try the raspberries in season, the cream cake, but she ate carefully and would not be persuaded.

'Do you come here often?' she asked.

'Often enough. I work near here, round the corner, in Kildare Street. An old civil servant.'

'You don't look the part at all, but James White did say you worked in the civil service. He said you were quite high up,' she smiled teasingly. 'What do you do?'

'Nothing as exciting as medieval poetry. I deal in law, industrial law in particular.'

'I could imagine that to be quite exciting.'

'Interesting maybe, but mostly it's a job – like any other.'

'Do you live in the city, or outside?'

'Very near here. I can walk most places, even walk to work.' And when he saw her hesitate, as if she wanted to ask something and did not think it right, he added, 'I have a flat. I live by myself there, though I was married once.'

'Are you divorced? Or am I allowed to ask that?'

'Of course you are. Divorce isn't allowed in this country. We are separated. For something like twenty years now we haven't laid eyes on one another. And you? Do you have a husband or friend?' he changed the subject.

'Yes. Someone I met at college, but we have agreed to separate for a time.'

There was no silence or unease. Their interest in one another already far outran their knowledge. She offered to split the bill but he refused.

'Thanks for the lunch, the company,' she said as they faced one another outside the restaurant.

'It was a pleasure,' and then he hesitated and asked, 'What are you doing for the afternoon?' not wanting to see this flow that was between them checked, though he knew to follow it was hardly wise.

'I was going to check tomorrow's trains to Dundalk.'

'We could do that at Westland Row around the corner. I was wondering if you'd be interested in going out to the sea where the world and its mother is in this weather?'

'I'd love to,' she said simply.

It was with a certain relief that he paid the taxi at the Bull Wall. Lately the luxury and convenience of a taxi had become for him the privilege of being no longer young, of being cut off from the people he had come from, and this was exasperated by the glowing young woman by his side, her eager responses to each view he pointed out, including the wired-down palms along the front.

'They look so funny. Why is it done?'

'It's simple. So that they will not be blown away in storms. They are not natural to this climate.'

He took off his tie and jacket as they crossed the planks of the wooden bridge, its legs long and stork-like in the retreated tide. The rocks that sloped down to the sea from the Wall were crowded with people, most of them in bathing costumes, reading, listening to transistors, playing cards, staring out to sea, where three tankers appeared to be nailed down in the milky distance. The caps of the stronger swimmers bobbed far out. Others floated on their backs close to the rocks, crawled in sharp bursts, breast-stroked heavily up and down a parallel line, blowing like walruses as they trod water.

'I used to swim off these rocks once. I liked going in off the rocks because I've always hated getting sand between my toes. Those lower rocks get covered at full tide. You can see the tidal line by the colour.'

'Don't you swim any more?'

'I haven't in years.'

'If I had a costume I wouldn't mind going in.'

'I think you'd find it cold.'

She told him of how she used to go out to the ocean at the Hamptons with her father, her four brothers, their black sheep Uncle John who had made a fortune in scrap metal and was extremely lecherous. She laughed as she recounted one of Uncle John's adventures with an English lady.

When they reached the end of the Wall, they went down to the Strand, but it was so crowded that they had to pick their way through. They moved out to where there were fewer people along the tide's edge. It was there that she decided to wade in the water, and he offered to hold her sandals. As he walked with her sandals, a phrase came without warning from the book he had been reading in Webb's. 'What is he doing with his life, we say, and our judgement makes up for the failure to realize sympathetically the natural process of living.' He must indeed be atrophied if a casual phrase could have more presence for him than this beautiful young woman, and the sea, and the day. The dark blue mass of Howth faced the motionless ships on the horizon, seemed to be even pushing them back.

'Oh, it's cold,' she shivered as she came out of the water, and reached for her sandals.

'Even in heatwaves the sea is cold in Ireland. That's Howth ahead – where Maud Gonne waited at the station as Pallas Athena.' He reached for his role as tourist guide.

'I know that line,' she said and quoted the verse. 'Has all that gone from Dublin?'

'In what way?'

'Are there . . . poets . . . still?'

'Are there poets?' he laughed out loud. 'They say the standing army of poets never falls below ten thousand in this unfortunate country.'

'Why unfortunate?' she said quickly.

'They create no wealth. They are greedy and demanding. They hold themselves in very high opinion. Ten centuries ago there was a national convocation, an attempt to limit their powers and numbers.'

'Wasn't it called *Drum* something?'

'*Drum Ceat*,' he added, made uneasy by his own attack.

'But don't you feel that they have a function – beyond wealth?' she pursued.

'What function?'

'That they sing the tired rowers to the hidden shore?'

'Not in the numbers we possess here, one singing down the other. But maybe I'm unkind. There are a few.'

'Are these poets to be seen?'

'They can't even be hidden. Tomorrow evening I could show you some of the pubs they frequent. Would you like that?'

'I'd like that very much,' she said, and took his hand. A whole day was secured. The crowds hadn't started to head home yet, and they travelled back to the city on a nearly empty bus.

'What will you do for the rest of the evening?'

'There's some work I may look at. And you? What will you do?'

'I think I'll rest. Unpack, read a bit,' she smiled as she raised her hand.

He walked slowly back, everything changed by the petty confrontation in Webb's, the return to the flat, the telegram in the hallway. If he had not come back, she would be in Dundalk by now, and he would be thinking about finding a hotel for the night somewhere round Rathdrum. In the flat, he went through notes that he had made in preparation for a meeting he had with the Minister the coming week. They concerned an obscure section of the Industries Act. Though they were notes he had made himself he found them extremely tedious, and there came on him a restlessness like that which sometimes heralds illness. He felt like going out to a cinema or bar, but knew that what he really wanted to do was to ring Mary Kelleher. If he had learned anything over the years it was the habit of discipline. Tomorrow would bring itself. He would wait for it if necessary with his mind resolutely fixed on its own blankness, as a person prays after fervour has died.

'Section 13, paragraph 4, states clearly that in the event of confrontation or disagreement . . .' he began to write.

The dress of forest green she was wearing when she came down to the lobby the next evening caught his breath; it was shirtwaisted, belling out. A blue ribbon hung casually from her fair hair behind.

'You look marvellous.'

The Sunday streets were empty, and the stones gave out a dull heat. They walked slowly, loitering at some shop windows. The doors of all the bars were open, O'Neills and the International and the Olde Stand, but they were mostly empty within. There was a sense of a cool dark waiting in Mooney's, a barman arranging ashtrays on the marble. They ordered an assortment of sandwiches. It was pleasant to sit in the comparative darkness, and eat and sip and watch the street, and to hear in the silence footsteps going up and down Grafton Street.

It was into this quiet flow of the evening that the poet came, a large man, agitated, without jacket, the shirt open, his thumbs hooked in braces that held up a pair of sagging trousers, a brown hat pushed far back on his head. Coughing harshly and pushing the chair around, he sat at the next table.

'Don't look around,' McDonough leaned forward to say.
'Why?'
'He'll join us if we catch his eye.'
'Who is he?'

'A poet.'

'He doesn't look like one.'

'That should be in his favour. All the younger clerks that work in my place nowadays look like poets. He is the best we have. He's the star of the place across the road. He's practically resident there. He must have been thrown out.'

The potboy in his short white coat came over to the poet's table and waited impassively for the order.

'A Powers,' the order came in a hoarse, rhythmical voice. 'A large Powers and a pint of Bass.'

There was more sharp coughing, a scraping of feet, a sigh, muttering, a word that could have been a prayer or a curse. His agitated presence had more the sound of a crowd than the single person sitting in a chair. After the potboy brought the drinks and was paid, the poet swung one leg vigorously over the other, and with folded arms faced away towards the empty doorway. Then, as suddenly, he was standing in front of them. He had his hand out. There were coins in the hand.

'McDonough,' he called hoarsely, thrusting his palm forward. 'Will you get me a packet of Ci-tanes from across the road?' he mispronounced the brand of French cigarettes so violently that his meaning was far from clear.

'You mean the cigarettes?'

'Ci-tanes,' he called hoarsely again. 'French fags. Twenty. I'm giving you the money.'

'Why don't you get them here?'

'They don't have them here.'

'Why don't you hop across yourself?'

'I'm barred,' he said dramatically. 'They're a crowd of ignorant, bloody apes over there.'

'All right. I'll get them for you.' He took the coins but instead of rising and crossing the road he called the potboy.

'Would you cross the road for twenty Gitanes for me,

Jimmy? I'd cross myself but I'm with company,' and he added a large tip of his own to the coins the poet had handed over.

'It's against the rules, sir.'

'I know, but I'd consider it a favour,' and they both looked towards the barman behind the counter, who had been following every word and move of the confrontation. The barman nodded that it was all right, and immediately bent his head down to whatever he was doing beneath the level of the counter, as if to disown his acquiescence.

Jimmy crossed, was back in a moment with the blue packet.

'You're a cute hoar, McDonough. You're a mediocrity. It's no wonder you get on so well in the world,' the poet burst out in a wild fury as he was handed the packet, and he finished his drinks in a few violent gulps, and stalked out, muttering and coughing.

'That's just incredible,' she said.

'Why?'

'You buy the man his cigarettes, and then get blown out of it. I don't understand it.'

'It wasn't the cigarettes he wanted.'

'Well, what did he want?'

'Reassurance maybe, that he still had power, was loved and wanted after having been turfed out across the way. I slithered round it by getting Jimmy here to go over. That's why I was lambasted. He must have done something outrageous to have been barred. He's a tin god there. Maybe I should have gone over after all.'

'Why didn't you?'

'Vanity. I didn't want to be his messenger boy. He could go and inflate his great mouse of an ego somewhere else. To hell with him. He's always trouble.' She listened in silence as he ended. 'Wouldn't it be pleasant to be able to throw people their bones and forget it?'

'You might have to spend an awful lot of time throwing bones if the word got around,' she smiled as she sipped her glass of cider.

'Now that you've seen the star, do you still wish to cross the road and look in on the other pub?'

'I'm not sure. What else could we do?'

'We could go back to my place.'

'I'd like that, I'd much prefer to see how you live.'

'Why don't we look in across the road, have one drink if it's not too crowded,' and he added some coins to the change still on the table. 'It was very nice of them to cross for the Gitanes. They're not supposed to leave their own premises.'

The door of the bar across the way was not open, and when he pushed it a roar met them like heat. The bar was small and jammed. A red-and-blue tint from a stained glass window at the back mixed weirdly with the white lights of the bar, the light of evening from the high windows. A small fan circled helplessly overhead, its original white or yellow long turned to ochre by cigarette smoke. Hands proffered coins and notes across shoulders to the barmen behind the horseshoe counter. Pints and spirit glasses were somehow eased from hand to hand across the three-deep line of shoulders at the counter the way children that get weak are taken out of a crowd. The three barmen were so busy that they seemed to dance.

'What do you think?' he asked.

'I think we'll forget it.'

'I always feel a bit apprehensive going in there,' he admitted once they were out on the street again.

'I know. Those places are the same everywhere. For a moment I thought I was in New York at the Cedar Bar.'

'What makes them the same?'

'I don't know. Mania, egotism, vanity, aggression ... people searching madly in a crowd for something that's never to be found in crowds.'

She was so lovely in the evening that he felt himself leaning towards her. He did not like the weakness. 'I find myself falling increasingly into an unattractive puzzlement,' he said, 'mulling over that old, useless chestnut. What *is* life?'

'It's the fact of being alive, I suppose, a duration of time, as the scholars would say,' and she smiled teasingly. 'Puzzling out what it is must be part of it as well.'

'You're too young and beautiful to be so wise.'

'That sounds a bit patronizing.'

'That's the last thing I meant it to be.'

He showed her the rooms, the large living-room with the oak table and worn red carpet, the brass fender, the white marble of the fireplace, the kitchen, the two bedrooms. He watched her go over the place, lift the sea shell off the mantelpiece, replace it differently.

'It's a lovely flat,' she said, 'though Spartan to my taste.'

'I bought the place three years ago. I disliked the idea of owning anything at first, but now I'm glad to have it. Now, would you like a drink, or perhaps some tea?'

'I'd love some tea.'

When he returned he found her thumbing through books in the weakening light.

'Do you have any of the poet's work?'

'You can have a present of this, if you like.' He reached and took a brown volume from the shelf.

'I see it's even signed,' she said as she leafed through the volume. 'For Patrick McDonough, With love', and she began to laugh.

'I helped him with something once. I doubt if he'd sign it with much love this evening.'

'Thanks,' she said as she closed the volume and placed it in her handbag. 'I'll return it. It wouldn't be right to keep it.' After several minutes of silence, she asked, 'When do you have to go back to your office?'

'Not till Tuesday. Tomorrow is a Bank Holiday.'

'And on Tuesday what do you do?'

'Routine. The Department really runs itself, though many of us think of ourselves as indispensable. In the afternoon I have to brief the Minister.'

'On what, may I ask?'

'A section of the Industries Act.'

'What is the Minister like?'

'He's all right. An opportunist, I suppose. He has energy, certainly, and the terrible Irish gift of familiarity. He first came to the fore by putting bars on the back of a lorry. He did handstands and somersaults before and after speeches, to the delight of the small towns and villages. Miss Democracy thought he was wonderful and voted him in top of the poll. He's more statesmanlike now of course.'

'You don't sound as if you like him very much.'

'We're stuck with one another.'

'Were you upset when your marriage failed?' she changed.

'Naturally. In the end, there was no chance. We couldn't be in the same room together for more than a couple of minutes without fighting. I could never figure out how the fights started, but they always did.'

'Did you meet anyone else?'

'Nothing that lasted. I worked. I visited my parents until they died. Those sort of pieties are sometimes substitutes for life in this country – or life itself. We're back to the old subject and I'm talking too much.'

'No. I'm asking too many questions.'

'What'll you do now that you have your doctorate?'

'Teach. Write. Wait on tables. I don't know.'

'And your husband or friend?'

'Husband,' she said. 'We were married but it's finished. We were too young.'

'Would you like more tea, or for me to walk you back to the Clarence? . . . Or would you like to spend the night here?'

She paused for what seemed an age, and yet it could not have been more than a couple of moments.

'I'd like to spend the night here.'

He did not know how tense his waiting had been until he felt the release her words gave. It was as if blank doors had slid back and he was being allowed again into the mystery of a perpetual morning, a morning without blemish. He knew it by now to be an old con trick of nature, and that it never failed, only deepened the irony and the mystery. 'I'll be able to show you the city tomorrow. You can check out of your hotel then if you wish. And there are the two rooms . . .' he was beginning to say when she came into his arms and sealed his lips.

As he waited for her, the poet's sudden angry accusation came back. Such accusations usually came to rankle and remain long after praise had failed, but not this evening. He turned it over as he might a problem that there seemed no way round, and let it drop. If it was true, there was very little that could be done about it now. It was in turn replaced by the phrase that had come to him earlier by the sea's edge, and had he not seen love in the person of his old mother reduced to noticing things about a farmyard?

'I hope you're not puzzling over something like "life" again,' a teasing call came from the bedroom.

'No. Not this time.' He rose to join her.

In the morning they had coffee and toast in the sunlit kitchen with the expectation of the whole day waiting on them. Then they walked in the empty streets of the city, looked through the Green before going to the hotel to bring her things back to the flat.

The following days were so easy that the only anxiety could be its total absence. The days were heightened by the luxury and pleasure of private evenings, the meals she cooked that were perfection, the good wine he bought, the flowers; desire that was never turned aside or exasperated by difficulty.

At the end of the holiday, he had to go back to the office, and she put off the Dundalk visit and began to go to the Trinity Library. Many people were not back in the office, and he was able to work without interruption for the whole of the first morning. What he had to do was to isolate the relevant parts of the section and reduce them to a few simple sentences.

At the afternoon meeting the Minister was the more nervous. He was tall and muscular, small blue eyes and thick red hair, fifteen years the younger man, with a habit of continually touching anybody close to him that told of the large family he grew up in. They went over and over the few sentences he had prepared until the Minister had them by note. He was appearing on television that night and was extremely apprehensive.

'Good man,' he grasped McDonough's shoulder with relief when they finished. 'One of these evenings before long you must come out and have a bite with us and meet the hen and chickens.'

'I'll be glad to. And good luck on the TV. I'll be watching.'

'I'll need all the luck I can get. That bitch of an interviewer hates my guts.'

They watched the television debate together in the flat that evening. The Minister had reason to be apprehensive. He was under attack from the beginning but bludgeoning his way. As he watched, McDonough wondered if his work had been necessary at all. He could hardly discern his few sentences beneath the weight of the Minister's phrases. 'I emphatically state . . . I categorically deny . . . I say without any equivocation whatsoever . . . Having consulted the best available opinions in the matter,' (which were presumably McDonough's own).

'What did you think?' he asked when he switched off the set.

'He was almost touching,' she said carefully. 'Amateurish maybe. His counterpart in the States might be no better, but he certainly would have to be more polished.'

'He was good at handstands and somersaults once,' he said, surprised at his own sense of disappointment. 'I've become almost fond of him. Sometimes I wish we had better people. They'll all tell him he did powerfully. What'll we do? Would you like to go for a quick walk?'

'Why don't we,' she reached for her cardigan.

Two days later she went to Dundalk, and it wasn't certain how long she intended to remain there. 'I guess I've come so far that they'll expect me to stay over the weekend.'

'You must please yourself. You have a key. I'll not be going anywhere.'

They had come together so easily that the days together seemed like a marriage without any of the apprehension or drama of a ceremony.

When he was young he had desired too much, wanted too much, dreaded and feared too much, and so spread his own fear. Now that he was close to losing everything – was in the direct path of the wind – it was little short of amazing that he should come on this extraordinary breathing space.

Almost in disbelief he went back in reflection to the one love of his life, a love that was pure suffering. In a hotel bedroom in another city, unable to sleep by her side, he had risen and dressed. He had paused before leaving the room to gaze on the even breathing of her sleep. All that breath had to do was frame one word, and a whole world of happiness would be given, but it was forever withheld. He had walked the morning streets until circling back to the hotel he came on a market that was just opening and bought a large bunch of grapes. The grapes were very small and turning yellow and still damp, and were of incredible sweetness. She was just waking when he came back into the room and had not missed him. They ate the grapes on the coverlid and each time she lifted the small bunches to her mouth he remembered the dark of her armpits. He ached to touch her but everything seemed to be so fragile between them that he was afraid to even stir. It seemed that any small movement now could bring calamity. Then, laughing, she blew grape seeds in his face and, reaching out her arms, drew him down. She had wanted their last day together to be pleasant. She was marrying another man. Later he remembered running between airport gates looking for flights that had all departed.

It was eerie to set down those days beside the days that had just gone by, call them by the same name. How slowly those days had moved, as if waiting for something to begin now all the days were speeding, slipping silently by like air.

Two evenings later, when he let himself into the flat and found Mary Kelleher there, it was as if she had never been away.

'You didn't expect me back so soon?'

'I thought you'd still be in Dundalk, but I'm glad. I'm delighted.' He took her in his arms.

'I had as much of Dundalk as I wanted, and I missed you.'

'How did it go?'

'It was all right. The cousins were nice. They had a small house, crammed with things – religious pictures, furniture, photos. There was hardly place to move. Everything they did was so careful, so measured out. After a while I felt I could hardly breathe. They did everything they possibly could to make me welcome. I read the poems at last,' she put the book with the brown cover on the table. 'I read them again on the train coming back. I loved them.'

'I've long suspected that those very pure love sonnets are all addressed to himself,' McDonough said. 'That was how the "ignorant bloody apes and mediocrities" could be all short-circuited.'

'Some are very funny.'

'I'm so glad you liked them. I've lived with some of them for years. Would you like to go out to eat? Say, to Bernardo's?' he asked.

'I'd much prefer to say home. I've already looked in the fridge. We can rustle something up.'

That weekend they went together for the long walk in the mountains that he had intended to take the day they met. They stopped for a drink and sandwiches in a pub near Blessington just before two o'clock, and there they decided to press on to Rathdrum and stay the night in the hotel rather than turn back into the city.

It was over dinner in the near empty hotel dining-room that he asked if she would consider marrying him. 'There's much against it. I am fifty. You would have to try to settle here, where you'll be a stranger,' and he went on to say that what he had already was more than he ever expected, that he was content to let it be, but if she wanted more then it was there.

'I thought that you couldn't be married here,' her tone was affectionate.

'I meant it in everything but name, and even that can be arranged if you want it enough.'

'How?'

'With money. An outside divorce. The marriage in some other country. The States, for instance.'

'Can't you see that I already love you? That it doesn't matter? I was half-teasing. You looked so serious.'

'I am serious. I want it to be clear.'

'It is clear and I am glad – and very grateful.'

They agreed that she would spend one week longer here in Dublin than she had planned. At Christmas he would go to New York for a week. She would have obtained her doctorate by then. James White would be surprised. There were no serious complications in sight. They were so tired and happy that it was as if they were already in possession of endless quantities of time and money.

MIKE McCORMACK

THE TERMS

ON THE VERY evening I burned down the left wing of our house my father told me that he hated me. He just stood there in the shadow of the gutted roof thumbing a shell into the rifle, making no bones about it nor putting a tooth on it in any way, just telling me quietly and for the last time that everything about me made him sick, everything: the massive dome of my head with its lank fringe, my useless legs and piping voice – most of all the lack of shame and outrage in my heart. He told me again that all the cruelty and misshapen ugliness of the world was summed up in my body and that he could not suffer it a moment longer. Then he told me that he was going to kill me. Frankly this wasn't news to either of us. Somehow we seemed to have always known that our relationship would come to this; it had been fated from the beginning to end in some swift settlement of accounts, some bloody reckoning. Putting it another way, neither our house nor our world was big enough for two people such as us.

Lately however, and for some reason I could not fathom, I had begun to dream of something else. My sleeping hours had been filled of late with shapeless images of truce and acceptance, compromises, it is true, which fell a long way short of love and redemption but nevertheless something to be getting on with. However, when I saw my father thumbing home that shell I realized that he knew nothing of my dreams.

'I'm going to shoot you stone dead,' he said evenly. 'And what's more, I'm going to shoot you in the back.'

'It's not going to be a fair fight then. I don't have any weapons to hand.'

'I'm going to give you a fighting chance,' he said. 'You're going to get a fifty-yard start over open ground and I have only one shot. If you make it don't come back. Here's two hundred and fifty pounds to help you make a start in the world just in case. Invest it wisely. I'd recommend government bonds.'

He handed me a wad of notes and I made some quick calculations. Normally my father was an excellent shot. In clear light I had seen him drop fleeing rabbits at one hundred yards. Now, however, there were other factors to consider. It was late evening and the autumn sun was well in decline. Shadows crawled everywhere and gave shapes and profiles an enormity they did not truly possess. Also I could see that my father's temper had begun to smoulder; little things gave him away. A tremor had entered into his white-knuckled hand as he gripped the rifle and a bead of sweat had broken out under his nose. Already I was beginning to fancy my chances but I still wanted further adjustments to be on the safe side.

'How about a head shot?' I said. 'You're always telling me that my head is too big for my shoulders.'

'Only at forty yards, beyond that whitethorn.'

'OK.'

'Plus ninety quid.'

'That's down to four pound a yard. It started out at five.'

'That's the law of diminishing returns. Take it or leave it.'

I thumbed the notes of the wad and handed them over. 'How do I know you'll only take the one shot?'

'One is all I'll need. Besides, I've only got one shell in the breech and if I have to reload you'll have gained another twenty-five yards. At that distance you'll be well in the clear.'

'What happens if I only get wounded? Suppose I take it in the lung and lie there bleeding to death?'

'Then I will leave you there and the crows will make short work of you. I'll walk out every day for as long as it takes and see how your death is progressing. On the day of your death I'll dump a bag of lime over you and within two weeks there won't be a trace of you except for a small, damp pile of chalk in the middle of that field.'

'A bag of lime isn't much of a memorial.'

'You're not much of a son.'

'Suppose I make a miraculous recovery and wake up to find that you have come and stolen my fortune? What then?'

'That won't happen. Whatever else I am I'm not a thief.'

'You won't try and profit from my death? A young, smooth body like mine would fetch a fair penny from research institutes or on the organ donor market. It would have considerable freak value. You might take off to Latin America with a mistress.'

'No, there will be no profiteering. This is a matter of principle not profit. Besides, there's not much of you in it and I'd prefer you to go to hell all in one piece.'

'I'm glad. I don't fancy the idea of some clueless medical student with a hangover poking around in my guts. The thought of it alone would put me off my stride. Nevertheless, you'll have a lot of explaining to do.'

'I'll tell everyone that you set fire to the house and took off in shame and fright. I'll dissuade any search party by telling them that you know every one of these hills and forests and that you will probably return in your own good time. I'll tell them that you were depressed lately on account of your condition.'

'That's a dirty lie. I've never once been depressed by what I am.'

'*You* haven't but *I* have. Every time I look at you I sink deeper into misery and despair. Right now I'm so low that if I sank any lower I'd disappear into the ground.'

By now the sun was a heavy rind over the hills and the earth glowered in shadow. The terms had been set out and I could think of nothing else I wanted to add to them. I was very calm and confident. I believed that at that moment I possessed every piece of worthwhile wisdom and knowledge in the entire world, every axiom and formula and instruction that was going to enable me to live longer. Nevertheless I wondered, did my father have any parting words to send me on my way?

'You're not going to wish me good luck or anything?'

'There's no point in wasting fortune on a dead man.'

'Then I guess I'll be on my way.'

'We seem to have covered everything.'

I jogged out to the starting post, moving at a steady lope, conserving energy. The ground was even and the going firm, a wide stretch of pasture sloping away from the gable of our house to a downhill finish running into the conifer plantation at its furthest edge, about one hundred yards distant. I had no worries that my father would cheat and shoot me in the back within the agreed range. This was his game and he had defined the terms and he would honour them with that vain integrity that only the truly wretched possess.

Ten yards from the whitethorn I burst into a sprint, running in a sharp zigzag from left to right and rolling my head. I passed the bush and veered wildly into its shadow, putting it between my father and myself. Ten yards beyond the bush and I was making good ground, breathing evenly and almost in the safety zone. Then there was a massive explosion in my head, a sunburst of white light and I was cast up into the air as if by a giant hand, hurtling forward almost on the verge of flight. I pitched through the gloom like a missile and then all was darkness.

Jesus, I had to hand it to the little runt, he wasn't going to make it easy for me. There he was, running faster than I would have thought possible on those useless little legs of his and jogging that massive head from side to side as if it were some sort of beach ball.

I knew the moment I lifted the gun to my shoulder that I'd been hoodwinked. The little bastard had kept me talking just long enough for the sun to disappear beyond the hills. His head was nothing more than a blur between the ridged walls of the gunsights and he was darting from side to side, shortening and lengthening each burst at random. He was now abreast of the bush and he suddenly veered behind it and disappeared from sight. The canny bastard had put the bush between us and, with the field dropping away behind it, he would now never emerge into the open. I would have to shoot through the tree. I saw a gap in the foliage and sighted through it, waiting for his head to bob into the open space. When it did, filling the bottom of the space, I waited a split instant before the rifle boomed and recoiled heavily in my shoulder. I saw his small body come hurtling sideways out of the silhouette, swimming through the air before crashing to the ground and tumbling head over heels in an untidy mess of arms and legs. And I knew then that it was all over; I knew that my son and only child, Edward Coon the second, was dead.

*

Edward was neither dead nor seriously wounded, he was just out cold with barely a scratch on him. The bullet had grazed the top of his head, parting his thick hair with a terrific red lesion which cut through to the bone of his skull. He just lay there on his back breathing lightly as if he had laid down for a nap.

I saw straight away that his condition placed him outside the terms of our agreement. He was neither dead nor seriously wounded but the danger now was that he might wake in a matter of hours and wander off into the world as an imbecile with neither wit nor memory, easy prey for thieves and malefactors. This was not what we had settled on. I wanted him either dead or alive, not queering up creation further as an idiot.

I picked him up and turned to the house. His head lolled heavily off my elbow and a thin rivulet of blood seeped through his hair. His tongue lolled thickly from his mouth. As I gazed upon him I saw for the umpteenth time how everything rank and misshapen in the world was summed up in this small bundle of flesh and bone. This child of mine seemed the very distillate of all the world's cruelty and malice. But beneath my disgust there welled also a deeper, more unspeakable feeling. It rose through my heart and leaked into my throat, swelling it and threatening to choke me. It had the same intractable presence as the rifle which lay across my son's chest.

For the first time in my life I recognized clearly that everything in my son which repulsed me was nothing more than my own mirror image.

I woke with a brutal headache; some implacable demon was working in my skull with a lump hammer. My room, a horrid prospect, smelled of charred timber and petrol. Shafts of light spilled through the shattered roof, settling in the room like converged lances. I walked through the ruined hallway and into the kitchen clutching my head in my hands. My father sat at the table cleaning the rifle, yanking a pull through from the barrel.

'You don't look like God and you're not forking stiffs into a furnace. What happened?'

'I creased your skull and you fell unconscious.'

'And you took pity on me?'

'No, I just honoured the terms of our agreement. Have a drink, welcome home so to speak.' He pushed a bottle of whiskey across the table to me.

'No thanks, you know well I'm only a minor.'

'Suit yourself. I would have thought that any man who had come within a hair's breadth of hell would want to celebrate his deliverance.'

'I'm not in the mood for festivities, I just want to get my head together.'

I pulled up a chair and watched him cleaning the gun. No matter how many times I had seen him do this simple task, the way he worked those stubby fingers of his still enchanted me. The guile and seamless grace of his movements. I had often reflected that somewhere in him there was a craftsman howling to get out, someone with patience and poor eyesight who worked with precious materials and terrifying degrees of accuracy. He laid down the rifle suddenly and stared into space for a long moment.

'We can't go on like this,' he said finally. 'It's nothing personal but this has got to end. People like you and me have no place any more in the world, Edward. We'd be better off dead.'

'Speak for yourself.'

'That's what I'm doing. I am so lost, so lost. It's a matter of scale, I think. We're told every day that the world is getting smaller and smaller and that distances are narrowing down, bringing the peoples of the world together in harmony. But for people like you and me it just gets bigger and bigger until we've dropped right through the meshes of it and into this pit. We have no life any more.'

'Was it ever any other way?'

'Yes,' he said vehemently. 'Yes, it was. There was a time when we had status and valuable skills. It's hard to believe that people like us were passed down from kings to princes as part of inheritances and that we were privy to their inmost thoughts. And it's harder to believe that some of us were real artisans and craftsmen, shoe-makers and fullers and spinners of gold thread, diamond prospectors even. Did you know our forebears trafficked in foundlings for depleted bloodlines and that we made ends meet with a bit of cradle-snatching? All honourable trades in their own worlds. But not any more, that's all gone now. Now we're not even good circus material. History has passed us by, Edward, and we're dead men, dead men both of us.'

'That's not unusual. The world is full of people who have been passed over by history – gypsies, tinkers and so on.'

'Yes, but none have fallen so low. We are the lowest of the low; right now we are neither men nor beasts, we're just nightmare creatures stalking a no man's land between myth and history.'

'You're just full of self-pity.'

'Don't patronize me, Edward. I've lived long enough to be able to distinguish pity from disgust. I cried for six months when your mother died and I couldn't eat for two after the first time I held you in my arms. I'm not likely to confuse the two. At this moment I'm so sickened by myself I couldn't summon up the energy to puke. And while we're on the subject of disgust, tell me, why did you burn down the left wing?'

'That was an incomplete job: if you hadn't come along I'd have burned down the whole house. I was hoping that when you came back the whole thing would be destroyed and we could go off together and make our way in the world. I wanted a new start. There was a time when I thought this house was our sanctuary and refuge. And it was too for many years – our own little scooped-out space in the world where we were safe and without enemies. But over the years this sanctuary has turned into our prison; there's no house around here for miles and we have no friends or function any more. Now I think it is time to up roots and move on. Somewhere out there, in the vastness of the world, I know there is a small place where we can find our niche.'

'Doing what?'

'I don't know. I was thinking in terms of adventure and destiny, taking every day as it comes, you and me facing fortune head on.'

He closed his eyes as if experiencing some vast weariness. 'That's a young man's game, Edward. I'm too old for that kind of optimism.'

He was right. I saw for the first time how all his years of rancour and bitterness had eaten away the fabric of his soul. He had about him now an air of utter defeat. It ran in every line of his body, coursing through his arms and legs and chest and into the curve of his blunt spine. Some terrible weight seemed to have settled upon him and it came as an immense shock to see that he was now almost shorter than myself.

By this time the gun was cleaned and he was tidying away the oil and the lint. I hadn't seen the hacksaw on the table and I noticed also that a piece of the barrel was lying loose beside it. He had sawn another inch off the stock, customizing the gun yet further. He handed it to me.

'Take it,' he said. 'It should handle lighter – I've shifted the balance nearer the stock. Today it's your turn. The same terms and no arguments.'

I felt my eyes start in their sockets.

'I can't do that,' I whispered in disbelief, 'I can't. It's just crazy.' I retreated a few steps from the gun he was holding at arm's length. 'I can't.'

'Take the gun, Edward,' he insisted. 'Take it.' He thrust it suddenly onto my chest.

'No,' I yelled, 'no!' I fended the gun off wildly with my hands.

'This isn't an order, Edward, it's a request.' He had me pinned against the wall now, laying the rifle across my chest. He took his hands away suddenly and I found myself holding it. A calm, solemn note entered his voice.

'I've hated you from the moment you entered the world and I've hated you all the more because you are my son. I didn't think the world could commit the same atrocity twice in the same place. But I was wrong. And worst of all I've felt neither shame nor remorse for my hatred. Now, not once in all these years have I ever asked you for anything, not once because what did a wretch like you have to offer, you who had less grace than I did? But now I'm asking you for this one thing. Take the gun and be my son, just this once and final time.'

The gun burned in my hand but I could not let it go.

'Is it what you really want?' I blurted.

'Yes, it's what I really want. I cannot suffer this any more.'

He turned and made his way quickly through the back door and outside he stood facing towards the field. The day was cruelly lit; a high, unseasonable sun flared in the sky like magnesium, casting neither shadow nor illusion. My father turned into the field and I could see by the way he moved, the slouched gait and the hopeless slope of his shoulders that he wasn't going to make it. I was filled with sudden panic.

'Dad,' I cried.

'Yes.'

'Run hard.'

He turned without a word and continued on his way and when he got to the starting post he just kept on walking.

CLAIRE KEEGAN

DARK HORSES

IN THE NIGHT, Brady dreams the woman back into his life again. She's out the yard with the big hunter, laughing, praising her dark horse. She reaches up, loosens the girth, and takes the saddle off. The hunter shakes himself and snorts. She leads him to the trough and pumps fresh water. The handle shrieks when pressed but the hunter doesn't shy: he simply drops his head and drinks his fill. Further off, the cry of hounds moves across the fields. In his dream these hounds are Brady's own and he knows it will take a long time to gather them in and get them home.

Waking, he finds he's clothed from the waist down: black jeans and his working boots. He gropes for the clock, holds the glass close, reads the hands. It isn't late. Overhead, the light is still burning. He gets to his feet and finds the rest of his clothes. Outside, the October rain goes shuddering through the bamboo. That was planted years ago to stake her shrubs and beans but when she left he took no mind, and the garden turned wild. On McQuaid's hill, through cloud, he makes out the figure of a man walking through fields greener than his own. McQuaid himself, herding, counting all the bullocks once again.

In the kitchen he boils water, scalds the pot. The tea makes him feel human again. He stands over the toaster and warms his hands. His aunt brought up marmalade last week but there's hardly a lick in the jar. With a knife he scrapes what's left off the glass and goes out, in his jacket, to the fields. The two heifers need to be brought in and dosed. He must clear the drains, fell the ash in the lower field – and there's a good day's welding in the sheds before winter comes on strong. He throws what's left of the sliced pan on the street and starts the van. One part of him is glad the day is wet.

In Belturbet, he buys drenching fluid, welding rods, oil for the saw. There's hardly any money left. He hesitates before he rings Leyden from the phone box, knowing he'll be home.

'Come up to the house,' Leyden says. 'I'm in need of a hand.'

It is a fine house on a hill, which his wife, a schoolteacher, keeps immaculate. Two storeys painted white look out over the river. In the yard a pair of chestnut trees, the horse lorry, heads over every stable door. When Brady lands, Leyden waves from the hayshed. He's a tight man, bony, with great big hands.

'Ah, Brady! The man himself!'

'There's a bad day.'

''Tis raw,' Leyden agrees. 'Throw the halter on the mare there, would you? I've a feeling she'll give trouble.'

Brady stands at the mare's head while Leyden shoes. The big hands are skilled: the hoof is measured, pared, the toe culled for the clip. On the anvil the shoe is held, hammered to size. Steel nails are driven home, and clenched. Then the rasp comes round, the shavings falling like sawdust at their feet. All the while it's coming down, gasps of sudden rain whipping the galvanized roof. Brady feels strange pleasure standing there, sheltered, with the mare.

When Leyden rasps the last hoof, he throws the tools down and looks out at the rain.

'It's a day for the high stool,' he says.

'It's early,' Brady says uneasily.

'If we don't soon go, it's late it will be,' Leyden laughs, his eyes searching the ground for nails.

'I've to get me finger out; there's jobs at home.' Brady puts the mare back in the stable, bolts the door.

'You'll come, any road,' Leyden says. 'I'll get Sean to change a cheque and we'll settle up.'

'It'll do another day.'

'Not a hate about it. I might not have it another day.'

'All right so.'

As Brady follows Leyden back to town, a burning in his stomach surges. Leyden turns down the slip road past the chemist and parks behind The Arms. It looks closed but Leyden pushes the back door open. The bulb is dark over the pool table. On Northern Sound, a woman is reading out the news. Long Kearns is there with his Powers, staring into the ornamental fishing net behind the bar. Norris and McPhillips are picking horses for the next race. Big Sean stands behind the counter, buttering bread.

'Is that bread fresh or is it yesterday's?' Leyden asks.

'Mother's Pride,' Sean smiles, looking up. 'Today's bread today.'

'But if we ate it tomorrow wouldn't it still be today's?' says Norris who has drunk two farms. Except for the slight shake in his hand, no one would ever know.

'Put up two of your finest there, Sean,' says Leyden, 'and pay no mind to that blackguard.'

'He's been minding me for years,' says Norris. 'He'll hardly stop now.'

Sean puts the lip of a pint glass to the tap. Leyden hands him the cheque and tells him to give Brady the change. The stout is left to settle, the dark falling slowly away from the cream.

'We got the mare shod, any road.'

'Did she stand?'

'It was terror,' Leyden says. 'I'd still be at it only for this man here.'

'It's a job for a younger man,' McPhillips says. 'I did it myself when I was a garsún.'

'After three pints there's nothing you've not done,' says Norris.

'And after two there's nothing you won't do!' says Leyden, raising the bar. 'Isn't that right, Sean?'

'Leave Sean out of it,' the barman says affectionately.

Norris looks at Brady. 'Is it my imagination or have you lost weight?'

Brady shakes his head but his hand reaches for his belt.

'It's put it on I have.'

Big Sean wraps the sandwiches in clear plastic and puts them in the fridge. Brady reaches out and his hand closes on the glass. The glass feels cold in his hand. It isn't right to be drinking at this hour, and the stout is bitter.

'Have you a drop of blackcurrant there, Sean?'

'What are you doing with that poison?' Leyden asks. 'Destroying a good pint.'

Brady swallows a long draught. 'At least I didn't destroy four good hooves,' he says, finding his voice at last.

Everybody laughs.

'Is that so?' says Leyden, smiling. 'And what would you know? There's nothing but cart horses in Monaghan.'

'Every good cart horse needs shoes,' says Brady.

'They wear around the Cavan potholes,' says McPhillips, a Newbliss man.

'Now we have it!' Norris cries.

When the banter subsides, McPhillips goes out to place the bets. Sean turns off the radio now that the news is over.

The silence is like every silence; each man is glad of it and glad too that it won't last.

As they sit there, Leyden's nostril flares.

'Which one of ye dug up Elvis?'

'Lord God!' Long Kearns says, coming suddenly to life. 'That would knock a blackbird off its pad.'

Leyden swallows half his pint. The shoeing has put a thirst on him so Brady, not liking to leave with the money, orders another round.

Out in the street, school children are eating chips from brown paper bags. There's the smell of fried onions, hot oil and vinegar. It is darker now and the rain is still falling. When Brady walks into the diner, the girl at the counter looks up: 'Fresh cod and chips?'

'Ay.' Brady nods. 'And tay.'

He sits at the window and looks out at the day. Black clouds are sliding over the bungalows. He thinks again of that night in Cootehill. There was a Northern band in The White Horse. They sat at a distance from the stage and talked. She had a thoroughbred yearling and a three-year-old she thought would make an honest hunter. As she talked, a green spotlight shone through her hair. They danced a little and she drank a glass of wine. Afterwards, she asked him back to the house. *If you bring the chips, I'll light the fire and put the kettle on.* They ate supper in the firelight. A yellow cloth was spread over the table. She put down wicker placemats, pepper and salt, warm plates. The cutlery flashed silver. Smell of deodorant lingered in her bedroom, a wee candle burning, and headlights were passing through the curtains. When he woke, at dawn, she was asleep, her hand on his chest. He was working then, full time, for Leyden. That morning, walking down the main street, buying milk and rashers, he felt like a man.

The girl comes with his order. He eats what's placed before him, pays up, and faces down the street. He has to think for a moment before he can remember where he parked the van. He passes a stand of fruit and vegetables, a bucket of tired flowers, boxes of Christmas cards, ropes of trembling red and yellow tinsel. When he is walking past the hotel he recognizes a tune he cannot name. He stops to listen, then finds himself at the counter ordering a pint. The day is no longer his own. A few more tunes are played. At some point he looks up and realizes McQuaid is there, in a dark suit of clothes, with his wife. Sensing him McQuaid looks over, nods. Soon after, a pint's sent down. On Brady's lips the stout tastes colder than the last.

'The bould man himself! Have you no home to go to?' It's Leyden. He takes one look at Brady, and changes. 'What's ailing you at all, man?'

Brady shakes his head.

Leyden looks over at McQuaid. The waitress is bringing serviettes, knives for the steak.

'Pay no mind,' he says. 'Not a hate about it. The land'll be here long after we're dead and gone. Haven't we only the lend of it?'

Brady nods and orders the drink. Leyden pulls his stool up close and waits for the pint to settle. Brady is almost sorry he came in. When the pint is ready, Leyden puts it on the beermat, turns it round.

'Never mind the land. It's the woman that's your loss,' he says unhelpfully. 'That was the finest woman ever came around these parts.'

'Ay,' Brady says.

'There's men'd give their right arms to have a woman

like that,' Leyden says, coming in tight and taking hold of his arm.

'They would, surely.'

The waitress passes with two sizzling plates.

'What happened at all?' asks Leyden.

Brady feels rooted to the stool. Back then some days were hard but not one of them was wasted. He looks away. The silence rises. He lifts his glass but he cannot swallow.

'It was over the horse,' he says finally.

'The horse?'

Leyden looks at him but Brady does not want to go on. Even the mention of the horse is too much.

'What about the horse?' Leyden persists but then he looks away to leave Brady some room.

'I came home one night and she told me I'd have to buy food, pay bills. She told me I'd have to take her out for dinner.'

'And what did you say?'

'I told her to go fuck herself!' Brady says. 'I told her I'd put her horses out on the road.'

'That's terror,' Leyden says. 'Did you have drink on you?'

Brady hesitates. 'A wee drop.'

'Sure we all say things—'

'I went out and opened the gate and put her horses out on the road,' Brady says. 'She gave me a second chance but it was never the same. Nothing was ever the same.'

'Christ,' says Leyden, pulling away. 'I didn't think you had it in you.'

It is well past closing time when Brady finds the van. He gets behind the wheel and takes the back roads home. It will be all right; the sergeant knows him, he knows the sergeant. He will not be stopped. There are big, wet trees at either side of these roads, telephone poles, wires dangling. He drives on through falling leaves, keeping to his own side. When he reaches the front door, the bread is still on the step. The dog hasn't come home but he knows the birds will have it gone by morning. He looks at the kitchen table, the knife in the empty jar, and climbs the stairs.

He gets into the wisp and takes his jumper off. He wants to take his boots off but he is afraid. If he takes his boots off he knows he will never get them back on in the morning. He crouches under the bedclothes and looks at the bare window. It is winter now. What is it doing out there? The wind is piping terrible notes in the garden and, somewhere, a beast is roaring. He hopes it is McQuaid's. He lies in his bed and closes his eyes, thinking only of her. He can feel his own heart, beating. He closes his eyes. Soon, she will come back and forgive him. The bridle will be back on the coat stand, the cloth on the table. In his mind there is the flash of silver. As sleep is claiming him, she is already there, her pale hand on his chest and her dark horse is back grazing his fields.

ANNE ENRIGHT

GREEN

I LIKE GERTIE, but she just doesn't get it. Her and that pair of vultures she works with, always sniping – a sort of dizzy silence when I walk into the restaurant and then all business as usual; wipe the fingerprints off a glass, smooth a tablecloth down just so. Of course they're jealous – the vultures I mean: young women you can see closing up over the years, getting bitter. But I expected more from Gertie.

Sometimes I feel like packing it all in. I said as much to my mother, I said I wanted to start over somewhere else. France – why not?

'Oh, this town is very small,' she said, and she looked out of the window at the passing street.

'No, Mam,' I said. 'That's not good enough.' But she is right, of course. It's the little things that get to you. It's the little things that make you turn to the window and wonder how long you have left, before you can decently die.

Mam was a beauty: she had that to contend with. There are still women who will not talk to her after Mass because of what their dead husbands said once, or did not say, when she walked by.

And of course I went to the 'better' school – St Matilda's. Years of chilblains and semolina; the French teacher whacking you over the head with Maupassant, in hardback – Miss Nugent that was, or should I say *Mamselle Noojong* – six years of misery so you could catch a man with a better-cut suit and maybe a four-wheel drive.

'You are the future,' said Sister Albert, sending us back to be hated in hotel bars from Birr to Crossmolina for our T-strap stilettos and our taste in Campari and lime. I'd rather be dead, I said. But, 'Why not?' said Mam. 'Why not marry a nice, well-to-do man?' I said there's better ways to earn your new Sanderson curtains than on your back – I'd get the money myself. Or no money, if that's the way I wanted to play it. And I packed my bag for uni and shook the dust of that damn town off my feet.

Now here I am. Back again.

Gertie was a Matilda's girl too, of course. She was three years ahead of me, and I thought she was really beautiful, and really dull. Or something worse than dull – the way Sister Albert smiled so sadly at her, and Gertie smiled so sadly back. Gertie was a saint. She tried to use a tampon once and fainted against the toilet cubicle door: ker-klunk. She never did leave the town. She married the man she was supposed to marry, and she got the curtains she was supposed to get: he drinks every day now from half past twelve, and Gertie says he's infallible when it comes to a good Bordeaux.

Go for it, Gertie. St Matilda's is proud of you yet.

She rang me up yesterday. She actually rang me up. She was terribly nice. I was terribly nice. I was smiling and nodding at the phone receiver like something demented.

'Aha!' I said. 'Unhum!' Then I put down the phone and went out and hacked down the sycamore that had suckered by the back wall. And of course it was too big for me, so the place is a mess of branches now, with an ignorant-looking stump left, all mutilated and half alive.

Because, strange to relate, I did marry a local man. And he does have a four-wheel drive. Which we need for the farm. But whatever way you cut it, eleven years after I left, I was back again in a white dress, walking down the aisle of the town church, that Gothic barn, the ghost of my childhood shifting her sticky knees on the green leatherette, *Behave yourself now*. The place was so cold my arms were mottled red and orange, poking out of the white dress like chicken legs. I was shaking – and not just with the cold. But sure they loved that too. Walking like something plucked in front of the sentimental, small eyes of that town. *Isn't she lovely?* Saying later I had terrible circulation problems because of the drugs I did in New York, was it? Or Paris? Believe me, this is an outrageous place. But all places are outrageous, and I was in love.

Still am.

I don't think Gertie understands 'organic'. She rings me up yesterday out of the blue, and says she wants enough radicchio for forty.

'Also,' she says, and then a list as long as your arm. *Well*, I thought, the pure gall of it. But, 'Aha!' I said. 'Unhum!' I said I'd see what I had, because 'with organic you don't always have it on demand'.

'Oh,' she said.

I went out to polytunnels and I couldn't find J.P. so I went to the toolshed and got out the handsaw and hacked at the poor sycamore until it was just a bleeding mess of green. It is very satisfying, cutting down a tree. You work small and the result is catastrophic: stand out of the way and, whoosh, the sky falls.

J.P. came up after a while.

'What gives?' he says.

'Gertie wants radicchio for forty,' I said.

'Well, that's good.'

'Jesus, J.P.,' I said. 'Never buy a chainsaw.'

*

That evening I was all depressed. I walked under the plastic and listened to the sprinklers. I am not sentimental about vegetables, but I think I was crying. All the beautiful rows of green. I felt like ringing Gertie and saying that rabbits had got into the crop, or sawfly. Paraquat in the irrigation system. Anything. No more radicchio. The radicchio is all dead, Gertie.

Mam said, 'Maybe it's the start of something new. A change of heart. She'll be ringing you up now, all the time.' I don't think Mam understands about the way my business is these days. I gritted my teeth and said, 'Mam . . . I have two refrigerated vans a day going up to Dublin. One of them goes all the way to the airport because they eat my *cime de rapa*, which are just fancy turnip leaves, let's face it, in effing London town. And now Gertie rings up *ten years too late* and says she wants my product. Ten years of her saying my carrots were delicious, of course, but a bit funny looking, and there was no demand for *cime de rapa* around here, and some of her customers actually picked the basil leaves out of their pasta and so what could you do?'

'So what?' says Mam. 'You've won now.'

But it doesn't feel like I've won. It didn't *sound* like I'd won when I was talking to Gertie on the phone. It was a wedding, she said. The bride wanted organic – was very firm about it. And why wouldn't she be, when her father ran half the cattle in the county? 'If anyone knows what's in the beef,' said Gertie, 'she does.' And we had a bit of a laugh about that, before I hung up and went looking for some implement of destruction – any implement of destruction – and a tree to cut down.

I'm throwing my radicchio before swine.

When I married J.P. and turned him organic, Gertie ran the only restaurant for fifty miles. For the first five years we put off having kids, worked all the hours God sent – all that – and Gertie did take some stuff, now and then, to help us out. But she had one cook who was a demon for 'posh' food, everything drowned in 'French' sauce, and lots of spuds of course, and *Has your daddy had enough?* I think Gertie was afraid of her, actually. The other one had done a course at Ballymaloe and was very uppity for the first while. Of course, my problem was that I was uppity all the time (thank you, St Matilda's) and so neither of them would touch one of my crooked, delicious carrots if her life depended on it. All that *cleaning*, they said. I know this because, for five years, every Saturday night, in the dim hopes of rustling up a bit of business, myself and J.P. took off our wellingtons, put on something half decent and went to eat in Gertie's restaurant in town. We ate until it choked us. We ate, more precisely, until the children came along. And when we stopped, I actually missed it – there was nowhere else to go.

We have sandy soil, red and light. I went all the way to Westmeath for the organic manure, and brought the first lot back by trailer. We couldn't afford a lorry. I made five trips.

'Muck into gold,' said J.P., shovelling it on. 'Muck into gold.' Now the tilth is so fine, it crumbles under your hand.

In year three I swung a deal with a small supplier in Smithfield. In year four I got our organic stamp. Prices went up. Over at Gertie's, Has-Your-Daddy-Had-Enough said that there were 'maggots' in the potatoes, and the uppity one said that she 'quite liked' organic, but 'you could get better organic elsewhere'. I bought my first van. I bought my second van. Every day they roared past Gertie's door.

'You know what kills me?' I used to say to J.P. 'If they started taking the stuff now, they'd say it was because it had improved. Or they'd decide the cos was OK, but the rest was as bad as ever. They'd tell me I should stick to cos.

And there I'd be, selling cos to them and smiling. That's what kills me.'

J.P. is out of sorts with all this. He is a reluctant sort of man. He likes working the land. I pretend this drives me mad, but of course it's the thing that keeps me sane. Tonight he takes off his clothes as though they are a trial to him, as though that shirt of his has been at him all day. He puts them into the laundry basket and slaps the lid shut. Then, naked, he gets into bed: my organic man. He closes his eyes, rolls over to kiss my shoulder, rolls back, and sleeps.

At four in the morning I look out the bathroom window and see the poor sycamore oozing sap under a scudding sky. Such greedy trees, sycamores, nothing grows in their shade. I look into the mirror and think about Gertie. The sight of her praying in the school chapel at fifteen, with those lumpy-looking white gloves that girls used to wear when they were all overcome by the Virgin Mary. I think about the little bully she married; her mother, who always had some vague symptom. Her mother's funeral, then, later. And my own father's funeral, later again. Shaking Gertie's hand.

'I'm sorry for your trouble.'

God, I hate that woman. I put my hands on the side of the sink and lean forward and close my eyes. And I think of the food I must gather for Gertie: the beautiful plump lettuces, the purple sprouting broccoli, the early beans. I think about pulling them from the earth when they are still cool with the morning; settling them into their boxes, with the sweet air trapped among their leaves. I think about how I will gather them up, and pick them over, and pack them with a little knotted sprig of rosemary and thyme. I think how Gertie will take this little bouquet, and look at it and like it. And I sigh.

Ronan, our youngest, comes in, holding the front of his

pyjamas, his face muddled with sleep. I help him go to the toilet and he says something about camels which makes me smile, about how camels hold their water for such a long time.

'Hydroponics,' I say to J.P. as I get back into bed. 'Ebb and flood.'

'You always say that,' he says. It is nearly dawn. He might get up now, and let me sleep on. The light outside our window is undecided and we lie there, intimately awake. J.P. has heard it all before – a dream I have of water, an infinity of lettuce, row upon row of the stuff, coming out of a lake smooth as glass, so all you see is the lettuce and the reflection of the lettuce. And maybe, as I fall asleep, me also, floating in there, utterly still amidst the green.

EDNA O'BRIEN

SEND MY
ROOTS RAIN

MEN AND WOMEN hurled themselves through the revolving door of the hotel with an urgency, and so quickly did they follow one upon the other that Miss Gilhooley imagined it was bound to end in a stampede. Discharged into the hotel lobby, they flung out their arms or tossed their scarves, triumphant at having arrived. Miss Gilhooley drew back, waiting, as she hoped, for a pause in the hectic proceedings. It was then that Pat-the-Porter noticed her, standing somewhat tentatively on the lower entrance step – not a young woman but a striking woman in a grey Cossack hat, such as he had seen on an actress in a Russian film many years before. He held the door and drew her in, as he put it, 'to the most distinguished address in Dublin'. He was an affable man, with sparkling blue eyes, proud of his girth inside that fine uniform and certain of the importance of his station. He had, as he soon told her, been working there for thirty-three-odd years, barring the two years when the establishment was closed for the massive revamp.

The hall was a veritable Mecca. Marble floors of shell pink, which an unthinking being could easily slide on, and countless chandeliers, blazed and gave out a beautiful light, that surpassed daylight and trembled within the many mirrors. A fire was blazing and on either side were dented leather buckets filled with consignments of logs and turf. The flower arrangements were particularly fetching – golden gladioli and lilies in high vases and then nests of littler vases, which had deep blue orchids that had been severed from their stems squeezed inside, their faces pressed close to the glass, chafing at their imprisonment.

Pat-the-Porter was regaling her with some of the hotel's history from the time when it had opened its doors in 1824 – the perilous days during the Rebellion of 1916, when gunfire whizzed in Stephen's Green across the road, and sure, wasn't the lounge famous for having been the very place where the Irish constitution was drafted. In between these snatches of history, he snarled at young boys, bellhops, with their grey pillbox hats set at jaunty angles; reminding them of their various charges and all smiles. The couple in the Horseshoe Bar, as Pat-the-Porter said, were still waiting for their oysters, and the front steps needed more salt; he didn't want people breaking their ankles or their hips or any part of their anatomy. He was able to change his manner at a wink, soft and confiding with her, severe with the underlings, and giving a knowing half nod to the various swanks and habitués who came skiving through the swing doors and headed for either of the two bars or the Saddle Room. He would give her a booklet later on in which she could read all about the hotel, from its inception to the present time as a hot-spot for movers and shakers, not to mention the English gentlemen who came for the stag parties.

Miss Gilhooley, he opined, would feel more at home in the sedate ambience of the Lord Mayor's Lounge, and so he escorted her to a table that was not too close to the entrance, in a recess, a little round table covered with a white linen cloth and on which there rested a folded menu. The elderly pianist, in an excess of energy, was bent over his piano, hitting the keys so fervently that a waltz sounded like a recruiting song. His bald pate glistened in the winter sun that poured through the bay window and onto his knitted grey-white eyebrows and his small purple dickie-bow.

It would be true to say that her heart fluttered somewhat. Strange to think that she was about to come face-to-face with a great poet whom she rated above all other poets and especially the young whippersnappers with their portfolios of clever words and hollow feelings. His poetry evoked the truth of the land, dock and turnips and nettles, men behind their ploughs, envying the great feats of Priam and Hector, tormented men in small fields battling their desires. Again and again she recommended his poems to borrowers in the library where she worked, and once, she organized a little entertainment, where there were readings of his poems and refreshments afterwards. The audience was restless, finding the poems too depressing, so that there was fidgeting and coughing throughout.

Each time a new poem of his appeared in a newspaper she cut it out, assembling a scrapbook of him. Finding one addressed to a woman, whose name he wrote, she thought, he is not made of stone after all. They had first communicated some years before when she asked if she could impose upon him to sign a copy of his collected poems, to be placed in a glass cabinet in the library hall. He sent a white, ruled, adhesive sheet, which carried his name and the date, February twenty-second. It was in deep black ink and the handwriting being so cramped and tiny she felt he had a reluctance in writing it or sending it at all. The photograph on the back cover showed a formidable man, his forehead high and domed, the eyes hidden behind thick horn-rimmed spectacles.

One autumn night, in an expansive mood, she sat down and wrote him a letter about the white mist. It appeared from time to time, wraith-like, twining the three adjacent counties: frail as lace and yet sturdy as it wandered, or rather seemed to float above the fields, above the numerous lakes and separating into skeins and then meshing again. He wrote back warning her not to get too carried away by the mist and concluded by saying, 'I reject miracle in every form and shape.'

Now, she was here, picturing him arriving, somewhat awkward, in a long overcoat, looking around and being looked at, because he was famous and rumoured to be fiercely abrupt with any who ventured near him. She had come for poetry and not love, as she kept reminding herself. Miss Gilhooley had had her quota of love, but had never managed to reach the mysterious certitudes of marriage. In her small town she was mockingly referred to as the Spinster.

She began imagining things they might talk about at first, the changes that had occurred in their country, changes that were not for the better, bulldozers everywhere and the craze for money. Money, money, money. The rich going to lunch in their helicopters, chopping the air and shredding the white mist, their wives outdoing each other with jewellery and finery, stirring their champagne with gold swizzle sticks, and Mrs Ambrose boasting about their drapes from the palazzo of a gentleman in Milan and a tea-set shipped from Virginia that had once belonged to a president of the United States. Pictures on their walls of bog and bogland, where they no longer set foot, priceless pictures of these lonesome and beautiful landscapes and pictures of bog lilies that lay like serrated stars on pools of purple-black bog water. It was not only the rich but those who aped them that were also money mad. That little hussy who sued the Church Fathers because the sleeve of her coat singed as she was lighting a candle, actually employed the family solicitor to press for compensation and he did, egging her on, encouraged her in this rotten ploy.

The invitation to meet had come some weeks after Christmas, but the stamps on the envelope had pictures of various snowed-on Santa Clauses, so it seemed that he had deliberately delayed posting it or else it had lain in his coat pocket.

Though frozen, when she arrived, one of her cheeks was now scalding from the blaze of the fire and the pile of ash under the grate that was a molten red. She moved her chair back a fraction, as she did not want to be flushed when he arrived. She reckoned on his being late, poets always were. Her bus journey had been long and cheerless, the fields along the way flecked with snow, and in places small mounds of snow lay like hedgehogs crouching inside their own igloos. She had walked briskly from the bus station through the busy streets, strains of music, melodeon and guitar, fraught young mothers wielding their pushchairs, and beggars of various nationalities. She stopped by one older woman because of the little begging bucket, a blue bucket such as a child would take to the seaside with his spade to make a sand castle, and soon regretted her mistake in trying to have a conversation, as the woman had a cleft palate and could scarcely pronounce her own name, which was Mary. A frost, sheer and unblemished, coated the bonnets of the cars that were like sentinels around the grand garden square, and the railings, clad with icy snow, felt damp through the palm of her glove. She stopped a second time to admire a statue of Wolfe Tone, flanked by tall columns of stone, the valorous figure sprung, as it were, from earth, the green-bronze of his boots, his jacket and his torso, curdled and glinting in the wintry sun.

Though feeling hot she felt too constrained to remove her

coat, merely opened the top buttons and let it fall capewise over her shoulders as she gradually eased her arms out of the sleeves. Under no circumstances would she mention the fact that she had written snippets of her own locality, little nothings for which she had received a flurry of rejection slips, polite and useless. There was one literary editor who had befriended her and who believed that one day she might become a Poet and in his tutoring of her became a little smitten. He would take her for a drive each week, to discuss this or that piece of writing and always on the dashboard there was a packet of toffees or glacier mints for her to take home. Eventually, they drove a distance away to the seaside, whence they would get out of the car and look or listen as the Atlantic waves vented their fury and now and then surprise them with a rogue wave that sent them toppling. One evening at dusk, when she could not see his face, he said that he was happy with the woman to whom he had been married for many years, but that those drives, the two of them witness to the hungers of the sea and the cry of the seagulls, were dear to him. Though young, she sensed for the first time how inexplicable love was.

She had been in love more than once, gloriously, breathlessly in love, but it was the last attachment that had been the deepest, that was as she believed, ordained. Such happiness. The long walks at weekends, scaling mountains which she would never have done alone, but she felt safe and confident next to him, and indeed if she missed her footing, as she often did, he was there to catch her and plant a kiss. Once they were loaned a grand house in County Galway and in the evening went to the pub in the hotel and talked with the beaters and the gillies and it was there she learned the yodel used to raise woodcock – 'Waayupwaayupwaayup'. It became their favourite password. By the open fire she read poetry to him, read from a book of foreign poets with the English translation on the opposite page and they swore that they would learn languages, that she would learn French and he Spanish and would converse in their adopted tongue. In one letter she was rash enough to tell him that she would walk water to reach him and he replied in kind. It was reciprocal.

His letter breaking it off was wedged half in and half out of her letterbox. She thought that he was merely postponing a date they had made to meet in Dublin at the end of the month, but she was wrong. He praised her qualities in English and in Irish and she cursed him for not having had the gumption to tell her in person. She hid it so as to return it to him in due course, but put it somewhere so safely that she could not remember where that safe place was.

'They'll find it, when I'm dead,' she said spitefully.

After the initial shock she felt the magnitude of the loss, and her whole will was directed towards getting him back. She so convinced herself of this that she bought wooden tubs to plant bulbs in the garden and new towels that were stacked in the bathroom, on a stool, waiting for him. They were a beautiful oatmeal colour. She lost friends, having no time for them and they, for their part, were aghast at how she was letting herself go, hair wild and uncombed, her clothes streelish, she who had once been so proud of her appearance. Her boss in the library – a sombrous man – asked if she had had a bereavement, to which she could only reply, yes, yes. After work she went straight home and locked her door and before sleep she would wait for his footsteps, thought she heard a friendly tapping on the windowpane. How often did she switch on the light, stare into the empty room and curse her daft imaginings. She turned to poets as she would to God. Gerard Manley Hopkins was her favourite poet at that time and the line she repeated again and again and which incurred much disparagement, was 'O thou Lord of life, send my roots rain.'

Hearing of a psychic in another county, who lived on a caravan site, she drove there one Saturday and begged, yes begged, for a reading. How her spirits lifted when the woman described in detail things that had actually happened, a hand-painted scarf which her lover had given her and which he placed shyly on her head in the shop, and the time that they had met by surprise in a hotel, their astonishment as they withdrew to an alcove and without exchanging a word, his placing his hand on her chest to calm the violent heartbeats. The psychic then foresaw them setting up house together. It was a cottage by the sea, which they would do up and extend. She drew a picture of their future life together, one or other, whoever got back first of an evening, kneeling to light a fire and praying that the chimney would not smoke, though at first it would, but in time that would clear, once the flue had its generous lining of soot. So real did this become for Miss Gilhooley that she began to furnish the imaginary house, choose wallpapers for various bedrooms, bathroom tiles with specks of gold, such as she had seen in a catalogue and she also added a balcony to the main bedroom where they would stand at night and hear the roaring waves and in the sunny mornings watch the several waterbirds wade gracefully on the soft muddy shore.

Her only sensible action during that wretched time was not to take the pills the doctor insisted she must take. One evening at dusk she drove to the lake, unscrewed the can and dropped the contents into the dark water that was scummed with debris. Many secrets lay hidden in the depths of that lake, condoms, unwanted pups, unwanted kittens sewn into sacks, and incriminating letters. In time, she would bring her own batch of letters, written on sleepless nights, some proud, some craven, all foolish, and assign them to this watery pyre.

She became more and more isolated, but the one person she did not shrink from was Ronan. He was a young man who lived in a caravan on the back avenue of the manor house where Mr and Mrs Jamieson lived. In return for being able to park there, he did odd jobs, cleared the woods, sawed timber, walked the greyhounds and lit the fires if the family was home of an evening. Now and then Mrs Jamieson gave him one of her husband's cast-offs but warned him not to let Sir know, as he was very sentimental about his belongings. Ronan and she made a pilgrimage together, for their special intentions, climbing up a steep mountain in Mayo, on a hot June day, with a busload of people who had been driven from the south. How relieved they both were that there was no one from their own vicinity, no one to spy on them. Often she wondered which of the locals had set upon the idea of torturing her with anonymous calls. They would come at all hours and always concerned Emmet, because Emmet was her lover's name, in honour of the hero Robert Emmet. Emmet, she would be told, had just got engaged to be married, Emmet was dating a dentist, Emmet was seen with a famous actress in Dublin, Emmet was seen in a shower with a brunette in a new spa in Westport. She knew they were lies, and yet to hear his name uttered and in such vile connotations, she longed to speak to him and warn him of these terrible calumnies.

It began to lessen. In her small gardens, one Sunday, she saw the stirrings of spring, the leaves of the camellia bush green and glossy, white buds, tight and tiny as birds' eggs, poised to open. She skimmed the sodden leaves from the rain barrel and standing there, looking, seeing, feeling the world around her, she realized that it was the commencement of her convalescence. A blackbird had found a luscious morsel of pink worm and was gobbling it, yet glancing left and right in case a fellow creature would snatch it away. Then, at the car boot sale, to which she went to pass the time, not one, but three different men smiled at her and she smiled back.

On the night when she gave herself to the minister, she believed, indeed knew, she had turned a corner. In their teens and while he was still a student, the minister and herself had met at a dance hall, had clicked and later sat in his motorcar, fondling and reciting poetry. She knew from the annual Christmas card down the years that he still remembered her and that he hankered in some way. When they found themselves at the same Summer school their joy at being reunited was immense. He was opening the event and she was giving a paper on the occult in Yeats's work. During the formal dinner, to which he had her invited, they exchanged glances, the odd word across the table, and eventually, not without a little detour, they found themselves in the same elevator and thence in his suite, which was so vast they had to grope their way to find a table lamp. Their lovemaking was at least twenty years too late, and they were too shy, lying in that enormous four poster bed, to laugh about it. At breakfast they were already on their separate ways, he to his house outside Dublin, and she further north, to the seat of the white mist.

She re-established friendships, went back to playing whist on Friday evenings and made a rhubarb jam flavoured with ginger, which she distributed among those who had been spiteful to her. Only Ronan knew. Ronan with his sideburns, dreaming of Elvis, of doing gigs in small towns, then graduating to big venues and finally to Dublin and afar. One night they watched a video of Elvis that she had hired, sitting in her front room by a warm fire and drinking red wine from the good cut glasses. There was Elvis, like a midnight God, in a midnight blue leather jacket and sideburns, wooing the world, Elvis asking a female member of the audience for the loan of her handkerchief to dab his brow, Elvis shivering as he half sang, half spoke, 'Are you lonesome tonight?' Ronan later strummed a song that he had written on his guitar, which he hoped would be a sensation at one of these imaginary gigs –

> Oh hollow heart you were so real
> I put my hand there
> I could feel
> Your hollow heart . . .

He looked at her, blinking – Ronan blinked out of nerves – and waited. She had to admit that it was not catchy enough and was somewhat bleak. Young people went to gigs to get high, to forget heartbreak and tedium.

'I can't do that . . . I can't forget,' Ronan said.

'Then don't,' Miss Gilhooley replied. But beyond that they did not dare go.

She came across her lover at a function a few years later, as she was wending her way through a room full of people, to table twenty-four. There was a priest with him and a young girl, perhaps his fiancée, though she could not tell. She stopped to say hello, not recalling a word of what was said, but she did and would remember how his arm, with a stealth, coming around the back of her waist and resting there for an instant, saying, without the words, what now would never be said. She drank somewhat immoderately at table twenty-four and kept repeating a line of Yeats's – 'A sweetheart from another life floats there' – much to the bafflement of the people around her.

At home she would mostly quell her desires, but when she went abroad in the summer, they ran amok. In that town on the Mediterranean, in stifling heat, everything quivered, even the knotted gauze scarves that swung from one of the stalls. The chrome of cars and motorcycles seemed to rasp in the head and in the jeweller's windows gold chains and gold wedding rings were at melting point. It was a crowded market, with a glut of goods – meats, fish, shellfish, fruits, vegetables, clothing, cutlery, handbags, seersucker skirts the colour of cotton candy, the locals knowing exactly what they had come for, steering their way with a certain pique through the loitering swell of visitors. The sun through the slits in the canvas awnings beat down relentlessly. A man wearing a faded blue shirt appeared as from nowhere and slid between the milling crowd with a curious, knowing smile. He was dark-skinned, his left jaw showing a strawberry mark, fiercely vivid, as if just slashed. He stood right before her as if she had willed him there, the encounter so thrilling and so unnerving, his eyes, which were a soft brown, moist and lusting, asking her to say yes. On one arm he carried a willow basket filled with gardenias, the smell so intoxicating, adding to her fluster and on the other arm there lay a snake, coiled and inert, its scales iridescent in that hot light. She drew back startled and he made some barely audible sound in order to reassure her. And yes, she would have said yes, gone down one of the narrow alleys, followed him to wherever he silently bade her, to lie with him. All that stopped her was that her friend Amanda was nearby, trying on different straw hats and beckoning her across. He took the measure of the situation and sauntered off with the ease of a panther.

The poet was late. The tall manageress blamed this lateness on the hopelessness of the train service. She herself had been five hours getting home to her parents the weekend previous.

'Where is home?' Miss Gilhooley asked.

'North east Galway,' she was told and tried to imagine the little townlands on the big map in the library hall, their names squeezed together in a cluster. After chatting to Miss Gilhooley, the manageress insisted on bringing one order of afternoon tea, saying that she would bring a second pot of tea when he arrived. She somehow guessed that it was a man. Presently a banquet was set before Miss Gilhooley – dainty sandwiches on white and brown bread, warm scones with helpings of clotted cream and raspberry jam, slices of rich fruitcake dense with raisins, currants, candied peel, cherries, and green strips of angelica and on the very top tier, as a final arpeggio, small gateaux of a sweet lemon flan, that trembled as the cake plate was put down. Except that she was not hungry.

She consulted her watch, regularly putting it to her ear to listen for the almost imperceptible ticking. A bellicose man at a centre table kept calling every other minute, to voice his complaints, addressing each of the passing waitresses as 'Serving person, Serving person.'

'An oddball ... comes every day ... lives alone somewhere in Ranelagh,' the manageress said, and hastened to his table, removing the cup and the saucer that was slopped with tea and speaking to him pleasantly.

People were munching and chatting, some consciously over-reserved, and from one table loud guffaws and peals of laughter at the richness of their jokes. She debated whether she should look, in the two bars and the Saddle Room, but the truth was that she did not feel confident enough to wend her way past all those people. The heat in the room was now quite oppressive and a mobile phone rang repeatedly from the depths of someone's handbag. The pianist, sensible to the fact that he was being ignored, ran his hands along the keyboard with a flourish, then stood holding those self-same hands out, as for a requiem.

All of a sudden, she pictured her own hallway, with the storage heater about to come on and the radio playing full blast in the kitchen, a deliberate ploy, as there had been several break-ins in the town of late. The bellicose man was reading a newspaper, when suddenly he bashed his hand through the centre pages, shouting as obviously he had read something which infuriated him. His face was moist with rage and his ears, which were a blazing red, stuck out from his head as he looked around for an opponent to argue with. It was not at that precise moment that she admitted to herself that the poet was not coming. It was fifteen minutes later.

A little girl wearing a tam o'shanter came across and asked if she would care to buy a raffle ticket for an extension to be built at their school. As she wrote her address on the counterfoil, lest she came first, second, or third, the little girl rattled off the prizes, which were all of a culinary nature. As she walked off, her parents waved their gratitude and at that precise moment Miss Gilhooley put her arms back into the sleeves of her tweed coat, rising with as much composure as she could muster.

She paid at the cash register near the arched entrance and asked for the tip to be left on her table as she dreaded the embarrassment of encountering the manageress, who was bound to be sympathetic.

Pat-the-Porter met her beaming. He had the booklet, the very last one, staff always swiping them, but he had it for her to take home as a souvenir. She mentioned the poet's name.

'Our Laureate,' he said, misquoting a line about a sod of earth rolling over on its back from the thrust of the plough.

'We had a . . . rendezvous,' she said, smarting at the

pretentiousness of the word, and for a moment he was lost in perplexity, then drew her aside and in a low confidential voice began to mutter – 'Look . . . it's like this . . . I know the man . . . I can vouch for his honour . . . he comes here all the time with them bowsies . . . the bar-stool poets as I call them . . . and he sits like a man in a trance . . . he'd have every intention of meeting you . . . he'd want it . . . I can just see it . . . him shaving . . . putting on a clean shirt and tie, getting the good overcoat and setting out . . . coming as far as the corner by Wolfe Tone and all of a sudden . . . balking it.'

'But why . . . why would he balk it?'

'Shy, shyness . . . the shyest man I ever came across . . . I'll bet you he's walking the street now or maybe on a bench by the canal, reproaching himself for his blasted boorishness . . . his defection.'

It was left like that.

He steered her through the revolving doors and watched her go down the street. She held herself well, but there was a hurt look to her back.

The air in the bus was freezing, passengers not nearly so buoyant or talkative as they had been on the way down in the morning. She was glad that no one had sat next to her. In the various towns through which they passed, Paud, the young driver, drove with caution, because he had been stopped several times by the sergeant, but once onto the country roads he was reckless, the bus trundled, raising slush out of the ruts, grazing the hedges and twice coming to a skidding halt when a vehicle met them from the opposite side. Passengers were flung forward and afterwards there were irate calls to him 'For feck's sake, cool it, cool it.'

The dark seemed to get deeper and darker and the land itself swallowed within a primeval loneliness.

She had been dozing on and off, when suddenly, she came awake with a start. What an awful dream and where had it come from. She had been drinking the hot blood that spurted from the throat of a wounded animal, a wolf she reckoned. It was in a strange forest, the trunks of the trees massive and covered with white fleshy toadstools, a forest that was already receding from her mind, but the taste of blood lingered in her mouth. The horror. The horror. Was this the true her, a she-wolf drinking blood. Looking around, she sought in vain for deliverance, then wiped the window and saw that they were passing the low white building that had once been a creamery and was about twenty miles from home.

Home, the small town that so cried out for novelty that a few fairy lights, since Christmas time, still dangled from the lower branches of the big chestnut tree in the market square, home to the loamy land and the brown-black lakes fed from bog water, home to the rooks convening and prattling at evening time in the churchyard grounds and home to the intangible white mist. Pressed to the window she said aloud the name of the man she had so loved, a name that had not passed her lips in almost twenty years, and all of a sudden she was crying, soft, warm, melting tears and she thought of the poet, that lonely clumsy man, walking streets in Dublin or, as Pat-the-Porter said, sitting on a bench staring into greenish canal water. She knew then, and with a cold conviction, the love, the desolation that goes in to the making of a poem.

'Welcome to Mullaghair . . . and all in one piece,' the grinning Paud said with Olympian pride.

People were slow to get down as the steps were slippery and so was the pavement, the goodnights were cursory and everyone, including her, drew up the collars of their coats, to guard against the biting wind.

COLM TÓIBÍN

THE EMPTY FAMILY

I HAVE COME back here. I can look out and see the soft sky and the faint line of the horizon and the way the light changes over the sea. It is threatening rain. I can sit on this old high chair that I had shipped from a junk store on Market Street and watch the calmness of the sea against the misting sky.

I have come back here. In all the years, I made sure that the electricity bill was paid and the phone remained connected and the place was cleaned and dusted. And the neighbour who took care of things, Rita's daughter, opened the house for the postman or the courier when I sent books or paintings or photographs I had bought, sometimes by FedEx as though it were urgent that they would arrive since I could not.

Since I would not.

This space I walk in now has been my dream space; the mild sound of the wind on days like this has been my dream sound.

You must know that I am back here.

The mountain bike that came free with the washing machine just needed the tyres pumped. Unlike the washing machine itself, it worked as though I had never been away. I could make the slow dream journey into the village, down the hill towards the sand quarry and then past the ball alley with all the new caravans and mobile homes in the distance.

At the end of that journey I met your sister-in-law on a Sunday morning. She must have told you. We were both studying the massive array of Sunday newspapers in the supermarket in the village, wondering which of them to buy. She turned and our eyes locked. I had not seen her for years; I did not even know that she and Bill still had the house. Bill must have told you I am here.

Or maybe not yet.

Maybe he has not seen you. Maybe he does not tell you every bit of news as soon as he knows it. But soon, soon, Bill and you must speak and he will tell you then, maybe just as an afterthought, a curiosity, or maybe even as a fresh piece of news. Guess who I saw? Guess who has come back?

I told your sister-in-law that I had come back.

Later, when I went down to the strand, using the old path, the old way down, when I was wondering if I would swim, or if the water would be too cold, I saw them coming towards me. They were wearing beautiful clothes. Your sister-in-law has aged, but Bill was spry, almost youthful. I shook hands with him. And there was nothing else to say except the usual, what you often say down here: you look out at the sea and say that no one ever comes here, you say how empty it is, and how lovely it is to be here on a bright and blustery June day with no one else in sight, despite all the tourism and the new houses and the money that came and went. This stretch of strand has remained a secret.

In strange, odd moments I have come here over all the years. I have imagined this encounter and the sounds we make against the sound of the wind and the waves.

And then Bill told me about the telescope. Surely, he said, I must have bought one in the States? They are cheaper there, much cheaper. He told me about the room he had built with the Velux window and the view it had and how he had nothing there except a chair and a telescope.

Years ago, as you know, I had shown them this house, and

I knew that he remembered this room, the tiny room full of shifting light, like something on a ship, where I am sitting now. I had cheap binoculars to watch the ferry from Rosslare and the lighthouse and the odd sailing boat. I cannot find them now, although I looked as soon as I came back. But I always thought a telescope would be too unwieldy, too hard to use and work. But Bill told me no, his was simple.

He said that I should stop by and check for myself, anytime, but they would be there all day. Your sister-in-law looked at me warily, as though I would be needing her for something again as I needed her all those years ago, as though I would come calling in the night once more. I hesitated.

'Come and have a drink with us,' she said. I knew that she meant next week, or some week; I knew that she wanted to sound distant.

I said no, but I would come and see the telescope, just for a second if that was all right, maybe later, just the telescope. I was interested in the telescope and did not care whether she wanted me to come that day or some other day. We parted and I walked on north, towards Knocknasillogue, and they made their way to the gap. I did not swim that day. Enough had happened. That meeting was enough.

Later, it became totally calm, as it often does. As the sun shone its dying slanted rays into the back windows of the house I thought that I would walk down and see the telescope.

She had the fire lighting, and I remember that she had said their son would be there, I cannot remember his name, but I was shocked when he stood up in the long open-plan room with windows on two sides that gave on to the sea. I had not seen him since he was a little boy. In a certain light he could have been you, or you when I knew you first, the same hair, the same height and frame and the same charm that must have been there in your grandmother or grandfather or even before, the sweet smile, the concentrated gaze.

I moved away from them and went with Bill, who had been standing uneasily waiting for me, to the small stairs, and then down towards the room with the telescope.

I hate being shown how to do things, you know that. Wiring a plug, or starting a rented car, or understanding a new mobile phone, add years to me, bring out frustration and an almost frantic urge to get away and curl up on my own. Now I was in a confined space being shown how to look through a telescope, my hands being guided as Bill showed me how to turn it and lift it and focus it. I was patient with him, I forgot myself for a minute. He focused on the waves far out. And then he stood back.

I knew he wanted me to move the telescope, to focus now on Rosslare Harbour, on Tuskar Rock, on Raven Point, on the strand at Curracloe, agree with him that they could be seen so clearly even in this faded evening light. But what he showed me first had amazed me. The sight of the waves miles out, their dutiful and frenetic solitude, their dull indifference to their fate, made me want to cry out, made me want to ask him if he could leave me alone for some time to take this in. I could hear him breathing behind me. It came to me then that the sea is not a pattern, it is a struggle. Nothing matters against the fact of this. The waves were like people battling out there, full of consciousness and will and destiny and an abiding sense of their own beauty.

I knew as I held my breath and watched that it would be best not to stay too long. I asked him if he would mind if I looked for one more minute. He smiled as though this was what he had wanted. Unlike you, who has never cared about things, your brother is a man who likes his own property. I turned and moved fast, focusing swiftly on a wave I had selected for no reason. There was whiteness and greyness in it and a sort of blue and green. It was a line. It did not toss, nor did it stay still. It was all movement, all spillage, but it was pure containment as well, utterly focused just as I was watching it. It had an elemental hold; it was something coming towards us as though to save us but it did nothing instead, it withdrew in a shrugging irony, as if to suggest that this is what the world is, and our time in it, all lifted possibility, all complexity and rushing fervour, to end in nothing on a small strand, and go back out to rejoin the empty family from whom we had set out alone with such a burst of brave unknowing energy.

I smiled for a moment before I turned. I could have told him that the wave I had watched was as capable of love as we are in our lives. He would have told your sister-in-law that I had gone slightly bonkers in California and indeed might, in turn, have told you; and you would have smiled softly and tolerantly as though there was nothing wrong with that. You had, after all, gone bonkers yourself in your own time. Or maybe you have calmed down since I left you; maybe the passing years have helped your sanity.

On Saturdays before I came back, through the winter and right into early June, I would drive out from the city to Point Reyes, my GPS with its Australian accent instructing me which way to turn, which lanes I should be in, how many miles were left. They knew me by now in the Station, as the GPS called it, in the cheese shop there, where I also bought bread and eggs, in the bookshop, where I bought books of poems by Robert Hass and Louise Glück, and one day found William Gass's book *On Being Blue*, which I also bought. I bought the week's fruit and then, when the weather grew warm, sat outside the post office eating barbequed oysters that a family of Mexicans had cooked on a stall beside the supermarket.

All this was mere preparation for the drive to the South Beach and the lighthouse. It was like driving towards here, where I am now. Always, you make a single turn and you know that you are approaching one of the ends of the earth. It has the same desolate aura as a poet's last few poems, or Beethoven's last quartets, or the last songs that Schubert managed. The air is different, and the way things grow is strained and gnarled and windblown. The horizon is whiteness, blankness; there are hardly any houses. You are moving towards a border between the land and sea that does not have hospitable beaches, or guest-houses painted in welcoming stripes, or merry-go-rounds, or ice-cream for sale, but instead has warnings of danger, steep cliffs.

At Point Reyes there was a long beach and some dunes and then the passionate and merciless sea, too rough and unpredictable for surfers or swimmers or even paddlers. The warnings told you not to walk too close, that a wave could come from nowhere with a powerful undertow. There were no lifeguards. This was the Pacific Ocean at its most relentless and stark, and I stood there Saturday after Saturday, putting up with the wind, moving as carefully as I could on the edges of the shore, watching each wave crash towards me and dissolve in a slurp of undertow.

I missed home.

I missed home. I went out to Point Reyes every Saturday so I could miss home.

Home was this empty house back from the cliff at Ballyconnigar, a house half full of objects in their packages, small paintings and drawings from the Bay Area, a Vija Celmins print, some photographs of bridges and water, some easy chairs, some patterned rugs. Home was a roomful of books at the back of this house, two bedrooms and bathrooms around it. Home was a huge high room at the front with a concrete floor and a massive fireplace, a sofa, two tables, some paintings still resting against the walls, including the Mary Lohan painting I bought in Dublin and other pieces I bought years ago waiting for hooks and string. Home also was this room at the top of the house, cut into the roof, a room with a glass door opening on to a tiny balcony where I can stand on a clear night and look up at the stars and see the lights of Rosslare Harbour and the single flashes of Tuskar Rock Lighthouse and the faint, comforting line where the night sky becomes the dark sea.

I did not know that those solitary trips to Point Reyes in January, February, March, April, May, and the return with a car laden down with provisions as though there were shortages in San Francisco, I did not know that this was a way of telling myself that I was going home to my own forgiving sea, a softer, more domesticated beach, and my own lighthouse, less dramatic and less long-suffering.

I had kept home out of my mind because home was not merely this house I am in now or this landscape of endings. On some of those days as I drove towards the lighthouse at Point Reyes I had to face what home also was. I had picked up some stones and put them on the front passenger seat and I thought that I might take them to Ireland.

Home was some graves where my dead lay outside the town of Enniscorthy, just off the Dublin Road. This was a place where I could direct no parcels or paintings, no signed lithographs encased in bubble wrap, with the address of the sender on the reverse side of the package. Nothing like that would be of any use. This home filled my dreams and my waking time more than any other version of home. I dreamed that I would leave a stone on each of those graves, as Jewish people do, as Catholics leave flowers. I smiled at the thought that in the future some archaeologist would come to those graves and study the bones and the earth around them and write a paper on the presence of these stray stones, stones that had been washed by the waves of the Pacific, and the archaeologist would speculate what madness, what motives, what tender needs, caused someone to haul them so far.

Home was also two houses that they left me when they died and that I sold at the very height of the boom in this small strange country when prices rose as though they were Icarus, the son of Daedalus, warned by his father not to fly too close to the sun or too close to the sea, Icarus who ignored the warning and whose wings were melted by the sun's bright heat. The proceeds from those two houses have left me free, as though the word means anything, so that no matter how long I live I will not have to work again. And maybe I will not have to worry either, although that now sounds like a sour joke but one that maybe I can laugh at too as days go by.

I will join them in one of those graves. There is space left for me. One of these days I will go and stand in that graveyard and contemplate the light over the Slaney, the simple beauty of grey Irish light over water, and know that I, like anyone else who was born, will be condemned eventually to lie in darkness as long as time lasts. And all I have in the meantime is this house, this light, this freedom, and I will, if I have the courage, spend my time watching the sea, noting its changes and the sounds it makes, studying the horizon, listening to the wind or relishing the calm when there is no wind. I will not fly even in my deepest dreams too close to the sun or too close to the sea. The chance for all that has passed.

*

I wish I knew how colours came to be made. Some days when I was teaching I looked out the window and thought that everything I was saying was easy to find out and had already been surmised. But there is a small oblong stone that I have carried up from the strand and I am looking at it now after a night of thunder and a day of grey skies over the sea. It is the early morning here in a house where the phone does not ring and the only post that comes brings bills.

I noticed the stone because of the subtlety of its colour against the sand, its light green with veins of white. Of all the stones I saw it seemed to carry most the message that it had been washed by the waves, its colour dissolved by water, yet all the more alive for that, as though the battle between colour and salt water had offered it a mute strength.

I have it on the desk here now. Surely the sea should be strong enough to get all the stones and make them white, or make them uniform, as the grains of sand are uniform? I do not know how the stones withstand the sea. As I walked yesterday in the humid late afternoon the waves came gently to rattle the stones at the shore, stones larger than pebbles, all different colours. I can turn this green stone around, the one that I carried home, and see that at one end it is less than smooth as though this is a join, a break, and it was once part of a larger mass.

I do not know how long it would have lasted down there, had I not rescued it; I have no idea what the life span is of a stone on a Wexford beach. I know what books George Eliot was reading in 1876, and what letters she was writing and what sentences she was composing, and maybe that is enough for me to know. The rest is science and I do not do science. It is possible then that I miss the point of most things – the mild windlessness of the day, the swallows' flight, how these words appear on the screen as I enter them, the greenness of the stone.

Soon I will have to decide. I will have to call the car hire company at Dublin Airport and extend the time I am going to keep the car. Or I will have to drop the car back. Maybe get another car. Or return here with no car, just the mountain bike and some phone numbers for taxis. Or leave altogether. Late last night when the thunder had died down and there was no sound, I went online to look for telescopes, looking at prices, trying to find the one that Bill had shown me, which I found so easy to manipulate. I studied the length of time delivery would take and thought of waiting for this new key to the distant waves for a week or two weeks or six weeks, watching out from my dream house for a new dream to be delivered, for a van to come up this lane with a large package. I dreamed of setting it up out here in front of where I am sitting now, on the tripod that I would have ordered too, and starting, taking my time, to focus on a curling line of water, a piece of the world indifferent to the fact that there is language, that there are names to describe things, and grammar and verbs. My eye, solitary, filled with its own history, is desperate to evade, erase, forget; it is watching now, watching fiercely, like a scientist looking for a cure, deciding for some days to forget about words, to know at last that the words for colours, the blue-grey-green of the sea, the whiteness of the waves, will not work against the fullness of watching the rich chaos they yield and carry.

RODDY DOYLE

TWO PINTS ×4

14–10–11

— D'yeh ever read poetry?

— Wha'?!

— D'you ever—

— I heard yeh. I just can't fuckin' believe I heard yeh.

— Well, look it—

— G'wan upstairs to the lounge if yeh want to talk abou' poetry.

— Just let me—

— Unless yeh can talk abou' the football in rhyme. 'There was a young player called Blunt'.

— There's no player called Blunt – far as I know.

— You're missin' me point.

— I'm not. I heard yeh. Yeh didn't hear me.

— I did.

— You feel threatened by it.

— No, I don't.

— Yeh do. Yeh even moved your stool there.

— I didn't.

— Yeh fuckin' did. To get away from anny mention of poetry. It's mad.

— Well, it's a load o' shite.

— I agree with yeh. That's wha' I'm tryin' to say.

— Yeh've lost me now.

— So listen. My young's one's youngest lad, Damien.

— The kid with the cheeks.

— That's him. He's good in school – the great white hope. Annyway, he has to read a fuckin' poem an' write a bit about it. The homework, like.

— Okay.

— So, he's in our place, cos his ma's visitin' the da. An' asks me to, yeh know, look at the poem. So I get the oven gloves on an' I give it a dekko. 'The Road Not Taken' – some bollix called Robert Frost. Have yeh read it, youself?

— I won't even say no.

— Two roads diverged in a yellow wood. Stay where yeh are; I'm just givin' yeh a flavour o' the thing.

— And – wha'?

— Well, this cunt – Robert Frost, like – he's makin' his mind up abou' which road to take an' he knows he'll regret not takin' one o' them. An' that's basically it.

— He doesn't need a fuckin' poem for tha'. That's life. It's common fuckin' sense.

— Exactly. I go for the cod, I regret the burger.

— I married the woman but I wish I could be married to her sister.

— Is tha' true?

— Not really – no.

— Annyway. Yeh sure?

— Go on.

— So annyway, the poor little bollix – Damien, like – the grandson. He has to answer questions about it. An' the last one – it's really stupid now. What road do you think you should never take? An', like, I tell him, The road to Limerick.

— Did he write tha'?

— He fuckin' did. An' guess where the fuckin' teacher comes from? An' guess who's been called up to the fuckin' school, to explain himself to the fuckin' headmaster?

— Brilliant.

— Tomorrow mornin'.

— Serves yeh righ' for readin' poetry.

— I agree. A hundred fuckin' per cent. Two roads diverged in a yellow wood me hole.

12–2–12

— Poor oul' Whitney, wha'.

— Sad.

— Desperate.

— She was a great young one.

— She was forty-eight.

— But she was always a young one. D'yeh know what I mean?

— An' forty-eight's young these days annyway.

— True. She's at home, fuckin' devastated.

— Whitney?

— Stop bein' thick. The wife. She felt a special – I don't know – a link, I suppose. Our youngest, Kevin, yeh know – he was conceived after we saw *The Bodyguard*.

— In the fuckin' cinema?

— No, we made it home. Well – the front garden.

— Nice one.

— We stopped at the boozer – here actually, upstairs. An' the chipper.

— Romantic.

— Fuck off. The chips were her idea.

— The ride was yours, but, was it?

— No, no. She took the initiative there as well. Thing was, she thought the fillum was the best thing she'd ever seen an' I thought it was a load o' shite.

— Bet you didn't tell her that.

— I forgot. So anyway, Kevin arrived the nine months later.

— Hang on. Kevin Costner.

— Exactly; yeah.

— An' if he'd been a girl, it would've been—

— Whitney; yeah.

— Ah God. I'm sorry for your troubles, bud.

— Thanks.

14–10–16

— See Bob Dylan won the Nobel Prize.

— Which one?

— Wha'?

— There's loads o' them. Bukes, science, accountancy – there's rakes o' the things. There's even one for fuckin' peace.

— Science then – I think.

— Fuckin' science? He won the Nobel Prize for science?

— Has to be, I'd say. That song, 'Mister Tambourine Man'.

— What about it?

— Well, how can one sham play a song with only a fuckin' tambourine? It can't be done. It's like givin' some poor fucker one o' them Irish yokes—

— A bodhrán.

— Exactly. An expectin' him to play 'Bohemian Rhapsody' on it. It's just not possible.

— But Dylan cracked it.

— That's me theory. But seriously—

— Go on.

— He deserves it. The buke – the literature – prize.

— I'm with yeh.

— I remember when me brother brought home *Highway*

61 Revisited, when it came ou', like. Now, I love me music – always did. But The Beatles, like – 'Love Me Do' an' tha'. I mean, there wasn't much in the lyrics of any o' the songs back then. An' then I heard Dylan singin' about the postcards an' the hangin' an' tha'. 'Desolation Row', yeh know. An' it was amazin'. The start of me life, nearly. Even me da stopped complainin' about the noise. For a minute.

17–10–19
— See your man, Doyle, has a new buke ou'.
 — What's it abou'?
 — Two fuckin' eejits talkin' shite in a pub.
 — Are yeh serious?
 — Yeah.
 — Two shams like us?
 — Yep.
 — Talkin' shite.
 — Yeah.
 — Who'd want to read tha'?
 — No one is my bet.
 — Would you want to read a fuckin' buke with you in it?
 — I'd only be half the buke.
 — Wha'?
 — The other half would be the other cunt.
 — What other cunt?
 — The cunt talkin' to the other fuckin' eejit.
 — Hang on – me?
 — Spot on.
 — Fuck off now – wha' do they talk abou'?
 — Well – the ice-bucket challenge.
 — Ah, yeah.
 — An' David Bowie an' Prince.

—Ah, yeah.

—An' Robin Williams.

—Poor oul' Robin.

—An' Bill O'Herlihy.

—Ah, Bill.

—An' the same sex marriage thing.

—Ah yeah.

—An' the football an' tha'.

—Just like us.

—Yeah.

—Hang on, but. Is it actually us?

—The wife picked it up there – in Eason's. An' she had a flick through it. An' she says, Yeah – she recognized me.

—It's us?

—Yeah.

—It mightn't be tha' bad, so. Did she buy it?

—No, she didn't. She says she already has me on audio – why would she want the fuckin' buke?

ÉILÍS NÍ DHUIBHNE

A LITERARY LUNCH

THE BOARD WAS gathering in a bistro on the banks of the Liffey.

'We deserve a decent lunch!' Alan, the chairman, declared cheerfully. He was a cheerful man. His eyes were kind and encouraged those around him to feel secure. People who liked him said he was charismatic.

The board was happy. Their tedious meeting was over and the bistro was much more expensive than the hotel to which Alan usually brought them, with its alarming starched tablecloths and fantails of melon. He was giving them a treat because it was a Saturday. They had sacrificed a whole three hours of the weekend for the good of the organization they served. The reputation of the bistro, which was called Gabriel's, was excellent and anyone could tell from its understated style that the food would be good, and the wine, too, even before they looked at the menu – John Dory, oysters, fried herrings, sausage and mash. Truffles. A menu listing truffles just under sausage and mash promises much. We can cook and we are ironic as well, it proclaims. Put your elbows on the table, have a good time.

Emphasizing the unpretentiously luxurious tone of Gabriel's was a mural on the wall depicting a modern version of *The Last Supper*, a mural of typical Dubliners eating at a long refectory table. Alan loved this mural, a clever, postmodern, but delightfully accessible, work of art. It raised the cultural tone of the bistro, if it needed raising, which it didn't really, since it was also located next door to the house on Usher's Island where James Joyce's aunts had lived, and which he used as the setting for his most celebrated story, 'The Dead'. In short, of all the innumerable restaurants boasting literary associations in town, Gabriel's had the most irrefutable credentials. You simply could not eat in a more artistic place.

The funny thing about *The Last Supper* was that everyone was sitting at one side of the table, very conveniently, for painters and photographers. It was as if they had anticipated all the attention that would soon be coming their way. And Gabriel's had, in its clever, ironic way, set up one table in exactly the same manner, so that everyone seated at it faced in the same direction, getting a good view of the picture and also of the rest of the restaurant. It was great. Nobody was stuck facing the wall. You could see if anyone of any importance was among the clientele – and usually there were one or two stars, at least. You could see what they were wearing and what they were eating and drinking, although you had to guess what they were talking about, which made it even more interesting, in a funny sort of way. More interactive. It was like watching a silent movie without subtitles.

A problem with the arrangement was that people at one end of *The Last Supper* table had no chance at all of talking to those at the other end. But this, too, could be a distinct advantage, if the seating arrangements were intelligently handled. On this sort of outing, Alan always made sure that they were.

At the right end of the table he had placed his good old friends, Simon and Paul. (Joe had not come, as per usual. He was the real literary expert on the board, having won the Booker Prize, but he never attended meetings. Too full of himself. Still, they could use his name on the stationery.)

Alan himself sat in the middle, where he could keep an eye on everyone. On his left-hand side were Mary, Jane and Pam. The women liked to stick together.

Alan, Simon and Paul ordered oysters and truffles and pâté de foie gras for starters. Mary, Jane and Pam ordered one soup of the day and two nothings. This was not owing to the gender division. Mary and Jane were long past caring about their figures, at least when out on a free lunch, and Pam was new and eager to try everything being a member of a board offered, even John Dory, which she had ordered for her main course. Their abstemiousness was due to the breakdown in communications caused by the seating arrangements. The ladies had believed that nobody was getting a starter, because Alan had muttered, 'I don't think I'll have a starter,' and then changed his mind and ordered the pâté de foie gras when they were chatting among themselves about a new production of *A Doll's House*, which was just showing at the Abbey. Mary had been to the opening, as she was careful to emphasize; she was giving it the thumbs down. Nora had been manic and the sound effects were appalling. The slam of the door that was supposed to reverberate down through a hundred years of drama couldn't even be heard in the second row of the stalls. That was the Abbey for you, of course. Such dreadful acoustics, the place has to be shut down. Pam and Jane nodded eagerly; Pam thought the Abbey was quite nice but she knew if she admitted that in public everyone would think she was a total loser who had probably failed her Leaving. Neither Pam nor Jane had seen *A Doll's House* but they had read a review by Fintan O'Toole, so they knew everything they needed to know. He hadn't liked the production, either, and had decided that the original play was not much good, anyway. *Farvel*, Ibsen!

In the middle of this conversation Pam's mobile phone

began to play 'Waltzing Matilda' at volume level five. Alan gave her a reproving glance. If she had to leave her mobile phone on, she could at least have picked a tune by Shostakovich or Stravinsky. He himself had a few bars by a young Irish composer on his phone, ever mindful of his duty to the promotion of the national culture.

'Terribly sorry!' Pam slipped the phone into her bag, but not before she had glanced at the screen to find out who was calling. 'I forgot to switch it off.'

Which was rather odd, Mary thought, since Pam had placed the phone on the table, in front of her nose, the minute she had come into the restaurant. It had sat there under the water jug, looking like a tiny pistol in its little leather holster.

In the heel of the hunt, all this distraction meant that they neglected to eavesdrop on the men while they were placing their orders, so that they would get a rough idea of how extravagant they could be. How annoying it was now to see Simon slurping down his oysters, with lemon and black pepper, and Paul digging into his truffles, while they had nothing but *A Doll's House* and one soup of the day to amuse themselves with. And a glass of white wine. Paul, who was a great expert, had ordered that. A Sauvignon Blanc, the vineyard of Dubois Père et Fils, 2002.

'As nice a Sauvignon as I have tried in years,' he said, as he munched a truffle and sipped thoughtfully. 'Two thousand and two was a good year for everything in France, but this is exceptional.'

The ladies strained to hear what he was saying, much more interested in wine than drama. Mary, who had been so exercised a moment ago about Ibsen at the Abbey, seemed to have forgotten all about both. She was now taking notes, jotting down Paul's views. He was better, much better, than the people who do the columns in the paper, she commented excitedly as she scribbled. No commercial agenda – well, that they knew of. You never quite knew what anyone's agenda was, that was the trouble. Paul was apparently on the board because of his knowledge of books, and Simon, because of his knowledge of the legal world, and Joe, because he was famous. Mary, Jane and Pam were there because they were women. Mary was already on twenty boards and had had to call a halt, since her entire life was absorbed by meetings and lunches, receptions and launches. Luckily, she had married sensibly and did not have to work. Jane sat on ten boards and Pam had been nominated two months ago. This was her first lunch with any board, ever. She was a writer. Everyone wondered what somebody like her was doing here. It was generally agreed that she must know someone.

One person she knew was Francie Briody. He was also having lunch, in a coffee shop called the Breadbasket, a cold little kip of a place across the river. They served filled baguettes and sandwiches as well as coffee and he was lunching on a tuna submarine with corn and coleslaw. Francie was a writer, like Pam, although she wrote so-called literary women's fiction, chick lit for PhDs, and was successful. Francie wrote literary fiction for anybody who cared to read it, which was nobody. For as long as he could remember he had been a writer whom nobody read. And he was already fifty years of age. He had written three novels and about a hundred short stories, and other bits and bobs. Success of a kind had been his lot in life, but not of a kind to enable him to earn a decent living, or to eat anything other than tuna submarines, or to get him a seat on an arts organization board. He had had one novel published, to mixed reviews; he had won a prize at Listowel Writers' Week for a short story fifteen years ago.

Six of his short stories had been nominated for prizes – the Devon Cream Story Competition, the Blackstaff Young Authors, the William Carleton Omagh May Festival, among others – but he still had to work part-time in a public house, and he had failed to publish his last three books. Nobody was interested in a writer past the age of thirty.

It was all the young ones they wanted these days, and women, preferably young women with lots of shining hair and sweet photogenic faces. Pam. She wasn't that young any more, and not all that photogenic, but she'd got her foot in the door in time, when women and the Irish were all the rage, no matter what they looked like. Or wrote like.

He'd never been a woman – he had considered a pseudonym but he'd let that moment pass. And now he'd missed the boat. The love affair of the London houses and the German houses and the Italian and the Japanese with Irish literature was over. So everyone said. Once Seamus Heaney got the Nobel, the interest abated. Enough's enough. On to the next country. Bosnia or Latvia or God knows what. Slovenia.

Francie's latest novel, a heteroglossial, polyphonic, postmodern examination of post-modern Celtic Tiger Ireland, with special insights into political corruption and globalization, beautifully written in darkly masculinist ironic prose with shadows of *l'écriture féminine*, which was precisely and exactly what Fintan O'Toole swore that the Irish public and Irish literature was crying out for, had been rejected by every London house, big and small, that his agent could think of, and by the five Irish publishers who would dream of touching a literary novel as well, and also, Francie did not like to think of this, by the other thirty Irish publishers who believed chick lit was the modern Irish answer to James Joyce. Yes yes yes yes. The delicate chiffon scarf was flung over her auburn curls. Yes.

Yeah well.

He'd show the philistine fatso bastards. He pushed a bit of slippery yellow corn back into his sub. Extremely messy form of nourishment, it was astonishing that it had caught on, especially as the subs were slimy and slippery themselves.

Not like the home-made loaves served in Gabriel's on the south bank of the Liffey. Alan was nibbling a round of freshly baked, soft as silk, crispy as Paris on a fine winter's day, roll, to counteract the richness of the pâté, which was sitting slightly uneasily in his stomach.

'We did a good job,' he was saying to Pam, who liked to talk shop, being new.

'I'd always be so worried that we picked the wrong people,' she said in her charming, girlish voice.

She had nice blond hair but this did not make up for her idealism and her general lack of experience. Alan wished his main course would come quickly. Venison with lingonberry jus and basil mash.

'You'd be surprised but that very seldom happens,' he said.

'Judgements are so subjective vis-à-vis literature,' she said with a frown, remembering a bad review she'd received seven and a half years ago.

Alan suppressed a sigh. She was a real pain.

'There is almost always complete consensus on decisions,' he said. 'It's surprising, but the cream always rises. I . . . we . . . are never wrong.' His magical eyes twinkled.

Consensus? Pam frowned into her Sauvignon Blanc. A short discussion of the applicants for the bursaries, in which people nudged ambiguities around the table like footballers dribbling a ball, when all they want is the blessed trumpeting of the final whistle. They waited for Alan's pronouncement. If that was consensus, she was Emily Dickinson. As soon as Alan said, 'I think this is brilliant writing' or 'Rubbish, absolute rubbish', there was a scuffle of voices vying with each other to be the first to agree with the great man.

'Rubbish, absolute rubbish.' That was what he had said about Francie. 'He's persistent, I'll give him that.' Alan had allowed himself a smile, which he very occasionally permitted himself at the expense of minor writers.

The board guffawed loudly. Pam wouldn't tell Francie that. He would kill himself. He was at the end of his tether. But she would break the sad news over the phone in the loo, as she had promised. No bursary. Again.

'I don't know,' she persisted, ignoring Alan's brush-off. 'I feel so responsible somehow. All that effort and talent, and so little money to go around . . .' Her voice trailed off. She could not find the words to finish the sentence, because she was drunk as an egg after two glasses. No breakfast, the meeting had started at nine.

Stupid bitch, thought Alan, although he smiled cheerily. Defiant. Questioning. Well, we know how to deal with them. Woman or no woman, she would never sit on another board. This was her first and her last supper. '*I feel so responsible somehow.*' Who did she think she was?

'This is a 2001 Bordeaux from a vineyard run by an Australian expat just outside Bruges, that's the Bruges near Bordeaux of course, not Bruges-la-Morte in little Catholic Belgium.' Paul's voice had risen several decibels and Simon was getting a bit rambunctious.

They were well into the second bottle of the Sauvignon and had ordered two bottles of the Bordeaux, priced, Alan noticed, at €85 a pop. The lunch was going to cost about a thousand euro.

'Your venison, sir?' At last. He turned away from Pam and speared the juicy game. The grub of kings.

*

Francie made his king-size tuna submarine last a long time. It would have lasted, anyway, since the filling kept spilling out onto the table and it took ages to gather it up and replace it in the roll. He glanced at the plain round clock over the fridge. They'd been in there for two hours. How long would it be?

Fifteen years.

Since his first application.

Fifty.

His twelfth.

His twelfth time trying to get a bursary to write full-time.

It would be the makings of him. It would mean he could give up serving alcohol to fools for a whole year. He would write a new novel, the novel that would win the prizes and show the begrudgers. Impress Eileen Battersby. Impress Emer O'Kelly. Impress, maybe, Fintan fucking O'Toole. And the boost to his morale would be so fantastic . . . but once again that Alan King, who had been running literary Ireland since he made his Confirmation probably, would shaft him. He knew.

Pam phoned him from the loo on her mobile. She had tried her best but there was no way. They had really loved his work, she said. There was just not enough money to go round. She was so sorry, so sorry . . .

Yeah right.

Alan was the one who made the decisions. Pam had told him so herself. 'They do exactly what he says,' she said. 'It's amazing. I never knew how power worked. Nobody ever disagrees with him.'

Nobody who gets to sit on the same committees and eats the same lunches, anyway. As long as he was chair, Francie would not get a bursary. He would not get a travel grant.

He would not get a production grant. He would not get a trip to China or Paris or even the University of Eastern Connecticut. He would not get a free trip to Drumshanbo in the County Leitrim for the Arsehole of Ireland Literature and Donkey Racing Weekend.

Alan King ruled the world.

The pen is stronger than the sword, Francie had learned in school. Was it Patrick Pearse who said that or some classical guy? Cicero or somebody. That's how old Francie was, they were still doing Patrick Pearse when he was in primary. He was pre-revisionism and he still hadn't got a bursary in literature, let alone got onto Aosdána, which gave some lousy writers like Pam a meal ticket for life. The pen is stronger. Good old Paddy Ó Piarsaigh. But he changed his mind, apparently. Francie looked at the Four Courts through the corner window of the Breadbasket. Who had been in that in 1916? He couldn't remember. Had anyone? Éamonn Ceannt or Seán Mac Diarmada or somebody nobody could remember. Burnt down the place in the end, all the history of Ireland in it. IRA of their day. That was later, the Civil War. He had written about that, too. He had written about everything. Even about Alan. He had written a whole novel about him, and six short stories, but they were hardly going to find their mark if they never got published, and they were not going to get published if he did not get a bursary and some recognition from the establishment, and he was not going to get any recognition while Alan was running every literary and cultural organization on the island . . .

At last. The evening was falling in when the board members tripped and staggered out of Gabriel's, into the light and shade, the sparkle and darkness, that was Usher's Quay. Jane and Mary had of course left much earlier, anxious to get to the supermarkets before they closed.

But Pam, to the extreme annoyance of everyone, had lingered on, drinking the Bordeaux with the best of them. They had been irritated at first but had then passed into another stage. The sexual one. Inevitable as Australian Chardonnay at a book launch. They had stopped blathering on about wine and had begun to reminisce about encounters with ladies of the night in exotic locations. Paul claimed, in a high voice that had Alan looking around the restaurant in alarm, to have been seduced by a whore in a hotel in Moscow, who had bought him a vodka and insisted on accompanying him to his room, clad only in a coat of real wolfskin. Fantasy land. That eejit Pam was so shot herself she didn't seem to care what they said. Her mascara was slipping down her face and her blond hair was manky, as if she had sweated too much. It was high time she got a taxi. He'd shove her into one as soon as he got them out. He couldn't leave them here, they'd drink the board dry, and if they were unlucky, some journalist would happen upon them. He stopped for a second. Publicity was something they were always seeking and hardly ever got. But no, this would do them no good at all. There is such a thing as bad press, in spite of what he said at meetings. He paid the bill. There were long faces, of course. You'd think he was crucifying them, instead of having treated them to a lunch that had cost, including the large gratuity he was expected to fork out, €1,200 of Lottery money. Oh well, better than racehorses, he always said, looking at Gabriel's *Last Supper*. Was it Leonardo or Michelangelo had painted the original? He was so exhausted he couldn't remember. He took no nonsense from the boyos, though, and asked the waiter to put them into their coats no matter how they protested.

Pam had excused herself at the last minute, taking him aback.

'Don't wait for me,' she had said. She could still speak coherently. 'I'll be grand, I'll get a taxi. I'll put it on the account.'

She gave him a peck on the cheek – that's how drunk she was – and ran out the door, pulling her mobile out of her bag as she did so.

Not such a twit as all that. '*I'll put it on the account.*' He almost admired her for a second.

With the help of the waiter, he got the other pair of beauties bundled out to the pavement.

Their taxi had not yet arrived.

He deposited Simon and Paul on a bench placed outside for the benefit of smokers and moved to the kerb, the better to see.

Traffic moved freely along the quay. It was not as busy as usual. A quiet evening. The river was a blending delight of black and silver and mermaid green. Alan was not entirely without aesthetic sensibility. The sweet smell of hops floated along the water from the brewery. He'd always loved that, the heavy, cloying smell of it, like something you'd give a two-year-old to drink. Like hot jam tarts. In the distance he could just see the black trees of the Phoenix Park. Sunset. Peaches and molten gold, Dublin stretched against it. The north side could be lovely at times like this. When it was getting dark. The Wellington monument rose, a black silhouette, into the heavens, a lasting tribute to the power and glory of great men.

It was the last thing Alan saw.

He didn't even hear the shot explode like a backfiring lorry in the hum of the evening city.

Francie's aim was perfect. It was amazing that a writer

who could not change a plug or bore a hole in a wall with a Black & Decker drill at point-blank range could shoot so straight across the expanse of the river. Well, he had trained. Practice makes perfect, they said, at the creative writing workshops. Be persistent, never lose your focus. He had not written a hundred short stories for nothing and a short story is an arrow in flight towards its target. They were always saying that. *Aim, write, fire.* And if there's a gun on the table in act one, it has to go off in act three, that's another thing they said.

But, laughed Francie, as he wrapped his pistol in a Tesco Bag for Life, in real life what eejit would put a gun on the table in act one? In real life a gun is kept well out of sight and it goes off in any act it likes. In real life there is no foreshadowing.

That's the difference, he thought, as he let the bag slide over the river wall. That's the difference between life and art. He watched the bag sink into the black lovely depths of Anna Livia Plurabelle. Patrick Pearse gave up on the *peann* in the end. When push came to shove, he took to the *lámh láidir*.

He walked down towards O'Connell Bridge, taking out his mobile. Good old Pam. He owed her. 'For all men kill the thing they love,' he texted her, pleased to have remembered the line. 'By each let this be heard. Some do it with a bitter look, some with a flattering word. The coward does it with a kiss; the brave man with a gun.'

That wasn't right. *Word* didn't rhyme with *gun*.

'Some do it with a bitter look, some with a flattering pun.' Didn't really make sense. What rhymes with *gun*? Lots of words. *Fun, nun. Bun.* 'Some do it with a bitter pint, some with a sticky bun,' he texted in. 'Cheers! I'll buy you a bagel sometime.' He sent the message and tucked his phone into his pocket. Anger sharpened the wit, he had noticed that before. His best stories had always been inspired by the lust for revenge. He could feel a good one coming on . . . maybe he shouldn't have bothered killing Alan.

He was getting into a bad mood again. He stared disconsolately at the dancing river. The water was far from transparent, but presumably the murder investigation squad could find things in it. They knew it had layers and layers of meaning, just like the prose he wrote. Readers were too lazy to deconstruct properly but policemen were probably pretty assiduous when it came to interpreting and analysing the murky layers of the Liffey. Would that Bag for Life protect his fingerprints, DNA evidence? He didn't know. The modern writer has to do plenty of research. God is in the details. He did his best but he had a tendency to leave some books unread, some websites unvisited. Writing a story, or murdering a man, was such a complex task. You were bound to slip up somewhere.

Perfectionism is fatal, they said. Give yourself permission to err. Don't listen to the inner censor.

He had reached O'Connell Street and, hey, there was the 46A waiting for him. A good sign. They'd probably let him have a laptop in prison, he thought optimistically, as he hopped on the bus. They'd probably make him writer-in-residence. That's if they ever found the gun.

JOHN CONNOLLY

A DREAM OF WINTER

WHEN I WAS a boy, I attended a school that stood by a cemetery. Mine was the last desk, the one closest to the graveyard. I spent years with my back to the darkness of it. I can remember how, as autumn neared its end and winter gathered its strength, I would feel the wind begin to blow through the window frame and think that the chill of it was like the breath of the dead upon my neck.

One day, in the bleakness of January, when the light was already fading as the clock struck four, I glanced over my shoulder and saw a man staring back at me. Nobody else noticed him, only I. His skin was the grey of old ash long from the fire, and his eyes were as black as the ink in my well. His gums had receded from his teeth, giving him a lean, hungry aspect. His face was a mask of longing.

I was not frightened. It seems strange to say that, but it is the truth. I knew that he was dead, and the dead have no hold over us beyond whatever we ourselves surrender to them. His fingers touched the glass but left no trace, and then he was gone.

Years passed, but I never forgot him. I fell in love, and married. I became a father. I buried my parents. I grew old, and the face of the man at the school window became more familiar to me, and it seemed that I glimpsed him in every glass. Finally, I slept, and when I awoke I was no longer as I once had been.

There is a school that stands by a cemetery. In winter, under cover of fading light, I walk to its windows and put my fingers to the glass.

And sometimes, a boy looks back.

KEVIN BARRY

THE APPARITIONS

IT WAS OCTOBER when the apparition of Samuel Beckett appeared on a gable wall in Ringsend. The spectral visitation was twelve feet tall and not quite inanimate – if you stared long enough, a strange flicker enlivened its hawk-like eyes. The apparition was faint in daylight but more obvious at night – come dusk, his form would somehow illuminate. The gable was of an old tenement that housed a 24-hour tanning salon and an infamous chipper. Soon it was noted that at a certain melancholy hour, Beckett turned by the merest fraction to look toward the Liffey's storied waters. By coincidence, the new Samuel Beckett Bridge had lately been slung across the river just west of Ringsend to link the Grand Canal Dock Redevelopment Scheme with the Irish Financial Services Centre, but let it be said that no apparent distaste clouded the falcon-like gaze of the stout-hearted old Resistance fighter.

The apparition caused immediate difficulties for the Dublin intelligentsia. This was no Blessed Virgin taking form upon a tree stump in front of syphilitic peasants out in the hungry districts of west Limerick. This was a secular apparition, and it was incontestable – Beckett was absolutely *there* on the Ringsend gable. The intelligentsia found they had nothing smart to say about the matter, and an amount of hand-wringing and beard-stroking went on in the thoughtfully renovated terrace houses of Portobello.

As for the particulars of the apparition, this incarnation

was of Beckett perhaps in his late fifties. He wore a trademark black rollneck sweater and a pair of thick-stemmed miserabilist corduroys. Gaunt as ever, he had that poised gentleness about him, too, a certain reserve – he was still every inch the ascetic Foxrockian.

In the early days, a steady stream of pilgrims flowed down Pearse Street. These were unhealthily thin young men who had lingered too long for their complexions' good in the reading rooms of Trinity College and the National Library. In an expectant hush, they gathered around the apparition, and little moans of ecstasy escaped their throats at every shimmer of the profoundly depressed dramatist's osprey-like glance. Perhaps his sharp gaze was seeking on the southern horizon the great peak of Djouce in the Wicklow mountains, where he had trailed as a boy after the bootsteps of his cheerful father? So the young men mused as they rolled cigarettes from their tobacco pouches and drifted into an almost post-coital fugue state.

Slowly, though, as the weeks of early winter passed, we grew accustomed to the apparition. Certainly, if you were on the No 2 bus heading home to Sandymount, you'd turn your head to have a quick look, as young women came and went from the tanning salon, tangerine-faced in their Ugg boots, and as the occasional brawl erupted outside the chipper, and you were reassured that no matter how grim you were feeling yourself, Beckett felt worse. But the gathering of pale young devotees with each passing day diminished, and the apparition became just another of those oddities of Dublin life that its people find are as well left unremarked.

Then Beckett spoke.

It occurred at precisely five o'clock on Tuesday evening in the last week of November. He said:

'Oh I have an itchy, *itchy* anus.'

Things became awkward. As anyone who has read his *Selected Letters* will attest, the fact that Beckett suffered the not-inconsiderable trial of an itchy anus is hardly news, but to have him state the fact in plain hearing of the citizenry was unfortunate, and frankly a little uncouth. Especially as it became the apparition's custom to repeat those words, like an irate mantra, every hour and on the hour.

It was at this point the city authorities put a call through to my PR consultancy.

Rikki, they said, we need your help.

The Beckett apparition had of course attracted an amount of international media coverage. Ireland is always favoured as a source for skewy colour pieces, and throughout the early weeks, global news crews were frequently on the scene in Ringsend. The apparition was a boost to our tourist numbers, certainly, though of course a smallish one – a ghostly visitation from an avant-garde dramatist will realistically only do so much for bed-night figures. Still, it was coverage, and the authorities were now concerned that having Beckett whinging about his arsehole on an hourly basis wasn't an ideal projection of the city's image.

We thrashed the matter out during an emergency late-night session at a discreet hotel on the quays. I tried to keep things calm. I suggested a number of reasonably innovative PR solutions, but just then a messenger lad came from across town, panting, and he brought fresh news:

James Joyce was after putting in an appearance on Clanbrassil Street.

We pelted through the rainy nighttime streets in our macs and galoshes, and it was breathlessly remarked that Mr Joyce had notable connections with his point of apparition. His character, Leopold Bloom, in the novel *Ulysses*, lived at 52 Clanbrassil Street. This direct link to the work suggested at once a more promising heritage opportunity. It was thoughtful of Mr Joyce, we remarked, to allow such a connect.

Then we saw him. He was above on the gable end of a poledancing and private-room emporium called Fun-time Kitty O'Reilly's All-Nite Slaghouse. In the window of which a flashing neon sign promised:

'Fresh Ukrainian Snatch Daily.'

Now Beckett was one thing. He has a certain snob value, but Joyce, to this day, is box office, and we knew his apparition would attract massive attention. And this is where he chose to appear?

Plus, he was shitfaced.

He swayed dangerously, and the eyes behind the wire-rimmed spectacles were watery and roving. And, unlike Beckett, who in due fairness had maintained a dignified silence for a few weeks anyway – at least until his piles started to play up – Joyce was mouthing out of him from the get-go. He was tappin' passers-by for change in a slurred and unpleasantly melodious tone. And he was sizing up everything in a skirt. Ankles to nape, they took the rake of his beady little masturbator's eyes. Anything aged sixteen to sixty-four. Lascivious, unkempt, drunk – this was our Joyce apparition.

'Ah, don't, please!' we beseeched the passers-by as they reached politely for change. 'He'll only drink it!'

We were only beginning to come to terms with the Joyce disaster when word filtered down from the northside reaches of the city: William Butler Yeats had arrived. His apparition was on the gable end of a methodone clinic on Talbot Street. He couldn't have picked a section of the city with more fucking skangers per square fucking foot. He was speaking, yes, but in a well-mannered whisper.

'Nodge?' he wafted. 'Would you have a nodge spare for me at all?'

We retreated to our discreet hotel on the quays.

So what's a 'nodge' exactly? a representative of the city authorities asked.

From what I gather, I said, it means a small chipping of hashish or cannabis resin – perhaps just enough to make a single cannabis 'cigarette'.

From our subsequent enquiries, it turned out, sadly, that WBY had form in this regard – he used to buy 'tincture of cannabis' from a chemist shop in Sligo.

At least he's not on the smack, an authorities man remarked.

Not yet, another sighed. But the hash is a gateway drug . . . The cunt will be robbin' people on the Luas by Christmas.

Rikki, they all pleaded, it's time for action!

And it was later – much later – whilst abed, in a flop of night-sweat, that the solution came to me:

Screens!

I remembered the fabric screens they used on the gable ends of pubs for big sporting occasions. A gauzy screen that pulls down and hides an entire gable for you. No bother.

I put the notion to the members and they barked like seals.

Quickly, we had the screens made up, and an explanation was offered to the city in a special broadcast that went out simultaneously on all channels.

It had been established, we said, by scientific evidence that the apparitions were starting to fade into the brickwork. This was not yet visible to the naked human eye but our surveyors were in no doubt. The fading was due to the workings of the pale Dublin sunlight. If the matter were to go unchecked, we would lose the apparitions entirely within a year or two. So the apparitions had to be protected by special screens, and the words spoken – such a gift from the otherworld – must be protected also. By being drowned out.

The Beckett screen was a rendition of the playwright gazing into a Parisian morn, outside a café, while a tape played loudly on an endless loop a rendition of 'I can't go on . . . I'll go on . . . I can't go on . . . I'll go on . . .' as performed by a rotating cast of stars of Irish television and radio, including the man who does the Brennan's Bread ad.

The Joyce screen was a vision of the novelist in blazer and strawboater, while a tape played (eternally) the closing paragraph from 'The Dead' as recited by An Especially Soulful Actor of the Dublin Stage.

The Yeats screen was an image from his dope-free early twenties, on the beach in Sligo, as a musical adaptation of 'Inishfree' was sung by Westlife.

We announced that the actual apparitions, and their voices, might yet be allowed to appear for special occasions.

But no particular dates were set.

LUCY CALDWELL

HERE WE ARE

'HERE WE ARE,' she said, as we faced each other, and my whole body rushed with goosebumps.

The summer is a washout. Every day the heavens open and the rain comes down; not the usual summer showers with their skittish, shivering drops but heavy, dull, persistent rain; true dreich days. The sky is low and grey and the ground is waterlogged, the air cold and damp, blustery.

We don't care. It is the best summer of our lives.

We go to Cutters Wharf in the evenings because nobody we know goes there. It's an older crowd, suits and secretaries, some students from Queen's. Usually we sit inside but one evening when the clouds lift and the rain ceases we take our drinks out onto the terrace. The riverfront benches and tables are damp and cold but we put plastic bags down and sit on those. It isn't warm but there is the feeling of sitting under the full sky, that pale high light of a Northern evening, and there is the salt freshness of the breeze coming up the Lagan from the lough.

After we leave Cutters Wharf that night we walk. We walk along the Lagan and through the Holylands: Palestine Street, Jerusalem Street, Damascus Street, Cairo Street. We cross the river and walk the whole sweep of the Ormeau Embankment. The tide is turning and a two-person canoe is skimming downriver, slate grey and quicksilver.

When we reach the point where the road curves away from the river, the pale evening light still lingers so we keep walking, across the Ravenhill Road, down Toronto Street and London Street and the London Road, Willowfield Drive and across the Woodstock Road and on, further and further east until we are in Van Morrison territory, Hyndford Street and Abetta Parade, Grand Parade, the North Road, Orangefield.

There are times in your life, or maybe just the one time, when you find yourself in the right place, the only place you could possibly be, and with the only person.

She feels it, too. She turns to me. 'These streets are ours,' she says.

'Yes,' I say. 'Yes, they are,' and they were. The whole city was.

She was a celebrity in our school, in the way that some girls are. She was the star musician and always played solos at school concerts and prize days and when a minor royal came to open the new sports hall. One year in the talent contest she played the saxophone while another girl sang 'Misty'. They didn't win – some sixth-formers who'd choreographed their own version of 'Vogue' got more votes – but they were the act you remembered. She wore a white suit and sunglasses, but it wasn't that: it was the way she bent over her instrument and swayed, as if it was the most private moment in the world.

It was a few weeks later that her mother was killed. She was out jogging when a carful of teenage joyriders lost control and careened up onto the kerb. They didn't stop: if they had stopped, or at least stopped long enough to ring an ambulance, she might have survived. As it was, she died of massive internal haemorrhaging on a leafy street in Cherryvalley, less than a hundred metres from her home. Her husband was a local councillor and so it made the headlines: the petite blonde jogger and the teenage delinquents.

Her entire class went to the funeral, and the older members

of the orchestra, too. I was only a second year and had never even spoken to her, so I just signed the card that went round. She didn't come to practice for several weeks and there were rumours that she had given up music for good. You'd look for her in the corridors, her face pale and thin with violet bruises under the eyes. Then one day she was there again, sitting in her usual place, assembling her clarinet, and if the teacher was surprised or pleased to see her he didn't let on, and none of the rest of us did, either.

She smiled at me sometimes in orchestra practice but I knew she didn't know who I was. I was two years below, for a start, and she had no way of knowing my name because the music teacher called all three of us flutes, Flutes. She smiled because he would make silly mistakes, telling us to go from the wrong place or getting the tempo wrong, and there'd be exaggerated confusion in the screeching, bored, lumbering ranks while he flustered and pleaded and tried to marshal a new start. People were cruel to him, sometimes even to his face. She never was: she just smiled, and because of the way the music stands were laid out I happened to be in the direction of the smile.

I used to say her name to myself sometimes. Angie. Angela Beattie.

What else? She cut her own hair: at least, that's what people said, and it looked as if it could be true, slightly hacked-at, although the mussed-up style made it hard to tell. Her father was a born-again Christian – he belonged to a Baptist church that spent summers digging wells in Uganda or building schools in Sierra Leone – and when our school joined up with another in west Belfast to play a concert at St Anne's Cathedral, she wasn't allowed to take part because it was a Sunday, even though it would be in a church, even though it was for peace.

There was so little I knew about her then.

In the summer term of fourth year, everyone took up smoking, or pretended to. The school was strange and empty that time of year, the upper sixth and fifth form on study leave, the lower sixth promoted to prefects and enjoying their new privilege of leaving the grounds at lunchtime. It was ours to colonize. We linked arms and ducked behind the overgrown buddleia into the alley behind the sports hall, boasting that we needed a smoke so badly we didn't even care if anyone caught us.

The day they did, it was raining and so we weren't expecting it: but all of a sudden there they were, coming down the alleyway, one at each end. I was holding one of the half-smoked cigarettes and I froze, even as all the others were hissing at me to chuck it away.

The prefect walking towards me was Angie.

I could feel the flurry as those with cigarettes or a lighter scrambled to hide them and others tore open sticks of chewing gum or pulled scarves up around their faces, but only vaguely, as if it was all happening a very long way away.

Angie stopped a couple of metres away. My hand was trembling now.

'Oh my God,' I heard, and, 'What are you at?' and, 'Put it out, for fuck's sake.' But I couldn't seem to move.

Angie looked at me. The expression in her eyes was almost amused. Then, ignoring the nervous giggles and whispered bravado of the others, she took a step forward and reached out for the cigarette. Her fingers grazed mine as they took it from me. She held it for a moment, then let it fall to the ground, crushed it with her heel. She looked me in the eye the whole time. I felt heat surge to my face.

'You don't smoke,' she said, and then she said my name.

I felt the shock of it on my own lips. I hadn't known she

knew it: knew who I was. She gazed at me for a moment longer in that steady, amused, half-ironic way. Then she said to the other prefect, 'Come on,' and the second girl shouldered past and they walked back the way Angie had come.

'It's not cool, girls,' she called, without turning round. 'You think it is, but it's not.'

There was silence until they'd turned the corner. Then it erupted: 'What the fuck?' and, 'Oh my God,' and, 'Do you think she's going to report us?' and, 'I am so dead if they do,' and, 'What is she like?' and then, 'Do you reckon she fancies you?'

It was the standard slag in our school. But out of nowhere I felt my whole body fizz: felt the words rush through me, through and to unexpected parts of me, the skin tightening under my fingernails and at the backs of my knees.

'Wise up,' I made my voice say, and I elbowed and jostled back. 'It's because of the music. My lungs will be wrecked if I carry on smoking, I actually should think about giving up,' and because we were always talking about having to give up, the conversation turned and that got me off the hook, at least for the moment.

For the rest of term I agonized over whether to stop hanging out with the smokers at lunch or whether to keep doing it in case she came back. In the end I compromised by going behind the sports hall as usual, but not inhaling, so I could say with all honesty, if she asked, that I didn't smoke any more. My days became centred on those ten minutes at lunchtime when I might see her again. I would feel it building in me in the last period before lunch, feel my heart start to flutter and my palms become sweaty. But she didn't raid the alleyway again. There was nowhere else I could count on seeing her: orchestra practice had ceased in the last weeks of the summer term – the assembly hall was used for examinations and there were too many pupils on study leave, anyway – and the sixth-form wing, with its common room and study hall, was out of bounds to fourth years. I passed her in the corridor, once, but she was deep in conversation with another girl and didn't notice me. On the last day of term I saw her getting into a car with a group of others and accelerating down the drive, and that was that.

The summer holidays that followed were long. My father, a builder, had hurt his back a few months earlier and been unable to work so money was tight: there wasn't even to be a weekend in Donegal or a day trip to Ballycastle. The city, meanwhile, battened down its hatches and I was forbidden to go into town; forbidden, in fact, from going further than a couple of streets away from our house. All my friends who lived nearby were away; I was too old to ride my bike up and down the street like my younger sister.

'Why don't you practise your flute?' my mother would say as I sloped endlessly about the kitchen. Normally I'd roll my eyes, but as the days stretched on I found myself doing it. I didn't admit to myself it was because of Angie Beattie, but as I practised I couldn't help thinking of her. When you first learn the flute, you're told to imagine you're kissing it. Now, every time I put my mouth to the lip plate I thought of her. I'd think of her mouth, the curve of it. I'd think of the times I'd watched her at the start of orchestra practice, how she'd wet the reed of her clarinet and screw it into place, test it, adjust it, curl and recurl her lips around the mouthpiece. I'd let my mind unfurl and soon I'd think other things, too, things that weren't quite thoughts but sensations, things I didn't dare think in words and that afterwards left me hot and breathless and almost ashamed.

I got good at the flute that summer. When school started up again the music teacher noticed. He kept me back after the auditions and found me some sheet music, asked me to learn it for the Christmas concert. Then he said he'd had a better idea and rummaged in his desk some more. A sonata for flute and piano, he said: we were short on duets. Angie Beattie could accompany me.

'She might not want to,' I said.

'Nonsense,' he said.

I don't remember much about the first few lunchtime practice sessions we had together. Each one, before it happened, seemed to loom, so inflated in my mind I almost couldn't bear it; then, when it was happening, it rushed by. At first I could barely meet Angie's eye: it was mortifying, the extent to which I'd thought about her, let myself daydream about her, and more. But the music was difficult – for me, at least, which made it hard work for her as my accompanist – and that meant there was no time to waste; we needed to get straight to work. After the first week I found I was able to put aside, at least when I was actually with her, the memory of the strange summer's fantasies. But sometimes, late at night, I'd be consumed for an instant with an ache that seemed too big for my body to contain.

One evening we stayed late practising after school and, completely out of the blue, she invited me back to her house for dinner. My heart started pounding as I tried to say a nonchalant yes; I'd imagined her house, the rooms she lived in, so many times; I'd imagined so often a scenario in which she might ask me back there. I phoned my mum from the payphone in the foyer and then we walked back together, down the sweep of the school's long drive, through the drifts of horse chestnut and sycamore leaves in the streets, swinging our instrument cases. There was mist in the air, and as we turned off the main road, the taste of woodsmoke from a bonfire in a nearby garden. The Cherryvalley streets were wide and quiet, thick with dark foliage, lined with tall, spreading lime trees. It was a world away from my street, its neat brick terraces and toy squares of lawn. The gnomes and mini-waterfall in our neighbour's garden that I used to love and show off to school friends, before I realized they weren't something to be proud about. Cherryvalley seemed to belong to somewhere else entirely.

'It's nice around here,' I said.

She glanced at me. 'D'you think so?'

There was something in her expression I couldn't read and I remembered – of course, too late – that her mother had died here, maybe on this very street, or the one we just walked down. The streets felt not quiet, but ominous, then, the shifting shadows of the leaves, the plaited branches.

'I meant,' I said, flustered, 'the streets have such pretty names.'

She didn't reply and I tried to think of something else to say, something that would show I was sorry, that I understood. But of course I didn't understand, at all.

We walked on in silence. I wondered what had made her ask me back and if she was already regretting it.

The Beatties' house was draughty and dark. Angie walked through flipping on light switches and drawing the curtains. I thought of my house, the radio or the TV or often both on at the same time, my mum busy cooking, the cat always underfoot. Angie made me sit at the kitchen table, like a guest, while she hung my blazer in the cloakroom and made me a glass of lime cordial, then hurried about getting dinner ready. She turned on the oven and took chicken Kievs from the freezer, lined a baking tray with tinfoil. Boiled the kettle to cook some potatoes, washed lettuce in a salad spinner and chopped it into ribbons. I had never, I realized, imagined how her home life actually worked.

I felt shy of this Angie: felt the two years, and everything else, between us.

When Mr Beattie got back he looked nothing like the man you used to see shouting on TV or gazing down from lamp posts. He was tall and thin and washed-out-looking; his shoulders were stooped and his hair needed cutting. He shook my hand and I found myself blurting out, 'My dad used to vote for you.' It was a lie: my dad never bothered to vote and my mum, even though Dad teased her about it, only ever voted Women's Coalition. I felt Angie looking at me and I felt my neck and face burning.

'Good man,' Mr Beattie said. 'Every vote counts. These are historic times we're living through.'

'And history will judge us,' I heard myself say. I have no idea where it came from. The car radio, probably, the talk show Mum always had on and always turned off.

Mr Beattie blinked and Angie burst out laughing.

'Indeed,' he said. 'Indeed.'

'He likes you,' Angie said, when Mr Beattie had left the room. 'He really likes you.'

I wasn't sure what there had been to like, but before I could say anything, she said, 'If he talks about church, don't say you don't go.'

'OK,' I said. 'Why not?'

'Oh,' she said. 'It's just more trouble than it's worth.'

When everything was ready and the three of us sat down at the table, Mr Beattie bowed his head and clasped his hands and intoned a long grace. I looked at Angie halfway through but she had her head bowed and her eyes closed, too.

I took care to chime my 'Amen' in with theirs.

As we ate, Mr Beattie asked questions about school, about music. Often Angie would jump in with an answer before I had a chance and I couldn't work out if it was for my benefit or her father's. When he asked what church I went to, Angie said, 'She goes to St Mark's, don't you?'

'St Mark's Dundela,' Mr Beattie said.

'That's right,' Angie said.

'That's the one,' I said. St Mark's was where our school had its Christmas carol service, the only time of year my family ever set foot in a church, and only then because I was in the choir.

'Good, good,' Mr Beattie said, and I made myself hold his gaze. All that nonsense was just hocus-pocus, is what my dad liked saying. Once, when some Jehovah's Witnesses knocked on our front door and asked if he'd found Jesus, my dad clapped his forehead and said, 'I have indeed, down the back of the sofa, would you believe.' My sister and I had thought it was the funniest thing ever.

'St Mark's Dundela,' Mr Beattie said again. I started to panic then, trying to remember something, anything about it. But he didn't ask any more. 'C.S. Lewis's church,' was all he said, and I smiled and agreed.

The meal seemed to go on forever. The St Mark's lie had made me feel like a fraud: but it wasn't just that, the whole situation was putting me on edge. Angie was more nervous than I'd ever seen her: in fact, I couldn't think of a time when I had seen her nervous, not when she confronted the smokers, not even before a solo. I must be doing everything wrong, I thought. I had the horrible feeling, too, that Mr Beattie could see through me, or worse, could see into me, into some of the things I'd thought about his daughter.

For dessert there was a chocolate fudge cake, from Marks & Spencer, shiny and dense with masses of chocolate shavings on top.

'Dad has a sweet tooth, don't you, Dad?' Angie said. She

cut him a slab of cake and they grinned at each other for a moment.

'We used to have chocolate cake for dinner sometimes, didn't we?' she said. 'Or cheesecake.'

'Strawberry cheesecake,' Mr Beattie said.

'We reckoned,' she said, turning to me, 'that because it had cheese in, it was actually quite nutritious.'

'A meal in a slice,' Mr Beattie said.

'Protein, fat, carbohydrate and fruit,' she said, turning back to him.

'A perfectly balanced plate,' he said, and they smiled that smile again, intimate, impenetrable.

When the meal was finally over, Mr Beattie said, 'Well, after all this talk of the duet, you must give me a concert.'

Without looking at me, Angie said, 'Another time, Dad, we're both played out today,' and I knew she was embarrassed of me. I felt tears boil up in my eyes and I stood up and said I needed the toilet. I took as long as I could in there, soaping and rinsing my hands several times over, drying each finger. I'd say I had homework, I decided. I'd say my mum didn't like me being out after dark. Both of these things were true.

When I told Angie that I had to go, she looked at me, then looked away. 'Oh,' she said. 'Right.'

Mr Beattie brought my blazer from the cloakroom and said he'd see me to the door.

'It's nice to see Angie bringing a friend back,' he said. 'I look forward to hearing this duet of yours one of these days.'

The whole way home I felt a strange, fierce sense of grief, as if I'd lost something; a possibility; something that wouldn't come again.

After that I avoided her, concert or no concert. I went with the smokers at lunch, half-daring her to come and find me, half-dreading it. Thursday and Friday passed without my seeing her. An awful weekend, then Monday and Tuesday, and on Tuesday afternoon I knew I had to skip orchestra practice. On Wednesday she came to the mobile where my class did French, in the middle of a lesson, and said to the teacher she needed to speak to me. She was a prefect and it was known that we were both musical; the teacher agreed without any questions. The shock and relief and shame of seeing her coursed through me and I had to hold onto the desk for a moment as I stood up. As I followed her out of the classroom and down the steps and around the side of the mobile I couldn't seem to breathe.

'How long are you planning on keeping this up?' she said.

'I don't know,' I said.

I could see her pulse jumping in the soft part of her neck. A horrible, treacherous part of me wanted to reach out and touch it.

'Angie,' I said, and from all of the things that were whirling in my head I tried to find the right one to say.

The trees and glossy pressing shrubs around us were thrumming with rain. All the blood in my body was thrumming.

'Look at me,' she said, and when I finally did, she leaned in and kissed me. It was brief, only barely a kiss, her lips just grazing mine. Then she stepped back and I took a step back, too, and stumbled against the roughcast side of the mobile. She put out a quick hand to steady me, then stopped.

'Oh God, am I wrong?' she said. 'I'm not wrong, am I?'

Two weeks later, in my house this time, a Saturday night, my parents at a dinner party, my sister at a sleepover. In the living room, in front of the electric fire, we unbuttoned each other's shirts and unhooked the clasps of each other's bras. Then our jeans and knickers: unzipping, wriggling, hopping out and off. We kept giggling: there we were gallivanting around in my parents' living room in nothing but our socks.

'Here we are,' she said, as we faced each other, and my whole body rushed with goosebumps.

'Are you cold?' she said, but I wasn't: it wasn't that, at all.

Afterwards we pulled the cushions off the sofa and lay on the floor, side by side. After a while we did start to shiver, even with the electric fire turned up fully, but neither of us reached for our clothes, scattered all over like useless, preposterous skins.

'We're like selkies,' she said, 'like Rusalka, do you know the opera?' and she stood up and struck a pose and sang the first few lines of the aria, the water nymph's song to the moon, she told me later, and I jumped to my feet and applauded and we started giggling again, ridiculous bubbles of joy.

'Here we are,' she said again, and I said, 'Here we are,' and that became our saying, our shorthand. Here we are.

All love stories are the same story: the moment that, that moment when, the moment we.

We were *we* through Christmas, and into the spring. It was so easy: the music had been the reason, and now it was our excuse. We used one of the practice rooms each lunchtime and sometimes after school, and no one questioned it. Sometimes we'd play, or she'd play and I'd listen, or we'd both listen to music, and sometimes we'd just eat our sandwiches and talk. I'd go to hers after school, although I never quite felt at ease there, and I preferred it when we'd go for drives in her car, up the Craigantlet hills or along the coast to Holywood. I drifted from my friends, and she from hers, but the music practice hid everything.

And then we had the summer and we were freer than ever, completely free, and I lied blithely to my parents about where I was going and who with, using a rotating cast of old friends, and neither of them ever cottoned on, and I assumed it was the same for Mr Beattie, too.

I don't want to think about the rest of it: the evening he finally confronted us; walked right in on us. I don't want to give any room to the disgust or the revulsion. To the anger and the panic that followed, and the tears, our tears, our wild apologies, when we should have been defiant, because what was there, in truth, for us to be apologizing for, and to whom did we owe any apology?

Both of us, tears streaming.

'I have to do it,' she keeps on saying. 'I'm all he's got. It won't change anything. But I have to do it.'

I don't want to think about any of that, either.

That winter, my English class studied Keats. I wrote a whole essay, six, seven sides, on the final stanza of 'The Eve of St Agnes'. *And they are gone: aye, ages long ago / These lovers fled away into the storm.* In the stanza before, the lovers are gliding like phantoms into the wide cold hall and the iron porch where the porter lies in a drunken stupor. His bloodhound wakes and shakes its flabby face but doesn't bark. The bolts slide open one by one, the chains stay silent and the key finally turns, then just as they think they've made it the door groans on its hinges. You think it's all over for them but then you read on and you realize they've slipped away, out of your hands, before your very eyes, a miracle, a magic trick, a wormhole to another place, another time, where no one can ever follow.

The teacher kept me after class. She didn't believe I'd written it, at least not alone. I opened my lever arch and showed her my notes. Page after page in my crabbed, self-conscious writing. Ending rights the focus, I'd written, does not leave us in too cosy a glow but reminds us of age/decay/coldness of religious characters. I left this part out: I finished my essay with the lovers escaping. We talked about the real ending, Keats's ending, and we talked about his drafts of the ending, some of which were printed in the footnotes of the cheap Wordsworth edition.

'You've really thought about this,' she said. 'You've really taken this to heart.'

I started to cry.

'Oh dear,' the teacher said, and she found me a tissue from a plastic pouch in her desk drawer, and she came round and sat on the front of her desk and asked if there was anything I wanted to talk about. I shook my head and held out my hand for my essay, and I wondered how much she knew, or guessed, my whole body liquid with shame.

I looked up Angela Beattie on the Internet just once, some months ago, on impulse, spurred by the Marriage Equality march in Belfast. It instantly felt too easy: too much. She'd never made it as a solo or even an orchestral musician but she was a music teacher – and she was married; she and her husband ran a small music school together in Ayrshire. There were pictures of them both on the website, taking group lessons, conducting ensembles, standing with students from the most recent woodwind summer school. She was still whippet-thin, no make-up, choppy hair. He looked younger than her: Doc Martens and skinny jeans, spiky hair, an earring. I clicked from one picture to the next. I don't know why I was so taken aback. I was engaged, after all. Engaged, happily engaged, and about to buy a flat. I just had never imagined it for her.

A memory came to me: one time in Ruby Tuesday's, or The Other Place, one of the studenty cafés across town in south Belfast where you could sit and eke out a mug of filter coffee for a whole evening. We'd said I love you by then: maybe for the first time, or maybe very recently; we were huge and important and giddy with it, with all of it, with *us*. I felt as if my blood was singing – that sparks were shooting from me – that everything I touched was glowing. I could have done anything in those weeks. I could have run marathons or swum the length of the Lagan or jumped from a trapeze and flown. And yet I was happy, happier than I thought it was possible to be, just sitting in a café, talking. We sat in that café and talked about everything and nothing, talked and talked, and we were us. I remember that; I couldn't get over that. The room and everything in it – the scuffed wooden booths, the chipped laminate tables, the oversized menus; the fat boys in Metallica T-shirts and Vans at the table beside us, the cluster of girls across the way still in their school uniforms, the waitress carrying a plate of profiteroles; the rain on the window, the yellow of the light – it seemed a stage set that had been waiting our whole lives for us and at last we were here.

The waitress at the table, splashing more coffee into our mugs: 'Anything else I can get for yous, girls?' and we say, 'No, thank you,' in unison, then burst out laughing, at nothing, at all of it.

For all the waitress knows, for all anyone knew, we're just two students, two friends, having a coffee.

'I want to tell her,' I say. 'I want to stand up and tell everyone.' And for a moment, it seemed as if it might just be that simple: that that was the secret.

'I don't want us to have to hide,' I went on. 'I want to tell everyone – my parents, your dad. Everyone. I want to stand in front of the City Hall with a megaphone and shout it out to the whole of Belfast.'

Suddenly neither of us was laughing any more.

'I wish we could,' she said.

We were both quiet for a moment.

'When you were older,' I said, thinking aloud, 'you could team up with a male couple and the four of you could go out together and people would assume, assume correctly, you were on a double date. Only the couples wouldn't be what they thought.' I was pleased with the idea, but she still didn't smile.

'Hiding in plain sight,' she said.

'You could live together,' I went on, 'all in one big house, so your parents wouldn't get suspicious. If you had to, you could even marry.'

I started laughing again as I said it.

'No,' she said, and she was serious, more than serious; solemn. She reached out and touched one finger to my wrist and all of my blood leapt towards her again. 'We won't need to,' she said. 'By then we'll be free.'

It all flooded back to me and made me indescribably sad.

That night, I walked the streets of east Belfast again in my dreams. Waking, the dream seemed to linger far longer than a mere dream. These streets are ours. I was jittery all day, a restless, nauseous, over-caffeinated feeling. I could email her, I thought, through the website. I wouldn't bother with pleasantries or preliminaries, I'd just say, There we were. Do you remember?

CATHY SWEENEY

THE DOOR

ON MONDAY 5/06/15, P—— was surfing the net during his lunch break when he saw a house to rent on Daft.ie. It looked perfect so he sent M—— an email with a link to it. M—— must have got on to it straight away because within the hour she texted P—— to say she had arranged a viewing for 7 o'clock. She reminded him that she couldn't make it because Thursday was kickboxing night, but P—— could go on his own. She ended her text with an 'x' which meant that she was in a good mood. In recent times P——'s lack of initiative had become an issue in their relationship so P—— was pleased at M——'s use of 'x' in her text and set out at 6 o'clock to view the house.

It was a long walk and the evening was cold, grey, and it was quietly raining. The agent was already at the house when P—— arrived and he introduced himself with a handshake. There was no one else at the viewing which surprised P—— as there was usually a long queue. While the agent showed P—— around, the two men chatted about hurling. P—— was wearing a Kilkenny jersey as he was originally from that county and, although the agent was originally from Galway, he agreed with P—— that 'The Cats' would bag it again that year. The house was nicely decorated with a modern-style kitchen and a balcony off the bedroom and P—— began to wonder if there had been a misprint on the website regarding the rent. Affecting a casual tone, he asked the agent what the rent was. The agent confirmed that it was as P—— had seen advertised on Daft.ie, at which point, unable to disguise his enthusiasm, P—— said that he would take the house.

The agent said that there was just one 'proviso'. What do you mean by 'proviso'? P—— asked. The agent explained that the rent was 'restricted' because of the access route required to the door at the end of the hallway. P—— did not understand what the agent was talking about, but when he looked down the hallway he saw a door at the end that he had not noticed previously. What do you mean by access route? he asked. The agent explained that every few months he would require access to the door at the end of the hallway. He assured P—— that he would not be inconvenienced in any way. He said, You have my word on that. I'll send you a text giving at least 48 hours' notice and then I'll arrive at a time of your choosing and access the door via the hallway. The agent said that he would have a person or people with him but that he would simply be escorting them to the door and that once they had gone through it he would leave via the hallway and that would be that. The entire process would take no more than a minute or two. Furthermore, the agent told P——, the soundproofing of the door at the end of the hallway was Grade A certified.

A lot of thoughts passed through P——'s mind. They passed through almost simultaneously and so the order in which they are presented below is purely arbitrary:

What person or people is the agent talking about?/ M—— won't like this 'proviso'./Where are the person or people going to?/M—— will be in a very good mood if we have a house like this./What is behind the door?/There is absolutely nothing else available to rent in this part of town that we can afford.

The agent waited. P—— reiterated that he would take the

house. Once more the agent shook P——'s hand heartily and the two men, having exchanged mobile numbers, parted by throwing genial phrases back and forth in the cold air. Talk to you./Mind how you go./Be good./And if you can't be good.../Up The Cats!

P—— and M—— moved into their new house on Saturday, 23/06/15. It was a warm day, although it clouded over in the afternoon. M—— organized all aspects of the move with the help of her father who owned a van. It went smoothly and by 9 o'clock that night the couple were in the living room, M—— unpacking the last few boxes, P—— setting up the new flat screen TV, a bottle of wine open and a lemongrass candle burning on the mantelpiece. Life was good.

P—— had not yet got around to telling M—— about the 'proviso'. In the weeks leading up to the move he had intended doing so, but something always got in the way. Either he was too busy or she was too busy, or M—— was in a good mood and P—— didn't want to ruin it, or M—— was in a bad mood and P—— didn't want to make it worse. P—— reasoned that since the 'proviso' was no more than a minor inconvenience, why make a big deal out of it. Sooner or later M—— would notice the door at the end of the hall and ask him about it, although it surprised him that she hadn't noticed it by now. When she did, he would explain it to her in a calm, reasoned way, exactly as the agent had explained it to him. He had already mentioned to her on more than one occasion that the agent was a decent type, originally from Galway, and a great man for the hurling.

M—— and P—— settled into their new house and life went on pretty much as it had before, except that now they shared bills and had to desist from habits such as shopping for superfluous clothes or masturbating in the shower.

M—— never mentioned the door at the end of the hallway and after a week or so P—— forgot about it completely.

On the morning of 27/10/15, four months after he and M—— had moved into the house, P—— received a text from an unknown number. It read, *What time Tuesday?* He stared at it for a long time before remembering that he had neglected to store the agent's number in his phone, and only then did he register its meaning. All through the day at work he thought about the text. He felt as if there was a bird dying in his stomach. He did not eat lunch. On the bus home he finally replied to the text. *3.30?* Almost instantly he felt his phone vibrate in his hand. It was a reply from the agent saying, *OK.

On Tuesday, P—— left work at lunchtime citing a toothache. He took the bus home. He was afraid to put on the TV or make a cup of tea or use the toilet in case the bell rang, so he sat on the second last step of the stairs and waited. Through the bubble glass in the front door he could see if anyone was approaching. Glancing down to the end of the hallway, he looked at the other door. He was perplexed as to how he could have forgotten about it. It was the same height and width as every other door in the house and was stained with the same brown varnish and had the same metal handle. There was no key in the keyhole.

The bell rang and P—— opened the front door.

The agent stood on the doorstep. Behind him was a woman with a sluggish face, as though she had just woken up or recently taken marijuana. The woman had a large baby in one arm and her other hand gripped the handle of a buggy. The buggy was stuffed with bags with more bags hanging from it. A small boy stood beside her. The agent winked at P—— and walked down the hall. The woman struggled to get the heavy buggy through the door and the boy followed behind her. The baby had a soother in its mouth and P—— noted that its face was very red. When the agent reached the door at the end of the hall, he whisked it open and the woman went in with the baby, the buggy and the boy. The agent closed the door and walked back along the hallway and out into the pleasant autumnal afternoon, calling as he went: Well, ye did it again. Two in a row for Kilkenny.

Long before Halloween the shops were full of Christmas decorations. M—— kept repeating the same phrase to everyone she met. The first Christmas in our new home. She explained to P—— how important Christmas was to her and insisted they go shopping most weekends. P—— was easy about Christmas. He could take it or leave it. But since it put M—— in a good mood, he was happy to go shopping most weekends. He was in the homeware department of Penneys in Dundrum Shopping Centre when he got the next text from the agent. It read, *Christmas Eve?* You have to be joking, P—— thought, even though he knew it was not a joke. While M—— was at the counter buying a set of four wooden napkin rings shaped like reindeers, P—— sent a reply text. *2.20. *M—— was going to her parents in Blanchardstown on Christmas Eve and he was going to his mother in Kilkenny. It had all been arranged months ago so that he and M—— could spend Christmas Day together. M—— would head off to her parents in the morning but he was planning to leave it until the afternoon to make the journey to Kilkenny. Two hours spent with his mother who was still sulking over the new arrangements for Christmas Day would be enough.* The agent texted back. *OK.

On 19/12/15, M—— went to her Christmas work party and told P—— not to wait up because it would be a late one. P—— planned to chill out, have a few beers, and watch an action movie on the flat screen TV, but he couldn't relax.

Around 10 o'clock he went out into the hallway. He put his ear to the door and listened. Nothing. He put his hand on the handle and slowly depressed it. The door opened and P—— looked inside. A small room, not much bigger than a porch, with the same laminate flooring as in the hallway, the same cream coloured paint on the walls, a picture on the back wall that looked like one from the set of impressionist landscapes that hung in the living room when P—— and M—— had first moved into the house and which M—— had promptly replaced with prints from Ikea. There was also a small potted plant in one corner and on the left wall, another door, just like this one, also with no key. P—— shut the door softly and went back into the living room where he crashed out on the couch. He was still there when M—— arrived home at four in the morning wanting to have sex.

When the doorbell rang at 2.20 on Christmas Eve, P—— opened it and greeted the agent, who shook his hand firmly. With the agent was an Arab man, mid-twenties, wearing jeans and a buttoned black jacket, carrying a rucksack. Without lifting his eyes, the Arab walked down the hallway after the agent, but when he reached the door he hesitated and mumbled something in what P—— presumed was Arabic, before the agent forced him through the door saying, C'mon now. No messing. On his way out, the agent smiled and wished P—— a Happy Christmas. As it turned out, however, it was not an especially happy Christmas. P—— and M—— got up very late on Christmas Day, both with a hangover, and ate their M&S dinner on their laps in front of the TV.

In the new year, P—— and M—— agreed to tighten their belts. P—— undertook 'Dry January' and M—— signed up for a spinning class on Mondays, Wednesdays and Fridays. She had tired of kickboxing. Whenever M—— was out,

P—— found himself thinking more and more about the door at the end of the hallway. Soon M—— had only to leave before P—— was in the hallway staring at the door. Questions about the door had come to P—— in the middle of the night when he couldn't sleep but couldn't get up in case he disturbed M——. Questions – again in arbitrary order – such as:

Where does the other door lead to?/ Who waters the plant?/ Do the Arab and the woman with the baby and the boy know each other?/How can a plant live in a room with no light?/Is the agent a good man or a bad man?

P—— began to open the door more and more. At first, just wide enough to glimpse into the room, but, gradually, wider and wider. The first time he went inside the room was on 5/05/16. He just stood in it for a minute or two. It was not until 18/07/16 that he began enacting what would rapidly become a ritual whenever M—— left the house for more than an hour or so. Stripping down to his boxers, removing his watch and glasses, P—— would open the door and step into the room, shut the door behind him, and then sit in the cool darkness with the wall at his back and his hands around his knees.

A lot happened in the first half of that year. The weather was unseasonably mild and P—— was promoted at work and, egged on by both his best friend and M——'s best friend, he proposed to M—— on 14/02/16 at a special dinner in an expensive restaurant. She said yes and was busy organizing the wedding, which was set for 21/06/18. Luckily M—— had a first cousin who was a wedding planner, because there was a huge amount to do. Also, the agent accessed the door at the end of the hallway on two further dates. On 22/02/16 he escorted a woman who looked Eastern European and who had a bruise on her right cheekbone and on 11/06/18, the day after P—— and M—— returned from a package holiday in Greece, he escorted a family of seven through the door. On that occasion M—— was upstairs unpacking their suitcases after the holiday. P—— had seen no reason to engage in elaborate schemes to get her out of the house since the entire process, as always, had taken no more than a minute or two. The family followed the agent down the hallway so efficiently that P—— just managed to do a head count and note that they looked Irish. The agent paused briefly at the front door to ask P—— if he thought Kilkenny were up to the three in a row. P—— replied, No better men.

P—— found himself going into the room more and more often. Sometimes he would go in at night while M—— was sleeping. She had read in a magazine that 'pure' sleep combated the signs of ageing and had taken to wearing earplugs and an eye mask in bed. P—— even went into the room when M—— was at home watching TV, or taking a bath, or – when work was particularly stressful – doing her mindfulness exercises in the bedroom. He would hear her calling him and reappear in the hallway. Where the fuck were you? M—— would say, but she didn't really want an answer. Once, when P—— opened the door, there were red/brown stains on the laminate floor and he didn't go into the room. They were gone a few days later when he opened the door again. Another time a half bottle of diet Pepsi was left beside the potted plant along with a clump of hair. But overall the agent was right, the door caused no real inconvenience.

In this way life went on. Things happened. Some good. Some bad. The agent arrived at the house every few months to escort a person/people through the door, but P—— no longer asked himself any questions. Kilkenny did not get the three in a row that year. P—— and M—— developed a routine that, while not entirely satisfactory, was not entirely unsatisfactory either, and included sex on one of the weekend mornings. Gradually they resumed their old habits of shopping for superfluous clothes and masturbating in the shower. One day they will move out of the house and someone else will rent it and accept the 'proviso'. Maybe P—— and M—— will save up enough money to buy a house in Kildare or Portlaoise or Arklow with a 35-year mortgage and a 4-hour commute. Or maybe they will break up before the wedding and one or other of them will emigrate to Canada or Manchester or Seoul. But before we leave P—— and M—— forever, let us pause on one final scene:

It is late afternoon on a Sunday and M—— is out at a family celebration. P—— is sitting in the room behind the door wearing only his boxers. His back is supported by the wall and the floor beneath him is cool. He reaches out and touches the leaves of the potted plant. They are smooth. Touching the leaves makes P—— believe he is in a dream, a dream in which he knows he is dreaming, and that if he wanted to, he could wake from, but he doesn't want to. In the darkness P—— closes his eyes. Everything is white and frozen and very silent, as in winter in some country that no longer exists.

SALLY ROONEY

COLOUR AND LIGHT

THE FIRST TIME he sees her she's getting into his brother's car. He's sitting in the back seat and she gets into the front, closing the passenger door behind her. Then she notices him. She cranes around, eyebrows raised, and then turns back to Declan and says, Who's this?

That's Aidan, Declan says. My brother.

I didn't know you had a brother, she says mildly.

She turns around again, as if accepting the inevitability of having to speak to him. Older or younger? she asks.

Me? Aidan says. Younger.

The interior of the car is dark, and she narrows her eyes before concluding, You look it.

He's only a year younger, Declan says.

The woman has turned away now to roll down her window. She has to wind it down using the small lever on the door.

Your parents were busy, she remarks. How many others are there?

Only us, Declan says.

They got it all out of the way quickly then, she says. Sensible. Declan pulls out of the parking space and back onto the main road. Cool night air floods through the open window. The woman is lighting a cigarette. Aidan can see only the back of her head and her left arm, elbow angled.

I'll drop this lad home and then we'll go for a spin, Declan says.

Sounds divine, the woman says.

On their right is a row of houses and shops, which tapers off as they reach the end of town. Then the caravan park, the golf links. Does the woman already know where Aidan lives? She doesn't seem curious about how long it will take to get there. She exhales smoke out the window. The surface of the golf course glitters darkly.

What do you do, Aidan? she asks after a minute or two.

I work in the hotel.

Oh? How long have you been there?

Few years, he says.

Do you like it?

It's alright.

She flicks the stub of her cigarette out the window and rolls the window up. The car is much quieter then and things seem to hang unspoken. Declan says nothing. Aidan bites gently at the rough side of his left thumbnail. Should he ask her what she does for a living? But he doesn't even know her name. As if apprehending this very problem, Declan says, Pauline is a writer.

Oh, Aidan says. What kind of things do you write?

Films, she says.

For some reason Aidan does not wish to seem surprised by this knowledge, though he doesn't think he's ever been in a car with a screenwriter before. He just makes a noise like: Huh. As if to say, Well, there you are. The woman, whose name is apparently Pauline, unexpectedly swivels around to look at him. Her hair, he notices, is pulled back from her forehead by a wide velveteen band. She has a strange smile on her face.

What? she says. You don't believe me.

He is alarmed, feeling that he has offended her and that

Declan will be angry with him later. Of course I believe you, he says. Why wouldn't I?

For a few seconds she says nothing, but in the darkness and silence of the car she looks at him. In fact she stares at him, right into his eyes, for two or three seconds without speaking, maybe even four full seconds, a very long time. Why is she looking at him like this? Her face is expressionless. She has a pale forehead and her lips are pale, so her mouth appears as one delicate line. Is she looking at him just to show him her face, the face of a screenwriter? When she speaks, her voice sounds totally different. She simply says, Okay. And she stops looking at him and turns around again.

She doesn't speak to him again for the rest of the journey. She and Declan start talking instead, about people and events that have nothing to do with Aidan. He listens to them as if they are performing a play and he is the only audience member. Declan asks her when she's heading off to Paris and she tells him. She takes out her phone and starts looking for a photograph to show him. He says that someone called Michael never got back to him about something and Pauline says, Oh, Michael will be there, don't worry. Outside the windows, the darkness is punctuated only by passing headlights and, far up in the hills, the flickering lights of houses, hidden and revealed through the leaves of trees. Aidan has a feeling of some kind, but he doesn't know what the feeling is. Is he annoyed? Why should he be?

Declan indicates left for the estate. The streetlights grow brighter as they approach, and then the world is populated again, with semi-detached houses and wheelie bins and parked cars. Declan pulls up outside Aidan's house.

Thanks for the lift, Aidan says. Have a good night. Pauline doesn't look up from her phone.

*

He sees her again a few weeks later, in the hotel. She comes in one night for dinner with a group of people Aidan has never seen before. She's not wearing a hairband this time – her hair is fixed quite high on her head with a clasp – but it's definitely the same woman. Aidan brings a carafe of water to the table. Pauline is talking and everyone else is listening to her, including the men, some of whom are older and wearing suits. They all seem fascinated by her – how unusual, Aidan thinks, to see grown men hanging on the words of a girl in that way. He wonders if she is famous, or somehow important. When he fills her glass she looks up and says thank you. Then she frowns.

Do I know you? she says.

Everyone at the table turns to stare at Aidan. He feels flustered. I think you know my brother, he says. Declan.

She laughs, as if he has said something very charming. Oh, you're Declan Kearney's brother, she says. Then turning to her friends, she adds, I told you I knew all the locals.

They laugh appreciatively. She doesn't look at Aidan again. He finishes filling the glasses and goes back to the bar.

At the end of the night he helps Pauline's party to get their coats from the cloakroom. It's after midnight. They all seem a little drunk. Aidan still can't tell what they are to one another – friends, colleagues, family? The men are watching Pauline, and the other women are talking and laughing amongst themselves. Pauline asks him to call some taxis for them. He goes behind the desk and picks up the phone. She places a hand delicately on the counter, near the bell.

We're going to have a drink at my house, she says. Would you like to join us?

Oh, Aidan says. No, I can't.

She smiles pleasantly and turns back to her friends. Aidan dials the taxi number, gripping the phone hard against his skull so the ringtone shrieks in his ear. He should have said thanks, at least. Why didn't he? He was preoccupied, wondering where her house was. She can't live in town, or he would know her. Maybe she's just moved to town, or maybe she's working on a new film. If she even really writes films. He should have paused for a second to think about her question, and then he would have remembered to thank her. On the phone he orders two taxis and then hangs up.

They'll be here shortly, he says.

Pauline nods without looking back at him. He has made her dislike him.

I didn't know you lived around here, he says.

Again she just nods. He has the same view of her now as he did in the car the other week: the back of her head, and her neck and shoulders. When the taxis arrive outside, she says without turning to him, Give Declan my best. Then they all leave. Afterwards the waiter who cleared their table tells Aidan they left a huge tip.

A few days later he's working the front desk in the afternoon, and a queue forms while he's on the phone. When he hangs up, he apologises for the wait, checks the guests out of their rooms, wipes their keycards, and then sits down on the wheelie chair. Guests really don't have to do that – wait to be checked out. They can just leave their keycards on the desk and walk off, without the formal goodbye. But Aidan supposes they want to get the official go-ahead, to have their departure acknowledged in some way. Or maybe they just don't know that they're allowed, and assume they're not without being told so, because after all, at heart, human beings are so extremely submissive. He taps his fingers on the desk in a little rhythm, distracted.

Declan and Aidan are in the process of selling their

mother's house. Declan has a house of his own already, a smaller one, closer to town, with a twenty-year mortgage. People thought Aidan might move back into the old house, seeing as he's renting outside town and has to share with housemates, but he doesn't want to. He just wants to get rid of the place. Their mother was sick for a long time, though she wasn't old, and he loved her very much, so it's painful to think of her now. And in fact he tries not to think of her. The thought creates a feeling – the thought might at first be only an abstract idea or a memory, but a feeling follows on from it helplessly. He would like to be able to think of her again, because she was the person on earth who loved him most, but it isn't yet possible to do so without pain – maybe it never will be. In any case, it's not as if the pain goes away when he doesn't think of her. A pain in your throat may get worse when you swallow, may be almost unbearably painful when you swallow, but that doesn't mean that the pain is gone when you're not swallowing. Yes, life is full of suffering and there's no way to be free of it. Anyway, they're selling the house, and Aidan will come into a little money, though not a lot.

That night Declan comes to pick him up from work very late, after two in the morning, and Pauline is lying in the back of the car, apparently drunk. Ignore her, Declan says.

Don't ignore me, Pauline says. How dare you?

How was work? Declan asks.

Aidan closes the door and puts his bag down at his feet. Okay, he says. The car smells of alcohol. Aidan still feels that he doesn't really know who this woman is, this woman lying on the back seat. She's coming up fairly often in his life at this point, but who is she? At first he thought she was Declan's girlfriend, or at least a candidate for that role, but then in the hotel the other night she seemed different – glamorous in a way, with all those men looking at her – and of course Declan wasn't there, and she even invited Aidan for a drink afterwards. He could ask his brother, How do you know this girl? I mean, are you riding her, or what? But Declan's sensibilities would be offended by that kind of thing.

How would you get home if you didn't have a lift? Pauline says.

Walk, Aidan says.

How long would it take?

About an hour.

Is it dangerous?

What? Aidan says. No, it's not dangerous. Dangerous in what way?

Ignore her, Declan repeats.

Aidan is my good friend, Pauline says. He won't ignore me. I left him a very generous tip in his restaurant, didn't I?

I heard about that, he says. That was nice of you.

And I invited him to my house, she continues. Only to be cruelly rebuffed.

What do you mean, you invited him to your house? Declan asks. When was this?

After dinner at the hotel, she says. He rebuffed me, cruelly.

Aidan's face is hot. Well, I'm sorry you felt that way, he says. I can't just walk out of work because someone invites me to their house.

I didn't get an invite, Declan says.

You were busy, Pauline says. And so was your brother, obviously. Can I ask you something about your job, Aidan?

What? he says.

Have you ever slept with any of the hotel guests?

For fuck's sake, Pauline, Declan says.

They are driving past the caravan park again now, where the smooth curved roofs of the caravans glow with reflected moonlight, white like fingernails. Beyond that, Aidan knows, is the ocean, but he can't see or smell or even hear it now, sealed up inside the car with Pauline laughing and the air smelling of alcohol and perfume. Doesn't she know that Declan doesn't enjoy that kind of banter? Or maybe she does know, and she's aggravating him on purpose for some reason Aidan doesn't understand.

Don't listen to her, Declan says.

A car flashes past and disappears. Aidan turns around to look at her. From this angle her face is sideways. It's actually quite long and oval, like the shape of a headache pill.

You can tell me, she says. You can whisper.

You're flirting with him, Declan says. You're flirting with my brother right in front of me. In my car! He reaches out and punches Aidan on the arm. Stop looking at her, he says. Turn around now. You're messing and I don't like it.

Who were all those people in the hotel the other night? Aidan says. Were they your friends?

Just people I know.

They seemed like big fans of yours.

People only act like that when they want something from you, she says.

She lets him continue staring at her. She lies there absorbing his look, even smiling vaguely, allowing it to go on. Declan punches him again. Aidan turns around. The windscreen is blank like a powered-off computer screen.

We're not allowed to sleep with the guests, he says.

No, of course not. But I bet you've had offers.

Yeah, well. Mostly from men.

Declan appears startled. Really? he says. Aidan just shrugs.

Declan has never worked in a hotel, or a bar or a restaurant. He's an office manager with a business degree.

Are you ever tempted? Pauline says.

Not usually.

Aidan touches the window handle on the car door, not winding it up or down, just toying with it.

We did have a writer in the other night who invited me back to her house, he says.

Was she beautiful?

Pauline! Declan says. You're pissing me off now. Just drop it, okay? Jesus. This is the last time I do you a favour.

Aidan can't tell if Declan is still speaking to Pauline now, or to him. It sounded like he meant Pauline, but Aidan is the one receiving the favour of a lift home, not her, unless there's another favour running concurrently to this one. Everyone falls silent. Aidan thinks about the linen room at work, where all the clean sheets are stored, folded up tight in the wooden slats, bluish-white, smelling of powder and soap.

When they pull up outside his house he thanks his brother for the lift. Declan makes a dismissive gesture in the air with his hand. Don't worry about it, he says. The shape of Pauline's face is visible through the back window, but is she looking at him or not, he can't tell.

Two weeks later, the arts festival is on in town and the hotel is busy. Aidan's manager has to call him in for an extra shift on Friday because one of the girls has laryngitis. He finishes work at ten on Saturday night and goes down to the seafront for the closing ceremony of the festival. It's the same every year, a fireworks display at the end of the pier. He's seen the display ten or twelve times now, or however many years the festival has been going. The first time he was a teenager, still in school. He thought that his life was just about to start happening then. He thought that he was poised tantalisingly on the brink, and that any day – or even any minute – the waiting would end and the real thing would begin.

Down on the beach he zips his jacket up to the chin. It's crowded already and the streetlights on the promenade cast a grey glow over the sand and the sea. Families pick their way down the beach with buggies, bickering or laughing, and boats clink in the marina, a noise like handbells ringing, but random and disconnected. Teenagers sit on the steps, drinking cans and laughing at videos. People from the festival hold walkie-talkies to their ears and stride around importantly. Aidan looks at his phone, wondering if Declan is around, or Richie, or any of the gang from work, but no one's said anything in the group chat. It's cold again this year. He puts his phone away and rubs his hands.

Pauline is already walking towards him by the time he sees her, meaning she has seen him first. She's wearing a big oversized fleece that drops down almost to her knees. Her hair is pushed back from her forehead by a hairband again.

So you do have days off, she says.

I actually just finished, he says. But I'm off tomorrow.

Can I watch the fireworks with you or are you with someone?

He immediately likes this question. Turning it over in his mind only seems to reveal additional angles from which it can be admired.

No, I'm on my own, he says. We can watch together, yeah.

She stands beside him and rubs her arms in a pantomime of being cold. He looks at her, wondering if the pantomime demands some kind of response from him.

I'm sorry I was such a mess the other night, she says. When was that? Last week, or whenever. I think Declan was annoyed afterwards.

Was he?

Did he say anything to you about it?

Me, no, Aidan says. We don't really talk about things. The lights overhead go down and the beach is in darkness.

Around them people are moving, huddling, saying things, taking out their phones and shining torches, and then at the end of the pier the fireworks begin. A line of golden sparks shoots upwards into the sky and ends in a coloured point: first pink, then blue, then pink again, casting its brief hypnotic light on the sand and the water. Then a whistling noise, as low as a breath, and above them in the sky, exploding outwards, red blossoms, and yellow and then green, leaving soft fronds of gold behind. When the fireworks burst, it's silent colour and light at first, and a second later the noise: a loud crack like something breaking, or a deep low booming that goes into the chest. Aidan can see the tiny missiles flying upwards hissing into the sky from the pier, almost invisible, and then shattering outwards into fragments of light, glittering like pixels, bright white fading to yellow and then gold to darker gold and then black. It's the darker gold, just before black, that he finds most beautiful: a low ember colour, darker than a glowing coal. Finally, so high above they have to crane their necks to see the whole shape, three dazzling yellow fireworks, consuming the sky, eating the whole darkness. Then it's over. The streetlights come back up.

Beside him Pauline is rubbing her face and nose with her hands. Cold again. Aidan realises, obscurely, that a lot depends now on Pauline's having enjoyed the fireworks – that if she didn't enjoy them, if she thought they were boring, not only will he no longer like her but he will no longer have enjoyed them either, in retrospect, and something good will be dead. He says nothing. Along with everyone else, they turn back and leave the beach. It's possible to walk at only one speed, the speed of the crowd, which seems like the slowest and least comfortable speed at which humans can move. At this pace Aidan keeps bumping into people, small children keep running out unexpectedly in front of him, and prams and people in wheelchairs need to move past. Pauline stays close by him, and at the top of the promenade she asks if he'll walk her home. He says sure.

She's staying in one of the houses on the seafront. He knows the street; it's where all the holiday homes are, with glass walls facing the ocean. As they walk, the rest of the crowd falls away behind them. When they reach her street it's just the two of them alone in silence. There's so much he doesn't know about Pauline – so much, it strikes him with a different and slightly surprising emphasis, that he would like to know – that it's impossible to begin asking questions. He doesn't know her surname, or where she's from, what she does all day, who her family are. He doesn't know how old she is. Or how she came to know Declan, or how well she knows him.

You know, as to what you were saying the other night, Aidan says, I actually did sleep with a guest at the hotel once. I wouldn't go telling Declan about it, because he doesn't approve of that kind of thing.

Pauline's eyes flash up at him. Who was the guest? she asks.

I don't know, a woman staying on her own. She was a little bit older, maybe in her thirties.

And was it a good experience? Or bad?

It wasn't great, Aidan says. Not that the sex was bad but more that I felt bad about it, like it was the wrong thing to do.

But the sex was good.

It was okay. I mean, I'm sure it was fine, I don't even remember it now. Something at the time made me think maybe she was married. But I don't know for a fact – I just thought it at the time.

Why did you do it? Pauline says.

He goes quiet for a few seconds. I don't know, he says. I was hoping you wouldn't ask that.

What do you mean?

You just seem like someone who understands these things. But when you ask that it makes me feel like I did something weird.

She stops walking and puts her hand on a gatepost, which must be hers. He stops walking, too. Behind her is a large house with big windows, set back from the street by a garden, and all the lights are switched off.

I don't think it's weird, she says. I used to have a boyfriend who was married. And I knew his wife – not well or anything, but I did know her. I'm not asking why you did it because I think it's sick that you would sleep with someone who was married. I suppose I just wonder, why do we do things that we don't really want to do? And I thought you might have an answer, but it's okay if you don't. I don't either.

Right. Well, that makes me feel better. Not that I'm happy you were in a bad situation, but I feel better that I'm not the only one.

Are you in a bad situation now?

No, he says. Now I would say, I am in no situation at all. I feel like my life basically isn't happening. I think if I dropped dead the only people who would care are the people who would have to cover my shifts. And they wouldn't even be sad, they'd just be annoyed.

Pauline frowns. She rubs the gatepost under her hand like she's thinking.

Well, I don't have that problem, she says. I think in my case there's too much happening. At this point everyone I've ever met seems to want something from me. I feel like if I dropped dead they'd probably cut my body into pieces and sell it at an auction.

You mean like those people you were with, at the hotel.

She shrugs. She rubs her arms again. She asks him if he wants to come inside and he says yes.

The house is spacious and, though furnished, appears curiously empty. The ceilings are high up and far away. Pauline leaves the keys on the hall table and walks through the house switching lights on in a seemingly arbitrary fashion. They reach the living room and she sits down on a gigantic green corner sofa, with a flat surface so large it resembles a bed, but with cushions at the back. There is no television and the bookshelves are bare. He sits down on the couch but not right beside her.

Do you live here on your own? he says.

She looks around vaguely, as if she doesn't know what he means by 'here'.

Oh, she says. Well, only for now.

How long is now?

Everyone always asks questions like that. Don't you start. Everyone wants to know what I'm doing and how long I'm doing it for. I'd like to be really alone for a while and for no one to know where I was or when I was coming back. And maybe I wouldn't come back at all.

She stands up from the sofa and asks if he would like a drink. Unnerved by her previous speech, about going somewhere alone and never returning, which seems in a way like a metaphor, he just shrugs.

I have a bottle of whiskey, she says. But I don't want you to think I have a drinking problem. Someone gave it to me as a present – I didn't buy it myself. Would you have even a small half glass and I'll have one? But if you don't want one I won't have one either.

I'll have a glass, yeah, he says.

She walks out of the room, not through a door but through an open archway. The house is confusingly laid out, so he can't tell where she's gone or how far away.

If you want to be alone, he says aloud, I can go.

She reappears in the archway almost instantly. What? she says.

If you want to be alone like you were saying, he repeats. I don't want to intrude on you.

Oh, I only meant that . . . philosophically, she says. Were you listening to me? That's your first mistake. Everything I say is nonsense. Your brother knows how to deal with me, he never listens. I'll be back in a second.

She goes away again. What does it mean that Declan 'knows how to deal with' Pauline? Should Aidan ask? Maybe this is his opening to ask. She returns with two half-full tumblers, hands him one, and then settles down on the sofa beside him, slightly closer than where she had been sitting previously, though still not touching. They sip the whiskey. It's not something Aidan would ever drink of his own volition, but it tastes fine.

I'm sorry about your mother, Pauline says. Declan told me she passed away.

Yeah. Thanks.

They pause. Aidan takes another, larger sip of whiskey. You're seeing a lot of Declan, are you? he says.

He's sort of my car friend. I mean he's my only friend who has a car. He's very nice, he's always driving me places. And he usually just ignores me when I say silly things. I think he thinks I'm a terrible woman. He wasn't impressed with me the other night when I asked you those vulgar questions. But you're his baby brother – he thinks you're very innocent.

Aidan pays special attention to the fact that she has

461

used the word 'friend' more than once in connection with Declan. He feels it can have only one meaning – a thought that makes him feel good. Does he? he replies. I don't know what he thinks of me.

He said he didn't know if you were gay or straight, Pauline says.

Ah, well. As I said, I don't talk about things with him.

You've never brought a girlfriend home.

You've got the advantage of me here, Aidan says. He's telling you all about me and I don't know anything about you.

She smiles. Her teeth are extremely white and perfect, unrealistic-looking, almost blue.

What do you want to know? she says.

Well, I'm curious what brings you to live here. I don't think you're from here.

That's what you're curious about? Good grief. I'm starting to think you really are innocent.

That's not very nice, Aidan says.

She looks wounded for a moment, stares into her glass, and says sadly, What made you think I was nice?

He doesn't think he can answer this question. In truth he doesn't think of her as particularly nice. He just thinks of niceness as a general standard to which everyone accepts they can be held.

She puts her empty glass down on the coffee table and sits back on the couch. Your life isn't as bad as you think it is, she says.

Well, neither is yours, he replies.

How should you know?

Everyone wants your attention all the time, so what? Aidan says. If you hated it so much you could fuck off on your own somewhere – what's to stop you?

She tilts her head to one side, places a hand gently under

her chin. Move to a remote seaside town, you mean? she says. Live the quiet life – maybe settle down with a nice country boy who works hard for a living. Is that what you had in mind?

Oh, fuck off.

She gives a light, irritatingly musical laugh.

I don't want anything from you, he adds.

Then what are you doing here?

He puts his glass down. You asked me to come in, he says. You asked if we could watch the fireworks together, remember? And then you asked me to walk home with you, and then you asked me inside. And I'm the one who's inserting myself into your life, am I? I never wanted anything from you.

She seems to consider this, looking grave. Finally she says, I thought you liked me.

What does that mean? If I liked you that means something bad about me?

As if she has not heard him, she replies, I liked you.

He now feels utterly confused as to why they seem to be arguing, confused to the point of abrupt despair. Right, he says. Look, I'm going to go.

By all means.

He experiences this parting with her – this parting he himself announced spontaneously and called into existence – as an excruciating ordeal, almost a physical pain. He can't quite believe he's going through with it, actually standing upright from the sofa and turning away towards the door they entered through. Why is everything so strange now? At what point did his relations with Pauline begin to violate the ordinary rules of social contact? It started normally enough. Or did it? He still doesn't even know if she's his brother's girlfriend.

She doesn't rise from the couch to see him out. He has to make his way through the half-lit, cavernous house alone, fumbling through dark hallways and at one point a dazzlingly bright dining room towards the front door. Why did she say that, about settling down with a 'nice country boy'? She was just trying to provoke him. But why? She knows nothing about his life. Why is he even thinking about her, then? At this moment, reaching the front door of Pauline's house, with its glazed glass reflecting back at him an unrecognisable image that he knows to be his own face, this strikes Aidan as the question without an answer.

Several weeks later he's in the back room trying to find a Continental power adapter for a guest upstairs when Lydia comes in saying that someone at reception wants him. Wants what? he says. Wants you, Lydia says. They're asking for you. Aidan closes the drawer containing the hotel's selection of adapters and, as if in a dream now or in a video game, his actions under the control of some higher intelligence, he stands up and follows Lydia out of the back room, towards the front desk. He already knows, before he sees or hears Pauline, that she will be there waiting for him. And she is. She's wearing a dress made from what looks like very soft, fine cloth. An older man is standing beside her with his arm around her waist. Aidan simply notices all this neutrally. His image of Pauline is already so confused and obscure that to see her in this situation cannot indicate anything really new about her.

Alright, Aidan says. How can I help?

We're looking for a room, the man says.

Pauline touches her nose with her fingertips. The man swats her arm and says, You're making it worse. Look. It's going to start bleeding again.

It is bleeding, she says.

She sounds drunk. Aidan can see that her fingers are bloodied when she draws them away from her face. He bends over the computer at the desk but does not immediately open the room-reservations interface. He swallows and pretends to click on something, actually just clicking nothing. Is Lydia watching him? She's at the desk, just a little way to his right, but he can't tell if she's looking.

For how many nights? Aidan says.

One, the man says. Tonight.

They're not going to have anything at such short notice, Pauline says.

Well, let's see, the man says.

If you'd told me you were coming, I could have arranged something, she says.

Relax, the man says.

Aidan swallows again. He's conscious of a kind of throbbing sensation inside his head, like the flicking of a light, on and off. He moves the mouse around the screen in a show of efficiency and then, impulsively, pretends to type something although there is no keyboard input open on screen. He's certain Lydia is watching him. Finally he straightens up from the computer and looks at the man.

No, I'm sorry, he says. We don't have any rooms available tonight.

The man stares at him. Lydia's looking over at him, too. You don't have any rooms? the man says. Every room in the hotel is taken? In the middle of April?

I told you, Pauline says.

Sorry, Aidan says. We can get you something next week, if you'd like.

The man moves his mouth like he's laughing, but no laugh comes out. He removes his hand from Pauline's waist, lifts it up in the air, and lets it drop against his own body. Aidan is careful not to look at Pauline or Lydia at all.

No rooms, the man repeats. All booked up. This hotel.

I'm sorry I can't help, Aidan says.

The man looks at Pauline.

Well, what do you want me to do? she says.

In response the man lifts his arm again to point at Aidan. Is this your boyfriend? the man says.

Oh, don't be absurd, Pauline says. Are you going to develop paranoia now on top of everything else?

You know him, the man says. You asked for him.

Pauline shakes her head, dabs delicately at her nose, and flashes a kind of apologetic smile at Aidan and Lydia across the desk. I'm sorry, she says. We'll get out of your way. Can I ask you to call a couple of taxis? I'd really appreciate it.

Oh, we can't share a taxi? the man says.

Coldly now, Pauline replies, We're going in opposite directions. Under his breath, with a kind of frozen grin on his face, the man says, I don't believe it. I don't believe it. Then he turns around and walks towards the large double doors of the hotel entrance. Lydia picks up the phone to call the taxi company. Pauline, without any change in her demeanour, lifts the hotel pen from the desk, takes the pad of paper, writes something down, and then tears the sheet from the pad. She takes out some money, encloses it in the note, and pushes it across the desk towards Aidan. Looking only at Lydia, she smiles and says, Thanks so much. Then she exits, following the man through the double doors.

When the doors swing shut, Lydia is still on the phone. Aidan sits down and stares into space. He hears Lydia saying goodbye, then he hears the faint click of the receiver replaced in its cradle. He just sits there. Lydia finds the note on the desk and nudges it in Aidan's direction with the end of a pen, like she doesn't want to touch it.

She left this for you, Lydia says.

I don't want it.

Lydia uses the pen to flick open the note.

There's a hundred euro in here, she says.

That's O.K., he says. You take it.

For a few seconds Lydia says nothing. Aidan just sits staring blankly straight ahead. Presently, as if making up her mind, Lydia says, I'll put it with the tips. She wrote you a note as well, do you not want that? I think it just says thank you.

You can leave it, he says. Or, actually, give it to me.

Lydia gives it to him. Without looking at it, he places it in his pocket. Then he rises from the chair to return to the back room to find the power adapter for the guest upstairs. He won't see Pauline again before she leaves town in a few days' time.

EOIN McNAMEE

SABLE

IT WAS THE funeral she would have wished on herself, sparsely attended, dim-lit figures adrift in cold side-chapels. Her brother came up behind her in the graveyard.

'You never said you were coming back,' he said. 'Of all things. Nora's funeral.'

'Long time since I had to report in.'

'The old witch.'

'I haven't seen her for twenty-five years. She kept something that belonged to me.'

'That's the reason you're here. You never do anything except for a reason.' She nodded. She had always been that way. She was faithless to herself and she was faithless to others.

'The mother said you'd never have children.'

'Did she?'

'She said you only had time for yourself.'

'She was right about most things.'

'So what does Nora have belonging to you?'

'I'm going to go down to the west end. I need to go to her shop.'

'You'd want to be careful. That whole street is condemned long since. Them buildings were put up on pure mud. It's no place for you down there.'

'I'm going.'

'They're saying she's in the right spot now. Six feet under.'

You're in the right spot, she thought, you look like you already died. You look like a morgue photograph of yourself.

'You know what they said about Nora?' Michael said.

'I know what they said about her.' It was a family trait to be knowing, to leave things hanging in the air.

She left Michael in the graveyard. She had no need of accusers. She had grown to be the evidence against herself. He looked old and broken and she knew what had happened to him. The wind here carried everything away, unremembered storms swept all consolation before them. Sooner or later you ran out of shelter.

She passed the Lido on the foreshore. The pool had been drained and there was tidal debris washed up against the outlet pipes. The diving platform rusted and tilted to one side. Through the empty windows she saw cracked tiles and broken stalls. Holidaymakers used to go to the car park beside the pool and sit in their cars facing the sea and the mountains across the lough. Then a boy had gone missing. She had seen the boy's mother in the back of a car in the corner of the car park night after night, her head bowed. There had been a chain of torches on the lower slopes of the mountains and you could hear men calling through the night, their voices coming back across the water.

Lillian had booked into the Liverpool hotel on the seafront. The car radio had said there was a storm coming. She rang the bell and stood in the glassed-in porch, the window putty loose, the glass shivered in the east wind, the salt-whitened panes. She felt as if she was standing in a tabernacle, solitary, revered.

There were elderly women playing bridge at a table in the foyer. They wore twinsets and their white hair was stiff with airborne static from the coming storm and they looked as though they had been given avian form, tiny and flightless. The owner gave her the key to her room.

'Bit of bad weather coming,' he said.

'I heard.'

'Talking about giving the storm a name.'

'They do that with the worst ones.'

'Used to be they gave them women's names. The way women would be. The way you'd never know what they might do one minute to the next.'

There had always been something feral about the men in the town. You always expected something underhand, glancing touches, an unwanted hand.

She could hear the women behind her, their voices rustling, collusive.

Before dark, she left the hotel and walked into the west end. Windows were shuttered. Alleys blocked with skewed hoardings. Gable walls leant outward. You expected to see marshlight seeping up through the pavements, wavering blue flame on the empty streets.

Nora had worn hats decorated with feathers and flowers, and fur stoles around her neck with the paws and heads intact. It was said in the school bathroom that the women of the town went to her when there was something that needed to be dealt with. That there was a room with a bath upstairs. That there were pessaries and coiled tubing. They whispered in school about what happened to the errant, the hollow-eyed girls who left mid-term, and now Lillian was about to find out for herself.

The sign outside said Nora Fashions, picked out in gilt. Lillian remembered frocks in the window, skirts hanging from racks in the doorway. Bolts of dress material, fabrics in gardenia and lily. Lillian could not have gone in. She had come to take a look. She had joined a guild of the blamed and she owed it to herself to view all outcomes.

'Yes?' Nora said. She wore a burgundy velvet hat with artificial lilies stitched low on the crown. A fur stole hung about her neck. Her face was gaunt, caved. Lillian tried not to look at the stole. The little paws, the little pinched weasel faces. They were sneaks, blood-drinkers. They stole fledglings from the nest.

'They said you could do something.'

'Do something about what?' Nora said. Lillian touched her stomach.

'You don't want to believe everything you hear about me. Nor half of it. Whose is it?'

Lillian shrugged. The boys of the town were like weather. You got into cars with them. They left you handled, sore, standing outside in the rain as they drove away. There would be laddered tights, nail varnish chipped against interior surfaces, you're always marked, the imprint of plastic seat covers on your skin, underwear balled in your handbag.

'Come back to me this evening after six.'

She had waited outside the shop in the dark that night for an hour before Nora returned, something spectral about the way she had come down the street, something of desolate encounters half-remembered, of love renounced. Nora reached into the letterbox and took out a Yale key on a string. She opened the door.

'I been standing in the cold,' Lillian said, 'I need to pee.'

'Come upstairs.' Nora climbed the stairs ahead of her. There were dresses in cellophane dry-cleaning wrappers hanging from the banisters, bales of taffeta and lining material on the small landing. She pointed to the bathroom door.

The porcelain bath was iron-stained, verdigris on the chrome fittings. Lillian looked at the cupboard. She thought of corrosive salts, cruelly shaped instruments. There was rubber tubing on a hook on the back of the bathroom door. There would be biting pain. There would be blood.

When she came out of the bathroom Nora was in a bedroom at the end of the corridor. Lillian could see a bed with a lace counterpane. There were roses on the wallpaper. Nora beckoned to her.

'They done a scan.' Lillian put the envelope from the hospital on the counterpane. She waited to be brought back into the bathroom. Nora knelt and took a tin out from under the bed. She took a small package from it and handed it to her.

'What's in it?' Lillian thought of powders, of the agonies foretold, bent double on the bathroom floor with cramps.

'An address and money.'

'An address?'

'The clinic is free. The money's for bus fare and you'll need a night in a bed and breakfast after.'

'I'll give you back the money.'

'You won't. You're not the type. If you were an animal you'd be one of these hanging round my neck. Take my advice. When you get out of the town keep going. There's too many like you round here. It gets hard to tell you apart.'

Lillian touched the fur stole around Nora's neck.

'What is it? What animal?'

'Fox.' Lillian ran her hand down to the fox's head. She thought she could feel the skull underneath the fur. The profane little face. What thoughts of wildness and of blood?

'Sable is the finest fur of all. Mink,' Nora said. Lillian had heard of mink.

'Why don't you wear sable then?'

'Too expensive.'

Lillian reached for the hospital envelope on the bed. Nora put her hand over hers.

'Leave it.'

As she left the shop, Lillian smelt perfume. It smelt of lost end-of-summer dances, of fading music, of ruined girls weeping bitterly on cold terraces.

Nora's shop had been closed for many years. The gilding on the sign had flaked. The front door was dented and gouged. Michael had told her of the decline. Nora had gone to a home and then a hospital. Lillian found the string in the letterbox and took out the Yale key. She opened the door. The shop stormlit through the dust-glazed fanlight above the door. A rack of satinette nightdresses shifted in the draught from the door then settled again. There were nylon demi-slips thrown over rails. Behind the counter a row of panelled girdles on hangers.

She walked to the door connecting the shop and house through an alley of water-stained frocks. She saw herself in the hallway pierglass, pale-faced in the vagrant dark. She climbed the stairs. Rain had entered the house and the walls were damp, streaked green and shone with a fungal effervescence, light coming from a corner of broken slates and from a buckled skylight.

The landing had been weakened by dry rot and had fallen inwards, carried down by the weight of baled fabrics. She looked at the ground floor. There were fragments of cloth mixed in with the broken joists and rotten planking, decayed material and cheesecloth.

One joist remained intact in the middle and she used it to step across the gap. The first of the night's wind rattled the slates above her head, old hollow spouting rung against the roofplate, the tolled instrumentation of loss gone by and loss to come.

She passed under a rooflight and heard the wind again. She thought she could hear voices in it. Nora had asked her if she had told her mother she was pregnant? No, she said, though she might know. That was the shadowy tradecraft of mothers, how they trailed you on the darkening streets of your promise. Knowing from the start that you would betray yourself.

She reached the corridor return and saw Nora's room in front of her. The floor shifted beneath her feet. Michael had been right. She had no call being here. Nora's room was in an attached annex, the walls subsided so that it had canted to the right, carrying the room away from the wall and expanding the planked gaps, cold filamented lights from outside penetrating the room, thread-like. She stepped across the gap. The double doors of the wardrobe had fallen outward, exposing the interior. Nora's hats were on hooks at the back of the wardrobe, a row of them across the top of the wardrobe, peacock and rooster feathers half-eaten and manged, night's pale emblems. The fur stoles were on a hanger beside the hats, the bodies knotted, the clawed feet interlocked, the little faces fierce and illicit, a blood rosette of them.

She crossed the slanted floor and knelt at the bed. The roses on the wallpaper were sunfaded, almost colourless now. She reached underneath and brought out the biscuit tin. She emptied the tin onto the bed. There were old bills in the tin, birth certificates, photographs that disintegrated as they fell, a smell of gone-off chemicals, the images barely visible, men in lounge suits and women in A-line skirts, their faces time-violated, sombre.

From the emulsified fragments on the bedspread she picked out a brown envelope. She took the scan out of the envelope and held it up, the small figure in it seen clearly as though the blanched roses held it in their own unwholesome light. The small unnamed carapace, formed from the darkness around it, gathered and held, fiercely willed.

She put the scan into her handbag. The floor of the annex flexed as the wind blew against it. She stepped over the collapsed flooring and went downstairs. It was almost dark in the shop. The rack of satinette nightdresses moved with her passing, moved and rustled. She ran her fingers over a rack of tights in cellophane, the packeted nylon crackling in the shop gloom. She imagined herself followed from the shop, night-gauds in decayed frocks, pale and animate in the derelict streets. She held the scan close and ran through the darkening town.

In her room she undressed and stood in the shower crying about promises she had made and forgotten. Love that she had begun and not finished. There were laws of possession and letting go. She had not attended to any of them.

She wrapped a towel around her and sat at the dressing table. She held the scan up against the light. The image in negative, spindly, unbroken, de-sexed. She wondered what it was thinking of with closed eyes that seemed grown shut, the deep unseeing.

She took her phone from her handbag and rang Michael.

'Do you remember the boy got lost on the mountain? The mother used to sit in the car in the Lido car park when they searched. Did they ever find him?'

'I don't remember if he was found or not. Word was he wasn't lost anyway. He was took by some man she was with. Wouldn't be the first was took around here.'

She put the phone down. She went to the window and looked out over the roofs of the west end towards the mountain, clouds gathered at the summits. Perhaps if the woman had waited long enough the boy would have come back, if anything could come back from those colours, the blue-black cosmos, anvil clouds massed.

She touched her stomach. The inside of her felt infinite, like a great constellated vault of night in which the stars were going out one by one.

Gales would soon move down through the valleys and across the lough. Named storms. The night would be rent with voices, wind hags. She would go to the Lido and she would wait with the unforgiven mothers and the little foxes would walk in their shadow, boneless, musked. They would wear sable and they would wait for the earth's taken children.

YAN GE

HOW I FELL IN LOVE WITH THE WELL-DOCUMENTED LIFE OF ALEX WHELAN

BY THE TIME Alex Whelan became part of my life he had already died. However, it was not until much later that I became aware of this fact.

I met Alex at a meeting of the Foreign Movies No Subtitles (FMNS) group. The date was 2 March. The movie was *An Autumn Afternoon*. The meet-up place was Eoin's (the organizer's) studio off Meath Street. And the fee was 5 euro per person (with a glass of red/white wine).

When I arrived the movie had already started. I stooped and sneaked in, taking a seat at the back. Alex was sitting right beside me but we didn't talk for the duration of the movie. Only when it was over did he turn to me and ask for the time. I checked my phone and told him it was 9.15.

'I like the song they sang at the end,' he then said. 'What do you think this movie is about?'

'It seemed the old man was about to die so he arranged a marriage for his daughter,' I said.

'I don't think so,' he disagreed. 'I think he liked that hostess woman and the daughter decided to get married so her dad could find his own happiness.'

'Wouldn't that be too much of a twist?' I frowned.

'It wasn't straightforward anyway,' he admitted. 'But isn't that what Japanese culture is about? The forbearance and the elusive love.'

'I don't know much about Japanese culture.' I gave him a smile.

'I'm Alex.' He grinned.

'Hello, Alex.'

'What's your name?' he asked.

I told him my name and briefly coached him on the pronunciation. Then he asked me what it meant. I in turn elaborated on my factually tedious name. In response, he said it was unbelievably beautiful and I nodded humbly to accept yet another round of applause for my culture and my smart-arsed ancestors.

It was all cliché. We then talked about the weather (wet and changeable), the place he came from (Kilkenny) and how long it took to drive there from Dublin (an hour and a half), among other things.

'How long have you been in Ireland?' he asked me at a certain point.

'Would you believe me if I told you I'm actually from Tipperary?' I said.

He laughed loudly. 'You must be kidding me!'

He checked his phone, saying he needed to head to Vicar Street to join the lads and he wondered if I had any plans.

'I need to go home now,' I said. 'It's too late.'

'It's not ten yet.'

'Long way to Tipperary, you know,' I said and picked up my satchel bag.

He wheezed.

'Add me on Facebook, will you?' he asked me before I left. 'The name is Alexander Whelan.'

'Sure.' I nodded and walked out the door.

Apologies if I have challenged your attention span. I admit the dialogue above isn't particularly interesting. However, I had to relay it in full detail because it was the only time we spoke. I'll go through the crucial part of the story very quickly now. What happened was:

On my way back to the apartment I added Alex on Facebook; it was approximately 10.30 p.m.

When I got home, my roommate was in her bedroom, having left some tortilla chips and hummus on the coffee table. So I sat down, had some food and lingered on Instagram for about half an hour before I went to the bathroom to pee. It was nearly midnight.

I had eaten too many tortilla chips and too much hummus to sleep. So I went back to my bedroom to work on my thesis/wait for the food to digest. I stared at the Word document for about twenty minutes and went to YouTube where I watched some old Chinese TV series for about three hours.

Eventually I decided to get ready for bed. I went to the bathroom to wash up and got caught up in a test ('Which Game of Thrones Character Are You?') and sat on the toilet for another thirty-five to forty-five minutes.

Then I lay on my bed, browsing through my phone to allow my day to sink in. It was 4.47 a.m. when I got the notification from Facebook. Alexander Whelan accepted your friend request. Good man, I thought. I wanted to click into his page and maybe send a message but I was too tired so I put my phone down and fell asleep.

The next day I woke up around 12 p.m. I was running around and doing whatnot for about five hours during which I routinely checked my phone every three to five minutes but there was no message from Alex.

I decided to PM him while I was preparing dinner, heating up a Tesco soup and buttering two slices of brown bread. So I went to his Facebook page and that was when I saw the posts coming up on his wall.

R.i.p.Alex. My heart was broken when I heard the news, one person posted. *R. I. P. Bro.*

Have a good one on the other side, another message read.

And many others.

It was 6.10 p.m., 3 March. I learnt from his Facebook that Alex had died that morning. There was an accident and he was sent to St James's Hospital and died there at 6.15 a.m.

I almost dropped the phone into my soup.

It wasn't the first cyberdeath I'd experienced. But this one also took place in real life. Or did it? I spent the whole evening questioning the authenticity of this news. Could it be a prank played by Alex and his friends?

This was how I pictured the situation:

Alex: So I just met this girl. She is kind of cute.

Friend A: Oh yeah?

Alex: She is Chinese. Actually I'm not sure. She said she's from Tipp. But she looks Chinese and her name sounds Chinese.

Friend A: Well, if it looks like a duck and swims like a duck . . .

Alex: Hey! . . . Wait, she just added me on Facebook.

Friend A: Cool. Show me her profile photo.

(Alex shows his friend my profile photo.)

Friend A: Hmmm . . . I don't know . . . You call this cute?

(Alex checks my profile photo.)

Alex: I don't know . . . Maybe? Ah never mind.

(Alex puts away his phone. They go drinking and then the gig is on so they enjoy the music until very late in the evening. Afterwards, they go to a friend's apartment to smoke some hash. It is around five in the morning when everybody is stoned and Alex cries out.)

Alex: Shit! I think I just accidentally added her!
Friend B: Who?
Alex: This Chinese girl I met.
Friend B: You were in China? China has good food.
Friend C: The moon is coming to get us!
Alex: Shit. Shit. I can't undo this now. What do I do?
Friend A: What are we gonna do? It's the moon man! Moon man is murdering the moon!
Friend B: Chill out. Watch me save your ass, loser!
(B takes out his phone and types.)
Friend B: Check your Facebook now, Alex.
(Alex takes his phone out and checks his Facebook. He laughs out loud hysterically.)
Friend A: What? Show us!
(A grabs Alex's phone and reads out: R.i.p. Alex. My heart was broken when I heard the news.)
Friend A: Epic! Wait!
(A takes out his phone and starts to post on Alex's wall. Then friends C D E F join in.)

The more I thought about it, the more it felt plausible. In this case, Alex would still be alive. He might be a dick but he would be alive.

Here is the fundamental question: if you meet a guy who you sort of like and he turns out to be a dick, would you like him to remain, unapologetically, a dick and pretend he is dead, or would you prefer he is actually dead, but possibly a good guy?

It was not entirely rootless speculation. For a start, Alex had 1,257 Facebook friends. And just in the last month, he had checked in at Vicar Street twice (Feb. 10th and 17th), Grogan's three times (Feb. 7th, 8th and 20th), The Lord Edward twice (Feb. 5th and 22nd), The Long Hall three times (Feb. 2nd, 14th and 25th), and Bowes four times (I don't even bother to recheck the dates).

I understand you might say: But sure it's February, where can he go if not the pub? But still. Plus, how would you feel if I told you that among the fourteen visits to local pubs, Alex was *feeling crazy* for seven of them, and *excited* on five of these occasions. There were only two times where he was tagged so I wouldn't be able to know how exactly he felt. But he certainly looked very well in the photos with his friends. And so did his friends.

So is it possible that he was a philanderer who played a prank on me via Facebook, because I was, according to Friend A, not cute?

On the other hand, there were things that suggested a slightly different lifestyle. For instance, he had read 572 books on Goodreads, rated 493 of them (3.73 avg.) and written eighty-nine reviews. He volunteered for numerous (twenty-three) events at Insomnia Ireland, helping people who suffer from either coffee addiction and/or sleep deprivation. He was the guitarist in a band on Bandcamp, where they had uploaded three songs ('How to Murder the Moon', 'Hippopotamus' and 'The Telly Is On'). He also hosted a tour on Airbnb, which was called Phoenix Park Walk: learn about Irish trees and shrubs. He charged thirty euro per person and had three five-star reviews.

And so on and so forth.

I slouched in front of my laptop, searching through all the online statistics of Alex Whelan. My roommate came over to knock on my door and she said: 'Would you stop watching Chinese soap operas? Work on your thesis.'

'Did my mother tell you to say this?' I asked her without turning back.

'No!' she exclaimed. 'She is only concerned about you, you know?'

'Relax. I am doing research for my thesis,' I said, scrolling down Alex's friends' pages.

'I can see from here that's Facebook!' she bellowed, and left.

Never mind the thesis. For now, I needed to get to the bottom of this. I needed to know what kind of person Alex Whelan was, whether he was really dead, and if so whether he had added me on Facebook right before the moment of his death.

I looked into his 1,257 Facebook friends. There were 202 of them living in Dublin. So I clicked into the profiles of these 202 people and finally found a Micheál Hannigan who shared his timeline with the public.

It seemed there would be a *Black Books* night at the Bernard Shaw on Friday evening and Micheál was going. So I went and got a visual on him after a few minutes of scanning the crowd.

'Hi! Micheál!' I approached and tapped him on the shoulder.

He looked at me and was for a second visibly confused. 'Hi?' he said.

'I'm a friend of Alex's. We met at Vicar Street a couple of weeks ago, remember?' He was at Vicar Street with Alex on 10 February.

'Oh!' He nodded. 'I remember now. Hello, how are you?'

I relaxed and poised myself. 'Good! I'm good, how are you?' I asked.

'Not bad. Not bad,' he said.

'So sorry about Alex. I couldn't believe it!' I sighed and shook my head.

'I know! I was just thinking. Jesus!' He rubbed his eyebrows.

I wanted to proceed but he asked: 'Sorry, can you remind me of your name again? I'm terrible with names.'

'I'm Claire,' I said.

'Oh,' he said. 'Claire?'

'Claire Collins,' I assured him.

He seemed satisfied. If it came with a surname it must be real.

And then we conversed. He'd had a very busy week programming, fixing a new application that was basically unfixable. 'The QA keep sending it back to me! I said send it to the engineers but nobody listened. It just keeps coming back to me.' My week hadn't been great either. After three nights of toil I sent in my thesis before the deadline only to find out that the professor was on strike. 'Would it kill him to let us know the week before so I could save myself a full tin of coffee?' Another cold wave was coming from Russia. There was an amazing sauna place on South William Street. 'Speaking of which, isn't it incredible, the emerging culinary scene in Dublin?' From there we slid into the friction-free zone of food talk, where I went on autopilot for about fifteen minutes before I seized a window to terminate the conversation.

'It was so nice talking to you. But I really need to run now,' I said. 'And, if you don't mind me asking, how did Alex, you know? I heard it was an accident. How did it happen?'

'Oh, you didn't hear? Right, they probably don't want to advertise it . . . He killed himself. Cut his wrist in the bathroom. Can you believe it?' he added, shaking his head.

I went numb and I heard him asking: 'So are we friends on Facebook yet? Add me if we're not.'

*

I learnt this from my mother: if you want to ask something really important, leave it till the end. 'Don't just go in and ask. It's impolite,' she said. 'You have to talk to people. You have to listen to them. You have to warm them up and show them you care. And then ask what you really want at the end of it. Ask casually.'

My mother is the most capable woman I know. She is bright, hard-working and unbelievably adaptable. She raised me all by herself after my father passed away when I was small (eighteen months, she told me). In 2005, she met a divorcee on the internet and they soon fell in love. He came to China to visit her in the summer and proposed at the airport before he left. They got engaged and tied the knot in the spring of 2007. Afterwards, my mother sold our apartment and we moved to Ireland with her new husband, Eugene Collins.

Mr and Mrs Collins still live happily in the picturesque town of Cahir, County Tipperary. She renamed herself Amy and introduced me as Claire. 'Claire Collins.' She tried to sell the name to me. 'It sounds right, don't you think?'

'That is just not my name,' I told her.

'But it'll be easier for everybody! Come on, Xiaohan. It'd be good for you!' she said.

My mother always knows what is best for me. In the end, I embraced the name and learnt to take pleasure watching people's faces change when I said I was Claire Collins. 'Yes, that's me. It's a bit mixed up. Long story,' I'd say. It was a great conversation-starter.

I didn't do this when I met Alex, though. For some reason, I told him my real name and coached him on the pronunciation.

'Sh-aw, H-ung,' I remembered him saying.

'That's perfect!' I laughed. I didn't let him know that I

couldn't really remember the last time someone called me Xiaohan.

After talking to Micheál Hannigan, I felt light-headed and took a taxi home. My roommate and her boyfriend were watching TV in the sitting room. 'Hi, Claire, how's your evening so far?' The boyfriend waved at me upon my entry. My roommate said: 'Can you call Amy later? She said you haven't called for a week.'

'I'll call her,' I said, and closed my bedroom door.

Alex posted this on November 2016:

Things we take for granted: A pint of Guinness. Packed and pre-washed spinach. Eight bananas from Costa Rica for one fifty. Sparkling water. Electric sockets. Toilet paper in public bathrooms. Short stories of Franz Kafka. Free streaming music. Google Maps. 4G data. Facebook friends. Being white. European Union. A Democratic president of the United States. Solidarity. Globalization. Rationalism. Freedom. Life.

It got 210 likes and three comments.

Sitting on my bed, I read it about ten times whispering the words through my lips, as if they were a spell.

I wanted to respond with something meaningful under the post. I tried and failed.

So I liked it.

211 likes.

I didn't think I would have been moved by Alex's post had he not been dead. Death was a titanic LOMO lens, through which every word and paragraph, every line of code and every algorithm looked solemn and prophetic.

In the early morning of 3 March, after watching the Japanese movie *An Autumn Afternoon* (without subtitles), after a few drinks at Vicar Street, and after accepting my friend request, Alexander Whelan sentenced himself to death.

What he left behind was this post, which was written right after the American presidential election, along with other posts about news he heard, books he read and music he enjoyed. There were also emojis, photos, video clips, events; in fact, his whole Facebook account, his Instagram, Twitter, Pinterest, Snapchat, Tumblr, PayPal . . . an entire world.

I believe I've made myself clear: this is a love story. This is a love story about boy meets girl. An Irish boy meets a Chinese girl in Dublin. They liked each other instantly and decide to be friends on Facebook. It won't be long before they start seeing each other but the boy is dead. Except that in this case he leaves behind an enormous and self-proliferating online archive with which the Chinese girl will find no problem falling in love.

This is what our first date is going to look like:

We are meeting for Thursday lunch at Mannings Bakery and Cafe on Thomas Street. Before I go, I check on Tripadvisor and learn most customers recommend their carrot cake.

Me: I'll have a slice of carrot cake, then. And a latte.

The waitress: Good.

(She repeats and writes down our orders and leaves.)

Alex: So you're having cake for lunch.

Me: Why not? It's Thursday.

Alex: What's special about Thursday?

Me: Its lack of identity.

(Alex wheezes.)

Me: So what do you do?

Alex: I work at Maniac and Anarchist Co.

Me: That's not a real company.

Alex: This is what my Facebook says.

Me: And what do you say?

Alex: I say we should just trust my Facebook.

(I laugh. The waitress arrives with our orders. She lays out the cutlery, the cups and the plates, and leaves. Alex takes a sip of his coffee. I cut a corner of my carrot cake with the fork.)

Me: If I could just read and trust your online profiles, why would we need to meet in person? Is there anything you can tell me in the flesh that your Facebook can't?

(Alex thinks for a while.)

Alex: Here's the thing: How do you define knowing a person? If we have spent, say, a month together, we share the space, we eat, we drink, we watch TV and we have sex. But we don't talk – we talk about basic stuff but we don't have conversations. You don't know what I like and dislike, which college I went to, who my favourite writer is, etc. But we spend tons of time together. In these circumstances, can you say you know me? Or, you've read my Facebook and other online archives, and we can trust all of them, okay? And you've learnt all about me. I like The Cure and I hate Maroon 5. I went to UCD. My favourite writer is Kafka. You know all my thoughts and understand comprehensively what kind of a person I am but you have never actually spent much time with me – like, we just met really briefly. Then, can you say you know me?

(I work on my carrot cake and finish it while Alex is talking. And I drink my coffee.)

Me: You are speaking hypothetically. But this is the reality: we are sitting here in your most visited café and I want to know something directly from you. Is that okay?

Alex: Shoot.

Me: Tell me, why did you kill yourself? And why did you add me right before you did it? If I had sent you a message there straight away, would it have made a difference?

Alex looks at me. And he smiles.

*

He posted this a week before his death:

I'm thinking about moving to a foreign country. I'm not talking about Canada, New Zealand, the UAE or Spain. I'm talking about REAL FOREIGN. Not any version of little Ireland. No bacon and cabbage, fish and chips or any comfort food for that matter. No English. What I want is to extract myself entirely from this life and to land in a brand-new one, in which I have no language, no clue of any cultural context and can find no trace of my own kind. People on Facebook, any recommendations?

Some suggested China. And one savvier and more cynical friend replied: 'North Korea?'

I knew exactly what he was talking about. It was precisely how I felt the first year I came to Ireland and studied at the language school. And then the second year. And then the third. And the fourth the fifth the sixth.

'Claire.' My roommate knocked on my door. 'Stephen and I are going to Grogan's to meet friends. You want to come? It should be fun.'

So I went with them to Grogan's. And there were their friends, sitting around two tables pulled together: beautiful blonde women in their shining jewellery, tall men and their scented hair gel.

I was directed to sit next to a smallish guy with a friendly smile. 'Alan,' he introduced himself.

'I'm Claire.' I smiled back.

'So how do you know Laura and Stephen?' Alan asked me.

'Laura and my mother are friends,' I said.

'Oh?' He paused and took a look at Laura.

'I was joking. I'm her stepsister.'

'I thought so. I've heard about you before.' He laughed with relief.

Stephen brought me a beer. I took a deep gulp out of thirst.

'So you're from China,' our conversation continued.

'Yep.' I nodded.

'Tell me, what's China like? I've always wanted to go there.'

'I can't really say. It's been almost ten years since I left. It is probably very different now.' I drank another mouthful.

'Wow, ten years. And do you miss China?'

'Sometimes.'

'And how do you find Ireland?'

'Good. Beautiful country. Nice people,' I said, and finished my beer.

'You're drinking fast!' He finally noticed. 'Can I get you another one?'

'Nope.' I put down my glass and sat back. 'I'm good now. Let's talk.'

After taking a moderate amount of alcohol I became interested in the conversation. We talked and laughed. And then we got up to go to the bar/toilet and switched seats subtly. New drink. New friend. Shake hand and smile. I'm Claire. I came from China. No, my English is not really good but thank you very much. Yes, I do like Ireland. Beautiful country. Nice people.

Later, in the cab home, Laura said: 'I'm glad you came. It looked like you were enjoying yourself.'

'Yes. I had a good time,' I said.

'So, how's Alan?' Stephen asked and turned around from the front seat.

'How's Alan?' I asked back.

'What do you think? Any craic?' he pursued.

'I don't know. I only talked to him for, like, ten minutes.'

'So no craic?' Laura said.

'No craic,' I said firmly, making sure she'd include this in her report to my mother.

I put 'Hippopotamus' on repeat, the song from Alex's band, and went on working on my thesis. It was a light song with subtle and intricate melodies, a sort of Scandinavian indie type.

> *Once upon a time I was about to die*
> *Fired from my job and kicked out by my girlfriend*
> *She said go to hell you asshole*
> *She said don't come back unless you buy me the Ferragamo*
>
> *Once upon a time I was about to die*
> *I sat outside Heuston Station, begging for change*
> *I said I'm starved please I am starved*
> *I said I want to have a spring roll or I am gonna die*
>
> *Eventually my way walked a man from Sligo*
> *He said here you go, son, a ticket for Dublin Zoo*
> *He said trust me you just need to see the animals*
> *You need to see the animals and you will never die*
>
> *Once upon a time I almost died*
> *I went to Dublin Zoo to see the animals*
> *I saw giraffes, elephants and monkeys*
> *Sea lions, zebras and flamingos*
> *And I didn't even forget the hippopotamus*
>
> *Giraffes, elephants and monkeys*
> *Sea lions, zebras and flamingos*
> *And oh don't forget the hippopotamus*
> *Hippopotamus, hippopotamus, hippo, hippopotamus*

It was not specified on the website but I believed it was Alex who wrote the lyrics. He seemed like the kind of guy who would not forget to see the hippopotamus when visiting the zoo.

I found myself roaming the internet again, tracing Alex's footsteps. It had been two weeks since he'd died. On his Facebook page, there used to be post after post of tributes, washing onto his wall like the most ferocious tide. And now his wall had gone quiet. Only once or twice a day, a casual *r.i.p.* would pop up, or a red candle emoji with praying hands.

Naturally, I decided to read all of these 203 posts, studying people's thoughts about Alex and their memories of him. He was described by lots of friends as *generous*. The word *passionate* came up fifty-two times. And then there were *adventurous* (thirty-one), *affectionate* (twenty-eight), *intuitive* (seventeen), *original* (fourteen) and *artistic* (ten). One said he missed his *whimsy*. Another called him *scintillating*. And a Susie Burns wrote he was *the most charismatic character in Dublin*.

We've lost the most charismatic character in Dublin. I don't know what you are gonna do people, but I'm getting DRUNK tonight, she posted.

The most surprising post came in three days ago. It said: *So I quit my job, ended my lease and bought a ticket to Bangkok. You were right, my brother. Our life here has turned into a monster and it's time to run. Get out before it eats you alive.*

It was from Micheál Hannigan. I clicked into his page and there he was, already checked in at Brown Sugar, Bangkok, wearing a salmon-pink short-sleeve and a pair of sunglasses, holding a tropical-looking cocktail, grinning at the camera.

I laughed out loud. I laughed so hard that I started

coughing. Struggling, I pushed myself up from the desk and closed my laptop.

It was late in the afternoon and I hadn't eaten. I went to the kitchen, scavenging for food. There was a half-eaten cheesecake in the fridge and the expiration date was today.

As I sat by the kitchen table, saving the cheesecake from decay, I thought of the monster of life. I thought it might be hiding, actually, in my bathroom. It was dark. It was heavy. Its skin hairless. Its breath foul. Its eyes small and vicious. Its mouth enormous and greedy. It was this monster that had devoured Alex's life and it was now hiding in my bathroom, watching me.

'Claire!' Laura called behind my back. I shivered.

'What? You scared me!' I turned around.

'It's not me.' She passed me her phone. 'Amy is on the phone. She wants to talk to you.'

'Hello, Claire.' My mother had the voice of the English listening test.

'Hi, Mum,' I said.

'Where have you been? You didn't call me last week. I asked Laura to tell you to call me,' she said.

'Yes you did. And she told me,' I said. 'I was just busy.'

'Everybody is busy. We all have different things going on. But I call you. I call you because I think it's important. I prioritize.' She laid out the principles.

'A friend of mine died,' I said.

'Oh,' she exclaimed lightly. 'Well, I'm sorry to hear that.'

I didn't know what to say and she continued: 'You know what we say in Chinese, that *the one who stays near vermilion gets stained red, and the one who stays near ink gets stained black*. You should be careful about whom to be friends with. Dublin is a very mixed city.'

Knowing my mother, I really shouldn't have been surprised, but I was still stunned. I took a breath and said: 'It's not what you think. He was a good person.'

'I'm sure he was,' she agreed. 'Anyhow, I just heard from Laura that you didn't like her friend. She said you think he is not very interesting? Claire, I cannot believe I'm repeating this to you: before you make any decisions, can you evaluate youself first? You are not a very attractive woman. You are a foreigner in this country. You are already twenty-seven and you're still in college, studying Journalism.' She stressed *Journalism*. 'So don't be silly, daydreaming about some Prince Charming – that's not going to happen for you. Be realistic and efficient. We've wasted time already. When we came to Ireland, you had to go to the language school and then back to secondary school for two more years. So now you must act. Listen, there are reasons I arranged for you to live with Laura . . .'

She went on and on. My understanding was she'd probably had a bad day and she missed me. Since I moved to Dublin for college, she had become more and more neurotic and then aggressive every time she called. Or it might just have been that Chinese, our native tongue, reduced us to the primitive form, made us incredibly susceptible and vulnerable. I felt a burning sensation in my throat. It was graphic.

The last time she'd called had been two weeks ago. It was the night of the FMNS meeting and I was running late but she wouldn't stop talking until after seven.

When I arrived at Eoin's I texted him and he came down to let me in. The movie had already started. There were six or seven people sitting in the room. Only silhouettes. On the big pull-down screen, a pale Japanese woman was staring blankly and uncannily. The buzzing sound of the projector rendered the space eerie and still.

It wasn't long before I realized the movie was about a father and a daughter, a widowed father and an unmarried daughter, living together in their old and run-down house. They sat by a small table and ate together, in front of each was a dish of vegetables and a bowl of rice. I started to cry. The movie was extremely quiet so I bit my lips and clenched my fists.

And that was when the strangest thing happened. There was this guy who was sitting beside me. I noticed his shoulder begin to tremble and his nose sniffing from time to time.

He was crying too. And tears were pouring out from my eyes. It was Alex and I, our silhouettes trembling, crying quietly while the Japanese father and daughter spoke, in a strange language, in black and white, without subtitles.

LUCY SWEENEY BYRNE

ECHOLOCATIONS

I GO TO see a film of a woman in a garden. It's showing in the Irish Film Institute in Dublin. The garden is that of her childhood home in Cork. It's a mansion, really. Anglo-Irish pile, Georgian, that kind of thing. Or maybe it's neo classical, I can't remember. She has been away, in London, I think. It's her first time back. She's been gone long enough to idealize the place. Her body language is all chest thrust forth, *mummy and daddy* and *oh yes let's find where the old pony's buried.*

There's no one else there; she has arrived a day before the new staff are due to come, left to enjoy her reunion with the place alone. She's at that age when she is still foolish but thinks she has grown wise. She's probably around my age, I realize, appraising her – lines, hips, hair. Or maybe I'm thinking wishfully.

It's thick and lush, the garden. Wetly gleaming in the morning light. A stream passes blindly through it somewhere down below, away from the house. She rushes out the door and down the hill the moment she confirms that there's absolutely no one else there: all she can see are her old dolls, the curved staircase, the dusty attic, the tidy, disused kitchen.

As she descends into the depths of the garden in this film I attend one afternoon, she is channelled through narrow pathways between high hedges, around whose corners it's impossible to see. The foliage shimmers. She runs her hands over it, touches everything as she goes. The garden is planted with the usual; dark stiff yews higher up the hill, enormous green gunnera down by the water, beneath which moss and ferns froth lowly. The hedges themselves are of box and beech, the latter still half brown, turning half green, with a mixture of last and this year's leaves. Above her are shadowed black trees, overwatching like gods, through which can be seen patches of clear blue skies; an elephantine cypress with a low branch like a curved seat; a side-leaning larch; a few horse chestnuts, and a warty, twisted oak. It's all hers, the whole place. Green, more green, blue green, yellow green, pale green, rich green, and the too-bright white of light reflected against dew.

She is narrating her memories, a voice-over voiced, according to the opening credits, by an actress different to the one filmed walking. The voice enunciates in the Queen's English. This does not feel incongruous. Even as a child growing up in Cork, in that place, it's likely she would have that voice. Coming from the Big House, with grounds like these, she would have grown up both of that place, from that place, and not. She could probably impersonate a Cork accent, and no doubt did for laughs at school, or back in London. Hers would inevitably soften into a hybrid when she spoke to the servants the following day, or in the local village – her 'o' sounds broadening into a wind-beaten *aeh*, a few *sures* and *thanks be to God*s thrown in where they don't, properly speaking, go.

The late forties, early fifties, it would have been, when this woman was growing up. A new time for her family: a time of transition – and transition precipitated by the external world is always experienced as a kind of loss. Perhaps they had all decided to leave, not just her. Perhaps, then, this film is not trying to suggest that anyone has died, that she is the only one left, but rather that she is the only one fool enough to come back. But why go back?

Something gone wrong for her in London, perhaps, the breakdown of a relationship, some dumb but suitably primed fellow with his own place in Kensington, who does something in banking and is a member of Hurlingham, from whom she'd been expecting a proposal any day now, for months, years, on end. All followed by champagne for one, then those last dregs of rum from the back of the cupboard, culminating in a series of indulgently suicidal phone calls. All as the moon, so sympathetic earlier in the night, gawped in at her through the tall, dirty windows of the flat.

I hadn't known what the film would be before collecting my ticket. It's one of those free lunchtime screenings, only half an hour long, chosen from the archive. I'd been waiting in a nearby coffee shop for a man I used to sleep with on and off many years ago, who hadn't turned up. Not even a text.

I am married now, as close to contented as my nature will allow. Therefore, I had been hoping with this meeting to convey this happy-adjacent state to him, this man whose initials I used to scratch along with my own into trees, desks, cubicle walls. This morning, before catching the train, I'd had my hair blow-dried. I'd worn impractical heeled boots and new, too-tight jeans that made my bum look like two ripe moons. *See?* I'd planned to convey to him, *I'm neither undesirable nor unhinged after all. Look how well I am. Look at how I've kept the weight off. Look at what your life could have been.*

I have escaped into the lunchtime screening to digest the new, sharp fact of his not bothering to turn up. It will provide just enough time for me to consume my own disappointment. At the very least, it'll offer a rest. Days out in Dublin – even those on which I don't hope to gloat across a coffee table from someone who used to orgasm at once within and without me – can be extremely tiring.

It is overstimulating for me, in that it often feels as though all the layers of memories I have of Dublin are humming and vying to be relived. Past selves, all those old, ill-dressed iterations, beat at the glass of my ears, jostling me into remembrance of things best left in the past; friendships lost, humiliations gained.

Dublin remains a velvet city, one that demands nostalgia, even of those who've never visited before. Overworn streets are made new and new again by minds and bodies growing older, over and over unto death, all as new bodies come to fill their still warm seats, to tell and listen in turn.

For me, it is always the same route; out the old bleeding side wound of Trinity by the empty gallery, pause for the *ding ding* of the Luas on the corner, across Nassau and up Dawson by the Hodges Figgis window, evoking the same thoughts each time a little more misremembered – 'but have you read his *A*? His *D* is very good.' Of how I'm as bad, how I always secretly felt there would be, should've been, for mine too: 'her *Green* isn't bad, but I think her *Blue* is better' – before turning right at Carluccio's, to stare in the window of the rare bookseller.

Erupting then into the overwhelm of Grafton Street, too busy, too bright, faces, memories – there I go with my mother down to have a coffee in Habitat before the Christmas sales on Stephen's Day; and there I go rushing to keep up with my father, late for a film, late for the train, late for something; there drunk running for the night bus, crying or laughing over something.

Too much, too many; escape off quick again out the

other side to peer passingly in the side windows of Bewley's, glance across to see the mystery of the angled church entrance, then back into the windows of the old jewellers, mercifully unchanged. Sparkle and shine, gleam and glare, and on along again, cobbled, to where – to where? – maybe over to George's Street and back around again, pass by the crowd outside Grogans who sit watching people watch them, right and then left onto Wicklow Street and in to admire the exotic, perfectly shaped fruit in Fallon & Byrne, on, onto where, Books Upstairs perhaps, and then to where, and again, and again.

And years will pass, and I will come back, and walk the same way, and breathe, until I, too, don't. And the last time will pass unbeknownst to me, and after it, the streets won't know I'm gone, they won't remember, and of my particular woven memories, my tread, nothing will be left in the city, not even whispers. No brown leaves will fall from me and clog up the gutters, nothing new to grow from my rot. No songs will be sung. And today, that day, this one, no one has come to meet me.

And yet, I am married now, with a house and a key that sticks and a particular breakfast I like eating in a particular way. I am a new, unexpected person in a new skin, a wife's skin. All that happened to me before this is now just that – things from before. They are not a part of this life. They have been left here somewhere, in Dublin.

No one told me and everyone did, of how, as I got older, life would become, in unexpected surges, desperately sad, even when it is happy, because of the accrual of memories of people and things irretrievably past. There's some niggling regret for what I've done and what was done to me, but mostly as I walk around the city, I experience both relief and a soft, permeating grief for all that pain now gone. Nothing shall ever feel as lusciously sharp again, I realize, as the romantic agony of my teens and twenties.

It is impossible to be in the same city twice. Although Dublin is a place in which plenty try. I see them everywhere, in old band t-shirts carrying guitars, or wrapped in tweed and oversized scarves. For these, time disperses on the air, slips out the cracked windows of pubs and cafés; it filters out with their breath on drunken dawns and out again with the yellow, rancid stream of their piss down back alleyways. Until one day there's a clean, bald pate where hair once thickly lustred; swollen blue veins rivering down calves; stiff, sore wrists and fingers. Damp now rises up the walls of the small flat that was once a temporary solution, perfect, they'd felt, for late night sessions and the swapping of joints and philosophies with beautiful, troubled women.

But the cinema is out of all that. The cinema offers a dark, warm hiding place, a place to absent the mind, to reset. It is still only lunchtime. There's much more day to come before home.

I live in a different city now, a train ride away, in my new, separate life, with my new, separate husband, who is not from Ireland at all, and knows Dublin only loosely. He sees it as just another city, neither historicized nor romanticized – touristy, over-monied, grasping falsely at a green and ginger-haired simulation of its past. I tell him of how it was before the money came and made it like everywhere else, and he listens patiently or talks of the same thing happening to his own home city, which makes me realize what a boring topic it is for the person who wasn't there.

It's just that, sometimes, my life now seems so completely cut off from the life I lived before that I can't remember what's real, and what is just some film I've seen once. I feel, occasionally, that I am waiting for this new warm, settled, pretend life to end, and to be told that now it's time to go back to the real one, the one in which Dublin is my city, its weathers my weather, its nights my night.

I am thirty-four, an age I never thought I'd be. But that only means I have accumulated thirty-four years of other ages, all of which brim and bubble within me, vying for attention. Now I am thirty-four, which means I am all at once newborn, six, sixteen, twenty-seven, and thirty-four. Sometimes even now, after all these years, I wake up in my bed beside my husband, and for a brief moment, I have absolutely no idea where I am or who he is.

In the lunchtime film, her path through the growth seems to grow narrower and narrower. There are large leaves that cast shadows, grasses that whisper and laugh. They move like people in crowds, swaying, dancing, leaning towards then suddenly away from her.

After a while, she comes to a locked gate. Through the gate is a man, rangy and unclean. This is the first other person we see in the film. Until then it has just been this actress (although there is, I suppose, the second actress too, the invisible one playing her inner monologue). He is clearly a workman.

Yes, there is a man, I remember that about the film; he is definitely there, but is he on the far side of the gate, or is he on this side? I can't recall. But I do remember that the gate can't be unlocked, that she is trapped, one way or the other, and that he – first seen, then, with a wave of dread, half remembered from before – is coming after her. She starts to run away, but he is a man, a native man, who has never left that place. There is no doubt that he will know its ways better than she ever could. He has worked it, still works it, by the looks of things. He has possibly been the one to plant those hedges, to lay the very paths she is trying to escape along. Or perhaps his father laid them, or his grandfather before him.

It's around this time that the mood of the film shifts. Although in truth, it has been unnerving all along, even when she's fondly remembering, flitting merrily from beloved nook to golden cranny. As she runs, something uncomfortably familiar runs cold fingers through me, and I shift in my seat. I am afraid for her. *Run!* I think, *run faster, you idiot, he's coming!*

Even though I know, of course, that this threat, whatever threat it is that this man embodies, has always been coming, and that it will get her in the end, whatever happens in the film. It has been there, latent, from the very beginning – it is the whole point, it's why they've made a film of her going back. They're telling us that this is both the draw and the danger of returning. It is, I'm told, what therapists often do with their patients – revisit, review, analyse past traumas. But then, therapists do it in sealed, quiet, private rooms, safely. As she runs, I curse the doomed image of her car pulling up on the gravel driveway, scorn her gormless glee of only a few minutes before, when she made her way up the steps and into the maw of the house.

Even as I sit there in the dark, I can feel it. Everywhere, the pulsing of what has been before: that is where we used to drink all together, twenty, thirty of us, there on those steps; and through that arch is where I used to rush from the train, forever in the rain, forever late for lectures; and that is where Bloom spoke to the lady about her mad husband, a riddle still unsolved, *U. P.: up*; and that is where Wilde liked to drink, apparently; and that's perhaps where Beckett threw up; and that could be claimed as precisely the spot where

Countess Markievicz once choked on a nut – *or was it a legume?*

And there, in that building behind the advertisement hoarding that promises insurance for me and my loved ones against whatever might befall us, is no doubt where Oliver Cromwell contracted syphilis from some great-great-grandmother of mine (*no wonder he was so cross*); and that is where they stood up on the roof and declared a republic, somewhat prematurely; and there, under my fingers, are the marks where the bullets hit. And as I touch them again in my mind, I think of how many of those shooting were Irish soldiers in the British Army, just following orders, trying their best not to starve to death, and of how we prefer not to think of all that.

It is too complex, too much like real life, the makings of a poor story. History, from the grand narratives of a nation right down to our own, is better told like a fable. It must be made into something that can be lived by. History is either something one has overcome, or it is a better time filled with better people, to whom pints can be raised of a Friday night. In truth, if we could look through all of history in one small corner of any city, we'd likely see little but rivers of blood, tears and faeces.

The woman has managed to lose the man. For now, she's safe. But he is out there somewhere, and she must find refuge.

All the while, she's striving to remember and to not remember. Images come to the screen in flashes. A woman in a large bright kitchen, large-bosomed – a servant. A little girl enters. She is happy. She sits at the oversized table and is given something good to eat by the servant woman. It's clear from the blurry, vignetted shots and the voice-over that this is her. It is clear, too, that this is the safe place she's seeking, and yet we know, as she does, that this servant woman is long gone, probably dead, and besides, she is not a little girl any more. She is thirty-four, like me.

There are two other people in the cinema that afternoon. The first is an old man who sits in the front row. He is neat, in a blue rain jacket and red wool hat that he does not remove. The moment he sits down, he takes from his backpack a Tupperware box containing a sandwich and a flask, from which I can see steam rising against the darkened screen.

The other person is a curiously anomalous seventies-style biker dude, with long, knotted blonde hair, leather apparel, and that wide-kneed, slumped way of sitting that makes me want to kick things. Unlike the first, this man greatly affects my watching of the film, and probably my remembering of both it and the entire day now.

He comes in last of the three of us, just after the film has commenced, and chooses for his seat, out of all the empty seats, the back row where I am sitting, just one along from me. Coupled with some pointed, wide-eyed glancing my way, this seat choice suggests a deluded notion that there is a chance of this being a different kind of lunchtime experience. Some sort of *opportunity*.

In response, I turn my body away from him, recrossing my knees, and do my best to radiate disdain. All as she, the woman on screen, begins her frolic through the gardens. I am pretty good at radiating disdain, and he soon gets the picture. This is a relief, and I try to settle into the film. It has just begun in earnest; there she is now disappearing behind the pampas grass. I watch her as she pauses, looks up, and makes a hammy romance of surveying the verdant splendour, clasping her hands before her chest. Watching her closely, I am trying my best to ignore the man entirely, and have just begun to forget he's even there.

But wait, what's that? That sound? What could that be? I can't quite believe it, but when I look to the source, only one seat away from myself, I see that, yes, he really is, he's – *biting his nails*. I am horrified. I raise my eyebrows and open my mouth as I turn my head side to side slowly, conveying my utter amazement to the audience of nobody watching.

This, then, is the issue that arises for me, that afternoon in the cinema, after the man I used to sleep with has not turned up. All through the film the biker man proceeds to bite his nails, loudly. The noise is insufferable. It's a quiet film. *Snap, snap, snap* go his teeth as he works his way slowly and diligently around the curve of each one. Then he peers down from the screen at his handiwork, and starts in again on the nails of the other hand. He does this over and over again, until there can only be flittered, bloody nubbins left. He takes his time. He luxuriates in it. Picturing his nails, even as I force myself to watch the screen, makes my stomach lurch. Remembering now makes it lurch again.

I can't believe it. I can't fucking believe it. There she is talking us through her memories of the old paths she played along as a child in her menacingly beautiful garden, and there he is, methodically biting his way through his thick, no doubt filthy, fingernails.

I turn my body back towards him to make a point of staring openly and noticeably in his direction, but now, of course, he affects to have no idea I'm there at all, despite his sitting so close to me that I could easily reach out and touch his knee. He simply cannot see me; I don't exist any more, as far as he's concerned. I clear my throat. Nothing. I shift irritably. Nothing. I sigh loudly through my nose. Nothing. Finally, I am forced to openly acknowledge the terrible predicament in which he has placed me: I am trapped. I can't change seats. It's a small cinema, and the rows go all the way to the wall on the left. The aisle is to the right, and he is blocking my way. I can't move without pressing past those awful, outflung, leather-clad legs.

And then, in spite of my best effort not to think the thought now hissing inside my mind, I become acutely aware of how he, too, must know this. And I fear that perhaps this is what he wants, this quietly torturous position I now find myself in. I wonder if this is some sort of revenge, this nail-biting, this drawing out of my attention. Is he trying to coerce me into moving seats, so that I'll have to endure the humiliation of our bodies, however briefly, touching? Surely not . . . But then, equally surely, no one past the age of twenty bites their nails for pleasure? In a cinema, loudly? But then *again*, I reason with myself – staring at him, praying he'll look back at me and, thus seeing himself seen, desist – he does have that hair, and wear those clothes, and sit in that flopped-down, sulkily pubescent way, so what can I know of how he sees the world?

I shake my head, try to forget about him, to instead return to watching the film. It's the kitchen scene now, the recalling of the bosomed servant, the incomparable safety of other women for women and girls. I think of how the light that shines down in triangles through the high kitchen windows is beautiful, the room warm and inviting in browns and ochres. It makes me recall my own grandmother's kitchen in turn, how it overlooked the golf course edged in woodland, with the plum blue mountains beyond. And I think of how she too is dead. I think of how that house was sold, of how the new people had a second storey put on and got the kitchen redone, no doubt in marble of white or black, with a double-doored fridge and a kitchen island, although I bet they kept her old Belfast sink.

Snap, snap snap . . . His nails, oh God. Fear, I feel it rise there in my chest, fear and rage intertwined. That old familiar. But what is there to be afraid of? Is this panic being caused by the film? I feel my breathing quicken along with hers on the screen, and I concentrate on slowing it down. *In-1-2-3, out-1-2-3, in-1-2-3, out-1-2-3* . . .

Perhaps he is sitting there, too close to me, because he's completely unaware of his surroundings. Perhaps he didn't think about the seat he took and doesn't even notice that he's biting his nails loudly, or that it's bothering me. Or perhaps he comes to these viewings all the time, and I have sat in his favourite seat, and he has positioned himself there, too close, because it's the closest he can get to the seat itself. Or perhaps this whole thing is in my head. Were I to confront him, that's definitely what he'd tell me. That would be his natural, default defence. I can hear it already, playing out as it inevitably would: 'What? You think I . . .? Holy shit, lady, you're fucking crazy. And anyway, you're not even hot!'

As I consider this imagined conversation, the humiliation I would feel (not that I would ever confront him anyway, that would be impossible), I glance over at him again. And it's then that I catch him watching me. And although I quickly look away from him towards the safety of the screen, immediately I know I have detected, or imagine I've detected – like hot, rancid oil seeping into my clothes – some little hint of triumph flicker across his eyes, there above the nails he still holds to his mouth, head twisting as he tears at them mercilessly.

The man in the film has reappeared, as we all knew he would. Now he seems to emerge from every corner, no matter where she flees. He clearly knows the garden too well. She is running again now. The sound of her heavy breathing, her feet thumping against the path, her frenzied thoughts, not quite willing to remember what she has so assiduously forgotten.

All is overlaid by the soul-destroying sound of the long-haired biker man's endless nail-biting. I cannot bear it, but I also can't get free, I can't get out past him. I will not. I will have strength, I will not run away, I will not 'make a scene'. I will not succumb to the ridiculousness – I can hardly bear to imagine it – of actually *leaving*. I'll do nothing, give him nothing. I'll wait patiently and quietly for the film to end.

Besides, why should I be the one to leave? To miss out? It would be unfair, another unfairness to add to all the others: not being able to travel to certain places without a man to accompany me, or to walk alone at night, or to fully forget myself in nature. Always this third eye, this watchfulness, this fear. But even if I could, I don't want to have to leave the film. The film is interesting, the film is evocative. I have every right to be here, in this seat. And it is only half an hour long, surely it'll be over soon anyway?

And there's also the fact that, if questioned, I would have no good reason to give for leaving. No one has touched me, no one has even spoken to me. Whatever I may have perceived, in truth, he's doing absolutely nothing. He's certainly not doing anything to me. No one, today, has done anything to me. That other one, he hasn't turned up, which is the definition of doing nothing. This one has, at most, sat too close. No crimes have been committed against me. Yes, okay, he's biting his nails loudly. But other than that, he's just watching a free lunchtime screening in the IFI. Same as the old guy eating his sandwich down front. Same as me.

I cross my arms and think of Dublin all around me, swelling and trembling in readiness, and I suddenly feel keen to be gone from the city altogether, to be away, back to my own, separate, adult life, out of the flow of all this remembering and reliving. I am not a woman on her own any more, however I may appear. I am not that girl, this one here, with all her glorious agonies. I think of home, of the place where home has become for me, it too ever-there, ever-passing, and a pang of joy runs through me.

But I must wait. I sit in the dark as the images glow and flicker, and I soothe myself by picturing my train ride home, pulling away, my face unknown to anybody. I picture the sea out the window, darkness falling, then the platform, the stairs, and there, my husband, waiting for me, in the bright lobby of the station.

He has her now, he has grabbed her in the dark cave of the bamboo grove. This has happened before, this is familiar – that is what we're supposed to understand. She has remembered too late. She should never have come here. *Well, duh*, I think. She is now herself as an adult, now herself as a child. Some sort of terrible violence is recurring. But I am only half there. *Snap, snap, snap . . . Snap, snap, snap . . .*

The film ends. Without a moment's pause the seventies biker nail-biter heaves himself up out of his seat, grabs his old, frayed backpack, and makes for the exit, head down. I sit and watch him go. He doesn't look up. Perhaps he doesn't dare.

After a moment, irrational relief coursing through me, I begin to stand, to look around myself in the newly lit room. I gather up my things: coat, bag, hat, gloves . . . The man below is doing the same. *Thwack* goes the catch on his lunchbox, closing again. The flask squeaks as he twists it tightly. I wonder if he is a widower, or just a lonely eccentric. I notice that he's getting his things in order faster than I am. Not wanting to be left there alone, I rush to leave at the same time he does, dragging my scarf behind me, coat only half buttoned.

As far as he's concerned, I think, taking the door he holds ajar for me, this has been a useful, warm way to eat his lunch in peace. After the brief interruption of the film, only half an hour long, he will continue on with his day: go see an exhibition, or meet someone, perhaps, for coffee, or dinner, or a drink – just the one – before getting the train or the bus home, to wherever it is that he lives. To his wife, or his husband, or his late husband or wife's ashes on the mantelpiece. Or to his elderly mother, or a sibling, or to the mewling cat. As will I. As will the other man, already gone. We will, all of us, go somewhere and sleep, and rise again, and sleep again and rise, and only perhaps, only ever in part, remember.

Walking down the long hall and emerging back out into daylight, I am momentarily dizzied, high and guileless on the winnowing out of stiff, sharp tension. I smile dopily as I stand blocking the doorway. A woman, around my age, taller than me, coughs irritably, and finally I move to the side, before slowly and without aim beginning my soft descent towards the river.

And there is The Ark, where years ago my own chubby face used to smile down from a windowpane, surrounded by other children. And here now is the river, where Viking boats came sailing in, came sailing in. And what about out the other way? Passing below bridges, 'sea air sours it', heard and – under she goes, and now, wait now, *there* – heard again. And now to where? Back into Dublin. Into Dublin, back. Even with all this rememorying, some things when gone are just gone, I think. All things, really, although it's easier not to know it. Nothing can be held. And perhaps that's why.

I wonder where the biker man is now, the tidy man who'd

been sitting down front, my ex, my beautiful husband. All out there now, far and close, growing older. And even though it is too obvious to think, let alone to say, the thought rises: how there is only this living blindly forwards and remembering back, and that this dull fact is, in a nutshell, the tragedy of the thing. However it all turns out.

ACKNOWLEDGMENTS

KEVIN BARRY: Short Story 'The Apparitions' as first published in *The Forge Magazine*, Jan. 25, 2016. Copyright © Kevin Barry, 2016. Reprinted with permission from C & W Agency.

SAMUEL BECKETT: 'Ding-Dong' from *More Pricks Than Kicks*, published by Faber and Faber Ltd. Reprinted with permission. Excerpt from 'Ding-Dong' copyright © 1970 by The Estate of Samuel Beckett from *The Selected Works of Samuel Beckett, Vol. IV.* Used by permission of Grove/Atlantic, Inc. Any third-party use of this material, outside of this publication, is prohibited.

ELIZABETH BOWEN: 'The Last Night in the Old Home' from *The Cat Jumps and Other Stories* (London: Jonathan Cape, 1934). Reproduced with permission of Curtis Brown Group Ltd, London, on behalf of the Literary Executors of the Estate of Elizabeth Bowen.

MAEVE BRENNAN: 'The Barrell of Rumours' from *The Springs of Affection* (Dublin: Stinging Fly, 2016). Reprinted with permission. Reprinted by the permission of Russell & Volkening as agents for the author's estate. Copyright © 1998 by The Estate of Maeve Brennan. Published in *The Springs of Affection* (Houghton Mifflin).

LUCY SWEENEY BYRNE: 'Echolocations' from *Let's Dance* (Dublin: Banshee Press, 2024). Reprinted with permission.

LUCY CALDWELL: 'Here We Are' by Lucy Caldwell. Published by Granta Magazine, 2016. Copyright © Lucy

Caldwell. Reproduced by permission of the author c/o Rogers, Coleridge & White Ltd, 20 Powis Mews, London W11 1JN.

JOHN CONNOLLY: 'A Dream of Winter' from *Night Music: Nocturnes Vol. 2* (London: Hodder & Stoughton, 2015). Reproduced with permission of the Licensor through PLSclear. 'Dream of Winter' from *Night Music: Nocturnes Vol. 2*, reprinted with permission from Darley Anderson Agency Limited.

RODDY DOYLE: 'Two Pints x 4' from: Roddy Doyle, *The Complete Two Pints,* published by Penguin Books. Copyright © 2020 Roddy Doyle. Reprinted with permission from C & W Agency. From *The Complete Two Pints* by Roddy Doyle, published by Vintage. Copyright © Roddy Doyle 2012, 2014, 2017, 2019 & 2020. Reprinted by permission of The Random House Group Limited.

ANNE ENRIGHT: 'Green' from *Taking Pictures* by Anne Enright. Published by Jonathan Cape, 2008. Copyright © Anne Enright. Reproduced by permission of the author c/o Rogers, Coleridge & White Ltd, 20 Powis Mews, London W11 1JN.

YAN GE: 'How I Fell in Love with the Well-Documented Life of Alex Whelan' from *Elsewhere*, published by Faber and Faber Ltd. Reprinted with permission. From *Elsewhere*, stories by Yan Ge. Copyright © 2023 by Yan Ge. Reprinted with the permission of Scribner, an imprint of Simon & Schuster LLC. All rights reserved.

NORAH HOULT: 'The Story of Father Peter' from *Nine Years is a Long Time* (London: William Heinemann, 1938). Reprinted with permission from The Estate of Norah Hoult.

CLAIRE KEEGAN: 'Dark Horses', © Claire Keegan. Originally published in *The Stinging Fly*, Issue 4, Volume 2 (Summer, 2006); also in Declan Meade and Sarah Gilmartin, eds, *Stinging Fly Stories* (Dublin: Stinging Fly, 2018), pp. 178–183; also in *Walk the Blue Fields* (Faber and Faber, 2007). Reprinted with permission from Curtis Brown Limited.

MARY LAVIN: 'In a Café' originally published in *The New Yorker* (February 5, 1960), p. 32; subsequently in: *The Great Wave and Other Stories* (Macmillan, 1961). Reproduced with permission of Curtis Brown Ltd, London, on behalf of The Estate of Mary Lavin. Copyright © Mary Lavin.

MIKE MCCORMACK: 'The Terms' from *Getting It in the Head*, published by Canongate Books. Reproduced with permission of the Licensor through PLSclear. 'The Terms' from *Getting It in the Head*, Copyright © 1996 by Mike McCormack reprinted by permission of Soho Press, Inc. All rights reserved.

JOHN MCGAHERN: 'Bank Holiday' first appeared in the *Irish Times* (Aug. 9, 1985); subsequently in *High Ground and Other Stories*, published by Faber and Faber Ltd. Reprinted with permission. 'Bank Holiday' from *High Ground: Stories*, published by Viking Books, an imprint of Penguin Random House, LLC.

EOIN MCNAMEE: 'Sable' by Eoin McNamee. Published by the *Irish Times*, 2020. Copyright © Eoin McNamee. Reproduced by permission of the author c/o Rogers, Coleridge & White Ltd, 20 Powis Mews, London W11 1JN.

ÉILÍS NÍ DHUIBHNE: 'A Literary Lunch' from *Selected Stories* (Newtownards: Blackstaff Press, 2023). Originally published in *The Shelter of Neighbours* (Newtownards: Blackstaff Press, 2012). Reprinted with permission.

EDNA O'BRIEN: 'Send My Roots Rain' first appeared in the *Sunday Times Magazine* (May 10, 2009); subsequently in *Saints and Sinners,* published by Faber and Faber Ltd. Reprinted with permission. 'Send My Roots Rain' from *Saints and Sinners* by Edna O'Brien, reprinted by permission of Peters Fraser & Dunlop on behalf of the Estate of Edna O'Brien.

FLANN O'BRIEN: 'John Duffy's Brother' published in *Irish Digest* (June 1940), pp. 69–73, and subsequently in *The Short Fiction of Flann O'Brien*, ed. Neil Murphy and Keith Hopper (Dublin: Dalkey Archive Press, 2013), pp. 54–8. Copyright The Estate of Evelyn O'Nolan. Reprinted with permission of Deep Vellum/Dalkey Archive, and approval from A. M. Heath on behalf of the Estate. HarperCollins Publishers Ltd.

FRANK O'CONNOR: Story 'Guests of the Nation' by Frank O'Connor reprinted by permission of Peters Fraser & Dunlop on behalf of the Estate of Frank O'Connor.

PÁDRAIC Ó CONAIRE: 'Knitting' [Translated by Thomas Murphy] from *Pádraic Ó Conaire: The Finest Stories* (Dublin: Poolbeg, 1982). Reprinted with permission from the Estate of Thomas Murphy.

SEAN O FAOLAIN: 'A Broken World' from *A Purse of Coppers* by Sean O'Faolain. Published by Jonathan Cape, 1937. Copyright © Sean O'Faolain. Reproduced by permission of the Author's Estate c/o Rogers, Coleridge & White Ltd, 20 Powis Mews, London W11 1JN.

LIAM O'FLAHERTY: Story 'The Sniper' from *Spring Sowing* by Liam O'Flaherty reprinted by permission of Peters Fraser & Dunlop on behalf of the Estate of Liam O'Flaherty.

JAMES PLUNKETT: 'Dublin Fusilier' from *The Trusting and the Maimed* by James Plunkett reprinted by permission of Peters Fraser & Dunlop on behalf of the Estate of James Plunkett.

SALLY ROONEY: 'Colour and Light' by Sally Rooney. Copyright © Sally Rooney, 2019, used by permission of The Wylie Agency (UK) Limited.

CATHY SWEENEY: 'The Door' from *The Stinging Fly* (Issue 37, Volume 2: Winter 2017–18). Copyright © Cathy Sweeney c/o Rogers, Coleridge & White Ltd, 20 Powis Mews, London W11 1JN.

COLM TÓIBÍN: 'The Empty Family' from *The Empty Family* by Colm Tóibín published by Viking. Copyright © Colm Tóibín, 2010. Reprinted by permission of Penguin Books Limited. From *The Empty Family: Stories* by Colm Tóibín. Copyright © 2011 by Colm Tóibín. Reprinted with the permission of Scribner, an imprint of Simon & Schuster LLC. All rights reserved.

Any third-party use of material published by Penguin Random House LLC, outside this publication, is prohibited. Interested parties must apply to Penguin Random House LLC for permission.